STRANGER
IN THE
TWISTED REALM

Published by Winterset Books
www.kaykenyon.com
Paperback ISBN: 9781733674676

Published in the United States of America

Cover by Deranged Doctor Design

Visit www.kaykenyon.com and join the author's newsletter for a free short story, and find out about new releases and reader perks.

Don't miss *The Girl Who Fell Into Myth*, the first book in the quartet, available in print and ebook at all online booksellers.

Also by Kay Kenyon

Coming winter, 2024: *Servant of the Lost Power*, the next book
in The Arisen Worlds quartet: *In a time of war and sorcery, Yevliesza, a
newcomer in the mythical realms, must undergo the ultimate test of her
resolve. One that can lead to knowledge—or madness.*

Fantasy Novels

THE ARISEN WORLDS QUARTET

The Girl Who Fell Into Myth, Book 1

Stranger in the Twisted Realm, Book 2

STAND ALONE FANTASY

A Thousand Perfect Things

Queen of the Deep

THE DARK TALENTS TRILOGY

At the Table of Wolves, Book 1

Serpent in the Heather, Book 2

Nest of the Monarch, Book 3

Science Fiction Novels

The Seeds of Time

Tropic of Creation

Rift

Maximum Ice

The Braided World

THE ENTIRE AND THE ROSE QUARTET

Bright of the Sky, Book 1

A World Too Near, Book 2

City Without End, Book 3

Prince of Storms, Book 4

Collections

Dystopia: Seven Dark and Hopeful Tales

Worlds Near and Far

STRANGER
IN THE
TWISTED REALM

BOOK TWO OF THE ARISEN WORLDS

KAY KENYON

Kay Kenyon

WINTERSET BOOKS

The Nine Powers

Foreknowing

Manifesting

Creatures

Warding

Healing

Verdure

Aligns

Elements

Primal Roots

Prologue

Pince Albrecht and his men had ridden hard from the
boundary gate deep into Volkia. It was nearly evening by
the time they rested their horses on the edge of a plateau
within view of the great manor house of Duke Tanfred Wilhoffen.
In the violet haze of dusk, the wide plains stretched before him,
an expanse that seemed to fill his lungs with cool relief after the
tight forests of Alfan Sih.

Behind the prince a horse snorted, impatient to reach the
stables. The creak of saddles was the only other sound. It was not
until this moment that Commandant Prince Albrecht von Treid
felt completely at peace. He loved these plains, broken sometimes
by canyons that sliced the flats like gaping aligns made visible.
Far away, the great Mist Wall, at this distance merely a hands-
breadth tall. It trembled with the pangs of birth as it slowly
extended the realm. He breathed in this power, or felt that he did.

Looking at the expanse before him, Albrecht felt a powerful
love beyond what he had ever known with parent or lover. *Volkia
now and forever*, the thought came, surprising him with its fervor.

But his party must move on without delay to meet Duke
Tanfred, who had sent a message that an urgent piece of intelli-

gence had come to him. If it affected the war, Albrecht was keen to hear it. Though the takeover of Alfan Sih had been swift, the rebels would not stand and fight, but struck at Volkish units and quickly faded into the glens and woodlands.

His gelding knew the way down the slope to the valley floor. Wilhoff Manor, forming a square with its three wings and courtyard wall, beckoned with the gentle light of torches. As they approached, the wrought-iron gate swung aside under the warding power of the gatekeeper, and they passed into the spacious courtyard. Stablers were waiting to take the horses, and the house steward stepped forward to welcome them.

Noting the duke crossing the courtyard toward him, Albrecht handed the reins of his horse to one of the servants and turned to greet his host. "How good to see you, my lord."

Duke Tanfred bowed. He bristled with energy, his patrician face barely containing some hidden excitement. "Prince Albrecht. Welcome to Wilhoff, welcome indeed." He led the way into the country manor with its timbered framing and mullioned windows, leaving Albrecht's officers in the charge of the steward.

They entered a reception hall with a high wood-beamed ceiling where manifesting globes hovered, shedding a pleasant glow. A servant took Albrecht's cloak, and Tanfred accompanied the prince deeper into the manor, the stone floor tiles echoing with their footsteps.

"Your suite is ready, sir," the duke said as they walked. "Would you care for dinner with your officers, or perhaps in your room?" He pushed a lock of sandy brown hair back from his forehead, a boyish gesture at odds with his formal jacket and trousers.

Albrecht waved the idea away. "Food can wait. You have news that could not be trusted in a packet?"

"Not in a packet, no. I would have come to the front myself, but I did not want to distract you. How do things go with the Alfan?"

"They are under control. Pockets of insurrection, but like moths around a fire, when they come into our light, they die."

Tanfred remained silent. The duke disapproved of the war, though he kept his opinions to himself. He was young to have come into his ancestral title, merely twenty-nine, and he had odd leanings, centering around primordialist beliefs. Tanfred's attachment to the legend of the ninth power was an embarrassment, but harmless. Prince Albrecht did not allow his command staff to belittle him. The man was a patriot and a dependable contributor to the general coffers. Given that, Tanfred could dance naked under the full moon or have conversations with his horse, and no one would even notice.

Tanfred led him out of the manor through a back door and across a formal garden toward a copse of trees with branches lit up with small manifesting lights like fallen stars.

"This is all quite mysterious, Tanfred."

"I do not mean it to be. But it is—an occasion—that should be given respect." He looked out the other side of the grove, where an opening among the trees gave a view to the Mist Wall. "My prince, in the eleventh month of last year, I had an unsettling experience. A distant tremor ran through me. I felt it in my very body, as though it echoed with a sound I could not hear. It came from the crossings.

"A few days later it happened again. Something of great import happened there."

Albrecht doubted that Tanfred had sensed anything in the paths between the realms. He sat on a bench, careful not to scoff. "We heard nothing of tremors or vibrations, Tanfred."

"But only a verdualist could detect it, sir. As you know, my affinity is very keen. It is said that the power most related to the crossings is verdure, the gift of growing things."

"It is also said," Albrecht pointed out, "that the most related power is aligns." A gift Tanfred did not have.

"But in the prophecy, it is an individual with verdure . . . *verdure* . . . who will detect a presence in the crossings. When a time of need arises."

By the First Ones, he was on about primordialist lore. The ninth power saving the Mythos, the favored one, and so on. Albrecht sighed, regretting that he had delayed dinner for this painful conversation.

The young duke rubbed his arms as though remembering the vibrations. "Still, it is my duty to report this to you, sir. I have never noted any perturbations in the crossings. And twice within so short a time!"

"And nothing since?"

"No. But is it not possible that when someone passed through the crossings at those times, I sensed them? And would that not be an extraordinary event?" He paused. "I believe that we may live in a time of the *Eibelung*. The one with the primal root power. The primal power that can effect a profound change in the Mist Wall."

"These ideas—" Albrecht began, but Tanfred interrupted.

"I know what it sounds like. Like a man raving, but might it not be true that in this time of upheaval we have been sent assistance? This individual has been in the crossings twice, and if he comes again, I will know it. And we must welcome him."

"We should welcome this person," Albrecht skeptically said, "because he will expand our lands beyond what we could ever see in our lifetimes, or the lifetimes of our children. . . ."

"Yes, my prince. Indeed yes." In the distance, the Mist Wall was merely a dark band on the horizon. It was slowly expanding Volkia even at that moment, leaving new land in its wake.

The cult of the ninth power was small, but even a few thousand of such believers could be a bothersome minority opposing the war. It was very pretty to think that the realm's growth, its natural growth, could intensify and provide more living space and resources. But it was nothing more than mysticism. He would handle Tanfred carefully, but now that Albrecht had taken Alfan Sih, he meant to keep it. Volkia's acquisition of the realm had happened in merely three days and with no help from prophecy.

But as Albrecht sat in the deeply shadowed grove, something gave him pause. He recalled that around the time of Tanfred's experience of the tremor, Volkish soldiers found a new path in the crossings. A path by which Lord Tirhan, prince of the Alfan, must certainly have gained access to his kingdom, since otherwise he would have been apprehended at any of the heavily fortified gates in Alfan Sih.

"You said that the event occurred on the first day of the eleventh month and five days later?"

"I noted the dates in my diary."

Albrecht recalled that he himself had been in the crossings on the latter date, the sixth day of that month. That was the day he was traveling to Alfan Sih with a battalion of fresh troops. The day he encountered a Numinasi woman. She was young and unaccompanied, looking slightly disheveled, and claiming to have come from a visit to Nubiah. He searched his memory for her name.

Ah. Yevliesza. House Valenty, she had said. He had since learned that early in the autumn she had been brought to Numinat from the origin world by order of Princip Anastyna.

This woman had been in the crossings when Tanfred detected a tremor. Coincidence? He recalled his strong impression that the reason she had given for being in the crossings was a lie. Perhaps she had brought some kind of small machine with her, and Tanfred had picked up on a disturbance that it caused. If there was the slightest possibility that the woman had something to do with the new path to Alfan Sih, he must find her, question her. And not about mystic prophecies.

After the insolent way she had behaved . . . what had it

exactly been? Ah, yes. She had suggested that his troops might lack honor. It was an insult he would not have endured from a man and had barely restrained himself with the woman of House Valenty. Now he would find her, and this time he would show less restraint.

"I must give your information more careful thought," he told the duke. "But now, sir, come." He put his hand on the duke's shoulder and led him from the grove. "I find that I suddenly have a ferocious appetite after all."

PART I
THE INFERNAL TRADE

Chapter One

Thirteen-year-old Pyvel rode his new horse at a trot, kicking up clods of snow from the trampled ground. Yevliesza watched him from outside the corral, happy that she could afford such a gift for him, the first person she had found to trust in Osta Kiya.

He was longing to try a gallop, but a trot was the fastest that his instructor, the *harjat* warrior Rusadka, would allow. Her flawless black skin was set off by the trim of ocelot fur on her cape. Strongly built, she carried off military dress impressively.

Yevliesza looked up at the palace commanding the hilltop, perched atop the great stone massif which held the seat of power and the thousands of inhabitants of Osta Kiya. This was her home. Medieval, brutal in some ways, but a place where she had found companionship as well as enemies; friendship as well as malice; perhaps love. Her heart swelled at the grandeur of the castle, bristling with factions, strange customs, and its bloody Tower. Things she had overcome or at least survived.

"Sit up straight!" Rusadka bellowed at Pyvel across the paddock. "Keep your feet in the stirrups!" She gave Yevliesza a long-suffering look. "Seems he cannot do both."

"You're making him nervous," Yevliesza said, amused that Rusadka had agreed to teach the boy, whom she now treated like a raw army recruit. If there was one person Pyvel feared, it was Rusadka, a woman who didn't hold with children, but managed to tolerate him because he was Yevliesza's steward. Or steward-in-training.

"He is nervous?" The *harjat* snorted. "What will he do when faced with enemy horsemen?"

"But we are in the paddock now," Yevliesza chided.

"Keep the reins low!" Rusadka called as the boy came by again, bouncing in the saddle and grinning.

Yevliesza enjoyed seeing her friend in the role of an instructor. She was one of only a handful of women to achieve *harjat* rank, much less pass arcana training in the power of aligns. They had been in the arcana triad together, and Yevliesza hadn't graduated, but the training had been worth it, because that was how the two of them had met. Rusadka, the only one who knew what Yevliesza really was. Not a master of aligns, but something far more imposing.

The burns on her arm and back occasionally pinched, as though the tracery embedded there was clamoring for attention. She would like to see them for herself, but there were no mirrors in Numinat.

Rusadka turned to note a horse and rider coming up the draw from the valley. Her eyes narrowed. It was Valenty, riding a tall chestnut stallion.

He joined them at the corral, greeting them, his eyes tender on Yevliesza, as hers were on him. She couldn't stop looking at him under ordinary circumstances, but on a horse, commanding it so well as he did, he looked smashing.

"May I join you?" he asked Rusadka, giving her deference since she was the teacher.

"Of course, my lord," she dutifully said. Valenty was a high noble, even if her opinion of him was low.

"I'll bring my mount to the stable," he said when Rusadka turned away. He exchanged glances with Yevliesza, his small smile making light of the woman's disdain and how he earned it by pretending to be less than he was. Rusadka took him at face value, a spoiled aristocrat with no decent trade and an indecent number of lovers. Now he was courting Yevliesza and, to Rusadka's annoyance, her friend encouraged him.

Pyvel came round again, appealing this time to Yevliesza. "A steward should know how to gallop, mistress!"

Rusadka muttered loud enough for him to hear, "A steward should not have a horse in the first place."

Yevliesza had taken the role of the boy's patron, including his room and board and education. She possessed a small stipend from her father's estate, a reputation as the person responsible for the dread Nashavety's downfall, and the tentative favor of Princip Anastyna. Tentative, because Numinasi politics were ever-shifting, especially in this time of Volkish aggression.

Valenty, having given over his mount to the stable hands, walked down to join the two women. Yevliesza was used to seeing him in court garb, but today he wore a fur jacket and leather breeches tucked into mud-smeared boots, and he stirred her with his dark good looks and the way he met her eyes. But she was still learning to trust him. He was in a trial period. She had made clear that she would accept his courtship—even after all that happened between them—but conquest was not guaranteed.

It greatly amused Yevliesza to have a lord of the realm accept patience and make an effort to show himself worthy. Now that he was free of the need to act a part—at least free to do so with her —she saw the finer side of him. The side that put honor before his own happiness; the side that was unaccustomed to the ways of a twenty-first-century woman, but one that also intrigued.

"Why Valenty, of all the men who admire you?" Rusadka asked with Valenty still out of earshot.

"No one else admires me!"

Rusadka smirked. "I assure you that is not the case."

"He loved me, but he was married. And then Dreiza released him. And he has set aside his . . . stable of women."

Rusadka muttered, "He better have."

"He worked for my release from Nashavety's hall. But I didn't tell him that the woman abused me. If he'd known, he would have demanded it."

"As though the princip would have listened to him!"

Yevliesza couldn't disabuse Rusadka of her ideas about Valenty. It was his role to play, a rich noble of no account. One who was actually the princip's chief spy. She had promised never to reveal this fact, never to reveal how few lovers Valenty had really taken—and all of them with the full knowledge and approval of his then-wife—as part of his role of the useless high lord.

Valenty had joined them, but his attention was on a group of people standing at the top of the long flight of stone stairs. "Sofiyana," he murmured. "And the *fajatim*."

Sofiyana, with hair the color of violets, was easy to identify in the distance.

Rusadka spat into the muddy snow, her only comment.

"They are coming down," he said, his face hard, eyes narrowing.

Yevliesza decided to head them off. These women who led the five great houses of Osta Kiya could be nothing but trouble for Pyvel and Rusadka. "I'll go up. See what they want." She nodded to Rusadka and walked toward the stairs.

Valenty accompanied her. "Let us discover their errand together."

"No. I have to do this alone."

"She is a *fajatim* now, not a hapless girl."

"I know what a *fajatim* is." God, she knew more than anyone the command and power they possessed. "If I show the least fear, she'll smell blood."

"Let me discourage her," he said darkly.

She locked gazes with him. "No. Let *me*." Seeing his expression, she softened. "You will not always be here to protect me." He was raised to protect what was his. But she wasn't his yet. And if she came to be, she'd still handle her own fights.

She left him standing on the stairs, trusting that he would stay behind.

Sofiyana noted her approaching and waited for her.

The five women looked like a gaggle of crows, each on their own step, black gowns flapping in the breeze. Four of them were looking out at the view, across the limitless plains in one direction, and into the profound, folded valleys on the other. Sofiyana watched as Yevliesza climbed.

"Well met," Yevliesza said when she reached the group. She bowed her head at Alya of Storm Hand and Ineska of Red Wind, those standing closest to Sofiyana.

"A good day for a ride, Lady Sofiyana?"

"Ah, Yevliesza," she responded. "Business keeps us occupied today, but we can take in the view." In contrast to the early days, Sofiyana wore her violet curls pulled back in as much restraint as was possible with her heavy locks.

It was still incredible to Yevliesza that the corrupt, rebellious Sofiyana had taken Nashavety's place at Raven Fell Hall. "I love it myself. I never tire of it."

Sofiyana cocked her head as though confused. "But you could not tire of a place you hardly know." She turned to Alya on the stair behind, sharing with her a patronizing smile. Turning back to Yevliesza, she said, "I see that you are indulging your servant with riding lessons. A pleasing gesture, unlike so much that you have done. Including against a *fajatim*."

"Lady Nashavety's disgrace was earned. Surely you agree?"

At this turn of the conversation, Alya and Ineska left them, climbing the stairs and marshaling the others to return to business or whatever plotting engaged them this day.

A few strands of Sofiyana's hair fluttered in the breeze, the curls bright as fire in the morning sun. "Lady Nashavety is banished, but she is not gone, not truly. She gave me her ring, and it gives me great comfort."

"I'm happy for you." Yevliesza knew that Sofiyana would never forgive her for bringing Nashavety to die in the Tower. And she *had* brought Nashavety to the brink of death. But at the last moment she had persuaded the princip to change her death decree. The *fajatim's* death sentence had been transmuted to banishment. And her left hand of power maimed. Nashavety was sent away on horseback with only a small purse of coins.

With Alya and the other *fajatim* well out of hearing, Sofiyana said, "I think you well remember the last words she said to you. It was a mighty curse."

Yevliesza wished that she did not have it by heart. *I consign you to the eight hells. May you hang over the jaws of darkness all your days, and at the end may they devour you. So I conjure the Mythos.*

Sofiyana went on. "You might think it has no power because her left arm was bound." She looked directly into Yevliesza's eyes. "But know that her desires find new life in me."

The words fell like shards of ice around her. Yevliesza had to answer this. "You have new rank, Sofiyana. You could make something of that. Something of your own, rather than that of a disgraced woman." She held Sofiyana's gaze. "You and I were friends once. Who poisoned that?"

"We believe you did."

We? Did she mean all the *fajatim*—or Sofiyana and her predecessor?

"And," Sofiyana concluded, "we mean for you to pay."

Yevliesza watched as the five *fajatim* climbed the stairs to the castle. She knew that Sofiyana would never have dared threaten her in front of Valenty. But then, it was better to know what she really faced with the woman.

A personal hatred, but also one linked to Nashavety. Gone but somehow, still there.

Chapter Two

Dreiza, at age seventy-eight, was a *satvar*. From her many years of life and from her handful of days in sanctuary, she knew how to release things. Like beauty, ambition, husband. Life, at least in the *satvary*, was about releasing, and it was not a bad path, since it did eventually prepare one to relinquish life. All this being true, how could she now sit in her small room and refuse to face the day and the loss it would bring?

When Dreiza had taken the pale the previous month, she had given up her fine apartments in Osta Kiya and her life as the cherished wife of the lord of House Valenty. She had given up fine dresses, court life, and old friends.

Now she sat in her oaten-colored tunic and trousers, her hair braided and coiled, and stared at her hands imagining that her heart lay in their clasp, struggling to beat.

A knock at the door. The High Mother came in, a gentle smile on her lips.

The Devi Ilsat might have sent a renunciate to fetch Dreiza, but she came herself, almost making things worse. Dreiza would not fall apart in front of her.

She sat on the bed facing Dreiza's chair. "The rider has come for Kirjanichka, my daughter."

They sat quietly a few minutes. Then Dreiza rose and, making a small bow to the High Mother, walked by herself out of the domicile and through the courtyard gate to the pen.

Her beloved dactyl squinted at the rider from Osta Kiya, considering whether to accept a stranger as a passenger.

She must give Kirjanichka back to the princip. The *satvary* could ill afford to keep her permanently, and it would not do for Dreiza to have such a privilege in the simple life she had chosen.

Kirjanichka's whiskers rose and fell with the creature's breath as she gauged the new woman's fitness to ride. Dreiza hoped she would accept the newcomer and not be recalcitrant, but the narrowed eyes did not bode well.

Dreiza approached the woman and handed her a small pouch. "She enjoys a few figs."

They would not have sent a man. Although many dactyls would eventually accept a male rider, Kirjanichka was not usually in a mood to do so, especially since she had been retired from service and had been gifted to Dreiza.

Standing next to Kirjanichka, Dreiza rested her hand on the great crest of her head. Dactyls did not love to be touched, but she felt she must have something of her in these waning moments.

Her large yellow eyes met Dreiza's. And she had thought the hard thing had been to relinquish her husband! She had bequeathed Valenty to Yevliesza, the young woman who came to the realm after growing up in the mundat, a world of few powers, and of those that remained, only small ones. Yevliesza had come to Numinat lacking her birthright power, and there was no end of trouble over that. But her power had found her at last—the aligns, it turned out to be—and it helped persuade her to stay amongst them. Dreiza was glad that she would, because Valenty had grown to admire her and must have her. It had been time for Dreiza to lose him, the second husband she had lost. So she knew about renunciation. Or thought she did.

As a gust of wind hit them, Kirjanichka lifted her wings. She had not flown for days and missed the sky, feeling the breeze in her broad, lovely wings.

"Yes, you must go, my dear," she whispered. "The day has come to fly high and strong. Remember me, Kirjanichka. I will never forget you."

She sang a parting song to soothe her.

> Take the days and moments, they are
> Yours to keep.
> Take the journeys and laughter, they will
> Stay with you.
> Take my care and devotion, may they
> Protect you.
> Take my heart, for it goes with you
> Now and forever.

And then they were gone, circling once over the *satvary* complex. Dreiza tried to keep them in view, but the sun cut into her eyes, and soon they had disappeared into the brightness of the afternoon.

⚜

SHE WENT FROM CHORE TO CHORE, RAKING THE COURTYARD, filling coal buckets for the *satvar* cells, folding laundry, and her favorite task, washing dishes, the never-ending dishes. When the cooks came in to prepare dinner, she took a few morsels of cheese up to Lord Woe's perch on the west wall, where he slept with slitted eyes, half-watchful for mice.

On her way, she noted that Kassalya's door was ajar.

After feeding the *satvary* cat and returning from the compound wall, she saw old Videkya coming out of Kassalya's room.

"How does our sister?" Dreiza asked. She hoped that Videkya noticed that she had been on an errand and had not come to try to see Kassalya. Dreiza felt she had a certain bond with the girl, but the High Mother had given strict orders for her—her especially—not to talk to Kassalya. The girl had lately been in an agitated state, visited as she was by unbearable foreknowing. Kassalya was the youngest member of their community, a wounded being, cared for by the renunciates. In fact, cared for by the Devi Ilsat's close circle, the *satvadeya*, one of whom was Videkya.

The woman closed Kassalya's door and turned to look at Dreiza knowingly. Videkya had lost weight during her long illness, but her eyes were still bright and keen. "She does well enough today. Few have found reason to use this corridor, and thus we preserve her peace."

Dreiza disliked being upbraided indirectly. She had been used to the city-palace of Osta Kiya where people generally said exactly what they meant."Then I will be on my way," she said with forced calmness.

"My sister," Videkya said, her face softening. "We are all so sorry that your Kirjanichka has gone."

Suddenly not in command of her voice, all Dreiza could do was nod, her throat tight, her face hot. Walking away, she considered how it was that she had maintained her equanimity perfectly through the day, only to have it collapse when someone was kind.

Chapter Three

Yevliesza greeted Valenty at her door. His smile stirred her heart, to think he was so glad to see her. He was dressed formally in rich browns and a dark vermillion doublet, as Numinasi men always outdid the women in glamour.

She now had three good gowns and tonight wore her black velvet. It was too fine for dinner in her quarters, but he had suggested last month when she agreed to let him court her, that they would dress for dinner, even if it was simple fare.

Her surroundings were simple, too. The main room had a finely tooled sideboard, long dining table, and several cast-off but still fine padded chairs. On one wall hung a lovely tapestry that the previous tenant had left.

She and Valenty seated themselves at the table as Pyvel—who had been standing at the sideboard—poured a dark wine, a bitter substance she drank solely for the sake of Numinasi custom. Then, as Pyvel had been instructed, he vanished into the kitchen.

"Anastyna has kept you so busy." Yevliesza said.

"These are dark times." He reached for her hand resting on the table between them, but only touched her fingertips. A contact as light as a bird's wing, but she felt the heat of it.

They sat in silence for a moment, conscious of the formality they had established. *She* had established.

"Prince Albrecht is massing soldiers at the Volkish boundary gate," Valenty said. "We think he will march soon."

"Which we know from our spies in Volkia?"

He made an expression she took for concurrence. They did not discuss the princip's business, but this was general enough to admit.

She had met Prince Albrecht, ruler of Volkia and commander of the Volkish army. A tense and unforgettable encounter in the crossings, when he and several Volkish officers stopped and questioned her.

"Where will he strike next?"

"Perhaps Norslad. It has few defenses."

It seemed so wrong that Volkia even existed. That its origins, like that of every realm, sprang from strong myths of earth. But in Volkia's case, it was the Aryan myth of racial purity and dominance. She had shared her surmise with Valenty, and he believed it, especially with the rumors leaking out of Alfan Sih that the Volkish used unnatural, machine-like weapons.

Valenty removed his hand away from hers, taking a sip of wine. "But I would much rather hear about you."

She realized how little she had been doing as Valenty worked his information network in Osta Kiya and beyond. "Like what?"

"Everything," he murmured. He leaned back in his chair, waiting, relaxed. For a moment she let herself admire him, his finely proportioned features, his eyes with enough violet in them to keep them from harsh black. His mouth, wide and expressive, his nose with a slight hook, his skin tanned from his love of horseback riding.

"I'm practicing reading Numinasi," she responded. "Grigeni says I'm a quick learner." Her father, as an envoy to the mundat from the Numinat realm, had made sure his daughter spoke the language. But not that she could read it. Thinking of her father brought a wistful mood. She still missed him greatly.

"I will bring you some books," Valenty said. Then with an ironic smile: "If that is allowed?"

"Perhaps a book or two would not be overfamiliar," she said with a straight face.

"Excellent. And Sofiyana's spies can report that I shower you with attention."

Pyvel served the bowls. A hearty soup made with barley and vegetables, almost the only thing she knew how to make. Along with that, a salver of dark bread and a ramekin of butter. Leaving the pitcher of wine, Pyvel departed to his room with instructions not to leave under any circumstances. Not that there *would* be circumstances.

Valenty lowered his voice. "Sofiyana is wearing the amber ring."

Yevliesza set down her wine glass with a slosh. "She *wears* it? She can't be seen to!" Nashavety had been required to leave all jewelry behind, including the prominent—some might say *evil*— ring with the immature dactyl claw embedded in amber.

"She wears it at night."

Apparently one of Valenty's people was a servant in Sofiyana's chambers. "Wears it to bed . . ." Yevliesza murmured. It was very peculiar. Disturbing.

"Perhaps it is best if you do not confront her. As you did on the valley stairs."

She continued eating her soup, pointedly not answering. She would not cower or hide in the castle. Not anymore.

He took the hint, changing the topic. "I have been thinking, about what you told me of life in the mundat. In Okla-homa. Where sometimes there are great spiraling winds that cannot be controlled. Very strange."

"No elementalists," she said. "People might someday control them by . . . science."

"Because there are no Deep powers."

"There might be some that remain from the old days. But if there are, they're greatly reduced. And not practiced openly." Even in the twenty-first century such abilities were often mistrusted, if not hated.

"You lived in a three-story house," he went on, "which you swept twice a week. And you had a suitor."

"I did?"

"The one who lived in the town and helped out at the house."

Shane. "Not a . . . suitor. I don't think he looked at me like that."

"Of course he did."

"He wasn't close to me. In any way."

He reached for her hand again, pressing his fingertips against her own, their only intimacy. Except for that moment in his study a few months ago, when she had been alone with him, and he had taken her in his arms and kissed her. She had wanted him, but he paused, thinking he had gone too far. He had Dreiza to consider, and he wouldn't take Yevliesza as a casual bed partner. Noble, maybe, but the beginning of their misunderstandings. Since then, Dreiza had become a renunciate. Their way was clear, or should have been.

"So I do not have to worry about this man," he murmured.

"No, and besides, he's a world away."

"It is only a long walk from here."

"Valenty," she firmly said. "I have chosen Numinat."

Her old home was in fact close, connected by a pathway of strange origin and power. But her memories of her home were fading in the intense light of a more vibrant world.

After their meal they talked late into the evening. He, of his parents, his father's early death, his mother's service at the court of the former Princip Lisbetha as translator of the several tongues spoken by Mythos diplomats to Numinat.

He spoke more freely than she did. She held back the largest truth, that she had one more power besides the aligns: the ninth power. The one that could alter the passages between the realms, the proof etched into the skin on her back for any lover to see. She wished she could trust that Valenty would keep that secret— unlikely, because he served the princip. And if Anastyna knew, she would use Yevliesza as a weapon in the Volkish wars. Perhaps for good. Perhaps.

For this reason, she wasn't ready to be his lover. And perhaps she never would be.

Chapter Four

L ate at night Valenty stood in Anastyna's deserted Numin Hall. He had been conferring with her and needed a moment by himself in darkness and quiet.

The numin pool lay still and deep. Above it, a circular opening in the ceiling revealed a cluster of stars, glazing the pool with silver. Some said the First Ones created the pool as deep as the oceans of Norslad. He gazed at the pool, sorting his thoughts about what the princip had commanded him to do.

Anastyna was a young ruler, open to new things as the old princip had not been. Anastyna desired the exchange of ideas with other Mythos realms. In extending her kingdom's vision outward, she was sometimes cautious, sometimes decisive. When the latter, her enemies at court despised her. Nashavety had nearly brought her down for her departures from the old ways. But Valenty had approved them. Had approved Anastyna's decision to welcome Yevliesza to Numinat, for one thing. For one bright and stunning thing.

He wanted her. Wanted to have her in every way he could. But she held herself apart from him, while inviting him in. He knew why. Because he kept secrets that did not include her. *Could* not include her. When he finally told her of his clandestine life, she understood him better. Still, she kept her distance.

She did not like that he served the princip. He had done so since she came to the silver collar, as his father had served Lisbeth before her. So when he went to Yevliesza tonight to let her know that he must go on a long journey, he hoped she would understand. What Anastyna wanted would drive both their lives. It could not be any other way.

His mission would be dangerous. It was possible he would not return, and the thought of never again seeing Yevliesza weighed heavily on him. The numin pool rippled with a current of air, deforming the polished surface of the water. He supposed that would mean something to a renunciate.

He made his way out of the royal precincts to tell Yevliesza of his departure. He had no choice but to withhold the true nature of his assignment. He would hint that he was going to Norslad to broker an alliance. But he was not headed to Norslad.

His mission was to Volkia.

IT WAS NOT DREIZA'S FAULT THAT THE SOUP POT NEEDED FRESH pepperleaves. Nor that, happening to be in the cookery at the time, she was sent to the greenshed to fetch them. And that Kassalya was there.

The girl was transplanting tiny starts of vegetables, her short black hair falling over her face as she concentrated, curtaining her off from eye contact with the other workers. Nearby, Dreiza harvested the best young pepperleaves, filling the small basket cook had given her. She smiled when Kassalya looked up, and the girl gravely nodded, holding her gaze.

It was difficult to break away from that long, dark look, the eyes that saw further than any foreknower anyone had ever heard of. In these days of the war in Alfan Sih, Kassalya's mind had become even more unseated, requiring the *satvary* to provide undisturbed quiet. The greenshed, though practical, was a retreat in itself, with its many panes of glass warming the winter garden.

Dreiza was startled when she heard Kassalya say, barely audible, "You are her friend. Yevliesza's friend." Her gaze drifted to the greenshed wall as though the future was just outside the glass.

"Yes, a friend. I wish her well." Then she blurted—it was a clumsy and unfortunate moment—but she asked, "Is she well?"

Remaining rigidly still, Dreiza hoped Kassalya would not answer. How could she have asked Kassalya to look into her fore-knowing?

Kassalya clenched her fist around the seedling she held in her hand. "Sacrificed," she murmured. "On a twisted altar." She opened her fist. "The poor thing. Pulled up by the roots."

Dreiza did not want to know, with all her heart, she did not. She did not have the courage to share Kassalya's visions, which often were of suffering. Yet now she asked, "Who uproots her?"

One of the sisters hurried toward them. Dyura. She put an arm around Kassalya and turned a concerned look on Dreiza.

Kassalya shook the *satvar* off and howled, "Anastyna, Anastyna!" The words broke through the humid quiet, resounding off the bright blue windows, traveling down the length of the shed.

Dyura took Kassalya firmly by the shoulders and walked her down the path to the door.

As they passed, Kassalya whispered to Dreiza, "Take the plant." She craned her neck to look back at the tray of seedlings. "Bury it."

෴

"AGAIN, MY DAUGHTER." THE DEVI ILSAT TURNED FROM THE window of her office, her plump form silhouetted against the light. She shook her head slowly. "Again."

Dreiza wanted to explain how it had happened, but what was the use? She had been the cause of Kassalya's alarm. Had asked, *Is she well?*

"What did Kassalya tell you?"

"That Yevliesza would be sacrificed. On a twisted altar. That Princip Anastyna would pull her up by the roots. Maybe killing her."

The High Mother's face remained calm. "Our purpose, my daughter, is to remove ourselves from the affairs of the realm. Kassalya cannot remove herself from anything. All things penetrate her to the core. But we . . ." Here she looked intently at Dreiza. "*We* have sequestered ourselves at this mountain sanctuary in order to keep far from the affairs of the world. Have you not come for the peace of Zolvina?"

Dreiza opened her mouth to assure the Devi Ilsat that she indeed had, but the old *satvar* raised her hand to forestall her, repeating more forcefully, "The peace of Zolvina." She went on. "The acceptance of our simple lives, the patience to allow things to unfold."

In other words, they would do nothing. Was this patience, or dereliction? Acceptance or complacency?

"May I ask a question, High Mother?"

She received a nod.

"By taking Kassalya in, you came to her aid and did not stand by to allow her condition to unfold as it otherwise would have. Because of the suffering. How is Yevliesza's jeopardy different?"

"It is different because when the girl Kassalya came to our hands she was without succor or custody. She was alone."

Dreiza would not presume to argue with the Devi Ilsat, at least not very much, but her expression must have been obvious. The High Mother waved her to speak.

"Are you sure that Yevliesza *does* have succor and custody? Are you sure she is not unfairly used by unscrupulous persons?" The High Mother remained quiet. "And so," Dreiza lamely added, "we should protect her?"

The old *satvar's* shoulders rose and fell in a long sigh. "You are right, my daughter. I cannot be certain." Her round features hardened. "But I must do my best."

She said no more, but led Dreiza into the hallway. The thick mud walls were uneven, and the corridors cramped in most places, but the spaces were warm and sweet-scented. Dreiza had never seen a *satvar* punished, but she imagined it would be something like plain water and crusts of bread for luncheon, or cleaning twigs and snow from the frozen numin pool.

Dreiza knew that the Devi Ilsat could not, by custom, interfere with royal affairs. But there was no stricture against *inquiring* about affairs, perhaps in a way that would make her opinion clear or provide moral guidance while seeming not to. And yet, she felt sure that the High Mother had not even done that much.

They walked past an open room devoted to spinning yarn and weaving. The sounds of laughter and the thudding of looms escaped into the hall, but it seemed that weaving was not to be her penalty. A shiver of cold came from an unwarded window where a *satvar* was feeding a hawk. *Sympats* were allowed if they did not require special treatment or extra work. Birds suited perfectly.

When they entered a long upper-story gallery, the Devi Ilsat walked to one of the glazed windows, looking out on the foothills. "This view is a special treasure. That is why we placed a hallway here, so one could only see the magnificent view when walking by. To avoid ruining the splendid with familiarity."

A lovely thought and probably a profound one. Dreiza began to hope the whole incident in the greenshed would be forgotten.

"You will spend a goodly amount of time in this gallery. But I hope it will be pleasant for you." She fixed Dreiza with a pointed look. "Tending the vine."

"The vine?"

The High Mother stepped back and gestured to a woody vine growing from a great earthen pot onto a trellis.

"It was a gift from the Irusen *satvary*. A rare *traveka* plant. It blooms every nine years, in great, fragrant blossoms. You have only four more years to wait."

Four years? "Mother, I do not have verdure."

"No. But the vine will accept your ministrations."

"How shall I minister to it?" Dreiza knew nothing about plants.

The High Mother's face dimpled with a smile. "Watch patiently, and you will discover what is needed."

Chapter Five

On the plain below the great massif of Osta Kiya, Valenty's escort of five soldiers were saddled and wearing fur-lined jackets and leather wrapped around their legs to the knees. Yevliesza held her cape close around her as a knifing wind raced down from the Numin Mountains. Tatters of clouds scudded across the plains as though fleeing winter itself.

Word had been passed that Lord Valenty would inspect the boundary garrisons on behalf of Anastyna, including Numin Pass Gate, under snow this time of year. But Yevliesza knew the truth: he was on a diplomatic mission to Norslad.

He was in close conversation with one of the soldiers, a *harjat* by his hair pulled into a knot in back. While she waited to say goodbye to Valenty, Pyvel approached.

"I brought your fur gloves, mistress." Pyvel watched the *harjat* and their mounts, keen on the military trappings.

Yevliesza was glad of the gloves but puzzled by his decision to come down from the palace.

"Maybe I could go with Lord Valenty," he said. "Everyone needs a steward."

"And so do I," Yevliesza pointedly said. "Do you really think Lord Valenty would take you with him?"

By his stubborn expression, he had thought so.

"Well. Thank you for the gloves, Pyvel. But return to our quarters, if you please."

Pyvel reluctantly left, his hair blowing wildly as he headed for the thousand-step ascent to the palace.

Valenty gave the reins of his sturdy roan to one of the soldiers and came to her side.

"I will see you in a tenday," he said. "Unless we are detained in the mountains by the weather."

"Don't be detained, my lord," she said, trying for lightness.

"All right." He allowed a smile to come. Then it left his face. "There is something I need to tell you," he began. "Something I have wanted to tell you. That I should have told you before that day in the Tower."

She waited, afraid of what it might be, if it had to do with *that day in the Tower*.

"Anastyna forbade me to tell you." He paused, looking toward the line of snow-mantled mountains. Then, meeting her eyes, "She said we had no proof and that you would hate us if you knew. But now that I am leaving, I cannot stay silent."

"Tell me, then. Quickly, please."

"I believe that Nashavety had your father killed."

In the icy wind, Yevliesza's face and hands were turning to stone. And now her heart.

"After you asked for her life in the Tower, it was too late to tell you. The princip had a chance to show favor to you and to mollify her enemies at the same time. I would have stopped you if I could have. I tried. But Anastyna withdrew the death sentence.

"You deserved to know the truth long before that. I am sorry, Yevliesza." Seeing that she didn't respond, he added, "Your father's guards left Osta Kiya shortly after he died. I felt that

Nashavety had outright ordered them to kill him or hasten his decline. She hoped to wear you down, take every support from you. She should have died, Yevliesza."

How infuriating to be counseled by a man who, for Anastyna's convenience, kept secrets about her own family. *She should have died.* Yes. And she had freed the woman. Her father didn't die of dementia, but at the hand of Nashavety or her proxies.

"So this was your idea of sharing, getting to know each other? Or was that just my idea?"

He bit his lip, taking his knocks. Not striking back.

It didn't help. His silence was infuriating. She had saved Nashavety from being flung from the Tower and now wished she hadn't. She wanted to hate the woman—*did* hate her—but thinking of her father being tormented in his cell opened a hot pit of anger in her chest.

So Anastyna had instructed Valenty to withhold this information which she thought would turn Yevliesza against the Numinasi? Is that how they thought of her, someone that had to be managed?

"Speak to me," Valenty murmured. Nearby, a horse stamped with impatience or nervousness in the wind.

"What do you want to hear?"

"That you forgive me." He glanced at the men waiting to take to their saddles.

At the moment she didn't want to forgive him, but he was leaving for another realm. This was not how they should part. "I do, Valenty. Forgive you."

She stood on her toes to reach his lips and kissed him, whether *harjat* and horses watched, or not. His lips were cold. One arm came around her as he pulled her closer. When he released her, she managed to say, "Don't be detained by the snow, my lord."

He nodded, his face losing an inch of the tension he held. He squeezed her hand. "It will take more than snow to keep me from you."

Chapter Six

The next morning Yevliesza woke to a calm day, the wind no longer rattling the shutters or sending veils of snow across the courtyard. Valenty would travel easier today. She rinsed her face in icy water at the basin, water brought up from the river by the work of elementalists. Her apartment had a spigot, allowing her to bathe in private, avoiding the communal baths and exposure of the tracery on her back. Lighting had etched that pattern, and time had altered it into a likeness of branching paths, like the crossings between worlds.

If she ever took Valenty as a lover, he would see this. The very reason why she might never be with him, or one of the reasons.

A knock at the door.

A servant sent by the princip.

SHE ATTENDED PRINCIP ANASTYNA IN A SMALL DRAWING ROOM, small compared to the halls where Yevliesza had stood in front of her before.

It was never a good thing to come to the princip's attention. The woman looked delicate with her slight build, her pale, heart-shaped face. But no one could mistake her for weak. She wore the silver torc around her neck, and Yevliesza thought her heart was of metal, too. Polished to look pleasing, but without true warmth.

The only other person in attendance was the Lord High Steward, Michai, his rotund bulk amplified by a padded velvet jacket and a shaggy white head of hair.

Anastyna greeted her warmly. "Yevliesza. How do you fare?"

"I am well, My Lady Princip." She had thrown on her everyday dress since it was the only one she could get into by herself, and hoped that her plain garment would not appear rude for a royal audience.

"We have tried to make you as comfortable as possible," Anastyna said. "Your rooms are favored quarters. We had them vacated for you." She smiled as though that was especially thoughtful, but now Yevliesza knew she had displaced someone.

Nodding a small bow, she tried to look grateful.

"And so." Anastyna glanced at Lord Michai.

The Lord High Steward cleared his throat. "We have had a request from a royal quarter and wish to graciously respond. The court asks you to assist in this matter, since it is about you in particular, but also because it bears upon matters of concern to the princip."

"It's about me, my lord?"

Pausing, Michai touched the medallion of office resting on his chest. "Indeed. And Prince Albrecht."

She stared at him in surprise.

"The Volkish Lord Commandant wishes for you to apologize."

"Surely there's nothing I could have done. . . ."

Michai silenced her with a wave of his hand. "You encountered Prince Albrecht last month in the crossings where you had gone for . . . the events that transpired. It seems that at the time a contingent of soldiers had recently passed through, and you admitted to the prince that you had hidden from them—because you were afraid of them."

"I wasn't—"

Michai interrupted. "Do you deny that you said that or implied it?"

Yevliesza thought back to that unnerving encounter. Prince Albrecht in a dress army uniform; his aides, in black uniforms of a modern cut, a style reminiscent of the Third Reich.

"You apparently said, when asked why you had hidden, that you doubted the soldiers were honorable men."

She remembered how Albrecht's eyes had narrowed to slits. How suddenly, he had dropped his pretense of graciousness.

The exchange didn't happen exactly the way Michai was saying. Albrecht had wondered aloud how she could have been uneasy to encounter his soldiers when they were honorable men. And she had said aloud that she wondered if they were.

"I didn't outright say so, my lord. I believe I said, I didn't *know*."

"Nevertheless. It was an insult, or it has been taken that way."

Anastyna looked at her with an expression of disappointment. Which inspired Yevliesza to say, "Please let Prince Albrecht know that I regret what I said." By the look on the princip's face, she had the uneasy feeling that it was not going to be enough.

"Yevliesza," the Anastyna said softly. "You would do me a good service if you explained your ungracious words and ask for pardon in person. In Volkia."

In *Volkia?* No. That was not going to happen. She must have looked stricken, because Anastyna motioned for Michai to bring a chair for her.

He did so. "It is a prince of the realm who has asked for this, Yevliesza."

"The leader of a vicious enemy!" she blurted.

Michai's voice now had iron in it. "And your princip requires it."

They were caving into the man. The prince's request was meant to humiliate. To agree to it showed weakness, even corruption. They had *invaded* Alfan Sih. She wouldn't do it.

In fact she *couldn't* place herself in their control in any way. Not with her power of the crossings. The very thing that Rusadka said shouldn't happen, the very reason Rusadka had advised her to admit to the princip what her second power was. So that she could be protected by all the force and wiles that Numinat could muster.

"My Lady Princip," she said, imploring her, "what if they don't release me?"

The princip looked at Michai again. He responded. "Fifteen days. We have the commandant's word he will escort you to the boundary gate after fifteen days."

Anastyna had already agreed to this. She felt events rushing toward her, all out of control.

"In return," Michai went on, "the prince will return the son of Iron River Hall to us. The boy who stole away to fight for the Alfans and who has been captured. His return is a gesture of good faith."

Oh God, so *that* was the plan. To trade her for that boy. To placate Oxanna, one of the five *fajatim* who had the power to bring down a princip. It was revolting. She dared to show her disgust, and Michai frowned.

Michai said, more sternly, "Yevliesza. Prince Albrecht believes that it would be proper for us to offer our own token of goodwill."

Goodwill? Toward a Nazi realm? She sprang from the chair. "I will not go."

Anastyna blinked. "*Will* not?"

"You can send me. But I won't apologize. These people . . . you know what they are."

Anastyna's voice went very soft. "They may well be what you say. But we are not at war. And this is a simple matter. Go for a few days. Make your apology, however painful that might be. Do it for my sake and your loyalty to Numinat."

Now was the time to say to the princip, *I have the ninth power. I can create or shut down access to the Mythos realms. Including this one.* But she said nothing. For one thing, Anastyna, by sending her into danger to apologize for a minor thing, had just shown how little she regarded her. She would think nothing of yoking Yevliesza to her ambitions if the ninth power came to light.

"Make yourself ready," Anastyna said. "Go and return. This is a small thing—"

"A *small* thing?" Yevliesza blurted with a harsh laughter. She realized that she had overstepped and dropped her gaze to the floor. God, they could have her beaten.

"A small thing," Anastyna slowly repeated. "And it must be done."

As she departed, she realized why Anastyna had sent Valenty away. In a vicious mood, she thought that if Valenty were here, he would have been forced to choose between an ambitious queen and the woman he claimed to love. His sure choice of Anastyna would settle things between them once and for all.

Returning through the drafty corridors of the castle, she shivered, thinking about walking into the arms of the Volkish military and, if they discovered what she was, how they would use her mercilessly to create new invasion accesses, hidden ones. She had to calm her alarm. If she could carry this visit off without betraying herself, she would be home in fifteen days. As bad as the Volkish were, they wouldn't dare harm her.

She tried to put a brave spin on her situation.

All she really had to do was keep her clothes on.

Chapter Seven

Alfan Sih was at war. Although the Volkish believed the realm was captured, Tirhan knew conquest depended on keeping what you stole. But today, as he and his partisans walked through a pillaged Alfan village, it did indeed look like conquest.

Smoke drifted around him as he walked through the village remains, hoping to find survivors. A few dogs barked from somewhere, warning their slaughtered masters of strangers. As if the Volkish swords were not enough, they had set fire to the great lodge and smaller dwellings, now nothing but ruins and embers.

He looked up to see his men checking the storage huts and barns. They emerged, raising no cry. Morwen walked a pace behind Tirhan, watching the hillside and every movement that might betray an ambush. Her face showed nothing. Only the blood in her hair betrayed how she had stooped to check on slain children and had killed a horse that still breathed despite mortal wounds.

There had been other villages. When the Volkish found that a settlement had hidden partisans, they killed all those who did not

escape and then set torches to the wooden structures. Here, everything was of wood.

The men were silent as they searched the rubble, faces grim,
hearts by now hardened against the slaughter. There would be
time to bring the fight to the Volkish. For now, Tirhan's band of
partisans struck quickly and disappeared, the only strategy they
had against an army of thousands. When Yevliesza had helped
him find a way back to Alfan Sih, he had thought that he could
rally the clans as a fighting force. But many had already been
cowed by Volkish brutality and overwhelming numbers. Still, at
least he was fighting and not living as an envoy in Numinat.

He thought of Yevliesza and her strange power, thinking how
she could create a sudden pathway in an unexpected place. She
could do so for Numinat forces to join the Alfan fight. That would
galvanize the clans. But would Anastyna bring a force of arms to
Alfan Sih? Why should they? Her own kingdom was not under
threat. He did not think that Volkia would dare march on them.
Yevliesza had told him she was going back to her first home, a
world where her powers would diminish and perhaps where they
would not even matter. He had tried to persuade her to stay. But
she would not. Numinat was the land that she loved, and Numinat
had turned on her.

Someone shouted, "A survivor!" It was Tirhan's captain,
Kierach.

He brought forward a girl, perhaps twelve years old. Stocky
and muscular for her age, her face bore streaks of dirt and smoke.
He quickly checked her for wounds, finding her apparently
unharmed. Future king or not, his gift of healing was often needed
as they fought in these forests.

"I pretended I was dead," the girl said.

"Your parents, child," Tirhan gently asked.

Her eyes were cold and steady. "They did not have to
pretend."

"How long since the Volkish left?" Kierach asked her. They knew it had not been long.

"The sun has moved half a hand." So they were still close by.

As Kierach slipped off the water pouch from his big frame and handed it to the girl, Morwen caught Tirhan's eye. "We take her to camp."

He nodded. Then to the girl: "You understand that you will leave with us?"

Her clear blue eyes held him. "Only if I can fight."

"Say *my lord*," Kierach snapped. "This is Lord Tirhan, who will be king."

"Can I fight, my lord?"

Morwen said, "I will teach her." And that was that. Most times he would not countermand Morwen. She was an able warrior, brave, if headstrong.

His small band—fifteen this day—left the remains of the village and went to find their horses in the trees. They had culled nothing from the ruins except a buried cache of potatoes discovered by their wolfhound.

Kierach brought his horse alongside Tirhan's. "We have no business with a child," he murmured, careful to keep the conversation from Morwen and the girl who shared her mount.

"We will wait and see," Tirhan said. If she did not fit in, they would bring her to Angewyst, the holdings of a large clan where she would find welcome.

Kierach's face clouded, but he nodded in acknowledgement and urged his horse forward. Tirhan knew his mind. Morwen had no royal status, but sometimes acted like she did. The men noticed. But they could rein in their opinions, including about who shared his bed. Kierach had been his father's highest advisor. He was now Tirhan's. Living in the wilds as they did, court formalities slipped away, and Tirhan allowed it, to an extent.

A chirrup from in front, the bird sound that warned of an

approach. They came to a halt and listened. The crash of some-thing large in the distant undergrowth. It might be a bear, but if it was, likely it would have smelled them coming and made no noise.

Morwen's hand came up to her shoulder to rotate the leather strap carrying her throwing knives so that they were close to hand. She sent the child to hide in a ravine.

A scout came back, bringing his mare close to Tirhan and Kierach. "An armored warrior, heading down the draw. The larger force has already reached the road."

Morwen had joined them. "So the cladder is alone." She was eager to strike at the thing—a warrior encased in metal—but Kierach conferred with three of the men, and they stole off to handle it.

Kierach saw Morwen's disappointment. "The iron warrior is descending a hill. Our men know what to do."

Tirhan motioned for Morwen to accompany him as he moved forward to take a position in reserve. One of her roles was to use her warding power to shield him, and from that they had become close, and then very close.

The Alfan fighters had already disappeared into the trees. They would have to move fast lest the cladder close the distance with the main unit.

Tirhan, along with Morwen and a few of his best men, crept silently along the heavily wooded hillside, unlike the cladder whose great bulk crashed in the underbrush like a laden wagon. They saw the iron warrior up ahead, balancing almost delicately as he placed one foot in front of the other, bearing a monstrous weight. From the rust on the armor, this was one that had been in the field for many days. The helmet had a slit for the man to see through, and a small breathing hole. The body suit enclosed his torso, arms, legs and even feet. The man inside the metal device breathed harshly, like a blacksmith's bellows.

The partisans sent to fell the giant approached from two sides, creeping along his uphill side. When they came at him, they used their bodies to simultaneously ram into the iron body. The warrior rocked but stayed upright. For a moment. Then he fell headfirst down the hill. Finding that the cladder's fall had exposed the skin of his neck, one of the Alfan warriors raised a pike and took his head off with a one stroke.

Approaching, Tirhan crouched down to look at the iron skeleton. He had never seen one close at hand. The joints were cunningly made to rotate and allow movement, but the body suit was a monstrous thing, a burden no warrior should be able to carry.

An *infernal device*, his people called things like this. The Volkish believed that their other hellish weapons, some of which moved on wheels, could not be called machines—*were* not machines, powered by oils of the land—and so their new weapons did not drive powers out of the Mythos as machines had done in the origin world. But, *infernal*, anyway. Unnatural, and therefore despised, especially here, where the natural world was all that Alfans knew.

Back at camp, the mood was high. As evening came on, they had a long-delayed meal. Morwen sat on a log with the girl— Eiwedd, her name was. When the girl had eaten, she slipped down to sit on the ground at Morwen's feet, falling asleep with her head on Morwen's knee. Meanwhile Kierach broke out a small cask of ale, and they passed it around, taking one swallow apiece.

When Kierach brought Tirhan the cask, he took a draught of it, wiping his mouth on his sleeve. In a low voice, Tirhan said, "Next we take the house at Glenir." Kierach met his eyes, skeptically. It was the great manor where Tirhan's mother and sisters were held.

"It is under heavy guard," Kierach said.

"No, the eastern clans tell me it is not. The Volkish are overstretched and deem Glenir too remote for us to muster an attack. They have left only a handful for security. Our people need a victory, not just the felling of a cladder, but something that shows our fighters, and all Alfans, that we are rising. Freeing the queen and my sisters would be that victory."

Kierach smiled in wolfish satisfaction. "Yes, my lord, that it would." They held each others' gaze. It was a risk, Tirhan knew, but Kierach held no doubts. He wanted to crush the Volkish, drive them limping back to the crossings, taking their abhorrent mechanicals with them.

Tirhan clapped Kierach on the shoulder. "A great victory," he said, and his captain broke into a grin.

Chapter Eight

Shortly after Yevliesza left Anastyna's presence, palace guards came to her door and informed her that she should be ready to depart that evening. They brought saddle bags and a large pannier for her dresses. Within minutes a servant came with a stack of clothes meant for winter travel: a heavy riding skirt, fur-lined boots and a heavy, hooded cape.

She jammed her belongings into the packs as she tried out various sarcastic apologies she could employ for Prince Albrecht. At last she had discharged much of her fury, such that when Pyvel showed up, she was able to appear calm, telling him where she had to go and why.

When she had changed into her wool shirt and riding skirt, she gave him her parting instructions. He was to inform Rusadka of her trip in the morning. Then it would be too late for Rusadka to make the mistake of complaining about Yevliesza's treatment. Her worst choice would be to tell her army superior of her concerns. She had come into favor in her unit, and she mustn't jeopardize that by appearing to involve herself in the princip's business.

"We should tell her right now!" Pyvel urged.

"No. Tomorrow, Pyvel." She held his gaze until he nodded his understanding.

※

AT THE STABLES IT WAS FULL DARK. FOUR HORSEMEN WAITED FOR her and began transferring her baggage to two packhorses. From Osta Kiya's many windows, the castle glowed on the heights like the abode of the gods. While she could see it very well, she and her escort wouldn't be visible, not even here on the close shoulder of the massif. It was the castle's one defensive weakness in what was otherwise an impregnable position. A stable hand came to assist, cupping his hands under her foot to help her into the side saddle.

Someone waited in the shadows of the barn doorway. Lord Michai approached, motioning the escort out of hearing range. She stared down at the old man, unable to bring herself to greet him.

"Yevliesza," he said in a softer tone than he had used in front of Anastyna. "Do this service, and you will have the princip's gratitude. Do not be concerned about the Volkish. They will be content with this gesture, and soon you will be home."

She couldn't stop the laugh that came out. "This is why you sent Valenty away. So he couldn't help me."

"That is not true. He had business that could not be delayed and in any case, he could not have persuaded the princip. Can you understand, girl, that a ruler keeps her torc at the will of the great halls?"

Of course Anastyna had been currying favor with the *fajatim*. She had to do so to some extent. But *this*. This was stupid and rash. Except that the princip did not know how much danger Yevliesza would actually be in. So she had brought this down on herself.

"I am so screwed," Yevliesza murmured. There was no translation for it in Numinasi, so she said it in English.

The use of a foreign language got the expected glare from Lord Michai.

But she was going on a diplomatic mission and was obviously *obeying*, if not with much grace. Abruptly, she turned her mount away from Michai and rode toward her waiting escort.

AFTER A LONG RIDE IN THE DARK, YEVLIESZA AND HER ESCORT OF four soldiers made camp. Her tent and heavy blankets made for a surprisingly comfortable rest. In the morning, she emerged feeling refreshed. The Numin Mountains, at first only a distant spine, now crept along the horizon like the backbone of an enormous, long-buried creature. Somewhere in those peaks was one of the three boundary gates of Numinat, where Valenty was headed. He said he would use Numin Pass Gate to enter the crossings. Her thoughts about him softened as she thought of the dangers he would face in Norslad. Still, she held onto her doubts about him. When he held things back from her, things that were her right to know, she felt the gap of power in their positions and feared it would fester between them.

As they rode through the steppe country with its rolling hills and occasional butte, her thoughts settled like water clearing after a storm. In the hypnotic sway of the horse, she fell into a clear awareness that an align was near, one of the networks of mysterious lines that crisscrossed the world, symbols of the Deep powers that resided not only in the people of the Mythos but in the land itself.

They rode across a strong align, which looked to her like a sparkling crack in the ground—and to those without align power, like nothing at all.

As evening came on and the men made camp, she sat on a rock and stretched out her legs. Not used to long rides, her body felt like it was carved from wood.

A soldier approached her, the officer in command. "Mistress," he said, pointing out to the flats. In the distance, a figure on horseback. After a few minutes, it became clear who it was. Pyvel. On his new horse.

She walked with the soldier to meet him. "Pyvel! Out here alone?"

He looked tired but happy. She held him with a wary gaze as the soldier took his reins and ordered him to dismount.

"Why are you here?"

"I thought you might need a steward. Rusadka was in a temper. Worried, she was. And I thought—"

"No, Pyvel, you didn't think. You can't come with me."

"The Volkish will not let these soldiers enter Volkia, but they would let a steward. And if you have trouble, then I could—"

"Could *what?*" She sighed. "No, Pyvel. Your motives are well-meant, but no."

The soldier took him firmly by the arm. "You will camp with us tonight. But you will return tomorrow, and for that"—his cold look caused Pyvel to wilt—"for that, I have to send one of my men to accompany you."

Pyvel had the grace to look chagrined.

She was disturbed at the thought of his long ride home in the morning. Even with a soldier, this was not a time for a youngster to be out in the wilds. Not in time of war.

Not that Numinat was at war with Volkia. But that war was approaching. She felt that she would be entering it herself, tomorrow, when they reached the gateway and crossed over to Volkia.

Chapter Nine

The next day, Yevliesza and her party came to Lowgate, the same boundary fort that she had passed through when first arriving in Numinat.

As she and her escort entered the crossings, its yeasty smell met her, releasing a rush of memory. She knew this place, knew it at a level beyond words. The footfalls of her soldier escort became a faint background to the innate sounds of the tunnels, softly clicking like baby birds within their shells, ready to fly free. It seemed that no one else could hear them, but the crossings had always called to her. She wanted to answer back, *What am I to do? Why did root power come to me?*

Almost unaware that she was walking, she stumbled. One of the soldiers caught her arm. "All well, miss?"

Yevliesza said it was, even if she had no idea if things were well or slipping inevitably into some place of hard consequence.

Tell me what to do.

But the crossings weren't alive. They had not bestowed this power on her, even if they spoke to her with strange sounds.

When her group approached the Volkia gateway, she almost

turned and ran to find a small cave and wrap herself in it. As she knew from experience she could very well do.

So when the soldiers on the other side of the great doors to Volkia met her, their gray-green uniforms without creases or grime, their boots polished, their hats with the insignia of eagles, the sides of their heads shaved close, and speaking Volkish—with which she had no familiarity—she felt she couldn't go farther. Unless she had an answer to her question of what in all the worlds she was supposed to do.

She needed an answer to steady herself. For comfort, she decided on one: Hide. Be in Volkia. But hide. Hide what you are.

❦

A HALF-DAY CARRIAGE RIDE THROUGH AN EVERGREEN FOREST gave Yevliesza the impression of entering a perpetual dusk. She saw no villages or farms, only the monotonous spikes of trees and, in the occasional breaks, distant low hills furred with myriad conifers.

With the carriage at last coming into a wide plain, her Volkish guide—speaking in halting Numinasi—told her they would soon arrive at Wilhoff Manor, home of Duke Tanfred Wilhoffen. And that Commandant Prince Albrecht would arrive the next day. They approached a grand home, low and timbered and surrounded by a walled courtyard large enough to hold a parade.

A maid led her to a suite of rooms with white plaster walls and rafters spanning the high ceiling. Mullioned windows peaked out from behind rich crimson drapes. Yevliesza admired the beauty of the home—even the set of antlers over the main living room fireplace—but never far from her thoughts was the likely belief system of its occupants, especially if they were opening their home to Prince Albrecht.

In the bedroom her maid, Anika, her brown hair braided and

clasped at the back of her neck, unpacked Yevliesza's things. She wore a long brown woolen dress with a tunic belted over it, a heavy garment, suitable for winter in a large, drafty house.

While Anika busied herself with shaking out the gowns and hanging them in an armoire, Yevliesza went to the room's double doors to step out on the porch.

Her skirts billowed in the wind, whipping in from what seemed an endless grass-mantled plain, its winter yellow like the long hair of Aryan maidens.

It was curious, why they had brought her here and not to a military complex where Albrecht might have assembled soldiers —or perhaps just his senior officers—to hear her public apology. Instead, she was in a remote manor of a local noble. Her host, Duke Tanfred, had briefly met her in the great hall and seemed pleasant enough.

Yevliesza was relieved that she wouldn't have to face Prince Albrecht right away, as the first meeting with him here had assumed large proportions in her mind. How he would act. How *she* would. The whole situation was awkward and laden with risk. But she reminded herself: Fifteen days.

In the far distance a low bank of clouds, heavily gray, stretched in a wide band across the horizon. Except . . .

She stared for a long minute. The clouds twisted as though at a slow boil but remained stationary. With a flicker of excitement, she identified it. A Mist Wall. The veil at the primordial edge of the world.

Anika was at the door. "Mistress, His Grace wishes you to know that the gowns in the armoire are for your use. A seamstress is at your disposal to assist you." Her Numinasi was heavily accented, but just passable.

Following Anika inside, she examined the gowns. Her eyes caressed the rich colors, the blues and violets and greens. After so long dressing in dark blues, black, and gray, they looked like costumes of some alien princess, lovely, but of no practical use. Next to one in burnt umber was her best silver and black gown, looking like a crow among parrots.

She had Anika lay out her dark gray dress, the one with small pearls from Norslad's great sea woven into the bodice. It made a statement: *I am Numinasi.* Perhaps even, *Princip Anastyna sent me, and she will be watching.*

❦

THE MANOR SPRAWLED, WITH TWO WINGS AT RIGHT ANGLES TO the main building. Windows on two sides of most of the corridors brightened the interior with a pleasing winter light. Carved beams supported the high ceilings, giving the manor a lodge-like feeling that was almost cozy, were the place not so large.

She walked through rooms adorned with paintings and furniture carved and upholstered in a masculine manner. For all its size, the mansion had only a few people in it, all of them servants except Duke Tanfred. They didn't make eye contact with her but they must have known who she was. No one else wore a gray dress with long sleeves and a high collar. She reflected that while their political and social outlook arose from a relatively modern culture, they had no technology, or none that she had seen. No radios, telephones, or central heating. The early inhabitants would have remembered machines, but they could not have them here.

She passed through a great room stuffed with books and scrolls. Standing against one wall, a clock in a tall cabinet. It gave her pause.

Numinasi did not have timepieces. In their world view, all complex machines were unnatural and threatening. But apparently the Volkish had other ideas. The clock was not a powered machine in the same sense as a car or an electric fan; they clearly made some distinctions. And it proved that simple machines could co-exist with the Deep powers of the Mythos, though her teacher Grigeni had never said so.

She didn't know why the Mythos was said to be vulnerable to advanced machines. Perhaps it was only a taboo. But during her time in Numinat she had imbibed the idea that such machines interfered with magic. In the corridors of Osta Kiya, people were alarmed by the rumors that the Volkish had powered machines. War machines.

As she continued her exploration, she found herself in a windowed foyer with double doors leading to a veranda. Glimpsing movement outside, she stepped into the fresh air and saw that dozens of people strolled a wide lawn stretching out in front of her.

Most of them were men; soldiers, she guessed. Some wore smocks over trousers, but most wore uniforms, gray, with jackets and trousers of a modern cut. One patient wore a plaster cast on a leg and several others, arms in slings. A woman in servant garb pushed a wheelchair along a paved path toward a one-story structure that might serve as some kind of hospital.

Nearby, a tall, solidly built man took note of her and left off his conversation with a young soldier. He approached her, dressed in a long robe belted with a woven cord.

"Good evening to you," he said in a deep voice and in Numinasi. "Welcome to our hospice." His dark hair fell to his shoulders, and his beard was long and untrimmed. "I am Father Ludving."

"Thank you," she responded. She was startled to think that Volkia had churches and to see a priest—or a monk, if there was a difference. "I'm Yevliesza, of House Valenty in Numinat."

"*Lately* of Numinat," he said, smiling. "And before, of the Firstland."

The Firstland—he must mean the mundat. So he knew a little about her. He placed his hand on a cross hanging around his neck.

She tried not to show her surprise. How odd to encounter this religious tradition here in the Mythos. But she was not in Numinat. Volkia would have its own ways.

"You're ministering to these soldiers?" she asked.

"We do what we can. They have suffered more than most. I see to their spiritual needs, but with my gift of healing, I am also a medicant."

These soldiers must be convalescing from the fighting in Alfan Sih. They had fought against Tirhan and his resistance movement. While her hope was for Alfan triumph, she was sobered by the view of these men who were definitely suffering from the war.

Father Ludving looked over the park-like lawn with its patients taking the air. "We owe this hospice to Duke Tanfred's generosity."

"Is Duke Tanfred's family here? I haven't seen many people. Hardly anyone."

"He is unmarried." Ludving's eyes crinkled, settling into creases that suggested his age was perhaps mid-forties. "Not for lack of interest on the part of high-born Volkish women."

He turned around to watch as the servants began escorting patients to the building on the other side of the lawn. Evening drew on. Most could walk on their own, but their movements were slow and sometimes halting.

"Does the duke have healing abilities?"

"No, his involvement with the hospice is in the role of patron. But he has a great gift of the verdure. Have you seen his work? His gardens?" He put up a hand to forestall an answer. "Likely you have not. You just arrived. I hope your journey was not a distressing one."

"Distressing?"

"Please forgive me. I do not mean to intrude on your . . . circumstances."

"Well. Prince Albrecht arrives tomorrow. So my circumstances could change in a hurry."

The priest nodded. "I am sorry. He is a complicated man. He loves his country, perhaps too much."

"Can one love too much, Father?"

He smiled. "It depends on whether love is broad or narrow."

"Isn't love of country broad?"

His dark eyes held hers. "One has to search one's heart to find that answer."

She thought of her love of the Mythos and whether disclosing her root power to Anastyna would be a broad or narrow love. "I don't want to be rude, Father, but I do wonder about Volkia."

"Ah. You wonder about Volkish ambitions." Despite the difficult topic, he seemed completely at ease. "Of course I can only speak of what I know."

"Well, you are at war. Volkia has taken Alfan Sih and might want more." He nodded solemnly. "Is this what God wishes to happen?"

In good humor Ludving said, "He does not usually speak to me, but I think perhaps you are asking, Do I, as His servant, approve?"

"You, or your congregation. Other people in Volkia."

He glanced up as someone came around from the side of the manor. Duke Tanfred. "One does not withhold compassion."

She lowered her voice, sorry that their conversation would be interrupted. "I don't mean to judge you. I'm just trying to understand."

"Of course," he said. "In my order, we encourage questions."

"But if no answers come?"

"Then prayer," he said simply.

"Ah, there you are!" Duke Tanfred said as he joined them. He bowed to Father Ludving, who extended his hand. Bending down, the duke kissed it.

He turned to Yevliesza. "I see that you have met Father Ludving."

"He was very kind to introduce himself and to tell me about the good work you're doing here."

His face brightened. "Excellent. You have no idea how much I have been looking forward to your visit." He shook his head. "No idea."

That she had no idea—that was true in a lot of ways. Not knowing what was going on had been true off and on since she'd first entered the Mythos.

❧

IN THE MORNING, YEVLIESZA WAS SERVED A BREAKFAST OF sausages and potatoes in her suite. Prince Albrecht would come today, presumably for the apology. She steeled herself for the job.

After breakfast she walked in the gardens to see Duke Tanfred's verdure handiwork and found herself entranced with the designs carved—or more accurately, coaxed—into hedge and tree, often in likenesses of animals and faces. Each turn led to another alley of green creatures, some looking so real it seemed that they might step onto the path before her. Before long, Duke Tanfred found her, and they walked together, their shoes crunching on the hoar-covered grasses as he pointed out his latest works.

Tanfred was boyishly handsome, his light brown hair cut very close on the sides and long at the crown, combed to the side. It was a look from the early twentieth century and jarred her a bit, though it went along with Volkia's origins. He wore simple trousers tucked into short boots, a shirt that buttoned up the front and a fitted leather jacket, altogether an almost modern look. Oddly, women's clothes, like the dresses she'd seen in the armoire and on Anika, were long and of a modest cut. Perhaps a reflection of a culture that kept women in inferior roles.

Duke Tanfred seemed eager for company and, she had to admit, so was she. He had heard much about the great castle at Osta Kiya and wanted her impressions of it and of Numinat culture and politics. She kept her responses positive, feeling suddenly more loyal to Princip Anastyna than was normally the case.

A servant found them on the wandering paths and spoke briefly to the duke. Translating, Duke Tanfred said that Prince Albrecht's entourage had been sighted on the road. He invited her to the rooftop to watch their approach.

They climbed narrow stairs to a small widow's walk framed with ornamental metal railings. A light snow drifted down, forming a scrim over the view of the distant riders and carriage.

In the opposite direction reared the Mist Wall, stretching out across the plain, its top flat as a butte and high enough even at this distance for her to detect its tremblings.

Tanfred noted the direction of her gaze. "My grandfather built this place to have the grand wall in sight. It has receded since then."

In the distance beyond the plains, Yevliesza could just make out a region of hills and valleys left behind by the strange engine of Mythos land formation.

"It's a little unsettling," she found herself saying.

Tanfred looked at her in surprise. "Do you think so? To me it is the great miracle of the kingdoms." As he gripped the railing, she noted that he wore a large gold ring with a cross in the middle of it. A devout man, as she had already seen.

"In my first home, there is nothing like a Mist Wall. It seems a complete mystery."

He watched her intently. "Perhaps you would be interested in riding out for a closer view. Do you ride?"

"I do, Your Grace. I would enjoy a ride very much."

"Excellent! I will arrange it. I place great hope in Volkia's continued growth. Who knows what we might become, what the wall will reveal?" He noticed her look of curiosity. "What I mean is, that Volkia must expand to serve our growing population, but in a natural way. The primordial way."

"The primordial lands don't grow very fast," she said. "In one person's lifetime . . ."

"There are many marvels in God's creation. Who knows what things may come to pass?" He smiled. "Forgive me. I am often caught by the wonder of it."

The riders and carriage were only minutes away.

"Who will be with the prince, Your Grace?"

"His officers. Also, his nephew Sigmar, on leave from the war zone. Evah Krim, who is often in the prince's company." He spoke reassuringly. "Evah enjoys a social engagement, and Sigmar is a decorated officer, even if he is just nineteen."

It didn't sound like it would be a court-martial. She breathed easier.

Chapter Ten

Valenty did up the last button of his Volkish uniform jacket and stretched out his arms to test the fit. His *harjat* aide, a tight-lipped and hardened warrior, also wore a Volkish soldier's uniform.

Palace tailors at Osta Kiya had copied the uniforms, having observed the cloth and cut from the entourage that had served the Volkish envoy in the days before his expulsion from Numinat.

Valenty watched as Urik belted his uniform. He had not known the man prior to this mission. These last few days they had been taking each other's measure. Urik was taciturn, but did not miss much of the land, the weather, or the worth of a man. As a *harjat*, he was a fighter of great skill. Valenty was his social superior, but in other respects Valenty thought that Urik might be the better man. He did not mind it. He needed someone very capable at his side.

The thick walls of the fort at the pass creaked from the cold like a crack stabbing through a frozen lake. Outside, two months of snow wrapped the garrison in a frigid blanket, deadening sounds, keeping the fort and its inhabitants in unforgiving isolation.

The narrow approach to it from the plain was kept open with the continual labor of elementalists. But as winter deepened, that effort would take more effort, necessary for food supplies and wood to burn.

The fort commander, with white hair and a well-lined face, joined them in their small room where they had spent the night.

"They are coming," the commander said.

Urik drew his knife. The roll of bandages lay on the table. He felt along his neck for the right place to make a cut, not a deep one, but not minor, either. Unflinching, he made the incision, making sure some of the blood fell on his jacket. The commander quickly dressed the wound, tying it off.

Leaving the room, Valenty and Urik strode through the narrow corridor into a dim staging area, where at one end was the great iron door to the crossings. There were no guards in the room which had been cleared for them. This was to be a secret mission, and the fewer who knew about it the better. The commandant nodded to them and wished them well.

They removed the bar securing the door. The steps led down into a region emitting a faint glow and bringing the unmistakable ripe smell of bread rising in a pan. They went down, hearing the heavy closing of the door behind them.

⚜

IN A CAVE-LIKE NODE OF THE CROSSINGS, VALENTY AND URIK waited as a contingent of some forty Volkish soldiers trooped through from Alfan Sih: those wounded badly enough to leave the field, but able to walk. Joining the group was the moment of most danger. Several such units of wounded had come through in the last day and a half, and the plan was that Valenty and Urik would move into place and wait for the next one, as though they had fallen behind from the last contingent.

A detachment of soldiers was almost upon them, their steps thudding in the close tunnels. Valenty and his aide crept out of the node and into the corridor, finding a place for Urik to sit with his back against the tunnel wall. As the group approached, Valenty helped Urik drink from a metal cup of the sort that Volkish soldiers wore strapped to their packs.

Valenty made a show of helping Urik rise and, supporting him, he threaded into the line of wounded and began the long walk to Volkia. Someone asked about their unit, and Valenty named one they knew was deployed in Alfan Sih, but his response was gruff to avoid further conversation.

Some of the troops around them bore the weary, distracted air of soldiers who had seen too much or done too much to join in casual talk. They might be fresh from action or suffer from unseated minds, or both. Valenty took on that demeanor when an officer came to walk at his side. After some time, a medicant made his way up the file offering water, and the officer told the man to change Urik's neck dressings, bloody as they were.

Valenty took Urik out of the line of march, and the medicant applied a clean white cotton bandage to his neck. As they had planned, Urik said thank you in Volkish, using a raspy voice that could suggest a throat wound. They rejoined their group and plodded on.

At an imposing tall cavern, several paths intersected, and the wounded took a rest, sitting against the walls. The tunnels glowed as Valenty remembered them, making the crossings less dreary than they might have been by torchlight. The soldiers broke out their rations wrapped in cloth and ate, disregarding the stench of wounds and sweat. A barrel was brought off a small wagon for the men to relieve themselves.

After the tension of joining the Volkish unit, Valenty found himself more at ease and able to surreptitiously listen to some of the nearby conversations. The war was not going well. Alfan fighters conducted quick raids and refused to meet the enemy head-on. They often got away, leaving damage behind, and affording no opportunities to exact revenge. He was gratified to hear it, but he knew that such tactics would not likely drive out the Volkish. Lord Tirhan, whom he knew well from his sojourn in Osta Kiya, would eventually have to pull the clans together into an effective army.

A group of officers came through from Alfan Sih, leading horses. These were High Command, Valenty knew, or at least one of them was. There could be no mistaking him. Marshal Walthar Reinhart. Short and thin as a bird, he had a narrow, hatchet-like face with a receding chin and a mustache clipped short. Famously ugly, he made up for these deficits with a uniform loaded with medals, braid, and silver buttons.

The soldiers sat up straighter, those that could, and Reinhart walked among them, chatting and smiling. Despite his reputation for cruelty, the common soldiers admired him. He was also the most powerful of Prince Albrecht's inner circle.

Reinhart made his way along the wall, heading toward Valenty and Urik. When he stopped next to them, Valenty made a show of trying to get to his feet, but the marshal said that he should remain seated. Valenty knelt and pretended to almost crumple from the effort. Reinhart, averting his eyes from this weakness, continued down the line.

Urik whispered, "A face like that could terrify children."

"And probably has," Valenty murmured.

A HARSH WIND BATTERED THE HOSPITAL POST AS VALENTY AND Urik shuffled forward to be seen by medicants, as the Volkish called them. The bivouac by the boundary gateway included hospital and mess tents and, dotting the broad field, officers' billets and tents for the rank and file.

They had emerged from one of the boundary gates giving access to Volkia. The question was, which one? Valenty noted the hills in the distance and, behind them, the crags of snow-covered mountains.

"I think it is Lassen," Valenty said.

"I agree," Urik said. In keeping with his guise of being wounded, he spoke barely moving his lips. Two soldiers moved along the line, passing out wool blankets.

Valenty and Urik had a guide waiting for them somewhere near there, but first they had to find a way to leave the line heading to the hospital tent. Any medicant would know immediately that at least Valenty was not incapacitated.

"On my signal," he murmured, "we will head off to the left, past the mess tent."

Urik nodded. Their plan was risky. Their detachment had come through the gateway in some disorder but were immediately ushered into the hospital queue, removing any chance for the two of them to easily slip away.

As they shuffled forward in the line, a fist of wind slammed into the hospital tent with a muffled thud. The soldiers in line pulled their wool blankets more firmly around them and kept their heads down.

Valenty and Urik had failed to shake off one of the soldiers who had walked with them through the crossings. Heinmann's hand was broken—in combat, he assured them—and he considered himself in bad shape, muttering about the pain as they marched. He had occasionally asked questions about their unit and what action they had seen, seeming to resent the shortness of Valenty's answers, but still keeping step with them. Now he was in line behind them.

"And my left hand," Heinmann groused. "A *left*-hand wound .

. . it got a bad correlation, like everybody says. You take a broken hand, now, like I got, they should put me at the front of the line."

"Well, you can move up, now," Valenty said sharply. "My friend needs the trench. His bowels are about to give way."

"So, where is the ditch?" Heinmann said without sympathy.

"We will find out and let you know." He pulled Urik out of the line before Heinmann could ask more questions, and they hobbled off, Urik bending over as though with cramps. Valenty expected at any moment they would be questioned, but they managed to put some distance between themselves and the hospital line and got directions to the latrine.

Several soldiers were standing and squatting along the edge of the trench, and Valenty kept watch for officers. This would be their best chance to slip away, even if it was second quarter of the day, with no shadows and few barriers to hide behind.

Valenty glanced at the junction of two saddles in the hills. "The confluence of the two hills out there," he said. "Our man should be in the thicket at the base of those hills. In a direct line from the gate."

"We will be spotted the moment we leave the camp," Urik said as he stood up, buttoning his trousers.

"Not if we march there in good order." He noted Urik's skepticism. "The forest perimeter might be patrolled. We could be relieving the sentries." Of course, if there *were* scouts or sentries, that would be trouble.

"It might work," Urik said. "Or we wait for nightfall."

"No. The longer we are here, the more questions. And some of them we will not be able to answer." *And you, my friend, without the language, cannot answer any*, he thought.

The latrine was empty of soldiers at last. As they began to head for a wood plank stretching over the ditch, they heard a man's voice.

"I thought you was going to tell me where they keep the shitter?" Heinmann was walking up to them.

"We got our own troubles," Valenty said.

"You two," Heinmann said, his face turning ugly. "None of the lads ever saw you before."

"As though *you* have a wagon-load of friends," Valenty cast back. He gave the barest nod to Urik. In a motion both swift and efficient, Urik stepped in back of Heinmann and, pulling the man backward, swiped a knife across his windpipe. As the man crumpled, grabbing his throat, Valenty and Urik tossed him in the ditch and hurried for the plank bridging the trench.

They crossed over the ditch and walked away, ears pricked for the sound of anyone entering the latrine and raising an alarm. If caught now, they would be seen as deserters and, soon enough, spies. The two of them dropped their blankets behind a shrub and struck out across a meadow well-trampled by a horse unit.

Maybe Urik was right, Valenty thought. They should have waited for dark, but it was too late now. A dead man lay behind them and they were headed away from camp. As they gained distance, Valenty felt as exposed as a bear in a courtyard. The sun shone down on the field, a cold glare bouncing off a thin crust of snow. Their steps punched through the crust.

They approached a dirt road and turned down it, their gait purposeful but unhurried, with Urik no longer the wounded soldier. They would reach the line of trees in a hundred steps, each one taking them further from a soldier's duty, a soldier's anonymity.

"If we hear a shout, we run," Valenty said.

"And make a stand in the trees," Urik growled.

At least they were well-armed. With Urik at his side, they could fight off twice their number. He thought of Yevliesza back at Osta Kiya. *Do not be delayed* was the last thing she had said to him, thinking he was going to Norslad. If he was spared, he would make it up to her; regretting his damn conviction that she must be protected from the truth. Lest Numinat lose her. Lest *he* lose her.

They reached the trees with no outcry or pursuit. Urik scanned the meadow. No one had seen them. But they must have found Heinmann's body by now, and perhaps someone had seen two soldiers marching away. Time to lose themselves in the forest, and quickly.

BY AFTERNOON, VALENTY, URIK, AND THEIR NAMELESS GUIDE scrambled up the side of a rock-jumbled hill into a small camp. They sat on a fallen tree trunk, weary from the fast pace they had maintained.

From this height, Valenty could see the field beyond the trees and the dark shapes of the Volkish encampment. They thought no one had followed them, but they might be, having set out when he and Urik were in the thick of the woods.

Their guide, tall and rangy, looked as though he lived in woods and had missed many a meal. Another guide had waited for them at Rorrs Gate in case the unit that the two of them had attached themselves to emerged there. All part of their elaborate scheme of infiltration, the camp contained the supplies they would need for the journey: winter clothes, fur-lined and sturdy, packs with rations, weapons, and supplies for making camp.

Their guide shared out skins of water and a portion of dried meat, and soon he and Urik were hunched over a map, conferring on the route.

It would mean a journey of several days. Of the two boundary gates, Lassen was the furthest gateway from the place where Nashavety was known to be hiding. Her holding was nestled far into the hills of the Breminger Forest, by reputation a forbidding land of fogs and trackless, dark woods. It was the sort of place their quarry would choose, bleak and murky like the woman herself. She had many guards, though the numbers were uncertain. Urik and he would use stealth, not force, to enter.

Nashavety had fled to Volkia and found a welcome there. In Numinat her sentence for trespass had been commuted from death to banishment, but only so long as she refrained from abuses of whatever Deep power remained to her after the severing of the small finger of her left hand.

The fiend had not refrained. Nashavety's powers were elements and creature power. Their spies had heard rumors that her powers, though diminished by the mutilation, were resurging. They did not know how, but Anastyna thought it could only be by means of dark arts. The princip's outrage flared higher when word came that the woman was advising Albrecht on Numinat defenses.

At this betrayal, Anastyna declared her pardon forfeit. Valenty's mission had latitude for circumstances on the ground, but foremost he was to reconnoiter and report what force would be required to flush her out and dispatch her. But if the chance arose, he was to kill her.

Valenty might have been an unlikely choice for the job. He was not a warrior, although trained in assassination, but he did have fluency with the language. As well, he possessed the complete trust of the princip in a mission that must remain secret. He believed they had every chance to succeed. Valenty had strong warding power and Urik, manifesting—helpful for entering Nashavety's stronghold unnoticed. But eclipsing all that, Urik was a *harjat*: an exceptionally skilled warrior.

Their Volkish guide had supplied Urik with a palm-sized mirror that he could use to send a message. A gifted manifester, he could send a visual impression, a display of a creature, a place, or even a route into a mirror and direct it into another. In Osta Kiya, the princip had often summoned Valenty with the mirrored impression of her *sympat* falcon. So the small mirror would allow them to provide at least some information back to the Numinat court if their mission failed and they were unable to return.

Valenty did not intend to fail. He would have undertaken this mission simply because the princip commanded him to, but the fire in his heart arose from a different source: Nashavety's responsibility for the death of Yevliesza's father. Her drive to bring about Anastyna's downfall. And most of all, her cruelty and murderous actions against Yevliesza.

Nashavety should have died at the door in the Tower. Now he would finish it.

Chapter Eleven

Despite the allure of the colorful gowns at her disposal, Yevliesza chose her black dress for Albrecht's gathering. It was a fine gown, with lace at the throat and cut velvet for the sleeves. As she sat before the bathroom vanity with an array of creams and powders laid out, Anika did up her hair in an elaborate twist, the closest she could come to the Numinasi style of hair folded into a strong net.

Yevliesza had grilled Anika about Prince Albrecht, discovering that he was unmarried, popular with the people and his officers, and an expert horseman, as would be expected of a man who had creature power. Coming face-to-face with him set her nerves racing.

When Yevliesza went into her bedroom, she found a woman looking into the armoire.

In fact, the stranger had dresses in her arms and, seeing Yevliesza, gave a start. She exclaimed something in Volkish and then curtsied, hugging the gowns.

Anika translated, saying, "Mistress Krim says that she did not know anyone was given this room."

Taken aback, Yevliesza didn't answer immediately, but there was no need, because Evah Krim was focused on the gowns she held.

"This . . ." Evah began, trying to speak Numinasi. "This green, so good! Is it, you think? Or the blue?" She laid them out lovingly on the bed, apparently past her embarrassment at being caught snooping.

"Very nice," Yevliesza said in Numinasi, since she had forgotten how to say yes in Volkish. The maid translated and closed the armoire doors, making clear that no more gowns would be coming out.

Seeing this, Evah smiled like a little girl caught taking cookies without permission. "I thought room empty."

Evah wore a cream-colored gown trimmed with fur at the scoop neckline and sleeves. Her small features were saved from plainness by her lustrous blond hair that fell in soft waves to her chin. Everything about the woman was small, meek, and soft except for her eyes, which held an impish sparkle.

Laughter from the hallway. It faded as people walked away.

Evah put a hand to her mouth as though she had said something she shouldn't have. She started toward the door, then turned. "I think, you wearing the blue? It is best." A scrim of light haloed the blue dress for an instant. Evah had the gift of manifesting.

The woman giggled, tossing her hair back. "Or the green." She took in Yevliesza's dark gown. "Better than old woman's dress." She slipped from the room.

Evah was not simply unpleasant, she was bizarre.

At the appointed hour, Yevliesza entered the dining room. On the longest wall a fire crackled in a fireplace, around which

Volkish army officers stood chatting. The only men not in uniform were Duke Tanfred and the man who must be Prince Albrecht. She did remember him now. He wore a long tailored jacket trimmed in black velvet, with a white shirt and lace at his neck.

"Ah, Yevliesza," he said as she approached. Her heart drummed in her chest, and she feared her smile wobbled. She joined the group, nodding a bow to Albrecht. His light brown hair was, as before, cut very short on the sides, but on top, slicked back. He was a handsome man, well built, with a forehead rather too high, his mouth expressive and full. But his most distinctive feature was the startling sky-blue of his eyes.

Albrecht noted her Numinasi gown and turned to Duke Tanfred. "She appears to be in mourning, my lord. Have you not put suitable attire at her disposal?"

Tanfred raised a hand in polite dismissal. She was grateful he didn't endorse the prince's rude remark.

Albrecht introduced her to his officers. Foremost, Marshal Kenrick, and also several colonels, their finely tailored uniforms studded with insignia and silver buttons. She memorized their names. They gave her formal bows, their eyes studiously gracious.

"And may I present Evah Krim." He gestured to Evah, who had been standing farther away. "Evah, this is Yevliesza of House Valenty."

"Evah and I have met, my lord," Yevliesza said. "She helped me select a gown for dinner."

Evah responded with a smirk.

Prince Albrecht raised an eyebrow at the apparent collusion between the two women. His blue gaze tended to hold a person's attention. She felt the man's presence acutely and drew herself up so that she wouldn't appear cowed, even if she was.

Turning to Evah, Albrecht said, "My dear, I had thought your taste in clothes was impeccable."

"I'm sure it is, sir," Yevliesza answered before Evah could. "But I made my own choice." Marshal Kenrick gave her a narrow, apprising look. Maybe she hadn't made a good beginning. Or maybe she had, because now Albrecht smiled in good humor and raised an eyebrow at his officers, who dutifully laughed at her apparently amusing self-assurance.

He introduced young Sigmar, wearing a beautifully fitted gray officer's uniform with some insignia of rank on his collar. He seemed merely a boy in a dress-up costume. But he reached out to shake her hand, his large brown eyes lit with pleasure. Albrecht clapped him on the back, and the group moved to the table in a better mood than Yevliesza had expected.

She was seated next to Sigmar on one side and Marshal Kenrick on the other and, across the table, Evah sat among the officers, a kitten among warriors. As servants poured wine and delivered soup, Tanfred announced that the evening's conversation would be in Numinasi in honor of their guest.

Albrecht inquired after her journey from Osta Kiya, regarding her carefully as she described the ride over the great plains of Numinat. Evah was ignored at the table, occasionally simpering at something she heard and casting glances at Yevliesza, perhaps desperate for attention.

Despite the carefully pleasant tone at the table, Albrecht's initial comments on her dress made clear that he wasn't above embarrassing her and making cutting remarks. Thank God that, for this opening gambit, she had worn the black. It signaled Numinasi strength. Women were not mannequins with nothing to say for themselves. At least she wasn't.

As the meal continued with another course—she barely registered what she was eating—she knew she had to make conversation and turned to the easier of her tablemates, Sigmar, asking how he was related to Prince Albrecht. He was the son of Albrecht's brother, who was envoy to the Jade Pavilion. She didn't ask about the war, but he was eager to tell her anyway, claiming that peace was being discussed. It was something he apparently thought she would approve, though it would mean the Alfan had given up.

Marshal Kenrick, heavy and barrel-chested, asked in halting Numinasi what she thought of the great Wilhoff Manor, and she praised it, particularly the gardens. Tanfred overheard and held forth on his plans for a folktale theme on the south grounds.

At last Evah managed to say that she and Prince Albrecht would spend a few days at his nearby country house, Treidenstag.

Albrecht waved this off, declaring that the ride would be too arduous for her this time of year, and that he would go alone.

"Oh?" Evah said in a crestfallen tone. "I would so like to go."

"Not this time," Albrecht said, directing his gaze at her and holding it.

"But my lord . . ." she protested.

"My lord *what*," he erupted, his fist crashing down on the table, causing the silverware to jump. The diners froze, especially Evah. "My lord, what, Evah? Do you intend to beg at the table? Perhaps shed tears into the poached fish?"

In a pleading voice, Evah said something to him in Volkish.

Albrecht made the slightest movement of his head toward a heavily medaled officer seated beside Evah, and the man stood, inviting Evah to leave with him. The chairs were soon straightened by a servant, leaving two holes in the seating arrangement and the table conversations muted.

Duke Tanfred gamely tried to salvage things, proposing a toast to Sigmar, referring to his bravery in combat. Everyone but Yevliesza raised their glass. She meant no disrespect to Sigmar, but she couldn't applaud the war. Albrecht didn't notice or pretended he didn't.

❦

AFTER DINNER THE ROOM EMPTIED, WITH DUKE TANFRED BIDDING her goodnight and saying that in the morning they could ride out for their excursion. She nodded her agreement and when she turned to leave the room, Albrecht said, "Stay a moment, Yevliesza."

She turned to him, defenses up, a calm demeanor firmly planted on her face. He gestured to the sofa next to the hearth and when she took a seat, he sat in a chair facing her. "I am sure the evening was trying for you, but that was not my intention. Perhaps I may make up for it now?" It seemed he was completely over his outburst and assumed everyone else was, too.

She responded, "If we can remain civil, it would go better."

He laughed at this. "I agree. Let us be civil. Sigmar was thrilled to meet you, even if you did not drink the toast. In fact, if you do not restrain him, he will ask you everything about your real homeland. Firstland."

"Numinat is my homeland, Prince Albrecht."

"Ah. I did not know how you regarded it, with your queen sending you on this unpleasant mission. And our first acquaintance being under difficult circumstances." He watched her calmly, his legs crossed, the fire throwing flickers of light on his face. He had two sides to his personality, and she was trying very hard to predict which one he would display next.

"The princip has many things to consider besides my convenience."

"Yes," he said with an ironic tone. "I hope to give you more respect than Anastyna has shown."

"As to that, Prince Albrecht, will your officers be the ones I will apologize to?"

He straightened up. "No. It will be to me."

"Then I do apologize. I apologize for my ill-chosen words, which I didn't mean to impugn your army's reputation." She had prepared a longer speech, but it had fled her mind.

Albrecht shook his head. "That is very well, but it does not satisfy." He drew his lips into a flat line. "I am not convinced your words are sincere. I am sorry, but I do not."

Of course they weren't sincere, but she had fulfilled her responsibility.

He went on. "You are an interesting and intelligent woman. Too intelligent to believe that an insult to my people can be laid aside so easily."

"What do you want from me, then?"

"That we come to an understanding. I would like you to meet more of the Volkish people."

"Duke Tanfred has been wonderful to me. And I have also met Father Ludving, who was very kind. I know one can't make blanket statements about a whole country."

"And yet you have." He held up a hand to forestall her response. "Since you are here, stay with us long enough to meet my people and then form a more nuanced view of Volkia. The agreement was for fifteen days, after all."

"I thought that I would be home in fifteen days, so given the four-day journey to and from, that leaves seven days."

"Come now, Yevliesza. Fifteen in Volkia is fair."

"Are you saying that it's a condition of the release of the young man of Iron River Hall?" *Fajatim* Oxanna's son.

"I am." He gazed at her calmly, waiting for her response. Knowing what it had to be but giving her the opportunity to willingly submit.

Yevliesza looked into the fire. A log collapsed, flinging out sparks. She should have known it wasn't going to be easy.

"Yes, then," she said in strict formality.

He signaled for a servant to bring wine, but Yevliesza excused herself, saying she was still recovering from her journey. Albrecht rose as she did and executed a short nod to her, by way of a bow, given the disparity of their stations.

If he expected to have engaging conversations and a meeting of the minds, she was delighted to prove him wrong.

Chapter Twelve

Through a curdling fog, Tirhan and his band crept across a bog to approach Glenir Manor. The great house held his remaining family: his mother and his two sisters, fourteen and seventeen years old. Lives would be lost this night, but it would not be just for his sake; it was for the hopes of the Alfan people, to see that the realm still had a queen, to know that Alfan Sih fought back.

Morwen, as always, was at Tirhan's side, ready to throw a warding. Two elementalists in their midst worked to thicken the fog across the flat terrain that otherwise gave little concealment. They needed the murkiness, but it clouded their vision as well as the enemy's.

Kierach, Tirhan's captain, led the way and would direct the assault. His wolfhound kept close to him, its ears forward with the concentration of a superb stalker. At his master's side, the wolfhound was trained to go to ground if it sensed a threat or attack if commanded to.

Glenir was no fortified dwelling, but a residence with porches and outbuildings that could give cover for sentries. They crept forward, watchful and silent.

Eiwedd followed the party, wearing Morwen's spare knives in a leather vest fashioned for the purpose. She would not fight—not yet—though she had been practicing with a sling and rocks, showing herself a deft learner.

The manor house loomed into view, a hulking shape two stories high, a few of its windows alight. Tirhan thought of his mother, Queen Gwenid, inside at the mercy of Volkish guards, bearing her grief for her husband and oldest son. She must wonder how her younger son—now her only son—fared, perhaps not even knowing that he had returned to Alfan Sih. His sisters, Hanavar and Cadris, were next in line for leadership, and therefore the Volkish removed them from the game board. He thought of Cadris, with her high spirits and her horsemanship, almost equal to her mother's, certainly better than his own. The memory of her winning her first race against him, and he, ten years her senior, had over time become a cherished one.

In a swift motion, the wolfhound lay down, its muzzle pointed to the left corner of the manor.

Tirhan and the raiding party crouched and watched, pulling their brown cloaks over their heads. Morwen drew a knife. Eiwedd handed her another to replace the empty sheath in her knife harness.

Kierach crept forward without the scout dog. After a time, he returned. "There are three sentries," he murmured. "Cynod and I will kill the first two, and Belwin will take the third one alive." They would force the sentry to enter the manor, a knife at his throat, and they would follow. Then Tirhan and the other fighters would pour in and fight past the soldiers stationed inside.

Morwen motioned Eiwedd back, and the girl retreated. Kierach signaled the wolfhound to stay behind with Tirhan and moved into position to take out his man. Soon he was lost in the fog.

"Once in the house," Morwen said, "keep me by your side. That is the dangerous part, inside."

Tirhan nodded. He had reluctantly accepted the need for a shield, and it happened that the best warder was Morwen. The men would not accept Tirhan being at high risk. But he knew he was a Volkish target, and therefore Morwen was as well.

The hound's ears pricked forward, and it crouched once more, watching a corner of the house. A soldier, one of the three sentries, had rounded the far corner. But he was not alone.

Under her breath Morwen swore. An animal was walking with the sentry, a brown and gray wolf. One that faded in and out of view.

"Wraith wolf," Tirhan whispered.

Despite its training, the wolfhound made a low growl at this apparition. The wraith wolf instantly heard this. The creature stopped and took a few steps toward Tirhan's position. The sentry pointed and the wraith wolf charged toward them. Another wolf had joined the first one and they plunged into the bog.

Tirhan hissed at the men to retreat into a tight formation, but some were too far to hear his command. He gave a shrill bird call to signal Kierach and Cynod to return. They were no match for wraith wolves, which could appear out of nowhere.

Morwen said, "Kill the sentry, the one who controls the wolf." She stood, her arm a blur as a knife left her hand and then another. The soldier was down, but now another wraith wolf came out of the fog and raced toward them.

Shouts came from near the manor, but Tirhan could not see if more soldiers had come from the house. Tirhan and his party retreated into the bog. One of the men let fly an arrow and, by the sound of a cry, it had found a mark. Morwen said, "They have the wolves under compulsion. The guards are sending them after us. We have to kill the controllers."

"No, fall back," Tirhan ordered.

In the next moment they had found a few of the others who formed a tight configuration of kneeling archers with some standing behind them, arrows nocked. Kneeling in front, Tirhan heard the sound of arrows on the fly.

Then, silence. Tirhan and Morwen found Eiwedd and hurried her along. One of the men chirruped a signal and soon several other Alfans joined them. At the edge of a line of trees, they spread out in a line and prepared to fight, using the trees for cover while the Volkish would be forced to approach them on the flats.

But the silence remained unbroken. After a time, Tirhan saw a wraith wolf come out of the fog a stone's throw away. Then it disappeared. But he knew it could still be approaching in wraith form. Eiwedd had drawn her rock sling and resisted being shoved to the back.

They waited. Kierach had not returned. He might have gone in a different direction to split the Volkish pursuit.

After a long wait, the archers relaxed. The Volkish were not pursuing. They had called their wraiths back. *Called* them, Morwen emphasized, though Tirhan had never known a wraith wolf to be under creature control. Wraith wolves passed easily between the world of the living and the land of the spirits, and when mortals saw them disappear, they were observing the creatures pass into that other realm, even if only for a heartbeat. He had never imagined that they could be subject to human control. It seemed even more wrong than the many other desecrations the enemy had committed.

Eiwedd moved closer to Morwen, handing her new knives. "You got one of them."

"One was not enough," Morwen said.

A shape came toward them and then another; two men approaching, but preceded by the bird cry that identified them as Alfan.

One of the shapes was Kierach, carrying a body. He lay it gently down. It was Belwin, his throat torn out. Another warrior bore Cynod, still conscious, but bleeding.

The men fashioned slings to carry Belwin's body and Cynod, and the party moved farther into the woods, navigating thickets that slowed them.

Eiwedd walked ahead of Tirhan and Morwen, keeping up with the rapidly moving party. The girl asked Kierach about the wolfhound, which she especially liked.

"He is dead," Kierach said. "But he died fighting." He put his hand on her shoulder.

Eiwedd shrugged him off. "That is all right, then," she said, pushing on.

TIRHAN KNELT BY THE STREAM, SPLASHING ICY WATER ON HIS face until it stung. They had made camp late at night, putting distance between themselves and any pursuit from Glenir. The fog lingered as though stuck in the naked boughs of ash and oak. They would leave at dawn for the main camp, but he could not rest yet.

The assault had been his idea, driven by desperation. His followers were eager to strike hard against the Volkish, but with so few fighters they were unlikely to do much more than harry the enemy. His people would fight on, even if they could not win. But some clan lords judged the Volkish too powerful. By remaining neutral they hoped to keep their ancestral lands, though the price would be fealty to Volkia.

Tirhan stood, brushing the mud from his knees. When he turned to go, he saw that he was not alone. Someone stood by a silverwood tree, although there had been neither silverwood nor a person there before. Tirhan's knife was in his hand, but he had no control over his arm and could not move at all, caught by some trance or spell.

As he took the stranger in—an older warrior, sword at his hip —the man said, his voice echoing among the trees, "I could have killed you already. But you will not need the knife." His hair hung long, the color of fog.

The stranger's face blurred and became younger, then older again, and Tirhan knew that he was facing a spirit from the otherworld.

Words came, though the old man's lips did not move. "Your people died today. Be assured that we have welcomed them into the depths of the silver forest. Here is why I have come, Lord King. Your mother, the Lady Gwenid, called upon us when you were a lad, one destined to overtake his brother. She foresaw this. She saw that you wanted great things, even if you had only your grandfather's bow and a handful of arrows. You would use them all up before their time."

What do you mean? Tirhan tried to say.

"I mean that patience flees you like a startled deer. And always has. If you stop running, perhaps it will come to you. When it does, son of Gwenid, you will find what you need."

Hearing his mother's name, his heart swelled. *How do I save my family?*

"The wolves, Lord King. They guard the prison. Know that they are also prisoners, and, in the Alfan forests, they must be free."

How?

"Set them free, though it take a hundred years. A hundred years. A hundred years." The warrior faded into the mist, taking the silverwood tree with him.

Tirhan flexed his fingers around his knife, his movements free again.

The air around him grew luminous, but it was not a mystical thing. It was dawn.

Chapter Thirteen

Father Ludving rode out with Yevliesza and Duke Tanfred early in the morning. At breakfast, it had been only she and the duke, as the prince and his officers were having a working breakfast in another room.

Cold wind gusted across the plain, ruffling Father Ludving's beard and making Yevliesza's eyes water. Ludving wore wool trousers and a heavy jacket instead of his priestly robe, but somehow, he still looked very much like a priest. Yevliesza had been provided trousers and boots for their ride, and had to admit that it was a relief to be wearing something sensible. Her glossy black mare was a beauty, as eager as she was for a good run. Duke Tanfred had said that their destination was a plateau from which they would have a better view of the Mist Wall.

"The wall looks like a windstorm approaching," she said.

"Except that it is going in the other direction." Father Ludving said.

The wall *was* receding. She kept having to remind herself of that.

Tanfred's dappled gray shied against the gusting wind, but the duke held him easily.

"Getting close is dangerous, isn't it?" Yevliesza asked. Lord Tirhan had said so when she first viewed the primordial lands in Alfan Sih.

"We will not go so near," Tanfred said. He cut a glance at her with a light in his eyes. "But perhaps you would like to?"

"Your Grace," Father Ludving admonished.

"Quite right, quite right," Tanfred said. "We have not the time today."

Yevliesza's attention was distracted by the sight of an align crossing their path with a fiery slash like a crack in the land. Other aligns came to her perception, four or five of them intersecting each other randomly. It was the most astonishing display she had yet seen in the Mythos, and it humbled her. She thought she knew what this world was, knew its magical state and its origins. But in the presence of the aligns and the Mist Wall beyond, she felt herself to be little more than a wanderer, a newcomer in a way that no one else here was or could even understand.

Hours passed, and the sun, blurred by a gathering cloud cover, rose toward noontime.

After they had taken a break and resumed their journey, Tanfred said, "Miss Yevliesza, I have a confession to make. I have brought you out here with a purpose, and I hope you will not fault me for it."

"I can't imagine finding fault, Your Grace."

"Good! That is excellent. I wanted to have time to speak with you in some privacy. I would like to tell you the story of the wall. Tell it in my way."

"The wall has a story?"

"It does. A legend, actually. My grandmother first told me of it. In some circles it is considered an obscure tale. But I assure you, a great many people take the legend as prophecy. The primordialist beliefs. What my grandmother told me was the legend of the ninth power and how it is ingrained in the nature of the wall."

Mention of the ninth power grabbed Yevliesza's attention. She listened warily.

Tanfred went on. "My grandmother said that she had learned from an aged retainer in her household that someday, in a time of peril, the wall would be a means of saving the kingdom. Saving it from dire threat."

He looked at her. "A dire threat such as we have now; the war in Alfan Sih. Where our young soldiers are dying and where many more will die when the other kingdoms come against us. As they surely will."

Yevliesza shivered as a finger of wintry wind probed into her borrowed coat.

"The legend promises that there is an alternative to wars of conquest. That Volkia can find room to expand because the wall will move on and reveal further landscapes."

"Reveal?" Yevliesza asked. "Or create?"

Tanfred smiled at that and glanced at Father Ludving, inviting him to join in.

"It is a common belief," Ludving said, "that the wall expands —and creates—the land we inhabit. But that is not quite the case. It is more accurate to say that it reveals what is already there." He noted her confusion. "Think of it as a curtain that parts to expose a stage. We of the Mythos inhabit the alter-realms of Firstland. What landscape our forebears had there, that is our inheritance, being slowly revealed."

"But what is revealed—the new lands—are barren of form," Yevliesza said. "That's not like Firstland." The Volkish didn't use a dismissive term for the origin world. They were more loyal than the Numinasi, who resented how their ancestors had been reviled.

"You are right, my daughter," Ludving acknowledged, "but

the new land becomes complete with time, like a child that has within him all that he will physically be."

She thought of Grigeni and wondered what her tutor would make of that.

"And what if the wall began moving faster," Tanfred went on. "What if it revealed more and showed not just a flat and simple territory, but its true shape? And on a timetable to discover room enough for all of Volkia's growing population?"

Yevliesza's gaze focused on the distant wall, its true length obscured by the limits of vision.

Tanfred went on. "There will be a person, the *Eibelung*. A person of uncorrupted sight who will have a—root power—that can bring the wall to its natural purpose. By this, we will achieve our destiny and avoid suffering and bloodshed. That is the hope and faith of the primordialists."

Father Ludving said, "But it is not a faith, Tanfred. Faith must be in God. This is a prophecy of the forefathers, what we might call a *prediction*. We do not imbue it with faith, but with hope and inquiry."

"Yes, Father," Tanfred said. "You are right. We do not worship the wall. How barbaric!"

Yevliesza hadn't heard anything they had said since Duke Tanfred's mention of a person possessing *root power*. Her mind raced. Tanfred knew something. Yesterday he had greeted her with an odd deference and had continued that treatment. She didn't like to imagine why that might be. What did he know about the ninth power?

They rode in silence, the subject large in their midst, with the time for a casual remark on Tanfred's legend idea fading fast.

Finally she said, "This person of legend, sir. The . . ."

"The *Eibelung*."

"Yes. You believe they could convince Volkia, Volkia's leadership, that—perfecting— the wall is a better way?"

"That is our great hope, yes."

Father Ludving said, "Even some in the cloisters hope that the legend reflects God's will."

Speaking as casually as she could manage, Yevliesza said, "It would be wonderful to think that the war could be settled that way." Which she didn't believe for a moment. Neither the part about the savior of the wall nor the Volkish military accepting it.

The sun was at its highest when they paused for a quick meal from Tanfred's pack.

Now that Yevliesza's initial alarm had subsided, she felt more confident. They didn't know what primal root power truly was. There were only three people who did: herself, Rusadka, and Tirhan. The other realms, the two that she had seen, were content with their own interpretations of the root power. Since it had an ambiguous name, people could assign it any meaning they fancied. But she *knew* what it meant.

After they resumed their ride, the vegetation grew more sparse and the land became soft, rolling hills dotted with patches of grass. The wall, now two hands high on the horizon, shimmered like a dark aurora borealis. Tanfred pointed to a steep promontory. Their destination.

Once they drew close, Tanfred led them up the side on a gentle incline that lay like a ramp to the narrow summit. At the top they dismounted. They stood on bare rock with a view in all directions. In the middle stood a stone arch about twelve feet high through which Yevliesza saw the Mist Wall. A shrine, Yevliesza thought. Peaceful, except for the wind, now blowing harder, swiftly unravelling her hair.

Tanfred looked at the sky. "I had hoped the weather would hold. We cannot stay long."

The three of them stood by their horses. Yevliesza sensed that Tanfred wished her to go to the arch alone. Stubbornly, she held back, waiting for him to lead.

At last, Tanfred walked to the arch and stood gazing at the wall.

Next to Yevliesza, Father Ludwig murmured, "He thinks you are the one."

So much for hiding. And of course Tanfred thought that. She would have to quash this as quickly as possible, but how to dislodge a mystical, desperate belief?

"I am *not* the one," she said to Ludving.

He nodded. "The soul must accept the role, or they are not the one."

But the duke would not be so sanguine. Wanting to get this over with, she joined Tanfred at the arch.

"It's a thrilling sight," she began. "But it isn't what . . . what I'm about. I'm sorry that I can't help, my lord, but you mistake me."

Tanfred didn't look at her, but watched the wall as it surged and dissolved, dancing to some rhythm or music only it could hear. "When you were last in the crossings, I felt your presence. It was in the twelfth month, the very day you met Prince Albrecht. I felt it, because the crossings are in synchrony with verdure power, which is my great gift."

He felt her presence. . . . And with *verdure* power? God, what was he trying to say? "It was a coincidence," she said, trying to keep the panic out of her voice.

Tanfred didn't believe this; she saw it in his face.

He went on. "I also sensed the same presence five days earlier. Perhaps it was when you entered the crossings on your way to Nubiah." He turned to her. "I do not mean to distress you. I know I may be wrong, but is it not my duty to speak up?"

The sinking feeling that had come over her now became a plummet. Foremost in her mind was the wild hope that Prince Albrecht didn't know any of this.

"There was one other time." Tanfred relentlessly said. "It was about the time you are said to have entered the Mythos from the Firstland. I felt a quake in my bones. In my heart."

The wall churned in front of her, as though at any moment the curtain would part and reveal something she hoped never to see.

Father Ludving, whom she suspected had come along on this ride to mediate this moment, joined them at the arch.

"My daughter," he said, "Duke Tanfred only means for you to examine your heart and allow the possibility to arise. He cannot force you, nor would he even think of it."

"And," Tanfred added, "Prince Albrecht does not believe it. So indeed, I may be wrong."

"Does not believe *what*?"

"That you are the *Eibelung*." He quirked his mouth. "Or that you fulfill the prophecy, for that matter."

Albrecht already knew. Knew about Tanfred's intimations and the meaning he assigned to them. She felt naked to questioning eyes on every side. Tanfred had perceived *something* about her. He had pinpointed her visits to the crossings, so he was bringing unwanted attention to her. If Albrecht was watching her for a power, he might well find one.

She looked at Father Ludving, noting the compassion in his eyes. But compassion couldn't help her. From this moment on, she would have to strive every minute to withhold her vital gift from Albrecht and his war machine.

Turning to face Tanfred, she said. "That belief—that mistaken belief—can put my life at risk. I'll be Prince Albrecht's hostage."

A sharp, wounded look crossed Tanfred's face. "He would never do that. There is Princip Anastyna. There is his sense of decency. And there is me. To protect you."

She stared at him. He wasn't going to protect her; he was going to expose her. And Albrecht's *decency*? Anastyna's? He was out of his mind. So clueless. So dangerous. *Get me out of here*, came her fervent thought.

Yevliesza left Tanfred at the arch and walked back to her horse, Father Ludving following. She swung into the saddle.

"My daughter," Ludving said as she mounted. "I will pray for clarity to come to you."

She looked down into his gentle gaze. She wanted to confide in him, because for some reason she trusted him. But all that came out was, "Better to pray I get out of here, Father."

PART II
A DANCE WITH VIPERS

Chapter Fourteen

I n the *satvary* of Zolvina, Dreiza shifted her kneeling pad to
start training the other side of the *traveka* vine. She had
wakened before dawn and lost herself in the painstaking
work of wrapping shoots around the trellis.

It was a devious punishment, one to which the other *satvars*
remained oblivious, traversing the sunny gallery and exclaiming
how dedicated Dreiza was and would it not all be worth it when
the plant burst into flower. In four more years.

She stood, stretching her back. Out one of the windows she
saw people in the yard, barely visible in the gloaming pre-dawn.
Six women passed in single file by the southern wall of the domicile just below her. Though true dawn was still to come, she could
make out that one of the *satvars* was the Devi Ilsat. Dreiza leaned
over the sill to see where they went, but they disappeared around
the corner of the compound.

The members of the Devi Ilsat's close circle, the *satvadeya*,
advised her on important issues and, by their presence in the
domicile and the fields, kept her informed of the physical and
spiritual health of the *satvary*. She wondered what they were
doing outside at this early hour. The compound lay in the foothills

of the Numin Mountains, in a region of rocky outcroppings sheltering valleys rich with black soils. There was nothing for six old women to do out there before sunrise. And one of them, Sofichka, was so elderly and infirm that it seemed unwise for her to be stumbling about in the dark.

It was none of her business. She watched out the windows as the eastern sky began to pale. She could just make out a bird soaring over the peaks. She thought of Kirjanichka, missing her terribly. But the dactyl could not live at the *satvary*, and she would be treated like royalty at Osta Kiya. Kirjanichka would be happy, and the idea comforted her.

When she looked at the vine in its pot, she sighed. The point of this exercise was patience, letting the things unfold, with attention, but not with force. Patience had always seemed like a fine idea that more people should develop, but one of them would never be her.

She felt weary. Perhaps, since the High Mother and her people were out of the compound, she would not draw attention by going back to bed until the breakfast gong. As she left the gallery, she took a last look out the windows. It was still quite dark, but the slopes of Zolvina's hill perch appeared empty of movement, as it usually did so far from human habitation.

She picked up the kneeling pad and left the gallery, rubbing her hands together to soothe her fingers from the aches of her task. If only the High Mother came by more often, catching her at work, but she seldom did.

That, too, could be a lesson. To do the work without reward. Dreiza sighed. In Osta Kiya such things would be written plainly down as ways and customs. No guessing required. But here things were different, as the High Mother was fond of pointing out.

Patience. No rewards.

And a good nap, she thought as she made her way to her room.

IN VOLKIA, TWO DAYS AFTER YEVLIESZA'S RIDE WITH DUKE Tanfred, she had left the relative comfort of Wilhoff Manor and now sat in a carriage alone with Prince Albrecht. They were bound for his headquarters in Volkia's capital city, Hapsigen, some sixty miles away.

The carriage rattled and swayed as it rolled over ruts in the road. Albrecht sat across from her reading paperwork. They had exchanged a few pleasant remarks, but fortunately Albrecht had not tried to engage her in conversation. Or interrogation.

He was in military dress, the gray-green uniform with epaulets edged in gold braid, and the collar of his belted jacket bearing an insignia of an eagle. Breast pockets with stitched emblems and medals. Trousers tucked into high black boots, but wide at the thighs like jodhpurs. The look was designed to convey power. And did.

The prince's headquarters in Hapsigen was the place where she would ostensibly get to know more of Volkia's people. Not that she believed that anymore. From Tanfred, the prince was alert to some connection she might have with the crossings. He apparently was not convinced by the primordialist beliefs, but his interest would certainly be aroused. In fact, this might be the real reason he had demanded she come to Volkia. She had hardly been able to sleep, thinking that her secret might be on the verge of exposure.

Albrecht looked up from his work. "Do you still have plans to marry?" he asked without preamble. "I was remiss in not inquiring earlier."

"It was an idea, not a plan." That had been her claim when she had met Albrecht in the crossings the month before, that she was returning from Nubiah after having met a prospective husband.

"Ah. The Numinasi idea that a woman chooses her mate."

She let that sit, hoping he wouldn't pursue the topic. Her claim that Lord Chenua of the Lion Court had suggested someone as a match seemed less believable now. Why would someone of his royal stature involve himself with her?

"Best to find someone more at your station, perhaps."

She pointedly looked out the window of the carriage. By *more at her station,* he likely meant more of her own race. The man could be gallant, but it was a show. His ugly ideas governed him.

To deflect the conversation away from her thin alibi for being in the crossings that day, she asked, "And you, Prince Albrecht, are you the marrying sort?"

He cocked his head. "I will marry when time allows. Volkia needs new sons. And daughters."

All for Volkia, then. Marriage for duty. It was all she could do not to roll her eyes.

"This world must seem very foreign to you," Albrecht said. "Allow me to say that you handle yourself with admirable poise, in what you must think of as strange lands. When I first heard of your summons to the Numinat court, I wondered why Princip Anastyna recalled your family."

How disturbing to think that he knew some of her history. He had spies in Numinat, no doubt.

Albrecht went on. "They were diplomats in the Firstland, were they not?"

"My father was, yes."

"And he died when he returned to Numinat."

"Yes." She did not want to discuss any of that painful time with Albrecht, so she deflected with, "How long a ride is it to the capital?"

"You find it aversive, to be in a carriage with me for too long?"

"Of course not. And you have your work."

He set aside his papers on the bench seat. "Since we are

condemned to sit in the same compartment for most of the day, we might get to know each other."

Oh, let's not. "If you like."

"I think you know something of me. You met my nephew, Sigmar von Treid. My brother's son, who, I assure you, has fallen under your spell."

"I have a spell?"

"Not that I have discovered," he said in a droll tone, "at least not around me. You do not find my company . . . relaxing, I think."

She tried out a small smirk, and he didn't react.

"My parents are at the family estate, Treidenstag, near Wilhoff. And I have several sisters. A large family. And you, without siblings. A lonely childhood, perhaps?"

"It taught me to be self-sufficient. But I've found a home in Numinat. House Valenty has been very welcoming."

"So all your loyalty is with Numinat," he said dismissively.

"Where else should it be?"

"Perhaps with people who respect you more." A sharp retort came to mind, but there was no point in angering him. He went on. "Duke Tanfred thinks you may be an extraordinary individual." His pale blue eyes held her transfixed. "Are you?"

She had a few ideas now about what to say when this subject came up. "I was really surprised when he told me his beliefs about the Mist Wall. I may not understand his ideas very well, but they don't sound believable."

"So you told him he was being foolish?"

"Of course not. Are you accusing me of another insult?"

"No, please excuse me. I did not mean to upset you."

"That's hard to believe, since you're refusing to accept my apology which Princip Anastyna understood you would welcome. And which you don't."

He bit his lip, looking away. "You mean to set a certain tone with me, Yevliesza."

She didn't like it when he called her by her first name alone. It took something away from her.

"I hope we can move past that," he added, picking up his paperwork. "At some point."

The carriage rolled on. She was his hostage. And it was all so . . . gentlemanly. And infuriating.

Late in the morning they passed through farming country, with fields harvested and the stubble bristling from the patchy snow. Here, the broad plain revealed hundreds of tidy farms laid out in precise squares. Homes and barns were made from some mud or adobe material, many with roofs of thatch or slate.

Despite the clear day, a reddish-brown haze pooled on the horizon.

Around a bend in a hill, Hapsigen came into view, a vast, low city where a reddish-gray fog swathed the air. A stone wall enclosed the city, broken in places by fortified gates. They passed through one, its iron and wood gate parting for the carriage.

When it shut behind them, Yevliesza tried not to consider it locked. Fifteen days, Albrecht had promised. Twelve days to go, by Albrecht's revised interpretation of the agreement.

Hapsigen was large—it must be one of the great cities of the Mythos—with two and three-story wood and brick buildings crowded together, mile upon mile. The streets were strangely empty except for uniformed men stationed at some of the inter-sections. Citizens that did go abroad walked with a discernible slump, as though trying to evade notice. Everywhere on the rooftops, stacks of chimneys trailed woodsmoke. Her eyes smarted from the acrid air.

"It is always worse in winter," Albrecht said. "But on the river, we will find relief."

They traveled through a more imposing central district with

large brick and stone buildings, some with grand porticos and arched windows crowned by ornamental moldings. One of the largest bore an impressive dome.

"The Church of All Graces," Albrecht said, noting her gaze. "You could join me on Sunday, but since you have made a home among . . . nonbelievers, I assume you would demur."

Being paraded around was not on her agenda. She noted that Albrecht referred to a day of the week—Sunday—and, again, the disparity between Volkia and Numinat jarred.

Down a side street she saw a wagon slowly drawn through the fog. Or pushed, since she couldn't see a coachman or horses. As it drew closer, she saw that nothing pushed it. Something inside it kept it moving. The front of it had a higher compartment, like the cab of a truck.

It was . . . it looked like . . . a machine. There had been rumors of war machines; could this be something similar? Yevliesza watched closely after that but didn't see others. Albrecht was tucking papers into a satchel, having taken no notice the conveyance or her reaction.

The wagon was just a small vehicle rolling down the street. But it seemed so wrong.

How strange to see the world through Numinasi eyes, she thought. The Mythos was threatened by technology, at least in some way—a way that clashed with magic—so that the sight of a powered vehicle plucked a string in her heart: *wrong, wrong*.

Chapter Fifteen

Valenty and Urik descended a talus slope, carefully picking their way down to the valley floor. The jumbled rocks would have been risky to traverse if they had been icy, but sun on the hillside kept them clear.

Once off the slope, the two of them picked up their pace. The terrain was creased by a narrow, rock-strewn river, and on the far side of it grew thick evergreens mantled in snow.

For three days they had pushed ever higher into the Breminger Forest, leaving behind ash and maple to enter woods of fir and pine. They tackled the hills when they failed to find a cut through them. It was cold, but their relentless pace kept them warm, and often they walked bare-headed and without gloves. Unsure whether they had been seen leaving the Volkish encampment, they sometimes traveled into the evening by the light of a moon close to full.

Urik had taken down two rabbits with his sling, but they had not dared make a fire. Perhaps tonight. As they made their way through thick underbrush and fallen tree limbs, Valenty thought about their close call at the boundary gate. And the moment when, in the crossings, they had actually spoken to Marshal Reinhart, the Volkish chief of intelligence. He was notorious both for his cruelty and a face that, as Urik said, could frighten children.

Walking along the side of the river afforded them a longer view of the territory ahead. The fogs that had stuffed the valleys had lifted that morning, giving them a sense for the first time of the vastness of the forest and its jumble of hills.

They filled their water skins from the river. Urik, hunched over the gurgling water, looked like a bear with his fur cloak hung about shoulders. As they continued on their way, Urik squatted down to examine prints in the light crust of snow. "Ice cat," he said. They were not the only ones that used this path.

"I've never seen one," Valenty said.

"You may get your chance," Urik said.

Though their guide had furnished them with supplies and weapons, Urik had made a spear for himself out of a fallen branch of ash, securing a knife at one end with leather cords. This, he said, would be their best weapon against large predators, although bears would be hibernating. Most would.

Surveying the area, his eyes narrowed as he looked up at the rocky incline down which they had come.

"What is it?" Valenty asked.

"Six men," Urik replied. "Coming down the slope." They moved quickly into thicker trees, dense with undergrowth.

So they *had* been seen leaving the bivouac. "They'll see our tracks," Valenty said.

"Not if we go to meet them."

"Walk up and introduce ourselves?" They had come so far, and now there was nowhere to hide. Six Volkish soldiers. It would be an ugly fight.

"We will take them on the lower scree slope," Urik said. "Swiftly, now." He slipped away, heading in the direction of their pursuers. Valenty followed, dropping his pack and making a quick check for the knife strapped into his boot.

At the bottom of the slope a tangle of bushes offered some cover, and they crept forward to hide there. Valenty could see the men picking their way down, the nearest soldier now two-thirds down the field of jumbled rock.

"Finish off anyone who gets past me," Urik said. "Use warding to protect yourself, but do not cast it for me." The *harjat* wanted no barriers in his part of the fight.

"There might be more soldiers over the rise," Valenty warned.

"And you might see an ice cat, too," Urik muttered.

Urik faded back, circling around to find another hiding place.

Going toward a superior force was not Valenty's idea of a good move, but now at the foot of the talus slope, he began to see the advantage. A man in the lead was carefully selecting his foot placement, sometimes stepping onto larger slabs and not looking up from the job of navigating the slope. The others were almost in single file and would be unable to work much in tandem.

When the lead soldier was close but still on the rock scree, Urik charged onto the slope. He had picked his route well and was upon the man in moments. Shouts came from above. Bringing his knife up, he slashed at the man's hand, cutting enough to startle him and causing him to stagger and fall. As Urik rushed up to meet the next soldier, Valenty found the first man struggling to rise and stabbed him in the eye. He crumpled. Looking up, Valenty saw Urik engaging with two men, lunging and ducking while skillfully finding his footholds.

One of the soldiers lost his balance and fell at an awkward angle downslope. As he lay trapped for a moment in a wedge of rocks, Valenty scrambled up to dispatch him. In their winter gear, the soldiers were not easy to take with knives, leaving hands and face the most vulnerable. Valenty kicked the man's weapon hand, sending the knife into a gap in the rocks and, as the soldier reached for another weapon, he plunged down his knife toward the man's neck, but he missed as his opponent twisted away. The soldier drew a knife from his belt as he rose. He was a bigger man than Valenty and jumped heavily down the slope at him so quickly that Valenty fell backward.

The man stomped toward him, his face obscured by the glare of sun directly behind him. Valenty threw up a warding just in time, a warding that made it impossible for the attacker's knife to penetrate, but also for Valenty to use his own weapon. As the soldier stooped over him, Valenty dropped the warding and thrust his knife into the man's stomach, sending him to his knees. Yanking the knife back, he scrambled to his feet and slit his opponent's throat.

Urik was a stone's throw away, facing off with the remaining soldier. The *harjat* moved slowly and deftly on the rubble and few flat rocks, changing places with his man in an elaborate dance.

As Valenty dashed up to assist, Urik shoved his opponent downslope. Flailing, the man fell headfirst and lay still.

Farther up the slope, two more bodies lay unmoving.

By the time Valenty reached the last man to fall, Urik was already kneeling at the soldier's side. Blood ran thick from his skull, streaming into the man's eyes. He brought a hand up to wipe the blood away but could not otherwise move.

"My lord," Urik said to Valenty, "translate for me." He looked down at the wounded man. "You are sorely wounded, and your leg is broken."

Valenty repeated this in Volkish.

"Your comrades are dead. Do you want to wait for an unlikely rescue, or make a quick end of it?"

The man looked up at Urik, fear and resignation fighting for dominance, looking for some other hope, some other way.

"We will leave you with water," Urik said. "Your choice."

The soldier could survive, but he could not get back to camp. It might not be long before wolves found him.

"Do it," the man said.

Urik did not need translation and struck immediately with a quick knife slash across the man's neck. Wiping his blade on the soldier's pant leg, he looked up at Valenty. "You were to stay below."

"I did. For a time."

Urik snorted a laugh and wiped his blood-spattered face with the back of his arm.

Chapter Sixteen

Albrecht's headquarters was a three-story, hulking palace trying for grandeur by sheer size. Battlements at the top gave it a fortified aspect. Flowing by it, and taking a yellowish tint from the sky, the great Danstree, a quarter of a mile wide. At a bow, it flowed past another side of the palace, almost seeming to surround it. As their carriage crossed the river over one of two bridges, Yevliesza felt that every turn of the wheels brought her farther into a stony nest of enemies.

Her oversized apartment had a spacious parlor with stone tile floors and a ceiling twenty feet high. The tapestries hanging on the walls did little to soften the effect of gigantism.

At her parlor's large window, she sat on a window seat and watched the cloudy Danstree as a long barge came by. If she was on that barge, where would she end up? Where did the river eventually flow to? Maybe the river flowed into some great sea of Volkia. Or through the Mist Wall. Behind which might be a sea. A sea not yet uncovered by the retreat of the great engine of land formation.

The room was cold despite a brisk fire in the broad fireplace.

To be fair, it was the dead of winter, but Osta Kiya had managed most times to feel almost cozy compared to this.

"Your bath is ready, mistress." Breta was a pretty young woman, her curly blond hair escaping here and there from her pinned maid's cap. She wore a sleeveless, belted tunic over a long brown dress and managed to look shapely in it.

"Thank you, Breta."

Though Yevliesza was sweaty and drained from the carriage ride, she had at first told the maid not to draw her a bath. Breta's puzzled reaction reminded her that unusual behavior on her part might bring unwelcome attention to her habits. It occurred to her that she might explain the tracery on her back as a tattoo—a strange custom of the mundat. And what else could the pattern be, except a tattoo?

The bathroom was steamy with the bath's heat. She thought of the consistent elementalist effort it must take to deliver any water to the pipe system, much less hot water. A bath—a private bath—was a great luxury. One she had done without for months.

Yevliesza let Breta unbutton her traveling dress. When she stepped out of it, she felt as though she were naked on a stage even though at the moment, she still wore her shift.

"Breta," she said, "do you know what a tattoo is?"

"Yes, mistress."

"I have a large one on my back."

"So I see, mistress."

"I suppose it's not customary in Volkia. But you've heard I come from . . . outside?"

"From Firstland, yes, mistress."

"Well, it's the custom there. But a lady's tattoo isn't ever discussed. Never brought up. Because it's personal and only seen when she is undressed. You see?"

"Yes, mistress. You have a tattoo, and it is nobody's business to know about it."

That was as much as Yevliesza had planned to say. To go into it any further would undermine her statement that a lady's tattoo was not discussed.

Once naked and her hair tied up, Yevliesza submerged herself in the glorious hot water. As Breta was leaving, she paused at the door. "Mistress, your tattoo. Did it hurt?"

There was a story to that. It had hurt like fire. It *was* fire.

Yevliesza sank up to her chin in the fragrant water. "Yes, it did. A bit."

⚭

WHEN THE BATHWATER HAD GONE TEPID, YEVLIESZA GOT OUT and toweled herself dry. There was a large mirror in the bathroom. It was startling to see, since in Numinat, people shied away from them. When she asked Breta if mirrors were commonplace here, she answered that common folk seldom had them in their homes, to fend off mischievous sendings by manifesters. But here in the palace of Rothsvund, no one would dare misuse them.

With a hand mirror in front and the bathroom mirror in back, Yevliesza looked at her back for the first time since the lightning strike.

Gray-blue tendrils appeared to sprout from the small of her back. They rose up the right side of her back and right arm all the way to her chin as though climbing a wall. Seeing it on her flesh, impossibly, but truly there, she shivered. Tirhan's drawing had revealed the pattern, but seeing it on her body, she stared in wonderment. It was strangely beautiful. And frightening. An emblem of the ninth power. *Why, though?* the inevitable thought came. *And why me?*

When she brought the hand mirror back to the bedroom, Breta ducked in. "Anything needed, miss?"

Long underwear and fuzzy slippers would be an excellent
start. "Just my dress, Breta."

As Breta held out the formal black dress for her to step into,
Yevliesza noticed red marks on the maid's left wrist. And then on
her other wrist.

"Breta . . ." Yevliesza paused. "You have bruises." Actually,
they looked like rope burns.

Breta pulled her sleeves more firmly down. "Oh, they are
nothing."

"They don't look like *nothing*."

"I am fine, miss. Truly."

Yevliesza felt she had to let it go. But someone had bound the
girl, she was sure of it.

৩৶৺

YEVLIESZA'S QUARTERS WERE IN THE CORNER OF THE SECOND
floor of the palace. Just outside her room were doors to a small
balcony overlooking the city. From her room she could walk
straight down a hallway to a game room with several square
tables set up. Farther on there was a door to a stairway—she had
seen a servant using it. When she tried the door, it was locked.
But if she turned left out her door, a wider, more grandly decorated hallway took her past several locked rooms to end in ornate
double doors behind which the hall likely continued. One of the
rooms down this larger corridor had an archway that opened to a
reception room with an elaborate fireplace.

She struggled to convince herself that Albrecht would allow
to her leave when the fifteen days was up. But he couldn't just
keep her. Even though Anastyna might not care about her, she
would be affronted, perhaps outraged, if Albrecht kept her from
returning. Surely she could keep her mouth shut and her clothes
on for nine more days.

At lunch Breta brought her a tray of fish in cream sauce, and busied herself tidying the bathroom and running a duster over the apartment furniture. When she left, Yevliesza went to the door, opening it quietly. Down the hallway she saw the door Breta left by, the one with the double doors.

After finishing her lunch, she strolled down the hallway, making her way to what she thought of as the reception room with its archway entrance. Through the tall windows, the setting sun glared off the river and cast a fervid glow into the room. Sitting in front of the cold hearth, her thoughts went to Tanfred and his strange ideas of the Mist Wall; Albrecht in the carriage probing about what she had been doing in the crossings that day; the Nazi-like uniforms of the commandant's military staff; the wounded soldiers at Tanfred's hospice. The sun fell behind the city and in the gloom, the hallway light fixtures began to glow. She rested her head against the back of the divan.

"Madam, you are well?"

Yevliesza started from her doze. A man in a black uniform stood in the doorway.

"I was going by," he said. "You are well?"

"Yes, thank you." She stood, smoothing her skirts. The man wore too much braid and insignia to be a common soldier. Short of stature, he had a long, thin face, a small mustache and receding chin. He strolled toward her.

"You are the woman Yevliesza from Numinat, I believe," he said in perfect Numinasi. His brown hair, shaved on the sides and longer at the crown, was slicked back so hard, it shone.

"Yes. Prince Albrecht invited me."

"I know this." The man flattened his lips, causing his small mustache to twitch, giving him the look of a rat. "Such grand quarters." He looked about the room. "They are to your liking?"

His words were inoffensive enough, but he delivered them with little inflection, giving his words a remote feeling.

"Yes, thank you."

He watched her carefully, just long enough to be rude, before saying, "This is the south wing of Rothsvund, or part of it. It was the palace of King Doermar in the old days. But I assure you, it is also a fortified garrison, for all its"—here he gestured at the furniture and tall windows—"embellishments. These are not your personal apartments. High Command staff and others will pass through here, so do not imagine you are alone. Do you understand?"

"I will be watched. Thank you for clarifying."

His face fell into a dark expression, further collapsing his already narrow features.

Yevliesza was alarmed by him but instinctively felt it was better not to show it. "I assume I shouldn't sleep on the divan?"

His mouth quivered. "Sleep where you please if you do not care who watches." He turned and walked to the door.

"May I have your name, sir?"

He stopped and looked back at her. "I am Marshal Count Walthar von Reinhart."

That was a lot of names. She managed to remember the last one: Reinhart. Watching him stride out of the room she thought that prior to this, she had met the nice Nazis. Here was the real thing.

Valenty, the thought came like a whisper. *Where are you?* Norslad. Perhaps already on his way home, but with no idea she could be a stop on the way.

Chapter Seventeen

After dinner served in Yevliesza's room, a young officer knocked and entered, introducing himself as Lieutenant Martel and saying that Commandant Albrecht would like her to join him in the salon.

"I can wait if you would like to change, mistress," he said in Numinasi with a strong Volkish accent. His light-colored hair had a hint of red in it and his face bore a smattering of freckles.

She thought she was dressed well enough. The black would do, though a few gowns hung in the wardrobe apparently for her use.

The lieutenant held the door for her, and they left the apartment. He led to her to one of the hallway doors—unlocked at the moment—and then down the stairs which, after a turn, became an open staircase to the main floor.

"What is your position here, lieutenant, if I can ask?"

"I think that you would say, undersecretary? For palace affairs, mistress."

"So that would be household things. Not military?"

"Yes. For now."

"You don't refer to Prince Albrecht by his royal title? You called him commandant."

"He sets his title aside for his military title. Leader of our military government and armed forces."

"And I should as well?"

"No, I think not. Your relationship is of a social nature."

She resisted the impulse to set him straight.

The hallway on the ground floor was a busy place, as men in uniform carried papers and briefcases between various offices. A few of them glanced sideways at her, taking in her gown that marked her as Numinasi.

Martel was explaining features of the palace. "Rothsvund has four hundred and twelve rooms. Many are converted into offices. Rothsvund was a royal residence in the days of the monarchy."

They passed through a grand entrance hall, with a large table that served as a desk, where people coming in stopped to state their business.

"Is Prince Albrecht alone?" She wondered if she was to be questioned again, or if others would be present, perhaps discouraging Albrecht from probing.

"Commandant Albrecht is seldom alone," Lieutenant Martel said. "In wartime."

He stopped outside a set of open double doors beyond which she could see a spacious sitting room. "You may go in, Mistress Yevliesza. May I say it is an honor to have met you." Suddenly awkward, he swallowed and ducked a bow.

She smiled at him, wondering what the honor was, unless she had some renown for having come from the mundat.

Turning into the salon, she saw Albrecht in uniform standing at a table with scrolls and bound folders. Around him several officers in black uniforms. Evah Krim lounged on one end of the table, ignored by the officers. As Yevliesza approached, she glanced up with a coy smile.

With a wave of his hand Albrecht dismissed the soldiers, who gathered their papers and left, barely glancing at her.

"Evah," Albrecht said, "pour Yevliesza a glass of wine." He turned to the blazing fire on the hearth and gestured for Yevliesza to make her way there.

"Alcohol doesn't sit well with me, my lord." She could barely stand Numinasi liquor.

"Nonsense. This is Volkia. You must try Evah's favorite." From the desk he brought his own glass, filled with a dark amber liquid. He indicated a couch facing the fireplace, and she sat, accepting a glass of wine from Evah. Her emerald-green gown was trimmed in fur at the neckline and the long, hanging sleeves flared at the bottom.

"You are comfortable in your quarters?" Albrecht asked Yevliesza. "You have all that you need?"

"Yes, thank you."

"And I believe you are meeting people. Lieutenant Martel, of course. Your maid Breta is satisfactory? She speaks excellent Numinasi, as should be helpful to you. And Marshal Reinhart said he came by to introduce himself."

"Yes. Charming," she managed to say with a neutral expression.

Albrecht crossed his legs and regarded her.

As he did so, Yevliesza took a wary sip of the drink. Surprisingly, it was exquisite. "Wonderful," she said, drinking a little more.

"Ah! The wine pleases. At least something does," he added, smiling at Evah, who trailed her hand along the fireplace mantel. Tiny sparks flowed from her hand, dissolving as she went. Childishly showing off her manifesting.

Albrecht went on. "I wanted you to know that the young man of House Iron River is now in Numinat, riding back to Osta Kiya." He raised his glass. "As promised."

Yes, the damn trade. "I'm sure Princip Anastyna appreciates the gesture."

"I am sure. So you see, your visit here is already creating advantages for your princip." Pausing, he savored his drink. "I have been thinking about Tanfred's story again. There is one detail that we have not discussed. It is his claim that he sensed you in the crossings a few days before you and I met that time. If he is correct, that would be when you were on your way to Nubiah."

"Perhaps it was near the time that Tanfred says he felt a . . . perturbation. I didn't keep track of his story that closely."

"But I am keeping track. And it happens that a new path to Alfan Sih was discovered on that day. I wish to hear what you know about that path. Since it is a remarkable coincidence that you were present at that time."

She produced a small frown as though she was confused. She wished she *were* confused, but now the new path to Alfan Sih was on his mind.

He sipped his drink, watching her. "The crossings grow and change, of course. But not quickly. How did you find it?"

"I didn't. I wasn't in Alfan Sih."

"Or perhaps it was someone you were with? Prince Tirhan? Or some verduralist who has managed to affect the paths?"

"You're saying that I must know something about a new path because at about that time Tanfred had an intimation of me in the crossings?" She put down her wine glass lest he see it shaking. "Is that why the simple apology isn't enough? Because you think I know about something important?"

He rose from his chair and went to the fireplace, putting a hand on the mantel and gazing into the fire.

Evah was floating around the room looking at things. With her yellow hair and green dress, she had the look of a parrot flitting here and there. Albrecht glanced at her with annoyance and jerked his head at the hallway, and she made her way out. Well trained.

When she had gone, he turned to Yevliesza. "You are right. A simple apology is not enough. A *heartfelt* apology would do." He held up a hand to stop her from speaking. "I know you are not ready to offer this. And I do not blame you. Our realms have competing goals, and I have brought you here where you find yourself amongst people you despise. What you may or may not know about access to Alfan Sih is of interest to me, that is true. But above all, I would like to present Volkia to you in a better light than you have seen it in the past."

A thin wisp of relief diluted her tension. But she had to keep up her stance of outrage. "A better light? By keeping me confined?"

"This is a military headquarters, and I naturally cannot let you roam freely. But if the south wing of Rothsvund is a prison to you, I beg you to understand that Volkia is at war, and few of even the most loyal Volkish women enjoy such luxury."

"I don't think it's going to work," Yevliesza said. "Delaying my departure. Not accepting my apology until I start appreciating Volkia."

"Delaying? But you have only been in Volkia six days."

She was well aware that this man could use force to compel her to confess things, though he would certainly be held back by the reaction in Numinat. She decided to soften her hostility. It wouldn't save her, but it might help.

"I did agree to stay for a little while. It's just that I am offended that my apology isn't accepted."

"We have been at cross-purposes," he said, relaxing a little.

She sipped her wine, letting silence enfold them.

"You might be glad to know that Duke Tanfred will be staying with us for a few days. I believe you enjoy his company?"

Yes, when he wasn't alarming her with his theories. "He was

very gracious to me at Wilhoff Manor. We went for a ride to the promontory with the arch."

"Ah, yes. The arch." He sighed. "But the duke failed to extract a confession from you."

"Because it's absurd."

He smiled ironically. "Well. In any case, I myself am more pragmatic. Let us leave the subject for now." Albrecht got up to refresh his whiskey or whatever he was drinking. He brought the wine bottle back from the sideboard and when she nodded, he topped off her glass. "In Numinat, Volkish wine is not served?"

"I'm not sure that they do. But this is very good."

He resumed his seat. "I believe Father Ludving joined you on your ride at Wilhoff. He is a man of great learning."

"Yes, he seems to be. And easy to talk to."

"Unlike me." His face was relaxed, but his eyes, icy.

"I didn't say that."

He paused, perhaps deciding whether he had been insulted or not. Then, a ghost of a smile. "I am not often in the company of women. No practice."

"But Evah Krim?"

"Well, yes. Evah. But I have something to ask you. I will attend church on Sunday, three days from now. Would you care to attend with me?"

"Well . . ." She glanced at him. "I have a choice?"

"Yevliesza," he chided. "Of course."

"Then, no. I'm uneasy to be in public. And I wouldn't understand the sermon in Volkish."

"Perhaps you should learn Volkish," he said softly.

It was exhausting to talk to him. More like chess than a conversation, and he had more pieces than she had. She stood up. "My lord, it's been a long day. I'm suddenly quite tired."

Lieutenant Martel escorted her back to her room. As they passed the front entrance with its tall windows, Yevliesza saw a delicate fall of white flakes. In this Volkish palace, it seemed more cold than lovely.

When they had turned at the landing, Martel said, "I am sorry that you are here under an unpleasant duty. Perhaps this evening, you found it more pleasing?"

"To be honest, I'm not sure. But I'm hoping to complete my . . . assignment in a few days and go home."

She was surprised at what the lieutenant had said. Even if her situation was generally known by Albrecht's staff, and even if she might have some prominence for having come from the Firstland, it was odd to hear someone express sympathy.

He escorted her to her room. When he left, she paused for a few moments and then silently opened the door a crack to watch where he went. It was to the double doors past the reception room.

That was nothing new. Except . . . had he left the door slightly ajar?

She walked down the now-empty corridor to see.

Chapter Eighteen

The door was slightly open. She hesitated, thinking that she probably should not go through. Since the door had always been locked, they obviously didn't want her in that section of the palace. Maybe a good reason, in itself, to go there. She was curious about the exits. At some point, she might need one.

Once through the door, she found herself in a continuation of the broad hallway she had just left. Moving down it, she guessed that she was right above the front entrance hall. She passed a junction with another corridor leading deeper into the palace. Staying in the main hallway, she tried a plain door, thinking it might lead to a staircase instead of an apartment.

Behind this door, a storage closet.

Voices came from the adjoining corridor, and boots clicked on the stone floor. In alarm, she turned to the next door and slipped inside. Her heart pounded in her chest like it wanted out, but as she leaned against the door, she quieted. She was in a well-furnished parlor. On a sideboard were glasses and a tray with the remnants of a meal.

A voice came from the next room. A man's voice. Quickly, she peeked into the hall. Several officers stood talking. Closing the door again, she heard from the other room, "Hermand?" The man asked for something in Volkish. She caught the Volkish word for *please*.

She could either be revealed as snooping or be seen by soldiers in the hall. Either way she'd be discovered.

"Hermand?" The voice came again.

She picked up a glass from the sideboard and poured it full from a pitcher of water. Walking to the door where the occupant was, she said, "Would you like some water?" Oh God, she had just spoken in Numinasi. "Water," she amended—too late—in Volkish, choosing from her few words and phrases.

"Come," the voice said, this time in Numinasi. She entered.

The room was beautifully appointed, with a bed occupying a small part of it. In it lay someone propped up on pillows. The room smelled of medicinals.

"Who are you?" the occupant asked in accented Numinasi.

"Yevliesza." She brought the glass of water to the bedside.

"I am Lothric." He gestured at his sunken body. "Or I used to be."

It was impossible to judge the man's age. Not elderly, she guessed. His skin had a pink, feverish glow rising all the way to the top of his head where a stubble of black hair sprouted half-heartedly. His arms lay outside the covers as though he'd given up on them.

"May I help you drink?"

"Please."

She assisted him to sit up straighter and brought the glass to his lips. Folds of skin slumped around his neck. He had once been heavily built.

He took a sip and nodded that it was enough. The man whispered with a half-smile, "I think you do not look so much like Hermand."

If the man could joke at her entering his apartment, it might bode well for him not exposing her.

"I was exploring," she said. "There were soldiers in the hall, and I didn't want them to see me. You don't need to call them. I'll just go back to my room with them."

"Not yet. If you do not mind? There is a chair."

She noted it next to the bed and sank into it, feeling light-headed after her rush of adrenaline.

"What is your name?" he asked again.

"Yevliesza."

"So . . . Numinasi," he said in a husky whisper. The man seemed not so much ill as exhausted. "I thought you were Hermand, my adjutant." He turned his head to look at her, but his gaze went past her, to the windows, or perhaps captured by other thoughts or memories. "My name is Lothric."

"Pleased to meet you." She cast about for something to say, but nothing seemed quite right, given that she was a complete stranger and had brought him a glass of water in his bedroom. Finally she said, "You speak Numinasi very well."

"Oh, yes, I have languages. Once I was an educated man." He brightened, making eye contact at last. "Now I remember. They took Hermand away. An elementalist. As am I."

"Why did they take Hermand away?"

"Oh! Needed at the front. Alfan Sih . . ."

She rose. "I should go. They won't like me being here."

He frowned. "Are they using women now? I would not approve it. I shall speak with Albrecht."

"I'd rather you didn't mention that I came."

He smiled. "Well. Our secret, then."

"Thank you for talking with me," she said, starting to back away. Then she paused. "But using women for what?"

"Oh, they would not employ women. Only men drive our weapons. For as long as we can."

"Is it hard work?"

"It is killing work."

A sound from the corridor jangled her nerves. "You don't need to mention I was here. I hope you don't have to. I'm a guest here."

"Albrecht is like a son to me. He is taking good care of me. He comes by every day."

That was enough to propel her from the room. "Goodbye, sir. I appreciated our talk."

"You could come back," he whispered.

"I'll try. But they watch me."

He made a scoffing noise that turned into a rumbling cough. "Do not let them. Women should have privacy."

Hurrying out of the room, she made her way through his sitting room to the outer door. She stopped, trying to hear any noise from the hall. Nothing. But that didn't mean the area was deserted.

There was nothing to be gained by waiting. She entered the hallway, finding it empty, and hurried to the double doors, slipping through them and making sure they were closed behind her.

As she approached her apartment, a man emerged out of it. Noticing her, he stopped. Reinhart. She hoped he hadn't seen her come through the door.

She also hoped he didn't think he could enter her quarters without her permission. But on further thought, of course he could.

Closing the distance between them, she asked, "May I help you, Marshal Reinhart?

"An excellent offer," he said casually. "What did you have in mind?"

They were the same height, and when their eyes met it felt like an invasion. She cast back, "That you refrain from prowling my room."

"You might remember that I said you would be watched. Where have you been, by the way?"

"I believe I have permission to walk the halls."

As his lip curled, his small mustache twitched as though it were alive. "I leave you to your walk, then." Except for the twitching, he seemed very relaxed. Confident. In control. She heard his boots clicking down the hall.

When she entered her parlor, she found Breta standing by the sofa, adjusting her dress.

"Mistress!" Breta moved away from the seating area, pushing strands of hair into her maid's cap.

"I came up to help you prepare for bed," Breta said. She smiled with practiced efficiency, but she had been crying.

She guessed the situation. Reinhart had used Breta against her will. And had taken advantage of Yevliesza's absence to do so in her apartment.

Breta hurried away to the bedroom to attend to her duties, leaving Yevliesza sickened with disgust. So much for the honor of Volkish soldiers.

Chapter Nineteen

In a lashing rain, Tirhan's partisans took shelter in the Creigath Hills, where caves gouged into a rocky plateau. They made camp in an immense, vaulted chamber where they could dry out after two days of evading a Volkish patrol and where there was room for the horses, as well.

In a chamber adjoining the main one, Morwen pushed off the fur cloak that covered her and Tirhan and lifted her tunic from the cave floor.

"Leave it off," Tirhan whispered, stirring from sleep.

"You cannot make the night last forever," she chided. But she paused.

"Then come to me." He reached for her, and she let drop the tunic, sliding next to him. He was ready for her, and she mounted him. Rocking, she leaned in, her long white-blond hair forming a curtain around their faces.

They were often desperate for each other. The tension of Volkish pursuit and skirmishes and the pain of lost comrades made their shared bed a refuge. "Let yourself go," he said as she made an urgent sound deep in her throat. He moved with her, losing himself when she did.

Presently the world came back to him. She hurried to dress and adjusted the knives in her cross-body strap.

"Morwen."

Something in the tone of his voice made her stop, and she approached the furs where he lay.

"Do not go."

"What, never?" she mocked. "When you are on the Silver-wood Throne, I will carry wine to the royal table."

"The throne is by no means assured."

"It is my watch; I have to go."

Morning was far off, and he did not rise with her. He could not share her watch; the men would not like it. They might like it even less if they thought he had strong feelings for her. They knew that he was expected to bond with Anwelyth, daughter of Clan Rhydwyn's clan lord. It was his father's wish, as Kierach often reminded him. But now his father was gone, and Tirhan could make his own choice.

A few hours later he woke to the sound of the men's voices in the large chamber. It must be morning, but this part of the cave system had never seen a dawn.

After he dressed, he went to the lip of rock at the cave's entrance where Morwen stood with Kierach. The ravine below glistened after the night's heavy rain.

"Walk with me," he bid them, and they followed him along the rocky ledge for a few paces. As they walked, Morwen said, "Eiwedd is missing."

"Missing?"

Kierach responded, "No one remembers seeing her bed down. I've sent two men to retrace yesterday's path."

"I will search on my own," Morwen snapped.

Tirhan nodded. "But first, listen. I want a few of us to go out to recruit. Now that we have found a secure camp, we will send people out to the clans. With wraith wolves protecting

Glenir Manor, we need our own men with creature power to set them free." Tirhan turned to Kierach. "Give me a list of your best woodsmen."

Morwen made an impatient face. "Recruiting clansmen with creature power? I thought you had let go that hope."

"No. The cave is a good place for now. You'll be able to bring recruits directly here."

"You do not mean *me*," she said in surprise.

"Morwen. You have a reputation among the clans. The woman who fights as fiercely as a man. They respect you."

"We should fight, not rest."

"Rest, but only for a time."

She shook her head. "We know the Volkish are nearby, hunting us. We should find them in the forest and pick them off one by one."

"If we are recruiting for fighting powers," Kierach said, "we would do better to find men with warding and elements. What use creature power?" He smiled ruefully. "Ah. Your spirit visitation."

Morwen whispered harshly, trying to keep their argument quiet, "And you do not even know it was a proper spirit! It might have been a skillful manifester."

"No manifester," Tirhan said. "He *spoke* to me. Whether it pleases the ancients or is just a test, I am to free the wraith wolves under creature control. And it happens that by freeing them, we tip the odds in our favor to free the queen."

"Then recruit for more fighters!" Morwen spat. "Instead, you wander after voices in the forest."

Tirhan let the comment go unchallenged. Faintly he heard, or remembered, the whisper of the otherworld messenger: *In the Alfan forests the wraith wolves must be free.*

"How is it even done—countermanding creature power?" Kierach complained. "And creature power is not common."

From up the hill, a lookout hailed them. "Our men returning."

When Tirhan walked to the cliff's edge to look down, the men had already disappeared into the boulder-strewn path to the cave.

"How many?" Morwen called up to the lookout.

"Two."

In a few minutes the men reappeared. They were carrying Eiwedd. Morwen took in a sudden breath.

Lodd came up the path first and looked at her, his face dark. A small shake of his head. Behind him, Demyr, a man so solidly built that he carried Eiwedd with ease. He took her into the cave and laid her down as the men silently gathered around.

Tirhan had seen enough bodies to know that she was dead.

Morwen knelt beside the girl's body, wiping the sopping hair from her face.

Lodd said low, "They used her badly."

Morwen looked at Lodd with as terrible a stare as Tirhan had ever seen.

Rage swelled in him. It was one thing to lose one of his men, men that he had lived with and fought with for many weeks. But Eiwedd was barely twelve years old. He clutched the handle of the knife at his belt.

When Morwen rose, Tirhan reached out to comfort her, but she shrugged away from him. "They will die," she spat before she stalked away.

The men were frozen in place, standing around the girl's body. Kierach looked at Tirhan, his eyes blazing. "My lord?"

Tirhan met his gaze, then turned to the men. "They will answer for this. Rest assured, she will be avenged."

He walked away, threading a path through the great chamber with its supplies and makeshift beds. At the embers of the previous night's bonfire, he set fire to one of the torches laid by for use and walked into the darkness at the far edge of the cavern.

Behind him, he heard the men talking and the whicker of horses as they sensed the tension around them. He found one of the side tunnels leading off from the main cave and strode down it, trying to shed his rage, but it followed him and urged, demanded, that he run his sword through the perpetrators.

The tunnel widened into a large room with light streaming from above. Looking up, he saw a hole in the ceiling and through it, the morning sky. The tunnel ended here. He sat, his back against the wall, laying the torch down and letting it gutter.

Morwen thought he did not fight hard enough. Now was the time to prove her wrong, to galvanize the men, to take the fight to the Volkish. His thoughts settled on the tactics of revenge, a subject that gave him some peace.

"You can kill them," a distant voice said, filling the rock cavity where he sat.

He rose to his feet. Turning to look down the tunnel, he saw that he was still alone.

"It would be justice," came the voice, sounding both far away and near. But no one was in sight. A sense of being underwater, but still breathing overtook him, and he fell into a trance-like immobility. It was the spirit again, reaching from the otherworld.

"But know this: it would not help you win."

Tirhan spoke, or thought he did. *To win we must fight.*

"Not only with swords," came the voice, "but with stealth and surprise." The words swept over him like a cold wind, tightening the skin on his face and hands. "Do you remember, Lord King, how you almost brought Yevliesza to her death? She of the ninth power?"

No, Tirhan protested. *I protected her.*

"By bringing her into the realm of the Alfan war? She might easily have been captured. Because you were in haste to fight no matter the cost to her."

In war, there is danger. Tirhan said, or thought. *But she was not captured.*

"Oh, but she was. She is in the hands of the Volkish because of your choice."

The words pierced him. Had the Volkish discovered her power? If so, a terrible turn of events. *Tell me. What has happened?*

"It happened long ago. Long ago."

What do you mean?

"Long ago and in days to come. It is difficult to keep events in the order you would understand." The voice was growing softer. "But I say to you, son of Gwenid, be patient."

In alarm, Tirhan called out, "Stay! Tell me what will happen to Yevliesza."

Very faintly: "She has not decided yet. But you must decide for the Alfan. Whether to rush to vengeance or to persist on the path."

But what is the path. . . .

A shadow appeared above, the shadow of a warrior standing on the edge of the cavity, black against the bright day, a sword hanging from his belt.

"The wraith wolves, Lord King," the voice came to him. "The wolves, the wolves." Then the shadow moved off and Tirhan saw clouds passing overhead, far away in the sky.

Chapter Twenty

"Eight hells," Dreiza muttered.

On her kneeling pad, she had been training a new sprout off the main stem of the *traveka* vine and broke it when she pushed it too hard. It was a shame to be in such a foul mood in this lovely setting: the long row of windows giving out onto the rocky hillside with the white peaks of the Numins like sentinels in the distance.

At morning meal, she had learned that Yevliesza had been made to go to the Volkish capital. And that somehow this had to do with the foolish son of a *fajatim*. Numinat might go to war with Volkia at any time, and here the princip had sent Yevliesza to Volkia without a care for her safety. It was outrageous, all the more so, since Valenty did not stop it. This was the *sacrifice* that Kassalya had foreseen. The fact that she had called it a sacrifice meant that Yevliesza would come to harm. And at Zolvina, they had known it would happen. Or suspected it would happen because of Kassalya's dread knowing.

Even if it might not have happened, the Devi Ilsat had done nothing to forestall it. Not that she *could* forestall it. There was no recognized connection between the Numinat court and the traditions of the *satvars*. They went their separate ways. But no princip could entirely ignore the High Mother of Zolvina sanctuary, a woman who eventually met some of the most powerful women in Osta Kiya, those who took the pale in older years.

Another stem broke off. Dreiza closed her eyes and let a pent-up breath clear her lungs.

Along the whitewashed corridor with its slate floor came a middle-aged *satvar*. She smiled in delight. "How patient you are, my sister! The vine will be so beautiful."

"Well, it is dropping new sprouts," Dreiza answered sourly, "so I am not that sure."

"Oh, the pity!" the *satvar* said, shaking her head and retreating down the corridor.

Dreiza made her way to the High Mother's office, hoping to find her in. She knocked at the heavy wooden door, but there was no answer. The next place to try was the cell where she helped tend to Videkya in her illness. The Devi Ilsat had great healing skills, but against the wasting disease, sometimes little could be done. Videkya was one of the oldest of the *satvadeya*, the Devi Ilsat's inner circle. She was fifteen years short of her allotted one-hundred and fifty, and everyone in the domicile was grieving already.

When she knocked again, the answering hail came from behind her.

"Ah, Dreiza," the High Mother said, smiling as she approached. She seemed genuinely glad to see her, although she must know why Dreiza had come. "Fetch your cloak," she said, "and I will meet you at the north gate. A walk will do us good."

A few minutes later, dressed in boots and woolens, the Devi Ilsat led the way through a stand of trees to the path up the hillside.

"How does Videkya?" Dreiza asked.

"She is cheerful. Knitting a scarf. She plans not to die until it is finished."

"May it be a long scarf, Mother."

"Indeed."

The Devi Ilsat was not a tall woman, so on the steep path, Dreiza kept her pace to match the older woman's.

"Yevliesza was traded to the Volkish," Dreiza bluntly said.

"So I heard. But we do not know what may befall, my daughter." As they climbed, the view down to the foothills began to emerge. Steeply pointed rocks reared up from the hillside like blunt spears, screening the views from time to time as they progressed.

The High Mother's statement seemed to sum up her position, and it might be pointless to complain. Nevertheless, she said, "Removal from the affairs of the world is a thin excuse for not helping."

"It is not a satisfying answer, is it," the High Mother said cheerfully. She threw her cape over one shoulder as the effort of climbing warmed her. At the top of the rise, they looked out on the valleys below and, behind them, the great peaks of the Numin mountains.

"Sometimes it is difficult to have a clear vision of what is going on," the Devi Ilsat said. "So we come here to see more widely." She sat on a rock ledge and gestured for Dreiza to join her. When Dreiza did so, she went on. "We have a knot, my daughter. Two strands, and we wish to untangle them."

By the Deep, a parable, Dreiza thought.

"One strand must be broken, and so we must decide which one."

"Why not just leave the knot as it is?"

The Devi Ilsat laughed. "Because you refuse, my daughter! And so we come to Yevliesza. Here is the thing you do not know.

Kassalya has told us that Yevliesza will be central to an event of great significance for the realm."

"All the more reason to protect her, then?"

"But protect her from what?"

"The Volkish, Mother. And Princip Anastyna's machinations."

The old *satvar* nodded, watching a large bird ride the updrafts. Suddenly it steeped into a dive, passing out of view as it plunged. "Yet anything we do may alter her destiny."

"But alter it for the good!"

"What is the good, my daughter?"

"We could have persuaded Anastyna not to send her to Volkia. You might have succeeded."

"Ah, Volkia." The High Mother turned to Dreiza. "But what if Yevliesza is supposed to be there?"

The question startled her. "Do you know that she is supposed to?"

"Goodness no. But we come back to the two strands. Suppose they are both good things. Suppose one is compassion for those in difficulty. The other is the freedom to find one's own way, even in danger and hardship. Sometimes we forgo the apparent act of kindness so we do not force outcomes. This is especially true when we consider people of great capacity. Their outcome is their own to forge."

"What if the girl is killed? Then so much for not forcing things."

The High Mother shook her head, a smile creasing her cheeks. "Now you wish to overcome death?"

Yes, she wanted to say. But even while she wished for Yevliesza's well-being, she could see the broader perspective. The girl of the mundat might have a high destiny, one that would affect the whole kingdom. And so the Devi Ilsat would not step in to push it along or interfere. Because it was possible that Yevliesza was supposed to be right where she was.

"Listen well, my daughter: Our words today must stay between us. No one must know." Dreiza nodded, mollified that the High Mother had shared so much with her.

The old *satvar* rose, brushing a crust of snow from her cloak and gazing out. "When the raptor falls from the sky, it may not break upon the rocks but find just what it needs."

The parable landed more softly on Dreiza's ears than usual. "Thank you, Mother. I think I understand."

"I am glad to hear it, my daughter." Starting down the hillside to the domicile, she gave a little hop over a few rocks jutting up on the path. Her voice floated up to Dreiza: "But you are still to tend to the *traveka* vine."

Chapter Twenty-One

In the hallway that had been allotted to her, Yevliesza walked, up and down, up and down. She hoped to talk to Lothric again. Passing the double doors to the rest of the second floor, she tried the latch. Locked.

She had begun this routine of walking because sometimes it was empty and at those times she tried the doors, noting which ones were locked. Near her apartment were doors leading to the balcony where she was allowed access, but the balcony was small and afforded no better view than from the windows of her suite.

She continued down the smaller hallway, which lay perpendicular to the larger one. The game-room tables so far hadn't been used and likely wouldn't be if they meant to isolate her. Out the windows she watched the courtyard below, where a stableman exercised a horse, leading it by the reins. Beyond the courtyard, she saw the many peaked roofs of the vast city fading into the hazy, polluted distance.

She noticed two men opening the wide iron door leading to the street. Presently, a dark shape appeared in the opening. It was a small wagon—or van, since it looked to be metal—moving on its own. Out of it protruded two bars. No, muzzles. Gun muzzles.

It noiselessly rolled into the yard, accompanied by a few soldiers on foot.

It came to a stop beneath her window. Out of the van stepped a soldier who disappeared into the palace with the others. Another wagon of the same sort approached from the street and, once it had entered the courtyard, the gate clanged shut behind it.

Yevliesza stepped away from the window, not wanting to be seen observing the devices. Clearly, they were weaponized machines. They were more than rumor; she had now seen at least two, and perhaps three, if the one she had seen when first entering Hapsigen had carried weapons. Machines under power, dark and lethal-looking. But under what power? They were silent and didn't belch steam or any kind of exhaust.

She remembered Master Lothric saying, *It is killing work.* Especially for elementalists. A thought arose, one she had been ignoring since her conversation with him. The machines were under some kind of power. Maybe it was the birthright power of their drivers. Powers like elemental ones. And it sickened them.

Anastyna had to hear of this. If the Volkish were engaged in a dangerous technology, the Mythos kingdoms might ally to stop them. Maybe the princip already knew. And yet she hesitated to send aid to Alfan Sih. The *fajatim* were against intervention, but would they be if they knew of this?

❦

Lieutenant Martel glanced at Yevliesza as he escorted her to the dining hall. "Are you well, mistress? Please pardon me if I am being forward in asking."

Yevliesza took a calming breath, trying to look relaxed when her thoughts were all of the machine and what fuel they might be using.

"It's nothing, Lieutenant." She forced a smile. "Who will be at dinner?"

"Just two others tonight besides you and Commandant Albrecht: Mistress Krim and Marshal Reinhart."

A meal from hell, then. "Thank you, Lieutenant."

At the open double doors, Martel left her.

In the cavernous dining room, the table was set for four at the far end. Fine glassware and silver settings glowed in the light of a candelabra. The only other person in the room was Evah, who stood before the fireplace looking into the flames. She turned as Yevliesza approached.

"Good evening, Evah," Yevliesza said in Volkish, having learned a few useful phrases from Breta. And then in Numinasi: "Your gown is lovely." It was palest blue velvet, with a neckline that plunged to show a bit of cleavage. Evah was turning up the heat.

Evah looked her up and down. "Choosing black dress always," she carefully pronounced in Numinasi. Her facial expressions seemed limited to a vacant calm interspersed with impish smirking.

Outside in the hall came the sound of arguing.

Albrecht entered the dining room with Marshal Reinhart. They joined the women as a servant appeared with drinks on a tray. Reinhart made a stiff bow to the women and took a glass of whiskey, downing it like medicine.

"Yevliesza, thank you for joining us," Albrecht said. "You have met Marshal Walthar Reinhart, I believe."

Yevliesza nodded to Reinhart, whose face was even more pinched than usual. "Of course."

"I apologize that I was not here to greet you. We had an incident."

He handed her a glass of wine from the tray. "You must try the wine. We have opened a special bottle for you."

"I'm afraid good wine is wasted on me," she said, but accepted the glass.

"The wine cannot be put back in the bottle," Reinhart muttered.

"I hope that you have taken care of your incident," Yevliesza said to Albrecht.

"No, we have not," Reinhart snapped. "But we shall."

"Oh, your poor horse," Evah said to him, looking sorrowful. "He a champion. Very expensive. But horse is . . . well?"

"No, Mistress Evah," Reinhart said, "the horse is not well. It had to be *shot*. Martel will have ten lashes for this."

"You can't mean to do that!" Yevliesza blurted.

He rounded on her. "Every soldier knows you do not reach for a stallion. One does not even approach a horse suddenly."

"But lashing is barbaric!"

Reinhart's face darkened, his mustache crumpling above his lip. "As a Numinasi, you are offended by barbarism?" He barked a laugh. "He will be whipped, for carelessness. I came back from a ride and still mounted, I spoke to the groom. Martel hurried up to hand me a dispatch and spooked the horse. When it reared, its foreleg came down on the carriage wheel. For that, Martel will be whipped."

"Surely not, for what was an accident?"

Reinhart tightened his lips and barely enunciated: "Do not presume to advise me, miss."

After a pause, Albrecht turned to Reinhart. "Walthar, it does not merit whipping." Reinhart's face stiffened. "The man made an error. I will speak to him, to impress upon him the severity of his mistake."

Reinhart drew himself up and smiled ingratiatingly. It was a brutal look. "As you say, my prince."

Making their way to the table, Reinhart slashed a look at Yevliesza. It was utterly calm but lit with fury.

Across the table, Evah bit her lip, trying to suppress a smile.

After dinner, the marshal took his leave and, perhaps by prior arrangement, Evah left with him.

Yevliesza took a seat on the divan in front of the fire and Albrecht joined her there, bringing her wine glass from the table.

"I am sorry if the dinner was difficult," he said. "An exceptional horse, though. A great pity."

"I'm glad you came to Lieutenant Martel's defense."

"We are not barbarians," Albrecht murmured, gazing at the fire.

"Would he really have had him whipped?"

"Perhaps. Military discipline is unforgiving. But you cannot pretend it is not the same in Numinat. I believe being pushed from a tower window is harsher than ten lashes."

A small shudder rippled over her, as she remembered the tower window. "Maybe I can't be too shocked. But you made the right decision."

"We are not a cruel people."

A log on the fire collapsed in a profusion of sparks. She had something to ask Albrecht, and now seemed a good time. "My lord, is there no place else that I can walk, aside from the second-floor hall? Perhaps outside, even?"

A small frown. "Outside?"

"I need fresh air once in awhile. The hall upstairs is too confining." She very much would like to know of an outside door besides the front portico.

Albrecht shook his head. "You must understand that Rothsvund is my military command center. Your, how do you say —confinement—is necessary under the circumstances."

"Of course, but is there nowhere appropriate?"

He watched her with an appraising look. "I will consider it."

"Thank you."

"You are not a prisoner, Yevliesza."

"Of course not," she blithely said.

"You do not sound convinced." When she didn't answer, he went on. "I thought we were building a degree of trust."

"Perhaps," she allowed.

"Well." He tossed off the last of his whiskey, setting his glass on the low table before them. "We are doing better. You have seen that I am not a monster, I think."

"Yes. You're not a monster." She felt she had to smile and managed a small one.

He nodded, seemingly pleased. Their eyes met for a moment, and she found herself trapped by his close regard. His gray-blue eyes held a flash of desire. Reaching toward her, he touched her cheek. She was so surprised, she didn't move, and he pulled her toward him.

She pressed her hand against his chest, but he had already taken her in his arms, drawing her closer. She pulled away from him, managing to stand up.

"My lord, no."

He ran his hand though his hair, pinning her with a hot gaze. She froze, afraid what would come next. But he calmly rose. "Please pardon me. For a moment I felt . . . invited."

"You weren't. And you're frightening me."

"Then I beg you, please excuse my behavior."

So he wasn't going to insist. It was a relief, but in the next moment he put his hand on her arm, still claiming that much. "I am a man of honor." Withdrawing his hand from her arm, he said, "You may not believe that."

"I believe you," she managed to say, hoping that was the right answer. She was so over her head.

That seemed to mollify him. "It is more important that we have mutual respect than anything else."

Strange that he wanted respect, that he valued the concept of honor. If he meant it, then it might keep him from his worst instincts. As it seemed it just had.

But then she thought about Albrecht's treatment of Evah. An unwelcome notion came to her that Evah's timidity might not be just a result of their different stations. She was missing something. Intelligence, self-respect . . . or her *will*. Albrecht had creature power. In Numinat, using powers against individuals was almost always a high Trespass. But maybe Volkish culture had a different view.

Had he intruded on Evah's mind? Did he take pleasure in that control?

With that thought, she said, "I think I'll retire for the evening."

He offered to escort her, but at the look on her face, he gave an ironic smile. "Would you rather I called Martel?"

"No, of course not."

At her apartment door, he stopped her from going in. "You have your own honor to maintain, Yevliesza."

When she looked askance at him, he said, "You were there when the new route to Alfan Sih unfolded."

He wasn't going to let it go.

"It troubles me," he went on, "that you deny this when I know it to be true. That event was an act of military intervention, allowing the Alfan prince to return home and galvanize an insurrection."

"I have nothing to do with military matters," she snapped. That was the truth. To avoid becoming a weapon was something she thought about every day.

"I am leaning toward believing you. But you do know something about how the new route happened. And you will share this with me before you leave."

With that, he left her, walking back down the hall to the stairs and taking out a key to unlock it.

When Yevliesza closed her apartment door, she leaned against it, closing her eyes to get herself under control.

Breta came up to her, her forehead wrinkled in concern. "Mistress?"

"I think he's going to keep me here," she murmured, more to the air in front of her than to Breta. That was why he didn't care that she had access to a window overlooking the courtyard with its devious machines. He was going to keep her.

"That is terrible, mistress," Breta said in distress.

"Tell me about it," she whispered in English.

Chapter Twenty-Two

Five men and one woman rode with Tirhan. Two were his escort, with the rest bound for the uplands where they would separately ride to the various clan holdings to recruit fighters. A particular kind of fighter, ones with creature power.

Morwen had agreed to help recruit, but she held strong doubts. Giving voice to them now, she said, "Why would anyone join us, when they have not yet done so?"

The youngest among the fighters, Bridan, thinking that Morwen spoke to the group, piped up. "That is what persuasion is for."

"And you have a gift for oratory," Morwen snapped, silencing the boy. Turning to Tirhan, she said, "Fighters have not come to us because clan lords say whether to fight or not. And the clan lords believe we have no chance against the Volkish."

"We only need those with an affinity for creatures," Tirhan said. "It is little enough to ask. If the clan lord says we may ask his people, then we will ask." He looked at her, sitting proud, her long hair clasped at her neck, out of the way of her knife arm. She wanted nothing so much as to fight the enemy, to make them pay for what they had done—to Alfan Sih, to Eiwedd. He knew that, and yet she was still willing to try this approach. The strategy of creature power.

The last visit of the spirit had greatly troubled Tirhan, when he learned that he had caused Yevliesza to be held by the Volkish. He did not know how she came to be captured, but he knew that her particular power would make her a great prize for Prince Albrecht.

Morwen wanted to know why the Volkish would risk their relationship with Numinat over the woman of the origin world. But he could not tell her. Neither she nor his men knew how he had really managed to return to his besieged realm from Numinat. He claimed that he had been smuggled into the realm inside an infernal machine with the aid of a sympathizer among the Volkish troops. But, as to the real method of his return—he had sworn to Yevliesza to keep that secret.

Now Morwen would go into the local holdings and speak for him, asking for any warriors who could help to release the wraith wolves from Volkish control. And she would do this for his sake, even if she thought it a waste of time.

One of the men chirruped a warning, and the party halted, listening. He heard one of Morwen's knives slip from its sheath.

The foremost warrior turned in his saddle and reported to Tirhan. "Four riders. Friends." He pointed into a draw. Soon a rider appeared, wearing the moss green cap of Clan Rhydwyn. In single file, others followed. Among them, Clan Lord Gryffyd and his daughter, Anwelyth.

Clan Rhydwyn was one of the unaligned holdings. Gryffyd, gray hair flowing, his body thin but still hearty, wore heavy furs against the cold. The clan lord now looked at the small party, assessing them. When he dismounted, he did not kneel to the presumptive heir to the Silverwood Throne, and this went over poorly with Morwen and the rest of Tirhan's party.

When Anwelyth was presented, they accorded the girl proper nods. Tirhan felt their sideways glances at him, watching how he would behave. The skirt of Anwelyth's silver-blue dress fanned out against her horse's flanks, and her pale skin had reddened from the cold. Tirhan remembered her as young girl, thin and energetic, when his father's entourage had visited Clan Rhydwyn. Now she was quiet and wary, old enough to understand what was at stake with the occupation. She was a woman of standing, and Tirhan greatly wondered why she accompanied her father so far from their holding.

After a meal was shared around, Tirhan's people moved off, leaving him to parlay. He bade Morwen stay, and they took seats on heavy fallen branches that his men dragged into place.

"My scouts said you camped at Creigath caves," Gryffyd said. "We were on our way there."

Tirhan responded, "If you knew we were there, perhaps it is time to move on."

"Come, my lord," Gryffyd said. "We know these hills, and my people range widely."

"As do we. I am sending some scouts into the holdings hereabouts. We are asking people to join us and, since you and I have met, allow me to include you in our pleas. So far our strikes have kept the enemy off-balance, but we could do much more with your help."

"So your people have said, Lord Tirhan. But the Volkish have fifteen thousand troops at Osian alone. Trained soldiers with mechanical weapons, and they punish attacks with reprisals against the holdings. Women and children. None spared."

"It is war, Lord Gryffyd."

"Your war. Do you think the clans will flock to you if you make an appeal with these few men . . . and a woman?" He glanced at Morwen.

"That is the plan," Morwen threw back.

Anwelyth watched all this carefully, her face revealing nothing. Tirhan noted her rich gown, the trappings of her horse, the several rings on her hands, the silver settings glinting in a shaft of sun. Tirhan's father and Lord Gryffyd had hopes for a union between them, but marriage had no claim on Tirhan's thoughts when he had the Volkish to fight.

Gryffyd narrowed his eyes. "You will not recruit on my lands, Lord Tirhan."

"Very well. We will continue without you. But I am not in your holdings now. So we will press on."

The old clan lord shook his head. "You were ever a son who went his own way."

Morwen made a small adjustment to her knife harness, and Gryffyd took note of this with a small smile. "And your partisans are loyal. They think they are fighting for the future king."

Tirhan raised an eyebrow. "And they are not?"

"The future king must win in battle. And to do that, my lord, you will need Clan Rhydwyn. If our men are to bleed for this one-sided war, we need assurances that our help will not be forgotten." Anwelyth sat still as a carving. A ray of sun that pierced the upper story of the trees frosted her blond-white hair and spilled over her dress. Tirhan remembered that she had chosen where to sit and saw how the whole visit had been carefully planned. First the clan lord was skeptical, then hostile, and then offered a bargain.

"I have many to thank," Tirhan said, locking eyes with the old clan lord. "And the people of Alfan Sih will remember who fought and who did not."

He got to his feet. The meeting was over, and he had not accepted Anwelyth in return for Rhydwyn's fighters, though she looked the part of a queen and might make a good one.

As Gryffyd and his party left the clearing for the long ride home, Morwen brought out her sharpening stone.

He watched her hone one of her knives. "Morwen."

Still working her whetstone, she said, "What would you have said to Gryffyd if I had not been here?"

"The same."

She slid the knife into her belt and rose to face him. "Tirhan. It is war. You cannot be led by your heart."

Bravely said. But it only made him more certain of what he had done. "Nor will I be twisted by an old man's ambition."

She narrowed her eyes, considering. She did not know his mind. *He* did not know his mind—not nearly—but sought his way through a thicket of swords and duty.

Morwen joined the men, who were with the horses. They accepted her as a warrior. But as a queen?

Chapter Twenty-Three

They were close to Nashavety's lair now. Valenty and Urik watched for guards who might patrol the vicinity, but as they carefully approached a clearing in the woods, they encountered none. Through the last line of trees, they glimpsed a strange three-story house, with a jumble of features, none of which seemed to belong together.

It was a brick, stone, and wood mansion with towers protruding from its corners, porches jutting from all three levels and, everywhere, a confusion of turrets, arches, vaulted roofs, and pillars. Massive and dark, the house looked like it had been cobbled together rather than built as one habitation.

With the day surprisingly warm, the last snowfall now sluiced down from the mansion's roofs as though the entire structure was melting.

"Not fortified," was Urik's only comment on the bizarre construct.

"No. But a puzzling layout."

"Meant to confuse." It was a good observation. If the inside was anything like the exterior, it would be a maze.

A guard stood on the main porch, standing rigid. "Still as a statue," Valenty whispered.

"It *is* a statue."

"Where are the guards?"

Urik snorted a laugh. "Inside." He looked up at the jumble of roofs. "No fires lit."

"Maybe they are all asleep."

"Or they do not need warmth," Urik muttered, a remark that reminded Valenty of what he had already surmised about Nashavety. She was a demon. Yevliesza refused to call her that since she did not believe in such things, but what other word was there for such as Nashavety?

The mansion looked out on an expanse of abandoned gardens and then a long slope into a valley surrounded by sheer cliffs. Nashavety's isolation was extreme, and if she had kept to herself, they would not now be trying to kill her. But she had defected to the Volkish and exposed the underbelly of Numinat to them. Though she had lost the small finger of her left hand, sources had told the princip that she had managed to summon her powers back. What those powers would look like now, Valenty was about to discover.

They split up to reconnoiter, taking separate routes around the house, but avoiding the front where most of the windows faced.

Meeting at the same place after their circuit, Urik said, "Go in from the top. Find an access to an attic." He noted Valenty's doubtful look. "There is a way up on the far side. Difficult but possible."

"Very well." Valenty scrutinized the mansion's upper story, where windows crouched under small, pitched roofs of both slate and thatch. "If they take me, and you can escape, my order is that you go."

Urik met his eyes and made an almost imperceptible nod.

Urik did not waste movement. But it might also be his way of saying *maybe*.

As though in answer, Urik unstrapped the spear from his back, stabbing it into the ground to make it easy to find. They left behind their packs and bulky jackets, and made their way around the rear of the great house to the place Urik had selected for their ascent.

As they climbed, Valenty felt a coil of fear in his stomach. It was too quiet, with not even the wind washing through the trees. The whole world seemed empty except for the two of them climbing the ornamental brickwork, sometimes finding footholds on ledge or sill. Urik led, more nimble than Valenty, with neither of them looking into windows lest they in turn be seen. The only sound was the trickle of water down the sides from the snow melt, slicking the stonework and creating the impression that they were climbing a great monster that had just emerged from the depths of a sea.

At the third story, Urik stopped, having found a window that he pried open. It swung out, but there was a matching window that connected with it, and it was locked. At last Urik had both of them open and, drawing his knife, he climbed in, followed by Valenty.

They were in an enormous and very dark top floor full of old furniture and chests crowded together or stacked. Windows let in slants of winter light that lit up great cobwebs like the sails of ships. No one had been up here for a very long time, Valenty thought. Maybe no one was in the house at all, for it was so quiet he could hear his own breathing.

Urik had found a door and motioned. As Valenty approached him, something under his feet crunched with a sound like a vase shattering. He froze, and the two of them listened for any response. Nothing.

The light here was just enough to see that he had stepped on something small and round. It was a face. He had stepped on a child's doll with a head made from a stiff material. The fleeting thought came that he had stepped on a child's skull, but he pushed the image away as Urik slowly opened the door, exposing a flight of stairs.

They crept down the open-sided flight into a long, narrow hallway with many rooms. A noise from nearby sent the two of them into a crouch against the shadows of the wall. Doors were opening and a few people emerged, coming toward the stairway which, after a turn into the hallway, continued down to the next floor. These were likely servants or guards beginning the morning duties. They did not speak or look up to where Valenty and Urik hid on the staircase.

After the column of men disappeared down the stairs, Urik whispered. "They are too quiet."

"Alert to the intrusion?"

"Not alert. Others might be." Urik crept down the stairs and approached one of the doors. Valenty was close by, and they entered with weapons ready. It was a small room with a cot and table piled with belongings. Extra clothes.

After combing several rooms, they found more clothes and changed into Volkish-looking shirts and leather, laced-up vests.

On the next floor down, they found a wide hallway, its ceiling lost in the heights. In the grime of the windows, the dawn barely penetrated.

The air of abandonment continued until, around a corner, the hallway became an open mezzanine. It looked down on a large parlor. Dozens of silent people milled or stood in the room crowded with furniture and statuary. Some stood at the windows, keeping watch.

In the center of the room at a huge table sat Nashavety, eating. Around her, people moved quietly as though afraid to make a sound. None of them made eye contact with each other or with her. Valenty could hear the click of her spoon against her bowl and a slurping noise as she ate. They watched this for a time, distinguishing those who were armed and those who were not. Valenty counted thirty-two people.

Though they could only see Nashavety's profile, she had greatly changed, her body almost impossibly thin, her face gray and bony. Her hair hung long down her back. Alarmingly, it snapped with movement.

She used her right hand to eat and rested her left hand on the table as though it was weak or useless. The hand was enclosed in a black glove, and even at this distance Valenty thought he could discern that the last finger of the glove was filled.

The woman had been born to two powers, elements and creatures. Valenty had seen Nashavety's finger severed from her hand, and now she wore a glove, perhaps to hide her loss. Or to replace it. Which could not be done. *By the Mythos*, it could not.

As they watched, she looked up from her bowl and noted a person walking across the room in a strange, shuffling motion. She pointed her left-hand small finger at him, and the man swayed and stopped. Then he backed toward the wall, where he stood along with others who appeared to await her pleasure.

"Creature power," Urik whispered into Valenty's ear.

Yes, creature power directed at people, many people, a trespass of breathtaking magnitude.

A young servant stood by Nashavety's side, ready with a pitcher. When the servant turned away from the table for a moment, Valenty recognized him.

Pyvel.

Urik saw him at the same time, and they retreated out of sight of the parlor.

Valenty murmured, "It is Yevliesza's steward from Osta Kiya."

Saying nothing, Urik regarded him closely, knowing that this might change things.

"We bring the boy out," Valenty fiercely said. "We cannot leave him here. I will go down. When he leaves the room, I will follow him."

Urik shook his head. He gestured toward the stairs to the attic.

All Valenty's thoughts had been focused on a way to kill Nashavety. And he could still wait for that opportunity, because surely, she was not always surrounded. But now there was Pyvel.

"He attends her in a special way," Urik said, once they had withdrawn from the mezzanine into a side hallway to talk in more privacy. "He is her particular slave."

Valenty had not noticed that, but he suspected it was true. She had snatched Pyvel from Numinat because Yevliesza was devoted to him. She would reserve a special suffering for him.

"We can get close to her," Urik said. "I will cast a manifestation on us to make our faces look like others here." He narrowed his eyes at Valenty. "We can still eliminate her."

"But if we fail, Pyvel stays enslaved." He could not leave him to be Nashavety's creature. He was not yet fully grown. And Yevliesza loved him. "No, Urik. We take the boy."

He regarded Valenty closely, leaving just enough time for him to change his mind. When he did not, Urik said, "Then we take him tonight. We will wait in the attic until dark."

Valenty nodded his agreement and turned toward the main corridor.

But it had vanished. The hallway they stood in now appeared long in each direction.

"Move!" Urik hissed and rushed down the hallway toward a source of light around a corner, Valenty following. The corridor was growing wobbly as though the walls and ceiling were not always in one place.

At the turn in the hall, they came to stairs leading down. "We do not go down," Urik said. "It is offering us stairs, but we do the opposite."

"The house is ensorcelled," Valenty said. "And we are discovered."

"The house knows we came in from the attic and should not be here," the *harjat* said. "It closes in on us like a plant folding up its leaves at night. But it has no volition." He moved down the hall. "This way."

Another corridor led off at a tangent from their present one. Urik shook his head but tried the closest doorway. It opened.

The room was small and empty, as simple and devoid of detail as the hallway they had just left.

"The further we go, the deeper the trap," Urik said. "Now we stay still. Keep your mind empty. Give it nothing to feed on."

After a few moments, Urik whispered, "It is trying to sense us. Ward yourself if you must think so loud."

Valenty wrapped himself in a warding. It did not make him invisible, so it might not help much, but Urik seemed to know something about sorcery.

The door rattled. Valenty's warding dissolved as he drew his knife.

Urik shook his head as the door quieted. He made a gesture for Valenty to sit down, and the two of them sat with their backs to the wall, listening and trying not to think.

☙❧

URIK SHOOK HIM AWAKE.

Falling asleep was a bad sign, Valenty thought. Nashavety might be aware the house was hunting them. Had she extended her creature power to him?

As Valenty shook himself awake, he glanced at the window, noting that dusk was coming on. Urik brought something out of a pocket. It was the small mirror their contact near the bivouac had given them. It was full of cracks. Useless.

Urik smirked. The man enjoyed nothing so much as a good enemy.

Motioning for Valenty to stand up, the *harjat* raised his left hand and drew a circle in the air around Valenty's face in a gesture of alteration. Valenty felt no different, but clearly Urik had conjured a mental impression of a different face.

"I have found something interesting," Urik said. He must have been out while Valenty slept. "The demon's cave. Her bedroom."

Down the hall they plunged, moving quickly through the gray tunnels of the corridor. Losing even more definition, the walls quivered and elongated, doors sagged. At a dead end, Urik drew his knife and pierced the wall, which had become merely a shadow. He walked through it.

Urik whispered, "When we stayed still, the house had nothing to chase." They emerged into a real corridor.

In moments they came to a small foyer with a large, carved door highlighted in flaking gilt.

Knives tucked up their sleeves, they entered a spacious chamber with a bed surrounded by curtains heavy with dust. Urik crept close and looked inside the drapery. Finding nothing, he turned to Valenty and pointed to an alcove. On the floor, a confusion of blankets. Lying upon the blankets, a leather collar on a chain affixed to the wall.

Valenty and Urik exchanged glances. This might be where Pyvel slept.

VALENTY WAITED. HIDDEN FAR BACK IN THE RECESS, HE watched the door. Urik had concealed himself behind a piece of furniture.

If Nashavety came in with Pyvel, they would kill one and grab the other. Valenty badly wanted that outcome.

Dusk darkened into night as the house settled into a ghostly semi-existence. Valenty wondered what Nashavety was doing in this remote place. If she had gone over to the Volkish, why was she not in their midst in Hapsigen? But clearly, she was ill and weak. Thin beyond any human form, her body eaten away by the re-creation of her hand or by the summoning of power into a wasted hand. If so, now might be the time to strike. But he and Urik might not survive the attack, and Pyvel would still be a prisoner. There would be other opportunities to carry out the death sentence Nashavety had earned. If not tonight, then the next mission.

A click. The sound of a door opening. The room was in heavy darkness, but Valenty saw a shape moving.

Pyvel. He approached the alcove. Valenty waited to see if anyone accompanied him. Long moments passed. At last Pyvel picked up the collar and placed it around his neck.

Valenty descended on him, grabbing him and covering his mouth.

"Pyvel. It is Valenty. I am taking you home."

The boy shrank away, but Valenty held him firmly. "The last time I saw you, I was leaving on horseback with the soldiers. You came down from the castle. Do you remember?"

Pyvel remained silent.

Urik had come out of hiding and stood with them. "He remembers nothing. Do we wait for her, or do we leave?"

"We leave."

With Pyvel following in a daze, the *harjat* led them to a tall window and unlocked the latch. Once Urik was outside, he braced himself on a ledge, and Valenty helped Pyvel to slip through.

Valenty was halfway out the window when the bedroom door opened. A piercing shriek. Outlined against the light of the hall was a thin woman escorted by two guards. She raised her left hand and a heavy gust of wind coursed through the room.

Two men rushed at him, their hair whipping around them in the wind.

Valenty swung himself back into the room. He grabbed the man who reached him first and swung him into the other one, who crashed to the floor. For a few seconds he had only one guard to deal with. The man kept his feet and, roaring like a bear, lunged at him with a curved knife. Valenty staggered out of the way and pivoted around to thrust his dagger up and under the man's chin.

Next, Nashavety, who had fallen to the floor. Valenty tried to pull out his knife from his assailant's skull, but it was still embedded and would not budge.

Heavy footfalls came from down the hall. He would not have time to get to the demon to finish her. Meanwhile the other guard had regained his feet and staggered toward him.

Valenty pushed himself through the window opening and, judging the ground to be almost too far to jump, launched himself out.

He hit the ground, falling hard.

Urik was running with Pyvel, but in the wrong direction. Instead of into the forest, he was circling around. Valenty followed. As they came to the other side of the house, he saw that Urik was throwing on his heavy jacket and pack. As Valenty followed suit, Urik grabbed his spear.

"The valley," he said.

As they ran past the front of the house, the statue left its position on the porch and rushed at them, sword raised. It was alive. Or alive enough to kill. Weaponless, Valenty lurched away, evading the worst of the strike, but the sword tip cut into his shoulder and then lanced into his thigh. Valenty went to his knees.

As the creature raised its sword arm again, Urik rushed up and thrust his spear into the swordsman's bowels. When he jerked it back, the statue fell.

Valenty got to his feet, and they ran, half-dragging Pyvel between them, just as the house let out an abysmal, shuddering growl that surged louder as it rode the wind and the night.

"The woods!" Valenty said, shouting over the roar of the house.

"No, that is what they expect." Urik did not alter his course. He thrust the handle of his spear into Valenty's hand on his uninjured side. "Did I ever teach you how to use a spear?"

"No," Valenty said, already breathing hard.

"You might have asked," Urik muttered, as they lurched down the steep hillside.

Chapter Twenty-Four

Yevliesza stood at her apartment window gazing at the river and, beyond it, the city with its haze of pollution turning the snowy roofs a sickly yellow in the sun. In the distance, a dactyl swooped low over the city like a bird of prey looking for a meal. She thought of Albrecht's possible creature-control of Evah. If he had stooped to that, would he be willing to use that power to force a confession from her or bind her to his military goals? That worry was ever-present now.

"Mistress?"

She turned to find Breta at her side. She was happy to be free of Reinhart, but wary of retaliation. It might have been a mistake to have told Albrecht, but the man was occasionally capable of doing the right thing. She thought Breta was safe. She hoped so.

"Lieutenant Martel is here to see you," Breta announced. When Martel came in, he relayed that Duke Tanfred was now in residence at Rothsvund and begged to see her later that afternoon.

"Please tell him that it would be a pleasure." She could hardly say anything else.

Martel nodded. His lips parted to say something, but nothing came out.

"Lieutenant?"

"About Master Lothric, miss."

"Who?" she asked, as though she didn't know who the lieutenant was referring to.

"Master Lothric. He mentioned something to me yesterday. That he was visited by a lovely woman in a black dress."

She couldn't think what to say; whether to deny her visit or make excuses.

Martel went on. "Lothric was the Master of Weapons before his illness, and I have had the honor of his tutelage." He glanced at the door and continued. "Since you went to see him, someone must have left the double door open. It should not happen, but it is hard to remember to close it."

"I see." Martel had left it open that night.

"Ask him why he has fallen ill. Old men like to discuss their health."

She suspected that Lothric was sickened by the machines. And Martel wanted her to know.

"Lieutenant . . . when might someone forget to close the door?" As Martel hesitated for a moment, she said, "Perhaps tonight?"

A slow nod. On Martel's youthful face a new, grim expression made clear they were entering dangerous territory. She felt it in the center of her body, a tight fist that might be fear—or excitement.

He departed, saying, "I will tell Duke Tanfred that you look forward to his company."

Her heart sped. Martel had turned against Volkia. He was risking his life.

She sat down on the nearest chair, gathering her thoughts. If Martel knew about using Deep power to run machines, why didn't he just tell her? Maybe he was terrified and wanted deniability, or maybe he didn't know an important detail. Or Lothric, as former

Master of Weapons, was a more credible source to convince whoever she told—Anastyna, for instance.

Was she going to manipulate a sick, injured soldier? As pathetic as that would be, her spirits surged. Albrecht had held all the power, all the board-game pieces, and she had parried his moves, keeping him off-balance. But she hadn't been able to make a move on her own.

That was going to change.

❦

WHEN, LATE IN THE AFTERNOON, DUKE TANFRED ARRIVED, SHE braced herself for more discussion of the Mist Wall legend, but her strategy was clear: deny, deny.

The two of them exchanged greetings, his pleasant, round face full of warmth. "How do you fare, Miss Yevliesza?" he asked.

She led him to the sitting area. "Well enough, my lord. But missing home."

"You have grown to love Numinat. And the Mythos. That shows a good heart."

"Well, I love some parts of it," she said, downplaying the idea that she was one who had a good heart, or whatever quality the hero of the primordialists should have. "Did Father Ludving come with you?"

"He sent his good wishes. But unfortunately, he has been called away. These days he is a great solace to me." He paused and his face took on a serious aspect. "There is news of the war. Have you been informed?" When she shook her head, he said, "Today Volkish forces invaded Norslad."

Oh God, Norslad. Valenty was there. "I don't know what to say, my lord."

"In your position, you cannot say anything, I know." He

wiped his hands on his thighs, looking distressed. His heavy gold ring caught the light from the windows.

She could say that the man she loved was in Norslad and might be taken as a hostage, even if he claimed he had gone there to see his mother. Norslad was suffering, perhaps terribly. But for the moment her heart could only hold Valenty.

Tanfred went on. "I have failed to convince Prince Albrecht that there is a better way. So many young men will die, suffer wounds . . . to body and mind." He paused, looking around the room as though searching for words. "I am sorry to burden you with these problems. It is presumptuous of me."

"No, I don't mind. I wish I could help."

"It is a catastrophe," he murmured, staring at the floor. When he looked up, his face tightened. "There is something I have to say to you."

She nodded but wasn't sure that she wanted to hear what it was.

"Miss Yevliesza, I detected—through my affinity of the verdure—that you entered the crossings seven days ago. When you came into Volkia. So not only on the other occasions I told you about, but again the day we first met." He fixed her with clear, brown eyes, filled with what looked like regret.

Her breath went shallow. The day she arrived in Volkia under Anastyna's orders . . . So now Tanfred had another data point in his detections.

He went on. "I do not wish to contradict you. But surely this is confirmation of all that I have been saying."

"Duke Tanfred, I believe that you feel these things. But when you say that the timing is because of me . . . that's just a coincidence. It must be, because I'm not part of, I'm not the answer to, the legend."

She had nothing to do with the Mist Wall. But he *had* tied her to the crossings, again. There was a time when coincidence became proof. Or as good as, for those who had to judge and who wanted to believe things.

"Did you tell this to Prince Albrecht?"

"No, God help me. I told him of the other times—which he is not convinced relate exclusively to you—but then this timing confirmed things." He sighed. "Well. I did not tell him."

She remembered to breathe. "Why didn't you?"

A lock of hair had fallen down on his forehead, and Tanfred brushed it back as though settling his thoughts. "Because you must be the one to say who you are. Not by proofs, but by your own volition. So Father Ludving has counseled me, and so I believe."

"I think I've said who I am and who I'm not."

"Yes, you have. No one can force you."

She looked into her lap. Unfortunately, that wasn't true.

But Tanfred had withheld crucial information from his prince. Tanfred might misinterpret the meaning of the information, but it could establish—with something close to certainty—that she had a tie with the crossings. That day on her ride to the Mist Wall with Tanfred, he had listed the times he felt perturbations in the crossings. But he didn't mention that on the day she arrived at Wilhoff Manor, it had happened again. He wasn't quite the simple, guileless person she had thought. He didn't want to push her too hard. Nor did he want to tell Prince Albrecht.

What would Albrecht make of this if he knew? But so far Tanfred was keeping her secrets, though unwittingly. She was grateful, but also distressingly aware that he held incriminating information about her.

"I would like to tell you more about the legend," he said. "If you are not tired of hearing about it."

"I do not mind hearing more."

He paused, looking grateful for this concession. "The legend of the ninth power has long been a part of our culture. We Volkish have a powerful hope that our small kingdom could grow and enjoy a sublime destiny. That hope combines the lost power, the ninth power, with the great mystery of the Mythos, the Mist Wall. The ninth power has a pull on our imaginations, and over time the legend has become associated with prophecy. Prince Albrecht calls it a cult. But those who believe it are fervent. Not that it is worship, of course. But Father Ludving does not forbid me from . . . investigating, he would say."

"Do you have a feeling of community with others of your persuasion? Do you meet? Discuss?"

"Yes, often. Sometimes at my home. Or on the plateau where I took you to view the Mist Wall." A self-deprecating smile. "I do not have a family, you see. The followers of the legend are my family. And we have become more so since war broke out."

"If the power comes," Yevliesza said, "I think it will be a dangerous burden for any person to bear. I hope you won't suggest to Prince Albrecht that I might have knowledge of such things. He might see me as . . . useful. Though I definitely would not be."

He looked concerned for her. She needed to encourage that in any way she could.

⚜

THROUGHOUT THE DAY THE HALLS BELOW SURGED WITH ACTIVITY, communications arriving by messengers on horseback, aides handling details, and officers meeting with the commandant prince. Albrecht now had two wars to fight. This might account for his increasing aggression about how the crossings had been altered.

She had considered a number of ways to escape, but none of them seemed even remotely possible in this fortress. If she could send a message to Valenty, if he was home by now, he might alert

Anastyna to her situation. But communication between the realms was cumbersome and, between Volkia and Numinat, almost nonexistent. She needed a collaborator. Martel might help. He had given her forbidden access, but he was fearful just to leave a door open. Breta had reason to hate this place, but Yevliesza couldn't put her at further risk. And Tanfred—although he meant well, he might turn against her once he realized she wasn't the *one*. And by herself, even if she could get into the city, how likely was she to find anyone to assist her?

Late that evening, she excused Breta for the night. She was going to see Lothric. He might tell Albrecht she had come. Still, Martel had provided an opening, and she intended to grab it.

Carefully opening the apartment door, she scanned the hallway. It was empty, and she stepped out. The double doors, when she reached them, were unlocked.

In moments she had slipped through and down the hall into Lothric's suite. Moonlight splashed onto the sitting-room rug. She made her way to the side table and found a pitcher of water and glasses, where she'd found them before. Filling one, she went to the bedroom door, knocking softly. And then again.

A voice called out in Volkish.

Lothric lay propped up in bed, and he waved at her to enter.

She came to the bedside and offered the glass of water. He took a drink as she held it for him. "You invited me to come back. Do you remember?"

He nodded, but his gaze wandered the room.

"How are you, Master Lothric?"

"Dying," he whispered. "But they take good care of me. You are the new nurse?" His gaze flitted here and there, as though there were several people in the room, and she was only one of them.

"No, I'm just a visitor."

"Hermand," he said, nodding. "Hermand would come, but I

fear he is not well." His Numinasi was so heavily accented, she had to concentrate to understand him. He reached for her hand, in sudden agitation. "They are not using women, are they?"

"I . . . I don't know."

She let him grasp her hand. His skin was dry and cracked, his grip trembling.

"But if they have elements?" His gaze finally locked on hers, his face full of distress. "Do they?"

"I don't know, but you're right, women shouldn't be used." She paused. "But is it only elements? Elementalists that can be used?"

He released her hand. "Yes, yes, of course. Elementalists can drive the weather, why not a war wagon?" He frowned. "You do not have elements, I hope?"

"Nothing so grand."

"Albrecht would not allow it, would he? They need everyone they can get to drive the machines, but women, that is improper. To expose them to . . . war."

A chair was close at hand, and she sat in it to speak to him better. "The elementalists who power the machines. They only last so long? They get sick?"

"We give what we can, but then we go to Wilhoff. For . . . how do you say, getting better?"

"To recover."

"Yes, recover. Some do."

The hospital at Duke Tanfred's estate. Was that where elementalists were brought to convalesce?

Lothric pressed back into his pillows, whispering, "Then they go back to the field, poor souls." His voice had gone so soft, Yevliesza leaned closer to hear. "But I would give anything to be in the fight. For the glory of Volkia."

He looked over at the door,

Albrecht stood there. So far from the moon-lit window, he

was only a silhouette, but she knew it was he. Yevliesza got to her feet.

"My boy," Lothric whispered.

Albrecht came to the bedside. "Rest now, my friend. Is there anything you need?"

"No, no. Does the war flourish?"

"Yes, very much. We have taken Norslad."

"Norslad . . . I went there once . . ."

Albrecht smoothed his blankets. Then he took Yevliesza's arm in a strong grip and marched her out of the sickroom, closing the door behind him. He steered her through Lothric's apartment and into the deserted hall.

She yanked her arm back, trying to get out of his grip. "Let go!"

He turned on her and backed her so forcefully against the wall, that her head snapped against it. He pinned her in place with his arm against her throat and his knee against her thigh. "Let go?" he said under his breath. "When you are interrogating a Volkish officer? Is this the behavior of a guest in my house?" The lights in the hall were very dim, but she could still make out the fury on his face.

"You're hurting me."

"Am I." The pressure against her neck tightened and she struggled for breath. Then he stood back, pausing. "You have disappointed me, Yevliesza."

She took in a shuddering breath, rubbing her neck.

"How did you get to this room?"

Warily, she watched him for signs that he would attack her again. She managed to say, "I couldn't sleep. I walked down my prison hallway and saw that the door was barely latched."

He took a few steps away, then swung around to look at her. "Your *prison* hallway. So now you will tell your princip that you were in a prison?"

Her heart stuttered with hope. Was he going to let her go? "I misspoke. You rattled me."

A short laugh. "Indeed?" He held out his hand to her. "Come away from the wall, since it will not protect you."

She was to come to him? Like a dog. Like Evah.

"I am waiting," he said with elaborate patience.

Taking a few steps toward him, she put her hand out—hating herself for doing it but remembering his stranglehold on her. Gently he took it, shaking his head. "Yevliesza, Yevliesza. Now I am not sure I can let you go home. Since you have been spying. It was not in the terms of our agreement, after all."

"I wasn't spying."

"But of course you were. In any case, I would be more forgiving if you told me what I wish to know."

"What?" she lashed out. "*What* do you want to know!"

He responded calmly. "Who was with you on that night when the path to Alfan Sih sprang into being? Who created it? Tirhan? And because you had fallen in love with him, as we hear, you are protecting him. Or . . . was it you?"

When she didn't answer, he set his mouth firmly and dragged her back down the hall. At the double doors, he pulled her through, slamming the doors behind him. Still gripping her hand, he brought her to her apartment and pushed her inside.

He faced her. "I did not wish to lose my temper. I am sure you wish I had not."

"You've succeeded in frightening me, if that's what you intended."

"Do you know the punishment for spying? It is hanging."

"I found a sick man who wanted company. We didn't talk about anything important."

His silent gaze unnerved her. He took a slow breath. "Yevliesza. I would like us to come to an understanding. You have learned some things tonight that I wish you had not. Now it is time for a trade. I must learn something from *you*."

"But what if I know nothing!"

"Then find something else to give me."

She threw back, "That's crude, even for a Volkish soldier."

His mouth tightened. "You insult me, miss. I was speaking of intelligence you might be privy to. If you continue in this manner, you will be disciplined."

She threw back at him, "This *manner*? This *manner* of thinking that you'll lash out, take advantage of me, after you've choked me and dragged me down the hall? And now *I* am to be disciplined!"

He came at her, and she retreated, but he had hold of her upper arm and pulled her across the parlor to the seating area.

"Sit," he told her. She obeyed as he took a chair opposite her.

He seemed to be making an effort to control his anger, and she began to believe he was not going to hit her.

"In wartime, you have been caught spying. If you think I hurt you tonight, you have led a very sheltered life. And you fight back by suggesting I am not, the Volkish people are not, honorable."

It was time to rip away his absurd claim of honor. "Is rape common in your household, Prince Albrecht?"

His eyes narrowed. "What can you possibly mean?"

"Because my maid is being raped by Marshal Reinhart. I saw her rearranging her clothes one night when I found Reinhart here."

He cocked his head in surprise. "He was in your apartment?"

"I saw him coming out when I was walking in the hallway."

"Yevliesza. You should know that in the realms, a man does not force a woman, or may carry the effects to his detriment."

That was true. Sofiyana told her—years ago, it seemed—that

women had control over their bodies, so no man would dare assault her sexually.

"Maybe a maid can't say no to a marshal of the Volkish army. The proof is, she has rope burns on her wrists."

Silently, Albrecht stared over her head. She let him absorb this news, expecting him to dismiss it, or ask for proof. How strange that, despite how the evening had gone, he seemed to care what she thought of him and his officers.

"That ends now," he finally said. He stood, the fight seeming to have gone out of him. "It is not *common* in my household, Yevliesza." He glanced at her to see if she would argue.

She stood, also, feeling like a storm had passed, leaving her limp. "I'm ready to believe you, Prince Albrecht. But he might punish Breta for revealing this."

"The maid is now under my protection. I will make him understand this clearly."

"What if he tries to harm her anyway?"

"Then I will send Reinhart to the front, to Norslad."

"Good." After a pause she added, "Maybe you should send him anyway."

A smile tugged at Albrecht's mouth. "You would make a good Volkish woman, I think. A fierce one."

Then he bid her good night and was gone.

Chapter Twenty-Five

"**M**y lord is bleeding again," Pyvel told Urik when he came back to camp.

Hearing voices, Valenty opened his eyes. Urik was crouching beside him, wrapping a fresh length of bandage around his shoulder.

He remembered, then, the long retreat down the heavily forested hillside, the piercingly cold wind, the pains in his shoulder and thigh. Pyvel had struggled to free himself from them, until he finally realized he had been flailing against a Numinat lord and a *harjat*.

Eventually Pyvel had described how he had been captured, having followed Yevliesza out onto the plains. When he had caught up with Yevliesza's party, she ordered him home, and a guard was sent with him. That night, a Volkish agent killed Pyvel's guard. The man took Pyvel to the nearest boundary gate, making clear that if Pyvel raised the alarm at the garrison, the Volkish would kill Yevliesza in retaliation. But why Pyvel, Valenty wondered? Perhaps he was just an easy target. Anyone that Nashavety could use to torment Yevliesza would do.

Foremost in Valenty's mind, though, was the news that

Anastyna had ordered Yevliesza into Volkia. For what purpose, Pyvel could not say. But what purpose could there possibly be? Anger colored Valenty's thoughts as he considered how Anastyna had made sure he was gone before sending Yevliesza away.

In his kit, Urik replaced the roll of bandages they had taken from the packs of the soldiers who had followed them from Lassen. Eventually Valenty was dressed and wearing Urik's fur cape, but he was still trembling from the exposure.

Pyvel said, "My lord is—"

"Shaking?" Urik interrupted, raising an eyebrow.

"Sorry, sir."

"You have left your sentry post. Go back and listen, both for what you hear and what you do not hear."

"How can I hear what is not there, sir?"

"Notice what you are hearing. When you stop hearing it, come and tell me." Urik was not greatly concerned that anyone was following them. It was likely Nashavety could not keep her people compelled with her dark powers if they were at a distance.

Urik dragged back the cedar boughs that had been covering Valenty's legs. "The thigh wound is the worst," he said. "Can you walk today?"

"Not far, I think." His leg had been almost useless by the time they had made camp.

Clouds shrouded the sky, shedding a few glitters of snow that drifted through the evergreens. The massive rock walls of the canyon loomed above them, as though they had been sheared off with a knife.

"I have spoken more with the boy," Urik said. "He describes how the demon is ailing. She cannot eat solid food and barely stands on her own. She wears a glove on her maimed hand, but she cannot grasp anything."

"The hand may be rotting," Valenty said hopefully.

"My lord, she has somehow preserved her hand of power. For at least one of her two powers. Creature power."

Valenty knew he was right, but murmured, "I saw her sever the left-hand finger. In the Tower that day." The belief was that a remnant of the Deep could remain, but only a shadow of it. Clearly, that was wrong.

Urik went on. "The boy says that sometimes the hand moves almost on its own. In sudden jerks. We should have killed her."

"We tried."

"*You* tried," the *harjat* said, as though he would have finished the task.

Valenty had always known that Nashavety was a fierce adversary, one who dared much to have her way. But *this*. Urik had not named what she was involved in, but the knowledge hung heavy in the air: Forbidden arts. Unthinkable trespass.

Urik looked up suddenly, his body still, his senses alert. After a few moments, he returned his attention to Valenty. "And then there is the house. It has been roused to do her bidding."

Valenty clutched the cape more closely around his shoulders, unsure whether he was cold from without or from within. The diabolical house was *roused*, somehow. An impossible thing, but he had seen it in the labyrinth of its corridors. It had stalked them, or at least altered itself to entrap them.

"How? How could she do this when she is so weak she can barely stand?"

"I do not know." Urik shrugged. "We should have killed her," he said again.

In shame, Valenty considered the enormity of his decision to bring Pyvel home. He commanded the mission and had turned away from it. For Yevliesza's sake. For her love of Pyvel. Urik would not say so, but he did not have to.

Urik stood up, stretching. "Now the question is, what is the demon capable of? If she stays in the forest, she is just a canker at its heart. But if she leaves . . ."

At the sound of crashing in the underbrush, the *harjat* unslung the spear from his back. Pyvel rushed into camp. "I stopped hearing," he called out.

Urik said, "But now our intruder has heard you shout and knows we are prepared."

Valenty labored to his feet, drawing his knife.

In another moment, a gaunt-looking man in old clothes emerged from the trees to stand on the edge of the clearing. His shoulders and long beard were dusted with snow. He spread his hands to show he had no weapon.

"You are . . ." he began in a thick, almost incomprehensible, accent, "you are Numinasi?"

"If you are a friend," Urik said, glancing at Valenty to translate, "you will not mind if we search you." At the man's nod, he sent Pyvel to pat him down and look in the pack he carried.

"He has a dead squirrel," Pyvel reported.

"I share what I have," the man said.

"A squirrel to feed four?" Urik said as he helped Valenty back down to the ground.

"To feed five," the stranger said. "We save some for my wife."

Chapter Twenty-Six

During a restless night, Yevliesza kept revisiting how Albrecht stood in Lothric's doorway; how he heard them talk about elementalists. *Might* have heard. His grip on her throat; his threat to keep her there. She was a spy. There was a punishment for that. She was convinced now that Albrecht would force her to reveal her power of the crossings, and soon.

She might say that the new crossing was Lord Tirhan's doing, but that would be a miserable betrayal. If he was captured, the future king of Alfan Sih would be tortured to confess. And if *she* was tortured, how long could she last?

Despite Albrecht's power over her, she had a recourse: to cut off the little finger of her left hand. She had seen by Nashavety's example how it was done. One should test the cutting edge of the knife first, she remembered.

Finding a good knife was the first challenge. It would be best to have it hidden close by, for when she needed it. She wondered if Martel would give her one. He might also help her escape, but leaving a door open might be as far as he would go.

Her mind, her thoughts, ran cold and clear. Maybe she was faking being brave. But the pretense helped.

❦

TANFRED CAME TO HER IN THE LATE AFTERNOON. SHE WANTED TO think well of him. He had a hospital for wounded soldiers— mentally, spiritually wounded, the condition that Master Lothric had described. She was sure that the hospital assuaged the duke's conscience about Volkia's wars. But he took little action against the kingdom's war-like prince.

Soon they were sitting by the fire, having a pleasant conversation, but tiptoeing around the subject that was always on Tanfred's mind. It wasn't long before he broached it.

"Have you never had . . . intimations of a different calling? Has it always been the aligns that the Deep bestowed on you?" He made a contrite face. "Forgive me if I am being too personal. Thoughts run through my mind like a deer hounded through a forest. I cannot bring them to a halt. I am poor company, I fear."

"I know how that is," she confessed. "Having your thoughts run wild."

"Do you?" He shook his head. "My life is not my own since the war began."

"Your charitable work, though. The hospital at Wilhoff Manor."

"It is little enough." He snorted a laugh. "Perhaps I imagine a more heroic role. Announcing the *Eibelung*, even."

Yevliesza poured him a little more wine from a pitcher that Breta had brought. "My lord, isn't it possible that the legend expresses a desire more than a prediction?"

"If that is the case, Volkia will be lost. My country will fall into war after war." He stared bleakly at the fire.

In the ensuing silence, a new thought arose. Yevliesza imagined a turn in her path. One that opened a whole different view of the territory.

They sat in silence for a time, as she considered the prospect of telling Tanfred what her true left-hand power was. The revelation might bring him to her side, or it might seriously backfire. The truth about root power would be an attack on his spiritual beliefs, the prophecy he thought she fulfilled; that God especially cared about this one kingdom of the Mythos and had planned to send a person who could deliver Volkia in a time of darkness. She knew how much comfort Tanfred took from these convictions.

If he believed her claim that the ninth power was really about the crossings, then he might come to her aid. He might see that if Albrecht controlled her, the prince could subjugate the entire Mythos.

But as she watched Tanfred sitting there, her fears of his reaction began to build. He was a Volkish nobleman, and she didn't know him, not really.

There was another piece to the Tanfred puzzle. Was he aware of the mental damage to the elementalists from powering the war machines? Surely he must know, but if he didn't, it would be time to tell him.

"Your Grace," she said. "I would like to know more about your hospice at Wilhoff."

He looked up at her. "The sanatorium?"

"If that's what you call it, yes."

"It is a small thing I do for the soldiers."

"Not a small thing at all. They're suffering, and you're helping them." By his expression, he thought it little enough. "Duke Tanfred. I know that those men are emotionally wounded."

"Perhaps. Not all."

"I believe they all are."

He rose and went to the fireplace. There he picked up a poker and jabbed at the logs. Flaring, they sank into a pile. He watched them for a time and then turned to her. "It has escaped my mind until now, but Prince Albrecht asked me to tell you that any time you wish, you may take a walk outside."

"Did he?"

"Yes. He said it was in answer to your request."

"Where?"

He glanced at the ceiling. "On the roof." Tanfred put the poker back in its stand. "Perhaps you would like to take a stroll now?"

AT THE TOP OF A SET OF STAIRS, TANFRED PUSHED OPEN THE door. The winter air swept over them. Yevliesza grabbed a lungful, feeling like she hadn't truly breathed in days.

They were bundled against the cold, an alarming, iron-fisted cold. Her face instantly lost its heat. Putting on her fur gloves, she moved out onto the enormous flat roof of Rothsvund. Battlements perched on the edges like gaping teeth. A half-dozen soldiers, stood looking out, keeping watch.

Numerous chimney stacks released bluish-black smoke, but since the chimneys were tall, the smoke fell away on the wind. Yevliesza clutched her wool cape more closely as she and the duke began to walk the perimeter.

"I hope the soldiers do not make you nervous," Tanfred said.

"Not at all," she lied. Some carried spears, others swords, or wicked-looking curved knives. The gray-green Volkish army uniform peeked out from beneath black woolen coats. After an initial glance, they paid the two visitors no attention.

From this viewpoint, the city of Hapsigen revealed itself to be even larger than she had imagined. It might have been a fine view under different circumstances, but at that moment the city looked only bleak and confining.

"I brought you up here for a reason," Tanfred said. "There are things that have brought me a great deal of sorrow. So now I will tell them to you. Because you, of all people, should know the truth."

With her entire attention she waited to hear.

"You asked me about the sanatorium," Tanfred began. "You visited there and are correct to say that the patients were hurt, emotionally." They passed a sentry, and Tanfred fell silent until they had gone some distance beyond him.

"It is because of the machines. Those patients used their powers to propel the military devices, or use them, or wear them for advantage in battle. That is why Alfan Sih collapsed, why Norslad was helpless at Volkish advances."

He looked out at the city as though he saw such machine in the streets. "These contrivances drain the men who use them. Drain them of their birthright affinity to the land and their very souls. They walk hollow."

Walk hollow. It was a phrase Rusadka had used about Sofiyana, figuratively. But now it was real. Her heart leapt with excitement that Tanfred was confiding in her.

"In Numinat we heard rumors of such things."

"Volkia cannot keep them secret now. The military has a goodly number of machines, and they build more every day." Tanfred gestured to the city with its heavy drape of acrid smoke. "Our forges work night and day."

So the pollution wasn't just from fireplaces.

He went on, "Armored soldiers encased in iron, gunners using projectiles, infernal wagons. All directing their element power toward fueling the devices. There are very many of these contrivances." He fell silent as they passed another sentry.

Yevliesza imagined the diabolical machines lined up and ready for their occupants, in warehouses and fields, perhaps even in side corridors of the crossings. It was a forbidding image, like a glimpse of the rats that would bring the plague to Europe.

She asked, "But what about the consequences? Aren't the Deep powers of the Mythos disrupted by engines?"

"That is true, but it seems only if the engines are run by fuels. Fuels of the sort that can be transformed into mechanical potency. But the prince has found a way to harness our birthright powers— which means, in essence, our very spirits—and he has personally assured me that this manner of propelling the machines will not poison the realms. Not that this absolves us of the crime."

They stood next to a deserted section of the battlements. Close by, Yevliesza saw the dome of the Church of All Graces just visible through the smoke. The church stood in a city drenched in fear, yoked to the industries of weapon-making, but there were patches of hope. There was always hope, she reminded herself, as she struggled to shake the darkness of Tanfred's words.

The thought came: *I am one of those hopes.*

Tanfred turned to her. "We have been building these devices for many months. We are ready to take them to Nubiah, the Jade Pavilion. And Numinat."

Albrecht would not stop; he would grasp more and more. Because he could.

After a pause, Tanfred continued. "A sorceress advises Albrecht, I am ashamed to say. She has devised this demonic scheme. Before meeting her, Albrecht had begun to experiment with ordinary machines, burning various oils. But when the lady came amongst us, she devised a way to fuel machines by the Deep power of elements. I warned Albrecht about these things, but he has developed great admiration for the woman."

A terrible conjecture took hold of Yevliesza's thoughts. "Tanfred. Is this woman a Numinasi?"

"I am sorry to say so."

"Oh God," she moaned. "Is her name Nashavety?"

He nodded.

Yevliesza blurted out, "Is she *here?* Here at Rothsvund?" She looked around, expecting to see her on the roof.

"No. She is staying in a secure location in Breminger Forest. Do you know her?"

"Princip Anastyna banished her for diabolical use of powers and attempted murder. My murder."

Tanfred looked stricken. "God in heaven." He shook his head over and over.

"Does she know I'm here?" If she did . . . No, if she had known, Yevliesza would have been under torture by now.

"I do not know if she has been informed," Tanfred said with some anxiety, seeing how Yevliesza had reacted. "Does she wish you ill?"

"Yes," came her whispered answer.

They resumed their walk so that they would not draw attention to themselves by stopping. Tanfred said, "I deeply regret that I have never spoken out against Albrecht and his plans. I could have done so, privately, or publicly. Perhaps you would do well not to trust me."

"But I do trust you," Yevliesza whispered. "I do trust you."

They walked back to the roof door, Yevliesza's mind churning with all that she had heard. Twilight was falling and the lights from the windows and factories of Hapsigen flickered like embers from a shattered sun.

"I am imperfect, too," Yevliesza murmured. "So that makes two of us."

A smile softened Tanfred's serious face. "I like the expression, 'That makes two of us.'"

"Well, don't admire me too much." Because she was terrified. Nashavety was back. Albrecht was tied to her. Her world had just turned inside out. *Valenty*, she called silently. *Rusadka. What shall I do?*

But she was the only one who could decide. The only who

could fight back. Hadn't she learned in the great Tower of Osta Kiya that she was the only one who could save herself?

They walked in silence—Yevliesza, trying to grasp what she had learned; and Tanfred, absorbed by the enormity of the secrets he had disclosed.

The sun was setting behind the great city as they left the roof. The two of them stood on the landing at the top of the stairway, thankfully out of sight of the soldiers whose presence keenly reminded Yevliesza of the odds against her.

"Who is the enemy that the sentries watch for?" she asked.

"The people of Hapsigen," he bitterly said. "The people who have lost their sons and brothers and husbands to the wars or seen them come back hollow."

She descended the stairs with Tanfred, thinking of the Volkish people and their great losses. And all the mistakes she had made, her failure to act, her naive attempt to fend off Albrecht's interrogations. Her trust that Nashavety was disempowered.

She stopped on the stairway. "Tanfred. There is more."

He would help her. If anyone could, it was this Christian duke. So she would remove her disguise. She would tell him.

Instead of the fear of her secret becoming known, she felt the urge to blurt it all out in a stream of words and have it over with. And then she would beg Tanfred for his help. But that wasn't the way to do it. She wouldn't come to him like a weakling, apologizing for not being the promised one and desperate to escape.

"Tanfred," she said again, this time whispering. "Come to me tonight. Like a lover."

He looked offended. "Miss . . ."

"We'll pretend. I have something to tell you, but not around soldiers and not in the open air. Come to me tonight, very late." She took his hand. "You aren't the only one with things to confess."

⟨⟩

Breta helped her into her nightgown and robe. But there would be no sleep tonight. She asked Breta if Reinhart was leaving her alone. *Yes, so far.* Breta left, leaving Yevliesza with her thoughts. The reply of what she learned on the roof: the stockpiles of mechanical weapons, Albrecht's ultimate ambitions, the perversion of natural powers, the servitude of elementalists, Tanfred's shame in not opposing Albrecht. And Nashavety. Nashavety, arisen again, more powerful than before. And the knowledge that if the woman didn't know Yevliesza was in Albrecht's possession, it couldn't be long before she did.

Breta had been gone for hours when a soft knock came to Yevliesza's apartment door. She let Tanfred in, closing the door behind him and locking it. She led him into the bedroom.

"Take off your jacket, if you would." If they were found together, it would help if they weren't fully dressed.

Tanfred uncomfortably complied, looking around for place to put his jacket. She took it from him and threw it on the bed. "Tanfred. May I call you that?" He nodded. "Tanfred, we are lovers. If anyone sees you leave, please protect my honor and confess only to Albrecht. OK?"

He frowned.

"Do you understand?"

He did. Then they had to decide where to sit. There were two chairs and the bed. She chose the bed, and soon they were propped up with pillows, and she was trying to find a way into her subject.

Turning to him, she whispered, "You hold my life in your hands."

She put a hand to his lips so he wouldn't swear to protect her. He should know the truth before he swore anything.

"Tanfred," she firmly said, "I am a weapon. What you felt in the crossings was me. But not because of the Mist Wall. I have no affinity for the wall, and I'm sorry that I'm not that person. The truth is that I am a weapon."

"Miss . . ."

"Call me Yevliesza. Please."

"Then, Yevliesza, please tell me how you can possibly be a weapon."

"I will. But first, you have to know this: If Albrecht forces me to serve him, I will maim my left hand rather than do it."

He reacted with dismay.

"I will. I have to. Because I won't give him easy access to the kingdoms of the Mythos."

Tanfred was watching her with stunned attention.

"Because I could give him that. You discerned me in the crossings, through verdure power. Because the crossings are related to roots."

"As I have said . . ."

"No, not as you've said," she responded, realizing that she was really going to do this. She had already begun and the further into it she got, the more it felt like the right thing. Like a burden cast off. Like freedom.

She began to untie the front of her robe. Tanfred was as quiet as a bird in the shadow of an owl.

Pulling her robe into a pile next to her, she turned her back to him and shrugged her nightgown down to her waist.

PART III
TO CROSS A PRINCE

Chapter Twenty-Seven

Dreiza hurried through the domicile halls in the middle of the night, clutching her heavy woolen shawl around her. Yarna, on night duty, had come to her room to awaken her, saying that the High Mother bid her to come quickly.

"What is happening?" Dreiza asked.

"I know not, except you are to make haste. The Devi Ilsat is in Videkya's cell."

Yarna left her then, and Dreiza made her way past other *satvar* rooms and down white-washed corridors, all silent and empty. Without taking time to dress, she had only her nightdress and shawl against the cold, and nothing on her feet. The icy stone floor was already sucking the heat from her legs.

Videkya might have died, or would pass during the night, and perhaps the entire *satvary* was to pay respects, given her position as a member of the *satvadeya*. Reaching the east staircase, she headed down the stairs to Videkya's cell, perplexed to find no one else stirring, much less gathering outside the room.

When she tapped at the door, she was met by the High Mother, who gestured her to enter. Videkya lay peacefully in her bed, but whether she yet lived, Dreiza did not know. To her surprise, along one wall sat the four other *satvadeya* in their pale tunics and trousers. Dreiza was still in her nightdress.

Several of the women smiled at her, small comfort for her embarrassment at arriving so disheveled. She clutched her shawl around her shoulders, her feet burning with the cold.

"My daughter," the Devi Ilsat said, "we are saying goodbye to our beloved Videkya." She brought Dreiza to the bed where Videkya lay, her eyes closed and her breathing labored, her face peaceful, as though her emotions were the first to leave and next would come her breath.

"We do not sorrow for her," the High Mother went on, "for she joins our ancestors in the realm of peace." The group was silent but relaxed, seeming to take more interest in Dreiza than their dying sister. Lusanya, a full-figured, almost round *satvar*, nodded at the High Mother's words. The hushed, peaceful scene seemed a little too contented. Dreiza hoped that when she died, people would be a little more upset.

"I suggest we give our sister some time alone with Videkya," Arlaty gently said, her dark skin saving her from the washed-out impression the others made in the oaten-colored tunics and pants and with faces wan with age. Arlaty's suggestion was odd, since Dreiza had only known Videkya for two months and could not be considered especially close to her.

"Of course," the Devi Ilsat murmured. She gestured for the sisters to rise and, when she opened the cell door, she insisted that they proceed her. Staying behind, she closed the door after them.

Videkya stirred, a low, musical note riding on her exhalation.

"You may take her hand," the High Mother told Dreiza.

She folded her hand around Videkya's. It was surprisingly warm, and a gentle squeeze showed that the *satvar* was at least partly conscious. Her gray hair had been combed across the pillow with great care, making a lavish frame for her face which, in the flickering light from the candle at the side table, suggested how lovely she had been in her youth.

"My daughter," the Devi Ilsat said, "Videkya has chosen you."

"Chosen?"

"Take the chair beside her, Dreiza."

She obeyed, startled by the High Mother having used her name.

The High Mother took a seat beside her. "The close advisors to a Devi Ilsat have, by our tradition, always been five in number. So when a *satvadeya* leaves the land of the living, it is our way that, if it is possible, she choose her successor. Videkya has chosen you."

A barely perceptible tightening of Videkya's hand around Dreiza's seemed to confirm that this was so, but her mind was swirling like a leaf in the wind.

"Why?" Dreiza managed to say.

"Well. I did ask her."

The frank comment took Dreiza aback just when she had begun to realize that she should feel happy about her promotion.

The Devi Ilsat went on. "She said that she thought you would be good at it."

"Ah." Of course competency would be the first requirement. Dreiza felt she had to say something, preferably something of wise import, but nothing was forthcoming. "I did not think she even noticed me."

"She sees a good heart in you. Better than most."

"I thought my good heart was getting me in trouble. Trying to repair things. Things that might not need repair."

"Nevertheless."

She did not want to seem ungrateful, but she did have questions, and now was the time for them. "I am too new to the *satvary*. People will not accept it. There are others more worthy."

"Nevertheless."

Dreiza removed her hand from Videkya's, knowing that she was not going to refuse this honor. "Does this mean that I will join the *satvadeya*?"

"Yes, dear one. It does."

"But I have a choice?"

The old *satvar* smiled pleasantly. "Not really."

It was settled then. The thought came that now she would know what the *satvadeya* were doing out after dark that time, slinking around the corner of the compound. She had seen many interesting things out the gallery windows while tending the *traveka* vine.

The two women sat at the bedside in silence for a long time. Dreiza's thoughts gradually quieted. "I fear," she murmured low, "that I will always be a thorn in your foot, High Mother."

"Yes. But a beloved thorn."

Through the window Dreiza saw the stars beginning to fade. The new day would find her life greatly changed. She had come to Zolvina for peace, not just the serenity of the domicile, but peace in her heart where most of the turmoil lived. She wondered if *satvadeya* duties and concerns would intrude on her small progress. As the stars left the sky, she spoke of this to the Devi Ilsat.

"My daughter," she replied, "a contented heart takes a strong muscle. You must challenge your spirit in service, even in difficulty." She chuckled. "And we have plenty of *that*."

Chapter Twenty-Eight

From the roof of the palace a feral dawn stained the sky, turning its yellow-orange haze a gloaming red. On the palace roof, Yevliesza and Tanfred walked the perimeter, their boots crunching through the crust of snow, the cold glazing Yevliesza's face into a freezing mask.

Tanfred had come for her early, eager to speak with her again. The disclosure of the markings on her back had at first disturbed him. She had watched him struggle to adapt to what it meant—for Volkia and for his primordialist beliefs. But in the end, he had promised to help her, despite his preconceptions about the ninth power.

As they came to the far side of the roof, they looked down on the Danstree, glinting in the cold dawn light.

"Tanfred," she began. "I know that what I revealed last night was hard to hear. I regret that." He had put all his hopes in the Mist Wall. He and the primordialists had clung to that solution to the war. But it could never have deterred Albrecht. The prince might claim Volkia needed resources and room to expand, but even for the Third Reich, that excuse had been a convenient fiction. The occupation of much of Europe had been about power and dominance. Tanfred's idea of the Mist Wall creating more territory was an idealistic solution to the wrong problem. Still, she had taken that prospect from him.

"I'm sorry that it's going to be harder than that."

He looked out over the city. "I still believe that you were sent to us. And if not, I still believe in you, Yevliesza. What you are capable of."

She wished she had that belief in herself. It was very difficult to understand why she had won the ninth power in the lottery of powers. Much less what she should do with it.

As they continued their circuit of the roof, they passed a sentry and Yevliesza commented on the dome of the church, and how impressive it was in the dawn. Once out of earshot, Tanfred said, "Our first need is to take you from danger. And I have an idea how to do it."

Her heart stuttered in her chest. He was talking about escape.

He went on. "I did not sleep after I left you last night. I was planning how to get you to the crossings."

To the crossings. To go home to Numinat and at last, to Valenty. Her heart lifted. Even if it was just a small chance, it was, at last, a *chance*.

But he would be exposing himself to terrible danger. "They would kill you, you know."

"They might. But I will leave with you, and we will be gone before they even notice."

"It will look like you've betrayed Volkia," she said.

"I know. But I am doing this *for* Volkia. As a patriot."

Despite the charged topic, they walked calmly, with him occasionally pretending to point out a sight in the city.

They watched as a dactyl came into view in the distance, its great wings barely moving as it headed toward them, riding the wind. Yevliesza could just make out the crest on its head and the rider on its back. As the creature loomed closer, for a moment its wings eclipsed the dome of the Church of All Graces. It lifted its wings high over its back to angle down onto the frontage lawn, out of sight from their viewpoint on the far side of the roof.

The spectacular arrival of the great beast wiped other thoughts temporarily out of Yevliesza's mind. She was started when Tanfred said, "Do you have to be in the crossings to affect them?"

"To affect the crossings? I . . . I think so. But I don't know."

His voice went so low she could hardly hear him. "Have you thought of how you could isolate Volkia? By shutting down the access paths?"

"I'm not completely sure that I could do that. I've thought about what root power might be capable of and how I'm the last person in the realms who should be wielding it. I'm not even *from* here. And what if the paths couldn't be opened again? How long would it be before all the crossing branches were closed, out of fear and suspicion? And the Mythos isn't . . ." She struggled to remember what Grigeni and Valenty had told her about the fragility of the realms. "It isn't resilient, like the Firstland. It could so easily be ruined. So if you want me to do something heroic—"

He interrupted. "I am not suggesting that you do it. I am looking at all the options for escape. Well, and perhaps a way to cripple Albrecht's ambitions. But you may be right, we cannot risk too much damage to the crossings. And it would leave thousands of Volkish soldiers in Alfan Sih and Norslad. With their war machines."

He was beginning to see the dilemmas that she faced. "I have no idea what I should do, only what I *won't* do. And I think absolutely no one will be happy with me when they know that."

"I am happy with you," he gently said. "But meanwhile, our task is to free you from this place."

"We can't just get in your carriage and pretend to be going to church or on a sight-seeing tour."

"No, but I think an emergency leave-taking would work. I will find a reason why I suddenly must leave, late at night. I will get an army uniform for you, one that I am afraid I will have to steal, and we will leave in my carriage." Tanfred's whole aspect had changed. No longer the careful, soft-spoken duke, whose greatest challenge had been to shape his garden. Now he was defying Volkia.

"We will have to adapt the uniform. Can you think of a reason to get needle and thread? I hope you know how to sew because I do not."

"I know a little." She had done simple mending. But somehow she would manage it. "When?"

"As fast as we can."

"And getting through the boundary gate?"

A lopsided smile. "People do not tend to question a duke."

She thought of the deference even Prince Albrecht gave Tanfred, and she started to believe that all this was possible. "But what shall we do about Breta? My maid," she reminded him. "They might think she helped us. Especially since I spoke out for her when I discovered Marshal Reinhart was abusing her."

He hadn't heard of that, and he shook his head. "Detestable."

"Come to my apartment tonight," she told Tanfred. "We need to think things through."

"We could tie her up and gag her," Tanfred said. "To make it look like we overpowered her."

"I think they'd see through that." Another idea arose. "Maybe she'd come with us."

"No," Tanfred said. "If it were possible to get a woman into the carriage at night, it would be you."

Breta was a serious problem. But she and Tanfred agreed to work things out that night. They were fellow spies now. Co-conspirators, partners in crime, even friends to the death if it came to that. She was no longer completely alone, and she savored the thought.

"Do you think Father Ludving would approve of what you're doing?" she asked.

"He would *urge* me to do it. I am sure of it."

Well, then, Yevliesza thought. *With God's blessing.* Now all she needed was a needle and thread.

Chapter Twenty-Nine

D ark, roiling clouds brought darkness early, as Tirhan watched a storm advance over the land. At the cave's entrance, he caught a sharp smell of lightning as brief flares lit up the black mass of clouds spreading toward the cave. Thunder trembled in the distance.

Kierach stood at his side. "It has only been five days. She will come."

Tirhan nodded. Morwen was the only one who had not returned from the mission to the local clans. "I should have sent them in teams."

"No, it was best to go singly. A man alone is harder to track."

A jagged slash of lightning plunged down from the storm clouds, revealing a forest shocked by light. A bellow from the sky.

"My lord," Kierach said, "the men have been too long idle. If she does not come by tomorrow, she can find us later."

Tirhan turned to him in exasperation. "Find us where, Kierach? Where shall we strike that makes a difference?" They could not target the place where his mother and sisters languished, not without the weapon they most needed.

"We harry them on their marches," Kierach said. "They take the main roads for the sake of their propelled wagons. We strike and fade into the woods where they cannot follow. It has served us well."

Tirhan did not answer. He had said before that they were not ready for decisive action. It was winter. They would bide their time. He watched the storm advance, plunging the forest into an early night. Fat drops struck the ledge in front of him, raising the smell of wet dust.

One of the recruiters had brought back a man with a strong hand for creatures, but still, he was only one. The enclaves might hold men eager to fight, but not without the clan at their side. Perhaps Morwen had been right, that if they were going to come, they would have done so by now. Yet his guide from the other-world, the spirit who sometimes appeared as an old man and sometimes as a warrior in his prime, would not have urged him to an impossible goal. So he believed, perhaps because the spirit had said his mother had called upon him.

Into these thoughts, his second-in-command intruded. "Are you determined to reject Anwelyth of Clan Rhydwyn, my lord?"

Tirhan knew Kierach's mind on this. Anwelyth was an old promise of the old king. But he would not be bound by his father's will. Morwen was the daughter of a minor clan, but in her bones she held all the fierceness and wisdom of Alfan women across the realm. She risked pain and even death for Alfan Sih. Who better to rule by his side? But he wondered if, as the spirit messenger had said, his impatience would bring harm to those around him. Kierach seemed to be suggesting that his favoring Morwen was yet another example of that rashness.

Kierach murmured, "It was your father's deepest wish. A strong alliance between the Silverwood Throne and Clan Rhydwyn."

No. He would not have the man carp. "Enough, Kierach. You

must decide whether you are my man or my father's. I would not compel your loyalty. But decide."

Kierach drew himself up, offended. "I can only be your advisor if I may speak freely."

"You may speak, but then I will also say my mind. You do not approve of Morwen; you have said as much, but that is not your place and so let us have an end to it. We are not at court, nor do we even have a crowned king. Let us keep our minds on a victory at Glenir."

"If we *can* strike at Glenir."

The man would not relent.

The forest went blue-white with a stupendous shear of lightning illuminating the valley and sending a roar to rattle the stones around them.

By its light, a lookout had seen something and called out, "Men approaching!"

Tirhan had seen them as well, a line of people threading through the trees.

"How many?" Kierach shouted.

"I cannot see," came the answer. "A handful in the forefront."

Behind Tirhan the men came to their feet, strapping on swords.

Then, a distant cawing sound, a signal from lookouts further down the hillside that the people were known.

The rain came. Torrents struck the ledge in front of the cave like fists, and a deluge cut off the outside view.

Tirhan and his men waited, now more curious than worried. At last a figure appeared in front of the cave opening, cloaked and drenched. Ducking inside, the visitor flung off the hood of the cape. Morwen.

"My lord," she said, seeing Tirhan at once. She shook the rain from her hair.

"Morwen," he said, keeping the relief from his voice. "You had no luck of the weather."

"No. We walked by moonlight, but when the clouds came, we made our way by the aligns."

"Of aligners, we have a surfeit," Kierach said.

Morwen heard him. "Well, but I have brought you seven elders."

Her companions were filing into the cave, shaking water from their winter cloaks and white hair.

"Old men and women?" Kierach murmured to Tirhan.

"They look robust, Kierach. And have managed what likely was a hard journey without collapsing at the end."

After Morwen introduced the newcomers, Tirhan stepped forward. "I am Prince Tirhan," he told them. "Be welcome here." They bowed to him, and he signaled to some of the men to bring warm drinks for the visitors.

"Was it a difficult journey?" he asked the group.

One of the elders spoke up. Lodwyn, a man of girth with craggy features. "Two days ago, lord prince, we set out from Talfyn Sid, the Temple of the Sacred Spring."

As Tirhan had guessed by now, Morwen had been to a renunciate sanctuary.

"And the Shrine at Belfour, three days hence," added a woman with her white hair cut short. All of the elders wore close-clipped hair, strange to see, but practical for their simple lives.

Morwen looked at her companions, who now were receiving dry blankets to wrap in. "And each of them, my lord, has a noble portion of creature power. And one of them, of aligns as well."

Tirhan looked at the seven of them in wonder and relief. With his one other recruit, they had eight. Two for each of the wolves at Glenir. He looked at Morwen, thinking how brilliant she had been to go to the one place not under the sway of a clan lord.

Lodwyn spoke up again. "We are more used to plying our

powers to care for goats, lord prince." He wiped the rain from his face with enormous hands and broke into a smile. "But we are not afraid of wolves—of any kind."

He frowned heavily and in a bass voice that carried through the cave, said, "It should not stand, that men have ensorcelled wraith wolves. They are sacred creatures who tread in both worlds."

֍

LATE INTO THE NIGHT TIRHAN SAT WITH LODWYN AROUND THE dying embers of the firepit. Morwen had long been asleep, and the men relinquished the circle around the fire for their prince.

Lodwyn prodded the remains of a log with a stick, answering a question Tirhan had asked. "We have had no word out of Volkia, my lord, but sometimes we are the last to have news."

It preyed on Tirhan that Yevliesza was in Volkish hands, as the spirit had told him. How her capture had happened, he did not know, but Yevliesza would never submit to them. He feared that if they could not take advantage of her skill, they would kill her. If they knew what her second power was.

"Do your foreknowers see an outcome, grandfather?" he asked, using a term of honor for the renunciate. Foreknowing might be unreliable, but the quiet of the cave and the growing dark set free his hidden thoughts.

"Foreknowing is a close thing. What may happen to our sheep grazing in the valley, whether a stranger will visit, or the storm come . . ."

Tirhan pressed on. "Nor any presentment, however small, of what may happen to the realms?" Surely the fate of their very existence might send a tendril of knowledge to those with the gift.

"Who knows but that there may be a select person who will be vouchsafed an arresting power, a power of foreknowing beyond the normal?" Lodwyn shook his head. "But not in our sanctuary, nor even in all of Alfan Sih that I have heard of. You have reason to think the Volkish will take other kingdoms, my lord?"

"I know not. But why should they stop? What have they gained in Alfan Sih that would not be thrice or five times enhanced by taking all? If they spread their diabolic machines, when might they surpass what the Mythos can bear?"

The elder held the stick across his knees, letting the embers sleep. "You have a personal reason entwined with all this, my prince?"

The word came to Tirhan in the next instant. Regret. His rash action in coming home—the *way* he came home—had exposed Yevliesza, left her open to danger, to the peril of them all and also to her person. His actions had benefited Alfan Sih. But at a price he should not have so carelessly risked.

"I have not always acted wisely, grandfather. It weighs on me."

"Then you are a better man than most."

Tirhan considered this but pressed on. "If a spirit brings a message to a man, does it mean he has strayed from a good path?"

"I would think perhaps the opposite, my prince."

"But do the spirits deign to speak to the living, grandfather? And should we listen?"

"It is a long journey from the otherworld." Lodwyn cocked a smile at Tirhan. "Perhaps they speak to kings."

Or queens, Tirhan thought, thinking of Queen Gwenid.

"But not to those in the temples?"

"Visions are for those who receive them. To tell others . . ." He shook his head. "It is like describing a song in the wind. But should you listen?" He paused, his already lined face wrinkling harder. "If a spirit found me, I would listen."

"Do you think I can I find peace with the things I have done?" Tirhan asked.

"Perhaps not, lord prince. Peace is hard work, and you have a kingdom to rule and your people to care for. Therefore, learn and grow and meet the future with what wisdom may come."

Tirhan smiled at this simple—and demanding—homily. "And you and the other elders will work hard at peace?"

Lodwyn stood, leaving the stick for the next man. "I have a hundred and four years, my lord. But I am making a little progress." He bowed to Tirhan and went to find his blankets.

Chapter Thirty

Valenty sat up against the cave wall, trying to clear his sluggish mind. He had slept for a day and a half, and now, as he looked though the curtain of snow that obscured the cave opening, it looked to be midday.

Leah—he thought that was her name—brought him a cup of something hot, smiling at him. She was a small woman, with arms as thin as poles, and when she smiled it was almost too broad for her narrow face.

"Thank you," he said as he cradled the warm cup.

She responded with a short acknowledgment, something in a foreign language he did not recognize. Then, in Volkish she asked, "Are you hungry?"

"Yes. If there is enough." He had seen three children playing. Now their raucous voices echoed from deeper in the cave.

"We can always feed one more," she said.

He, Urik, and Pyvel had been led there by the woodsman, Sam, a journey that Valenty remembered as a prolonged labor of climbing over rock slopes and forging icy streams. He had been at the end of his strength when they arrived at a rock wall that Sam declared was his home. Valenty hardly recalled being coaxed up a ladder and finding a nest of blankets in a cave where he collapsed.

He sipped the hot broth as Leah bustled about the cave. With his thoughts clearing, he wondered at the sense of menace that he had awakened with. An ugly thing that he did not want to remember. It came to him, then, what Pyvel had told him.

Yevliesza was in Volkia. Incredibly, Anastyna had sent her, and she had done so after he had already left the castle. Why had she done this? He could not put forward even one hypothesis. Pyvel did not know what her destination in Volkia was, much less her purpose in going. All these days on his mission he had thought Yevliesza was safe in Osta Kiya and now . . . now he was sick with worry. He wanted to go after her, bring her back, no matter what Anastyna's purpose was.

He was helpless to protect her, crippled as he was and ignorant of her location. His inability to help her was hard to bear. *Yevliesza, where are you?*

Pyvel appeared at the cave opening and, seeing Valenty had awakened, hurried to his side, eager to know how he felt. Better, Valenty told him. Physically, better.

"Where is Urik?" Valenty asked.

"He and some of the men have been out hunting since dawn."

"What men?"

"James and Aaron and . . . others. The families that hide here. I have been exploring. There are caves all over."

Leah returned, bringing fresh strips of cloth, and began to change his dressings, nodding in approval at the state of his thigh and shoulder wounds.

"How many are here?" Valenty asked.

"Sixty-one. Sixty-two in a few days when Charlotte has her baby." She looked around at the cave. "We are blessed to have this. And you are welcome to stay as long as you like."

"My thanks. You are very generous."

She shrugged. "We have all we need. Shelter, good hunting, a stream nearby. Even our own rabbi. We will survive."

Ah, so these were Jewish families. There were few of that tradition in Osta Kiya, but many more in the polities. It was strange that they were hiding in these caves, in winter.

"Is the rabbi your leader?"

Leah nodded. "A wise counselor. Since we have him all to ourselves, maybe we will not ever want to leave!"

As she turned to go, he asked, "Can I speak with him?"

"The rabbi? Not right now. He is out hunting. But later."

Pyvel helped him to stand, and they haltingly made their way to the cave opening, little more than a long crack in the stony hillside. The snowfall had abated, leaving the sun to take over the valley. Once outside, a slight incline led down to a shelf of rock where they could stand behind a jutting rock that shielded them from view. On the towering rock wall of the canyon, he saw several cave openings at different levels. Some were connected by cunningly disguised rope ladders embellished with branches.

Valenty walked to the edge of the jutting rock and crouched down to spy out the valley where it carved through the mountain terrain. Down-valley was the direction of the Rorrs boundary gate. The dense forest looked impenetrable. Like his future with Yevliesza. He could only hope and trust that she was safely back in Numinat. But that, he knew, was far from sure.

It was dusk when the hunters returned. Valenty had been dozing but awakened to the chatter of people greeting the men. Urik had come in with them and turned his sack over to waiting hands, and soon cook fires were kindled and pots brought forth.

Urik crouched beside him. "All well?"

"Much better. We have found a refuge."

"Yes. But we should leave tomorrow."

He seemed unusually serious. "Urik?"

"People here have had word: Numinat has declared war on Volkia."

Valenty was stunned. He was glad of it, but perplexed. "Has something happened to force Anastyna's decision?"

Urik shrugged. "Three days ago Volkia invaded Norslad. No kingdom is safe from them."

Anastyna now realized that Volkia had to be stopped. At last. But now he and his companions might encounter more serious scrutiny at the boundary gate. He thought he was fit enough to travel. A healer among the refugees had helped his hip wound to knit faster and the pain in his shoulder was greatly lessened.

"Before we leave," Valenty said, "I have to speak to the rabbi."

Urik narrowed his eyes. "To ask him about the demon."

Yes. The woman who could enliven a house of stone and timber, and cause it to hunt them.

❧

THE OLD MAN HAD BEEN BROUGHT HIS DINNER FIRST, AND HE insisted on sharing it with Valenty. Rabbi Neva was solidly built, looking more like a warrior than a scholar or teacher. Above his beard of gray and black, deep lines crisscrossed his face, but his eyes were lively.

As they ate, Valenty heard the story of how sixty-one people had come to live in the caves. How, in the larger cities, the Volkish had forced people into back-breaking labor in the forges creating metal wagons and weapons. How they kept the children of workers to make sure that no one shirked the labor or tried to escape. Many workers died from inhaling the smoke or from accidents at the forges.

"The skies of Hapsigen and Fornich are orange with the breath of the factories," the rabbi said. "Like the fires of hell. They save that work for people who have the blood they fear. The wrong blood. So we left before they could take our children and came to this place where we heard there was safety." He shook his head. "Now soldiers patrol the gates at Hapsigen. No one can leave. Leah and Sam were among the last to come. They were smuggled out in a garbage wagon. But then on foot it took them many days and, by the time they found us, the children were sick. They could have gone no farther."

Valenty remembered what Yevliesza had said about the myth she called *Nazi*. A mundat belief in pure blood, people more pure than others, and how the belief was used to justify appalling violence and murder. Yevliesza feared that Volkia had arisen from that creed and, when stories trickled out of atrocities and infernal machines in Alfan Sih, he had begun to think she was right.

The rabbi wiped his hands on a cloth, his face serious but not troubled. "We do not ask what you are running from. Everyone has a story, and the less we know the less we can reveal if we are discovered."

They sat in silence for a while. As young children played a game with twigs and rocks in one corner of the cave, Rabbi Neva watched peacefully, allowing Valenty time to get to his subject.

"Do you believe there are demons, Rabbi?"

The old man raised an eyebrow. "Demons? Yes." His eyes held Valenty's with a new intensity. "But they are human."

"Not arisen from the eight hells, then."

"When I mentioned hell earlier, I meant hell in the here and now." He raised an eyebrow. "Who do you call a demon?"

"A woman. She has committed terrible crimes and was condemned to death, but the sentence was withdrawn on condition that she not use her powers for evil."

"I think you have seen terrible crimes in your thirty-some years."

"I have, Rabbi. But never like this. This woman holds dozens of people captive in her stronghold. She bends them to her will with creature power. Power she should not have because she forfeited the small finger of her left hand."

Rabbi Neva narrowed his eyes but remained silent.

"Her stronghold is an evil house. A house that can change its shape to catch anyone who enters without her knowledge. A house that can listen for one's thoughts and lure one to . . ."

"To?" the rabbi prodded.

"We did not stay long enough to find out. The boy Pyvel was one of her captives, but we brought him out."

"Perhaps *demon* is a good word for her," the old rabbi said.

Yevliesza had said there was no such thing as a demon, but now Valenty knew it depended on what kind of demon you meant.

"Is there something you wish from me?"

"Yes, Rabbi, if you know which power she is using or perverting. She has elements and creatures, and neither has ever given a rock breath or made a house a raging beast."

"She is your enemy," the rabbi guessed. "And you need to know the nature of her power."

Valenty looked into the old man's face and was not entirely sure he wanted to hear the answer, if there even *was* an answer. But he thought a man who had spent a lifetime learning about what was good and bad for the spirit would know a great deal about the bad.

"Do you know what power she uses?"

The rabbi took his time before answering. "I believe that she is draining the powers of her prisoners. Feeding on them. And combining them."

"Feeding on them . . ." Valenty whispered.

"That is how she gives this stronghold, this house, a diabolical life."

"Can it even be done? Something so terrible?"

"I have seen worse, my son," the old man said. "But send Pyvel to me before you leave in the morning. If you would like me to give him my blessing?"

"Does he need such . . . such strong healing?" Valenty had thought Pyvel fully recovered.

"This demon took something from him," Rabbi Neva said. "And now he needs to grow it back."

Chapter Thirty-One

When Tanfred arrived that night, Yevliesza met him in her nightgown and robe. She managed to coax him to sit next to her on the bed, propped up with pillows. It would have to do, though she didn't know how Albrecht would react if he found them. She could picture him laughing or flying into a rage, but it didn't matter as long as he saw they were in bed together.

"I think I can steal a uniform," Tanfred said, adjusting his pillow. "They have plenty of those. But boots and a cape might be harder." He would at least bring the uniform so she could start altering it. She had already asked Breta for needles and thread.

In the hours since they had hatched their escape plan on the roof, Yevliesza was discovering the complexity of breaking out of a military headquarters in a paranoid realm. They compiled a list of concerns, and she and Tanfred took them one by one.

"We should drug Breta," Yevliesza decided. "If they find her insensible, it will be harder to think she was involved. Can you get a sleeping potion?"

Tanfred looked doubtful. "I have no knowledge of such things."

"They must have something in Hapsigen like a drug store, or whatever you call them here."

"I could visit an apothecary," Tanfred said. "Although a visit by a nobleman might draw attention. A servant should do it."

"Wear something plain? Don't shave that day?"

He frowned. He might whisk a prisoner out of Rothsvund by stealth, but not shaving . . .

"Very well," he said uncertainly. "I will do my best. And while I am out, I might also buy a pair of lady's boots."

He was nervous about the potion. It had been one thing to think of a grand overall escape, but quite another to think about the nasty deeds that went along with it. Whereas she was prepared to do most anything it took. "Remember that we're doing this so that Volkia can't use me. For the wars that are killing your young men. Those young soldiers at the hospice who might never recover."

"I know, I know," he murmured.

"While you're in the city, pick up an inexpensive bracelet or pendant. I could use it to distract Breta when the time comes." She was planning out the steps to getting the drug into the maid's drink.

"Yes, a pendant should be easy to find."

"Nothing too fancy. Something a maid might like. And we'll need rope to tie her up in case she wakes up too early."

"Rope?" Tanfred said in distress.

"OK, thick ribbon."

"Right, then. Potion, pendant, ribbon."

Potion, pendant, ribbon, to escape the Volkish military head-quarters? Doubts began stabbing at her.

"I have been thinking about the gateway," Tanfred said. "They might be on alert by the time we arrive there. It's a two-hour journey to the closest one."

"Could we steal a dactyl?"

"Yevliesza. That could never happen."

Actually, she remembered, the last time she had fled a hostile place—Osta Kiya—it *had* been on a dactyl.

"I am afraid a carriage is all we have," he went on, "but I will be there, and I will make clear to any who impede us that I am on a mission of great importance for the prince. But you will still be expected to answer the guards at the boundary crossing, at least the first interaction, after which I can reasonably intervene."

"But if we have a head start," Yevliesza began, "how would they be on alert?"

"Manifesting. Albrecht can have a signal sent by mirror. If fortune goes with us, we will be long gone by the time they discover you missing. Otherwise . . . otherwise, it would help to have some kind of incident to distract them."

Her mind was still back on the need to speak Volkish to a soldier. "I don't know if I can manage the right phrase, or even pronounce it."

"I'll teach you two or three phrases and we'll have a signal between us as to how you should answer a question. And then I step in."

"What can we do about an incident at the boundary gate? You can't just throw a noble fit. That would look desperate."

"There is another possibility. Leave this to me."

How lovely that he even had an idea about how to do that. Tanfred was turning out to be more devious than she had expected.

"And—oh! Someone must drive the carriage."

"Yes. That will be my man Eldrik."

"Even in the middle of the night?"

Tanfred gave her an amused look. "Have you never had servants who have been with you for years?"

"Actually, no."

"Eldrik will be at my disposal."

She was leaving a lot to Tanfred and had to admit that in fact everything hinged on him. A hug of gratitude would certainly not do. She thought he might yelp in distress. "Thank you, my lord," she murmured.

He smiled as though he was starting to enjoy himself. "You might remember that I am used to getting my way. But there is one thing you have to prepare yourself for." He hesitated. "You will have to shave off your hair."

Unconsciously, she put her hand to her head. "Oh. Of course."

"A soldier's cap will only cover so much."

When he seemed genuinely regretful at her having to cut off her hair, Yevliesza had to smother a laugh. It was the least of her concerns. "Easy come, easy go," she said in the best Numinasi approximation. "I'll use some scissors. And what about your coachman? He might be punished."

"When we are at the gate, I will give Eldrik the choice to come with us. But even if he does not want to leave, the authorities aren't likely to think I would have told a coachman my plans."

She greatly wondered how they had come to this place of reckoning. Looking at it overall, it seemed impossible. But if she thought of each step, she could imagine success with each one. Alter the uniform, cut her hair, drug Breta, learn a few Volkish phrases. Enter the crossings.

The *crossings*, now. Those she was sure of.

YEVLIESZA AND HER MAID SAT TOGETHER ON THE DIVAN, A SILK gown lying between them as they each worked a different part of the dress; Breta on the bodice and Yevliesza on the hem. Watching Breta sewing, Yevliesza could see that the bruises on her wrists were still angry but fading. And she seemed happier, as she must be, if that troll of a Volkish marshal wasn't using her.

The gown, an awful shade of green, provided the excuse to have needle and green thread for the project that was hidden under the chair facing the divan. The chair had a skirt of cloth around the bottom and behind that curtain lay a corporal's uniform of gray-green.

Breta had been surprised when, two days ago, Yevliesza had asked for her help to select a gown to alter. Yevliesza claimed that she would wear a Volkish gown to a dinner some evening as a surprise. Breta lobbied for a pastel blue dress to no avail, and now Yevliesza had needles and a plentiful supply of thread.

As Yevliesza worked, she silently repeated the Volkish phrases that Tanfred had taught her. The meaning of the first was, "I accompany Duke Tanfred Wilhoffen," and the second was, "Duke Tanfred wishes to speak to you." The phrases were simple enough, but she had to keep her wits about her to remember when to preface them with "sir" should an officer be the one who approached them. She wondered if, in the dark, she could identify an officer from a common soldier. Tanfred had drilled her on military insignia, of which there were a bewildering variety. Her accent, they would practice on the way to the boundary gate.

"Oh!" Breta exclaimed, having stuck her finger on a needle. "Are you sure the palace tailor would not do a better job?"

Yevliesza kept her face neutral, as though altering a big gown was a relaxing occupation. In reality, it was tedious work and the fact that it was pointless made it all the harder to keep at it when Breta was around. "I'm sure Master Lindvall would be helpful," Yevliesza said, "but at home I always sewed as a hobby. Since it appears my stay will be longer than I had planned, I must do *something* with my time."

When it came to the uniform, removing the trouser side-seam stitches was tricky because the stitches were very small and the fabric, not of very good quality, sometimes tore. It was especially difficult to work by candlelight when it was so late at night that the manifesting globes were not powered.

Yevliesza wanted to take a walk on the roof so that Breta would leave. But she had already gone for a walk that morning and she and Tanfred had decided that nothing should change in her routines. Except one thing: she and the duke would have to have a disagreement, a loud one.

They had staged it on the roof yesterday with an intense discussion punctuated by a few harsh interactions, ending in Tanfred storming away. They hoped the show—once reported to Albrecht—would remove any concern that Tanfred was becoming too friendly with the captive. If Albrecht asked, she would complain that Tanfred had pushed her too hard about the absurd legend and her being part of it. She hoped the guards made note of it and reported a disagreement between the two of them, though Tanfred was a terrible actor and overplayed his part.

As Yevliesza hemmed another inch of the seemingly endless dress, Breta said, "We had awful news this morning. Prince Albrecht's nephew Sigmar has been killed at the front."

"Oh, no!" That young man . . . she was genuinely distressed.

"Yes, it is terrible for the prince."

She remembered Sigmar from her first dinner at Duke Tanfred's estate, the young man seated next to her at the table, eager to discuss peace treaties and basking in Albrecht's approval.

"Very sad," Breta said. "He was serving in Norslad. Only nineteen, he was."

So the dark side of the glorious war had struck home. She could not be glad of it, no matter her opposition to Albrecht. But already she was thinking how to use the information. A gracious response on her part might help create the impression that she was moving toward a deeper respect for Albrecht. This could help establish the idea that he was wearing down her resistance and that she was on the verge of revealing more about the new branch in the crossings. It wasn't certain to put off harsh interrogation, but it couldn't hurt.

"I think I should convey my regrets to the prince, Breta. Please pass word to Prince Albrecht that I would like to express my condolences in person."

"Yes, miss. That would be very kind."

"But with this sewing, you mustn't stay to help me. Really, Breta, I insist. We are not in a hurry."

Breta looked up doubtfully. "If you insist, mistress. But I can come back this afternoon."

Yevliesza almost groaned. "No, Breta, look at your thumb. It's bleeding. We'd never get blood off the fabric." Laying down the hem, Yevliesza held Breta's gaze. "I insist."

Chapter Thirty-Two

It was not Martel who came for her this time, a matter of some relief as Yevliesza didn't want to distress him about how disastrously the last meeting with Master Lothric had gone. Martel had meant well, and she now had more details about an important secret, but she would have learned it from Tanfred in any case, so she had suffered Albrecht's rage for nothing.

Her soldier-escort brought her to the ground floor of the palace and through the increasingly crowded corridors of the headquarters. Passing by open doors, Yevliesza noted clerks hunched over papers, secretaries copying missives by hand, and officers conferring with staff and messengers.

She had never been to Albrecht's suite before. Since he had retreated there in the middle of the day, she thought he must be greatly affected by his nephew's death. The guard at Albrecht's door announced her, and presently she was ushered into the apartment.

Albrecht was standing at a window in shirt sleeves and casual trousers. He nodded at her as the door closed behind her. The spacious room was very much like her own parlor, with lofty ceiling and several seating areas, as well as a flank of windows overlooking the Danstree. She realized she had been given an apartment equal in luxury to the prince's.

"My lord," she said, when she came up to him, "I am so sorry for your sad news."

In her peripheral vision she saw a shadow coming at her. A large dog was streaking out of nowhere and, barring its teeth, lunged for her.

Albrecht spun around, slashing at the animal with his left hand. The animal skidded to a halt and hunched over, cowering. Albrecht spoke to it in Volkish, and it skulked away, its body thin, its legs spindly, but no less powerful for its wiry build.

A vein pounded in Yevliesza's forehead as she tried to calm herself.

"He guards me," Albrecht said unnecessarily. "I hope you were not too frightened."

"I was, actually." She looked across the room and saw the animal licking itself, as though needing comfort after its master's harsh command.

Albrecht turned to regard her, face drawn, eyes wary. "Have you come to rebuke me for sending my nephew to his death?"

"I would never do that, Prince Albrecht."

He turned to the window. "Then I stand corrected."

The river reflected a pewter sky tinged with a sickly orange. Occasional gusts of wind whipped it into crests that flew away in tatters. She wondered if Albrecht resented her condolences, but after a time, he seemed to shake off his ruminations and gestured her to the seating area before the hearth. A small fire crackled there.

She arranged her skirt on the divan, deciding that this visit should be a short one. "I wanted to express how terribly sorry I am. I know what it is to lose a loved one."

Albrecht did not join her immediately, but stopped at a side table and poured whiskey into two glasses, bringing one to her. He took a chair facing her, saying in a flat tone, "Please excuse my rude welcome."

"Of course. But if you rather I left, I would understand."

"No. I did not think I wanted to see anyone, but . . . perhaps it is better not to withdraw." He downed half the glass. "There is really nothing to say. With death. When someone is gone and all that they were is obliterated."

"I felt that way when my father died in a Numinasi prison. He was obliterated." She remembered, though, that people had been exceptionally kind. Valenty, Tirhan, Grigeni.

Albrecht nodded. "Good. You have no platitudes to offer. I appreciate that. Tanfred tried to speak of God's mercy, but it was no use to me. Not right now."

The mention of Tanfred gave her a start. Even his name spoken aloud reminded her of how they were plotting against Albrecht and, sitting in his apartment, she didn't want such things on her mind. She took a sip of the whiskey, if that's what it was. The taste was harsh, perhaps just the thing needed at such times.

"How is your brother doing?" she asked.

"Strong, as always, I would suppose. He has other sons." He finished off his drink.

How cold a summary. Perhaps he and his brother were not on good terms. She was about to bring up the topic that was always between them, but there came a knock at the door.

"Come," Albrecht said in Volkish.

An officer entered and Albrecht joined him at the far end of the room for a murmured conversation. As they conducted their business, Yevliesza went to the window, eliciting a low growl from the dog who was now paying strict attention to her.

Albrecht glanced at the animal and held its gaze. It quieted.

The window rattled in the wind and Yevliesza hoped the weather would hold long enough for a carriage to travel at night. A storm could delay everything for days, days she might not have, before Albrecht increased the pressure on her. She tried not to dwell on the types of pressure he might exert and the tools at his disposal. If only the weather could hold for a few more days. She thought she could be done with the uniform in three days if Breta did not hover so much, but if she did, then cutting back on sleep could make up the difference. Meanwhile, she had to keep Albrecht from any rash moves.

When the messenger left, Albrecht joined her at the window seat and gazed out.

"My lord," she began. "I've been thinking about the things you've asked me about. I'm trying to decide what I should do. Do you understand that I might have . . . many aspects of my situation to consider? That this will take a little more time because it's not simple for me?"

He turned to her in some surprise. "Yes." He narrowed his eyes, carefully considering her. "I can well understand."

"I hope that—soon—we can come to an understanding. If I can see my way clear. To my future."

He compressed his lips into a firm line and nodded slowly as though finally figuring something out. That she was coming around, she hoped.

"This calls for a drink," he pronounced. "Come. And bring your glass." She joined him at the sideboard, and he refreshed her drink that didn't really need it, pouring more for himself.

When they took their seats again, he took a place next to her on the divan. He raised his glass in a toast. "To a better understanding."

Her smile wobbled, but she held up her glass, finding to her dismay that her hand was shaking.

His pale blue eyes seemed to soften. "I know you are torn

with conflicting loyalties. All will be well in the end." He smiled indulgently. "You are shaking. Are you afraid?"

"Probably." She gulped her drink, letting him think it was because of *conflicting loyalties*.

Having swallowed the potent stuff, she felt slightly better, but she put the drink on the table. She needed all her wits about her, lest he suppose she was going to tell him *now*.

"I'm thinking things through," she said, making ready to leave.

"Yes," he said. "Yes, you are." His gaze held hers. His left hand touched his chin as he watched her. His *left* hand. That was never an accident.

She returned his gaze, knowing—and not greatly caring—that it was a bad idea. In his eyes, a keen attraction to her. His face was both strong and exceedingly gentle. In a rush of hot feeling, she found it welcome. He was masculine, handsome, and open to her. At some level she deeply hated herself for what she was about to do but was helpless to stop herself. She leaned into him, touching his upper arm. It surprised him just enough that he had to disengage to put his drink on the table. Then, rather than taking her into an embrace, he held her at some distance, regarding her with deliberation. It seemed he was making a point. *If you want me, come to me.*

When she moved the slightest bit toward him, it was all he needed. His arm came around her back, and he pulled her to his lips, kissing her hungrily, bringing his hand to the back of her head, allowing him to taste her deeply. This went on and, deliciously, on.

Must leave, a distant part of her was saying. *Must leave now.*

She did not want to stop. She must stop. Stopping was almost impossible.

"Yevliesza," he whispered, as his embrace tightened.

She pulled back, hating herself for leaving his arms. Her hand went up to rearrange her hair, as though that was the main issue.

He looked ready to pull her back into his arms, but she made a show of putting herself together, pulling down her sleeves and smoothing her skirts.

As he watched her with what she took for well-practiced self-control, she managed to say, "Not when you're grieving. It wouldn't honor Sigmar."

As she sat back on the divan, Albrecht watched her, biting his lower lip, regarding her intently. Even with that expression —*especially* with that expression—he looked incredibly handsome. What harm to give in to the man, when it might make him all the more reluctant to hurt her? Really, what harm?

But what was she thinking? What *harm?* That her first experience with a man would be with a Nazi? That she would betray Valenty?

She got to her feet. "I have to go. I'm not sure. . . ."

After a pause, he also rose. "No, you must be sure, Yevliesza. Not today."

And then she was fleeing the room, her thoughts clattering around in broken shards, her stomach knotted in fear and desire.

She was halfway down the corridor with her escort when she realized that Albrecht had used creature power on her. Flinching, she stopped in her tracks, causing her escort to look at her with concern.

"Miss? All well?"

Her voice came out in shreds as she resumed walking. "Yes, of course."

Even after suspecting that he used creature power to control Evah, she had failed to identify it when it happened to *her.* Universally, it was a trespass to exert birthright power over people's will. He was a man who pretended to honor, but transgressed decency when it suited him. Clearly it suited him in her case.

"You must take a seat, miss," the officer said in concern.

"No," she murmured. She didn't need to sit down. She needed to break out of the palace and flee for her life.

Chapter Thirty-Three

S unlight slanted low through the forest as Valenty awoke.
They had found a shelter under an overhanging rock with
just room enough for three, but Urik and Pyvel must have
risen early. Clearly he had not, as it was well into the first quarter
of the day.

Valenty stretched out his leg, still throbbing with pain. Fortunately, they were within a few days' hike of Rorrs Gate—a much
closer gate than Lassen Gate, where they had arrived.

Close by, he heard Urik and Pyvel talking. He found them in a
muddy clearing where the *harjat* and the boy, short sticks in
hand, circled each other in a practice knife fight. In a quick pivot,
Urik jabbed Pyvel with an elbow, hard enough to knock him
down.

From his position on the ground, Pyvel said, "You struck me
with an elbow!"

Urik nodded. "If you are close enough, punch or jab. You can
use your body faster than you can bring up your knife."

Pyvel looked at the stick he still held in his hand. "It was a
knife fight."

"No. It was a fight." Urik looked down on him. "Again."

As Pyvel rose, brushing the snow from his leggings, Urik said. "Look around you, boy. What do you see?"

Pyvel turned to take in the surroundings, noting Valenty standing nearby. "I see Lord Valenty has snuck up behind me and the two of you are going to attack all at once."

"He is just a distraction. Look once more."

"There are trees full of snow and, behind you, a patch of thick brambles."

"Another thing is that I have slowly been backing you toward that sapling." He cocked his head toward a trunk about a hand-width wide. Pyvel noted the small tree. "Everything around you is a weapon."

"A sapling?"

"Yes, a sapling. Or anything else you can slam your opponent against."

"I might lose my knife."

Urik nodded. "In this fight, you would have lost it within moments. Now grab me by the arm and swing me against that tree."

"You are too big."

"Good. What else can you do with the sapling?" Urik gave him a moment to consider, then said, "If I am already off-balance, kick me the rest of the way."

"Into the tree."

"Try it." Urik went close to the tree and feigned a stagger. Pyvel jabbed at him with his foot, and Urik crashed against the tree, losing his balance and falling to the ground.

"You are not really hurt."

"No, but I will be when you slam your foot into my head."

"And then what?" Pyvel said eagerly, liking to see the *harjat* sprawled out.

Urik got to his feet and wiped the muddy snow from his hands. "Then you draw your knife and thrust it into my eye."

He clapped Pyvel on the shoulder. "Two lessons from this fight: Awareness of your surroundings. And everything is a weapon: trees, walls, knees, elbows. Everything."

Valenty had watched all this with interest. It was not the same Urik he thought he knew.

As Pyvel went back to the rock ledge to pull a morning meal out of their packs, Valenty murmured, "Teaching him to take down a guard at the boundary gate?"

Urik watched Pyvel disappear through the trees. "Teaching him to respect himself." He frowned. "And to get up and try again."

๑๕๛

As they set out from camp, Urik led the way with Pyvel behind him, creating what path through the snow they could for Valenty.

They were leaving behind the mountains and the valley with its massive ramparts. As the landscape opened out before them, the conifers shared the terrain with aspen, maple, and birch, their bare branches piercing the bright sky.

Sam and Leah had given them hides to tie over their trouser legs and wool hats against the crackling cold. Pyvel had a heavy cape which they had cut down for him, a gift from Rabbi Neva. He had given Pyvel his blessing, and told Valenty and Urik to care for the boy's spirit as well as his physical safety. Pyvel had been under heavy creature control. Healing would take time, perhaps accelerated by fighting drills, since he had always wanted to go for a soldier.

For the next stage of their mission, the passage back to Numinat, Urik was clean-shaven, as was Valenty except for a small mustache. Their hair was cut short on the sides, with Pyvel's trimmed with care to chin length.

Their moods were sober, both for the journey ahead of them and for what they had seen of Volkia, with the ensorcelled house and the gruesome creature control that Nashavety exerted over the people there. The plight of the Jewish fugitives and what they had described of the treatment of fellow Jews in the cities was as dark as anything they had imagined Volkia capable of. These facts were not fully known outside of Volkia but would be if and he and Urik succeeded in getting through the gate at Rorrs. Their plan had seemed like a good one when they had worked it out in Numinat. But now Valenty saw its flaws. With Anastyna's declaration of war, the gate would be more heavily guarded. And they had Pyvel, making two of their number who could not speak Volkish.

By declaring war, the princip had made their passage more difficult. The military would be continually on alert. He thought she had finally done it because of the invasion of Norslad, which made clear that Prince Albrecht would not be satisfied with just Alfan Sih. But it was a harsh calculation when three of her subjects had been dispatched into enemy territory.

Valenty hoped that she had secured the participation of Nubiah. That realm's envoy, Lord Chenua, would doubtless have pressed his king hard on this action. Whether the princip would strike first in Norslad or Alfan Sih, he did not know. First, free one of the vassal states, combining military resources for the assault on Volkia. Unless Volkia attacked first. Prince Albrecht had begun with weaker kingdoms, but he doubtless wanted to occupy Numinat if for no other reason than to neutralize its military power. If Volkia attacked, which boundary gate would they attempt? Lowgate was the closest to Osta Kiya and Causeway Gate was within reasonable distance. Anastyna could split her forces or decide to concentrate on one gate. He thought Numinat could turn back a Volkish attack, but losses would be heavy.

Pyvel's presence required Valenty and Urik to take a short

detour. Leah and Sam had sketched a map of the route they must follow, both to get to Rorrs and also to skirt the edge of a village where they could find supplies.

A large bird glided over their heads, its wingspan blocking out the sun for moment. Urik stopped, watching its silent passage.

"What bird was that?" Pyvel asked him. His face was reddened from the cold, but he seemed energized by the hike.

"Frost owl," Urik said, eyes narrowed.

"I never saw a bird so large."

"A harbinger of death." He stared at Pyvel's wide-eyed reaction. "How fast can you find your knife?"

Pyvel fumbled for the dagger he carried. It fell into the snow. As he fished it out, Urik resumed walking, refraining from comment.

Valenty hardly registered their exchange. He was thinking of Yevliesza and how he had almost forgotten her face. Not that it had been so long, but the struggle at Nashavety's lair, the revelations of Rabbi Neva, and the coming war had gripped his mind for days. Yet how could he forget her face? Combined with the possibility that she might be in danger in Volkia and he, doing nothing, he felt alternately hotly angry and morally craven.

Underneath that was something else: a troubling idea that her heart might not have room for him. She kept herself from him. Sometimes he thought she had secrets. Rather than let those lie, his instinct was to discover them. When they were together once more, when she returned to Numinat—as she *had* to do, as he kept telling himself—he would get to know her all over again. If she would allow it.

❧

THE VILLAGE WAS TUCKED UP AGAINST ROUNDED, SNOW-CLAD foothills. It was a small hamlet, with twenty or thirty cottages, a main cobbled street, and nearby fields pockmarked with remnants of the harvest. The three travelers left their packs in a glen and crept up a knoll for a better view of the place. By their reckoning it was what they called Sunday in Volkia, a good time to find what they needed, if most people would be in church.

From a few of the cottage chimneys, smoke curled, promising cozy rooms with welcoming fires. A church spire and snow-laden roofs gave the village a peaceful look, suggesting simple, pleasant days. The scene contrasted with the harsh conditions at Sam and Leah's cave, where dozens of people had fled grim conditions in Volkia's forges and weapon mills. Valenty wondered what these villagers knew of what their leaders were doing and if they cared or would oppose it. Any of it. Even people of the *right blood* were sending their sons to war. And would not see them return.

Valenty and Urik planned to split up to find—to steal—better garments for Pyvel. He must look like an aristocratic young man; and if not wealthy, at least not like a pauper that had just spent a fiveday in the woods.

"Boots," Urik said. "Take those if nothing else. If he is to look like high folk, the boots must be good ones."

They needed clothes for him, too, though. Pyvel's tunic and jacket were mud-stained and in tatters.

"We must use our knives if it comes to it," Urik said.

Kill someone for their boots? But Valenty nodded.

They found a ditch that looked to carry water in warm weather. Backed onto the ditch, a row of small, tidy houses.

Leaving Pyvel with the packs, the two of them took different directions. Valenty stole alongside the ditch looking for a likely dwelling, one more prosperous-looking than the simple cottages. One of the houses had clotheslines bearing frozen bedclothes swaying in the wind. No smoke came from the two chimneys.

He went on, thinking if there was a landowner's house, it would not be amid these humble dwellings.

The backs of the houses were eerily silent. No children playing, or men chopping wood. At church, then. He should get on with his thievery before people came back. At the end of the row, he came to a snow-clad field with stalks of the fall harvest thrusting up from the white crust. Beyond, a larger dwelling with pitched roofs and a stable. Creeping up to it, Valenty watched the windows for a few minutes and, seeing no one, made his way through the spacious yard. Slipping through the door of a stone fence, he found himself in a small garden of dormant roses and vines.

The door to the house led into an empty kitchen, which he could see through the window. Pressing down the latch of the door, he pushed the door open enough to look past the kitchen and into a hallway. He listened for a long while, straining to hear the sound of conversation or footsteps. Satisfied that he was alone, he silently entered and made a quick appraisal of the layout. A dining room, parlor, study, and buttery. A small bedroom that might be for a maid. There was a second floor. He took the stairs rapidly, eager to rifle the rooms and be gone.

The doors on the upper floor were open, and he quickly judged the likely occupants by the furnishings. One room's wardrobe held a girl's frocks, but the next one in line was a boy's quarters. Boots lined up by the door, clothes in a chest. He took a shirt and long pants. Over the bed post, a jacket with buttons and braid. He laid it out on the bed and threw the clothes onto it, then rolled up the jacket. On his way out, he looked more carefully at the boots. All were dirty and scuffed, but he grabbed the best of them and moved swiftly through the house toward the door.

Someone was in the kitchen. A maid laying a fire in the stove.

He turned and slowly made his way toward the front door. If he was seen coming out with a pile of clothes and boots, an alarm would be raised. One look out the window showed that no one was on the street. He had Pyvel's new clothes. And he intended to keep them.

Leaving the house, he descended a few stone steps to the entryway in an easy manner so as not to draw attention. He walked down the cobbled street as though he had every right to do so and then turned into the empty field, making his way to the irrigation canal. No one hailed him, but a man shoveling coal into a bucket looked up at him and returned his wave.

At the meeting place, he and Pyvel quickly stuffed the clothes into one of the packs. Urik came soon after. The boots Valenty had found would not fit into a pack. Valenty held them up to Urik's skeptical judgment.

Urik's lip curled. "No one of high birth would wear them." Then, with a superior expression, he took from under his arm a pair of high, polished riding boots and held them up.

"Hurry," Valenty cautioned them. "Someone saw me. At a distance, but I was noted." He tossed the worn boots behind a bush, and they crept away, following paths already made in the snow.

"I could use those boots right now," Pyvel told Urik.

The *harjat's* expression was enough to silence him, and they left the environs of the village, putting distance between themselves and pilfered houses.

Chapter Thirty-Four

Dreiza stumbled over a root in the path. "Eight—" *hells*, she almost said, but refrained. At her side, Mitasha laughed. "Go ahead and swear. You are not a *satvadeya* yet!" Stinging cold swirled against Dreiza's thin wool trousers every time she took a step forward. She and Mitasha followed the High Mother as she made her way past the domicile wall in the abysmal dark, with Arlaty at her side. In the rear, Lusanya helped old Sofichka, holding her firmly by the arm and getting farther behind all the time.

Despite having to climb out of bed in the second quarter of the night, Dreiza was excited to be among the privileged group, but also a bit concerned about the initiation rites. In answer to questions about the ceremony, the Devi Ilsat had answered, "It is not usually onerous," which did nothing to set her mind at ease.

They began to climb. Overhead, the waning crescent moon sailed through shredded clouds, blown by gusting winter winds. *Let there be a cave,* Dreiza told herself. *A nice warm one.* But at least she had a heavy wool cape. She pulled it closer.

Behind, she heard the last two *satvadeya* trudging slowly and someone—probably Sofichka—muttering, "By the Nine, how far to go?" A soothing answer from Lusanya, answered by, "Colder than a serpent's kiss!"

Dreiza felt the strain in her calves, but imagined ancient Sofichka, by her muttering, was feeling it more.

When she and Mitasha climbed to a flat shelf of rock, they found it empty. Out of a hole in the rock face, a round figure appeared, waving them into a cave.

"Arlaty is laying wood for a fire," the High Mother said, "but we will have to wait for our manifester to light it."

At last Lusanya arrived with Sofichka, and everyone fussed over their oldest member, bringing her to a shaped log to sit on and offering a flask of what Dreiza suspected was spirits. The Devi Ilsat saw Dreiza's expression of surprise. "When you are a hundred and forty, you will warm your bones with the domicile's special liquor, too."

The group was now standing around the fire pit, and Lusanya conjured a flame under the logs. The High Mother directed Dreiza to sit on a log next to Sofichka and when she had done so, said, "This is our ceremony, my dear. I hope you like it."

"What do I do?"

"Do? Oh, nothing. But we have presents."

The fire began to crackle, throwing a warm light into the cave, revealing its considerable size. Though the ceiling was lost in darkness, the walls flickered with shadows. The group of women, all standing now except for Dreiza and Sofichka, formed a circle, their faces softened by the firelight. Each of them was distinctive. Sofichka, small and stooped, her thinning hair cut short; Arlaty's dark complexion highlighted by her white hair, braided close to her head like a crown; Lusanya's generous proportions, widened by her cape; and Mitasha, the tallest of them, her long hair wind-blown, whereas the others wore bound loops or braids tucked into a bun. Finally, the High Mother, with her ample curves and short stature.

"Well, I have a gift if no one else does," Sofichka snapped. She turned to Dreiza, and her face turned kindly. She reached out, holding something, and Dreiza cupped her hand to receive it: a bracelet made of tiny wires. Trapped within its web, glowing stones of amber.

"Oh!" Dreiza exclaimed. "Beautiful."

"It was my gift when I first was called to serve. May you attain one hundred forty-nine years, eleven months and thirty days, my sister."

Dreiza felt tears sting her eyes.

Arlaty came next. She held a packet in both her hands and presented it to Dreiza. "This is a pouch of herbs for an infusion to soothe the body and spirit. Dreiza, be welcome and know that I will always replenish its contents and care for your comfort." She smiled as Dreiza put the fragrant pouch to her nose and gratefully inhaled.

Lusanya approached and brought from under her cloak a thick stalk of braided lavender, interlocked so closely it appeared to be a miniature tree with leaves of violet. "May we weave our days together in beauty and strength, dear sister."

Greatly moved, Dreiza put the bundle in her lap and thanked her, as Mitasha, who she always thought of as Mitasha the Merry, came to stand before her.

"There is one who is missing in our circle," Mitasha said, "and I have the High Mother's permission to introduce this individual now." Shrugging down a strap from her shoulder, she opened a cylinder made of leather. She drew forth a parchment, handing it to Dreiza.

When Dreiza unrolled it, she stared at the artful drawing upon it. It was a picture of a dactyl soaring in the sky, silver scales flashing, a proud head crest like a crown, and great wings stretched to meet the wind. A shimmer of blue rippled across its back, colored by the sky. It was Kirjanichka.

She could not speak. After a few moments, Sofichka thrust a handkerchief toward her, and Dreiza wiped her eyes. "Thank you so much, Mitasha," she said, trying to master herself.

"You are welcome. I drew this during the dactyl's last visit." She added mischievously, "Kirjanichka did not seem to mind."

At last the High Mother approached. "Dreiza, my gift to you is a selfish one. I hope you will pardon me."

"Of course," she answered, but then wished she had not inferred the gift would *need* pardoning.

The Devi Ilsat handed her a disk the size of the palm of her hand. It was a mirror.

"Wherever our ministrations to the world may take you, may you always be able to reach out to me and me to you." A messaging mirror. The Devi Ilsat smiled. "You will need a manifester to help you." She added, "Usually."

Dreiza thanked her, and the High Mother gave her a cloth bag to put her gifts in.

"And now to business," she unceremoniously said, taking a seat before the fire.

Dreiza realized that the High Mother managed the *satvary*, but she was vaguely disappointed that her welcoming ceremony had been just one of several items to be dealt with. Still, she felt that the cave, with its shifting, fire-lit walls had laced her induction ritual with proper mystery.

Looking at Dreiza the old *satvar* said, "The time has come, my daughter, for you to know the great care that has come to rest upon the shoulders of the *satvadeya*."

Dreiza brought all her attention to the High Mother.

"It began with Kassalya," she said. "You have seen how she suffers from her foreknowing. When she first arrived here two years ago, we knew her for a rare soul of powerful vision. But then she told of one thing she saw, and we were profoundly shaken.

"She talked of Volkia and how it was not a normal realm. It had only arisen from the origin world some seventy years ago. And though young, it was exceedingly dark. A realm that could destroy the Mythos. She saw that its darkness would begin with the arising of machines and end with the poisoning of the Deep and the shattering of the realms."

"I could not eat for a week," Mitasha murmured.

The Devi Ilsat raised a disapproving eyebrow.

But Dreiza hardly listened because the High Mother had spoken of the *destruction of the Mythos*. It was a horrific claim, but she shoved the thought away to listen to the rest of it.

"Here is where Yevliesza comes into the story."

Ah. Yevliesza's important role, as the High Mother had hinted at before. Dreiza was now sitting very still lest she miss a single word.

"The *satvadeya* and I considered long and carefully. That was back when Videkya was amongst us of course, and it was she who suggested that now was a time when, if ever, we had need of the First Ones—and their ninth power, the power that had not been seen for a thousand years."

Mitasha piped up, "Let us turn to our youngest member and see what her intuition tells her about our dilemma." She turned to Dreiza. "My sister, if Volkia has arisen from evil, how could the ninth power help us?"

Dreiza's thoughts were whirling, but she caught one of them. "If the primal root power is a lost power, perhaps we have lost any understanding of what it can do. And so it might be something that can save us."

Old Sofichka had been nodding off, but apparently she was listening, for she muttered, "Ha! She has her wits about her after all."

"Indeed," the Devi Ilsat said. Turning to Dreiza once again, she continued. "But the meaning of the final power was never lost, not to us, though we respected the will of the First Ones never to reveal it. Primal root power disappeared from the Mythos after the first age because it was not needed. Its use had been to forge the paths when the First Ones fled the earth; the First Ones of all the traditions. Power over the crossings would never be needed again, for they would grow and adapt over time.

"No one imagined that the crossings would ever need to be constricted, much less cut off. But now we thought that Volkia might have to be isolated before its trespasses pulled the Mythos apart."

Dreiza tried to comprehend what she was hearing. The ninth power was the power over the crossings? "So it faded out of disuse?" she asked. "And now it is back?"

"Yes. Because we intervened."

Dreiza felt like she was standing on a great precipice, looking out on the entire world for the first time. "You gave it to Yevliesza!"

"Goodness, no. But in circle we invoked the ancients to help us. To bring back primal root power to defend against Volkia. And *they* invested her."

"So you did not let things unfold!" Dreiza blurted. "And the First Ones *listened*?"

The Devi Ilsat bowed her head, confirming this. "We six came into circle, we who had lived as contemplatives for a combined four hundred years, and asked the ancients for assistance." She looked around the cavern. "In this very place."

Dreiza frowned. What about giving her the vine to train, what about all the high-minded language of learning patience and letting people find their way, always the High Mother's response when Dreiza wanted action? "You forced an outcome!"

"A High Mother's prerogative," the Devi Ilsat answered, chuckling. Turning to Mitasha, the most voluble of the sisters, she said, "Perhaps you would continue the telling, my daughter."

"Gladly, Mother." Mitasha settled her skirts around her legs. "We had in mind for the power to be invested in a warrior who could rally the *harjat*, who could inspire the people to join the ranks of the army, who, by force of his personality could persuade young Anastyna to take action in defense of the Mythos." She sighed. "That is not how it turned out. We had to work with what we got. Yevliesza.

"We knew that root power was too dangerous to give to any one kingdom—since it could be a formidable weapon for trespass as well as defense. Anastyna was too new a princip to have the wisdom of its use; none of her subjects would be suitable, nor the subjects of any realm for that matter. It should be someone without a kingdom. We implored the First Ones to give us a newcomer. Someone who could be impartial. That is when things went awry."

Awry? Were they going to say that Yevliesza was the wrong choice? Dreiza wished that they would just get to the point. But looking around the circle and the serene faces of her sisters, she knew there was no way in the Mythos that they would hurry up.

Chapter Thirty-Five

L ate in the night, Tanfred came to her. In the bedroom, he took off his jacket and velvet waistcoat and tossed them on the bed with the air of an accustomed lover.

Out of his shirt he took two small pouches.

"Ribbons and a pendant," he said. He pulled out a bundle of red ribbon and a short chain from which dangled an ornament of silver filigree.

Her plan was to send Breta into the bedroom, where she would find a gift on the dresser. In the few seconds while she was gone, Yevliesza would stir the drug potion into whatever drink she was sharing with the maid. Tanfred handed the pouch with its contents to her, and she stuffed it under the mattress.

"Next," he said. He retrieved a small bag from his trouser pocket. "A sleeping powder. Use half of it in a hot drink or cup of wine."

"And the other half?" Yevliesza asked, taking the pouch.

"If she does not drink it and you have to try again another time."

"There can't be another time!" The idea of spending another day in Rothsvund was intolerable.

"What has happened?" Tanfred asked, frowning.

Yevliesza related how Albrecht had tried to compel her to have sex using his affinity with creature power.

An expression of disgust flared across Tanfred's face. "I cannot believe it."

"Believe it. He means to bind me to him with sex."

"But to compel you! How could you feel a bond with him after such defilement?"

"I couldn't. But he would at least have his pleasures without violence."

Tanfred ran a hand through his hair, pacing to the cold hearth. On his way back he said, "We should leave as soon as possible. Can you finish the uniform in two more days?"

It would mean working fast. But with Breta's day off tomorrow, she could make it happen. "I still have the jacket to do."

"The jacket does not need to look perfect, just so long as it does not draw undue attention." She nodded her agreement.

"We leave in two nights, then," he said.

Two nights. He must have noted her worried expression because he asked, "Is there any reason to wait?"

"No. Let's not wait." But her breath went shallow. They were really going to do this.

YEVLIESZA WOKE AT DAWN, HURRIEDLY SPLASHED WATER ON HER face, and dressed in her front-buttoning gown. Breta had the day off, so the day could be dedicated to finishing the uniform trousers.

She had set up her sewing space with care, with a side table in front of her chair to hold the voluminous dress and a straight-backed chair close to one side for her scissors and thread. It formed a barrier to anyone coming in. By the time they got around the barricade—aided by a divan for guests to sit—she would have time to push the uniform under her chair.

Ignoring the breakfast that was sitting under a serving dome that a maid had just brought in, she picked up the thread, cutting off a length. However, her shaking hands couldn't manage threading the needle. After several tries, she was swearing and gripping the needle so hard it fell into her lap. *Eight goddamn hells.*

Anger streamed forth from a hidden geyser. Anger at Albrecht. Albrecht treating her as a guest, using charm and cunning and finally creature power to have what he wanted. Albrecht breaking his promise to Anastyna of her swift return. Albrecht demanding that she betray Numinat. Out of fear of him, she had pushed away her anger and now, with the drop of a needle, it sprang forth.

She thought of Breta and Evah, both of whom could forestall rape if they lived in Numinat. But in this kingdom, a woman's volition could be undercut by the Volkish way and custom of celebrating manhood. By war, by domination. So a rape by a man of standing could not be punished with physical injury to his privates, or lack of vigor in sex, or whatever a woman's punishment would be. She wished she had learned more about how to do it. There was only one thing that soothed her and that was imagining Albrecht's stunned fury when he found she had escaped along with the richest man in the kingdom.

When she picked up a length of thread and moistened the end of it in her mouth, she got it through the eye of the needle on the first try.

On her third stitch, the apartment door opened.

Evah Krim. Yevliesza bent over and plunged the uniform under her chair, smoothing the chair skirt, and rose to greet the woman.

"Good morning, Evah."

In answer, a smile that came and went in a microsecond. Evah wore a white tunic belted over a sky-blue gown, her blond hair framing her face down to chin level, giving her a modern look despite her long garments. She slunk around the divan and began examining the dress draped across the small table.

"Why not nice yellow dress? This too big," she said in her halting Numinasi.

"A little. But I can fix it," Yevliesza said. "And how do you know there is a yellow dress? Have you been snooping again?"

"Snoop?"

"Coming into other people's rooms without their saying you can."

A smirk. "But this, *my* house."

"And this, *my* apartment." She pointedly held Evah's gaze. The woman must not come and go as she pleased. "Please leave, Evah. I would like to be friends, but not if you . . ."

Evah brightened. "Snoop. Not if snoop." Then, trailing her hand through the folds of the green dress, she languidly turned away, retracing her steps to the door just as Albrecht came in.

He carried a heavy-looking package wrapped in brown cloth and tied with ribbon.

"Evah," he said in surprise.

"My lord," she said in Volkish, curtseying.

He moved past her, joining Yevliesza at her chair. Glancing down at the heaped dress, he smiled. "What is this, you are left to do your own sewing?"

"No, my lord. It is a project I felt like doing." He put the package on the divan and Evah strolled over in curiosity. "Breta and I are working on a dress. So it will fit me."

A genuine smile came to him. "That is excellent."

It was odd how unattractive he seemed at that moment, now that she knew he had used creature power on her. The planes of his face were aristocratic but arrogant. His well-toned body was merely intimidating. His mouth, sensual in a debased way; the blue of his eyes, icy.

"I have brought you a present," he said, setting down the package on the divan.

"A present?" This was a new gesture.

Yevliesza sat on the divan, unwrapping the package and avoiding looking at Evah who might feel offended not only that Albrecht had given another woman a present, but chose to do so in front of her.

As the cloth fell away, Yevliesza saw that it was an elaborate clock of the sort made for a sideboard or mantel. It was housed in gracefully curving silverwood decorated with tiny carved birds. On the watch face, the hour and minute hands were of gold filigree, clicking as though counting off the minutes remaining to her.

"It's beautiful, my lord," Yevliesza murmured.

"Please. You must call me Albrecht."

Out of the corner of her eye, she could see Evah's stricken expression. Albrecht might be completely unaware of the effect of his behavior, or else he enjoyed making Evah jealous. The clock gently ticked. It was 10:34. If only they would both leave . . .

Albrecht glanced at the gown. "Am I to see you wearing this dress? Or is it for Breta?"

She pretended to be amused. "I thought I might wear it."

Evah, looking longingly at the timepiece, said, "Must go on fireplace."

Yevliesza rose. "Let's see where it looks best." She picked up the heavy clock and, as she went to the mantel, Evah trailed behind her.

"In the middle, do you think?" Yevliesza asked Evah. She was probably making Evah feel even worse, but she couldn't stand leaving the girl as a bystander.

When they had positioned the clock just so, Evah said, "Heavy clock. Hard to pack for traveling."

As though she would be allowed to leave. There was nothing to be said at that, except, *I'm going to leave in a great hurry and won't pack anything.*

Finding silence surrounding her, Evah shot an ugly look at Yevliesza and made her exit.

When they were alone, Albrecht said, "I know that Numinasi do not use timepieces, but that is just superstition. One must not be afraid of change. Of new things." The clock ticked as though it agreed.

"Princip Anastyna seems interested in new developments," Yevliesza said, "but her *fajatim* are not, and it causes no end of controversy. Some of it because of me."

"So I understand. Anastyna has treated you badly. Perhaps reason enough to . . . part ways with those who do not appreciate you."

"Well. That is my dilemma," she responded, giving him a sideways smile.

"Perhaps you feel some loyalty to this nobleman, Lord Valenty?"

Her smile faltered. "Lord Valenty?"

"He seemed interested in you. The man offered you a place in his household." Albrecht knew more about her than she wished he did. But one thing he appeared not to know: that she had been tried for treason for having gone to Alfan Sih. Which, if known, made a lie of her story that she had been to Nubiah when she first met him.

"Lord Valenty tended to be nice to many women." She trusted that Albrecht was getting the right picture, without her spelling things out and appearing to press her points too hard.

To her relief, Albrecht moved on. "I hope you enjoy the timepiece. It was made by a famous Volkish artisan. Meanwhile, I came by to say that I must travel for a few days.

She managed to react. *He will be gone.*

"When I return, perhaps we can have our conversation?"

"I hope so—Albrecht." To make it seem that his trip was of little concern to her, she responded, "I do have to think about what my future will be. I already have an enemy here, and if I am powerless . . ." She didn't need to say the man's name.

"He will not be a problem."

"But you keep him at your side."

"Because the troops are loyal to him. The common troops, not the officers. He comes from humble stock, but I cannot discount his influence." She must act as though it mattered. When he saw her deflate, he went on. "Yevliesza. Do not be concerned. I am planning for you to have a title. Countess, perhaps. It would signal your rising power, signal it not only to him, but to the people of Volkia."

"He will never tolerate me."

Albrecht's face stiffened. "He will do what I tell him to do."

She had played that out as far as she should. Albrecht did not like Reinhart's power. Perhaps the prince wasn't as confident of leadership as he appeared. "How far are you going?"

"Not far. I will be back soon." He looked at the gown under repairs. "Perhaps you might wear the dress when I return."

She smiled in what she hoped was a mysterious way. The green dress loomed in her mind as a symbol of complete abdication. And doubtless now, to Albrecht as well. If she was still there when he got back, she would have to wear it. Not only that, but submit to him taking it off her.

The image came to her mind of Albrecht's surprise to see the tracery on her back. What could she say, how could she lie, if he saw her naked back, or even the back of her neck or her upper arm?

Oh, it's just a tattoo.

How far does it go?

It goes everywhere.

But he was leaving, and she would not be here when he got back. "When do you leave, Albrecht?"

"In the morning. I will return in three days."

Perfect. She would be gone in two.

Chapter Thirty-Six

rlaty threw another branch on the fire, and the stack collapsed under its weight, setting free a flock of sparks to dance for an instant in the air. As the glimmers died and drifted down, the *satvadeya* flicked ash off their skirts and continued giving Mitasha their close attention.

"That is when things went awry," she was saying.

They had just gotten to the part where the *satvadeya* asked the spirits of the First Ones to bestir the Mythos into conferring primal root power on a newcomer, a person whose loyalty was not tied to any one realm, and preferably a strong leader or warrior.

"And what we got was a skinny girl!" old Sofichka rasped, shaking her head.

"But sister, she is a woman grown," Mitasha gently said. She resumed her telling. "It so happened that this was the time when Anastyna had undertaken a review of the envoys to the origin world and discovered that one was unaccounted for. Ansyl, of Iron River Hall, who had been on his mission for twenty-three years. Here at the *satvary*, we had no inkling that a daughter had been born to him on the origin world, nor that she was coming to Numinat."

Lusanya snorted, and Mitasha looked over at the rotund woman who, by her annoyed expression, was eager to speak.

"And if we *had* known who was coming," Lusanya said, "you may be sure we would have beseeched the First Ones to reconsider! But we did not know. Events came fast."

"Yes," Mitasha said. "Coming fast upon the messenger's return from the origin world, Yevliesza was headed for Osta Kiya on the back of a dactyl." A broad smile took over her face. "But one person knew what was happening."

Sofichka chuckled and roused herself, leaning forward to hear the next part.

Mitasha went on. "One person. And that was Nashavety. Her spy at the boundary gate saw that a stranger had come and with his mirror made a sending to his mistress, having discovered that the stranger came from the origin world. Such a visit had never been heard of, and he knew that the arrival of the foreigner would likely be unwelcome news to the *fajatim* of Raven Fell."

Dreiza broke in. "Did she know that Yevliesza was a Numinasi? And she was willing to attack her anyway?"

The High Mother answered. "Possibly, if her spy even knew. But whatever the case, Nashavety made a bold plan. If the girl was not of the realm, then she must not enter it. She must not enter the Mythos at all, it being against all custom. But if the newcomer turned out to be the offspring of the Numinasi envoy, then she would have standing in the realm—however regretful her upbringing. And though Anastyna might welcome her, the girl would still be—she must always be—a foreign influence, bringing inimical ways into the closed kingdom of Numinat and must be disposed of."

Mitasha eagerly went on. "Oh yes, such were undoubtedly the *fajatim's* reasonings. But when Nashavety brought the storm and the lightning strike . . ."

She paused for dramatic effect, and Dreiza whispered into the gap, "The girl's natural power rode in on the lightning."

A great sigh went up from the women gathered around the fire. They seemed to enjoy hearing this story that they knew so well.

Mitasha nodded to herself. "Not only her birthright power of aligns, but the second power that we so badly needed. And so, the very person who would most hate a foreigner having root power, was, in some ways, responsible for a foreigner having it!"

A long silence followed. There was something about the tale that left all of them in wonder, this story of misplaced plans, the price of meddling, or the irony of an evil woman's interference to create the very thing she feared. It was a story Dreiza could never have guessed at. Now she understood why Kassalya had been in such distress at Yevliesza's possible death at Nashavety's hands. Why Yevliesza's future came so keenly to Kassalya's unbearable knowing. Despite the dramatic revelation of Yevliesza's power, Dreiza found herself thinking of the confusion and fear she must feel. And the uncertain future she would have with Valenty. How could they ever have a normal life; and even if peace came to the Mythos, where could they go, where she would not be singled out by those who mistrusted other realms, or wished to have other realms? If only Ansyl had utterly disappeared and his daughter had found a life in her home world. Surely the First Ones could have asked the Mythos for someone else.

Perhaps the High Mother saw her worried expression, because she said, "You must understand, Dreiza, that we had no idea how the root power would be invested. As it turned out, lightning was not a very good choice; the girl almost died. And the princip has had no end of trouble with her and doubtless has regretted her decision to bring her home."

Arlaty broke in. "But it was not really the princip's decision. She sent the messenger to bring the *father* back. Anastyna could not have known that he and his wife had kept a *child* at their posting."

"Yevliesza was a complete surprise." The High Mother chuckled. "Even to Kassalya, although who can say what the poor creature knows and does not know. In any case, here we have our newcomer. Recovered from lightning, gaining the favor of Anastyna, and fending off Nashavety's further depredations."

"Only to be sent into the embrace of the enemy," Dreiza grumbled.

"Which only happened," the High Mother reminded her, "because Anastyna did not know about her great gift. Yevliesza chose not to reveal it."

"If she even knows it has come to her," Dreiza said. "For how *could* she know?"

The High Mother answered. "That is simple, my daughter. Because Prince Tirhan asked her to create a new route to Alfan Sih. And she did."

"But we heard that she claimed at trial to have entered Alfan Sih through a normal gate!"

"Simply put, she lied."

"How can you be sure?" Dreiza asked. "Perhaps they did enter through a normal gate."

"I suppose that is possible. But she was present on what appears to be the very day or very near the day when a new crossing path was discovered, the new path to Alfan Sih. At this same time, Kassalya began having lucid premonitions about Yevliesza and outsized fears about the dangers she was in."

Dreiza tried to make sense of it all. The general populace did not know of Yevliesza's new power nor, it seemed, did Anastyna or Valenty. But the *satvadeya* knew. They had asked that someone receive that power. And, by the Deep, it was Yevliesza.

The High Mother nodded and repeated to Dreiza, "And so,

yes, for her own safety, she lied." As though the lie was of any import, Dreiza thought. Of course the girl had lied!

Lusanya blurted, "Not a very noble beginning for our great defender." General murmurs of agreement around the circle reinforced her remark.

"And yet," the High Mother went on, "she it is who can bring the realms to peace. She it is who by happenstance may be precisely the person we need. But she must find her strength. Her will to use her power."

"What is her wise course, then?" Dreiza asked, hoping for a good end to the story.

The Devi Ilsat looked at her hands clasped in her lap. "We do not know, my daughter. We did not think that far ahead."

There was no plan? They went into this dangerous undertaking without a plan? Dreiza was stupefied. "But is it not true that you raised no objection when she was sent to Volkia so that under duress she would grow in strength and also, seeing the full evil of the realm, grow in wisdom?"

"Oh," the High Mother said as though she had not thought of that. "Perhaps you are right, my daughter." She smiled benignly at Dreiza. "Perhaps, as you say, we must let this play out for the greater benefit of all."

Sofichka sucked at her teeth, muttering, half-asleep. "Unless they kill the poor thing. Then where are we?"

Irritated by the casual discussion of Yevliesza's death, Dreiza said, "If she needed to develop courage, we could have brought her to Zolvina and come up with tortures of our own."

"Ah," the Devi Ilsat said. "But that would have been interfering."

Chapter Thirty-Seven

Yevliesza's fingers cramped as she worked on the jacket sleeve. Her stitches were longer, sloppier, but the sleeve hem didn't have to last long. It must all be ready tomorrow night. She had the trousers, boots, cloak, and also the things she needed to take care of Breta.

It would all be ready. She put the jacket under the chair and went to the window to check the weather. A high wind had cleared the city of smoke and for once she could see blue sky and a high, bright sun. Massaging her tired hands, she imagined herself in Tanfred's carriage leaving Hapsigen, never to return. The weather was perfect, clear and dry.

The door rattled and Marshal Reinhart entered the room.

"I didn't hear you knock," she said.

He smiled, an extraordinarily unpleasant expression. Walking to the divan, he examined the green dress.

"You have chosen to sew it yourself. Unusual."

She ignored the remark. In the cream-colored parlor, his black uniform made him look like a dark creature, out of place in this refinement. The features of his face were mismatched, the nose and forehead too prominent, the chin too small, the eyes recessed as though taking cover. He was the chief spy for Volkia, as Valenty was for Numinat, and the difference between their features seemed an emblem of their true natures.

He dropped the fold of the dress, his face showing distaste for what he might see as feminine things. "You will take a walk with me, Mistress Yevliesza."

"What you have to say can be said here, I hope."

"You might indulge me, to walk up and down the hallway here." He looked around the room, as though his true purpose was to find the hidden uniform.

"All right," she quickly said. A very bad thought came to her. He had something awful to say to her, she felt sure, and had waited to say it until Albrecht had left that morning. So it was going to be something that would be especially upsetting.

He opened the door for her, and she preceded him into the hallway. It was deserted, as it so often was. She chided herself for being afraid to walk there with the man. She wished Martel or Breta or Tanfred was around. Even Albrecht. Reinhart led her toward the reception room.

"How are you finding your stay with us so far?" he asked, walking at her side, his hands clasped behind him.

"Challenging."

"Perhaps a bit harder than challenging? Or does deception come naturally to you?"

"Since it's your line of work, maybe you could tell *me*."

"You are working very hard at charm with everyone but me. Does it occur to you that this is rather the opposite of what you should do?"

"I'm sure you're impervious to my charm."

He smiled, showing gray teeth. "I am that."

They came to the reception room near the double doors, and he turned around, leading her back down the hall. "Of course you do realize that your relationship with Duke Tanfred is known to me. We have tolerated this effort on your part to befriend him."

"I think if you look deeper, you'll realize he's been trying to befriend *me*."

"Oh yes. Because you are the *Eibelung*. Which you have no doubt reinforced with him."

"He thought so from the beginning and has put pressure on me to become a primordialist."

"To *lead* the primordialists, more like. He is susceptible to you, because he thinks you may be the answer to his pathetic hopes. And you have encouraged this, perhaps even inviting him to your bed to persuade him. I advise you to stay away from him or I will be forced to take steps against you. You have already spied upon us." He looked at her, waiting for a reaction, which was not forthcoming. "Perhaps you remember going into the private wing and questioning Master Lothric about military matters. You must have been happy to find him in a condition that you could take advantage of."

She didn't like the fact that Albrecht had told him about that. It was more fuel for Reinhart's suspicions about her. And Martel was in danger about the affair, as well. "I didn't take advantage of Master Lothric. I kept him company for a few minutes. Harmless enough."

"Harmless," Reinhart repeated in a flat tone.

They had reached the door to the veranda and took a turn down the hall toward the game room.

"You should be more careful. The commandant is capable of indulging women, but he would be ruthless with you if you betray us. Do you understand?"

"Yes." She did understand. The understanding had been gnawing at her for days.

He stopped before the game room door. "But I would like for

you to be more aware of my . . . determination." He went to the windows and gestured for her to approach.

As he pulled back the curtains at the window, Yevliesza hesitated. Then she willed herself to approach the window.

A body hung on the wall of the courtyard, suspended by the neck with a rope.

Yevliesza drew in a shocked breath. The face was blackened, but she knew, knew . . .

Reinhart said softly. "You went to see the Master of Weapons. And Lieutenant Martel encouraged you to do so, unlocking the door. It took a few days before he admitted it. But eventually it was clear how you managed it."

She retreated into the room, placing a hand on the back of a chair to steady herself. "Did Albrecht . . . did he . . ."

"Approve it? Of course. Did you think your influence extended that far?" He shook his head at her apparent naïveté. "And if you are a spy of Numinat, if I find that you are seeking or finding things to use against us, I will hang you as well. Slowly."

With that, he left her. She sank to her knees. *Martel. Oh, Martel.* She put her head in her hands. Her body spasmed violently and she threw up in repeated lurches of her stomach.

After a time, she got to her feet and went to her apartment to find cloths to clean up the mess. Later, Breta found her wiping the carpet. The maid led her away from the game room, holding her arm, opening the parlor door, bringing her to sit in the chair with the uniform under it.

Yevliesza stared out the windows. Eventually, her gaze fell on the scissors. She imagined using them on her hand. If she was ever too cowardly to use them on her hand when it was necessary, she would think of Martel's death, and then it would be easy.

Chapter Thirty-Eight

In the great hall of her abode in the woods, Nashavety gazed at the dozens of subjects assembled before her. Every day she convened them, seated on the floor in case, in her ministrations, some of them collapsed.

Her hand pulsed with a lacerating pain, as though the flow of blood was gouging its way into her small finger. Her healers made efforts to soften the agony, but their gifts must be administered by touch, and that she could not bear.

The thing that protruded from her hand could not really be called a finger. It was a blackened growth, without joints, but it fit nicely into a glove so that she did not have to look at it. Not that she was vain of her looks. She knew what she looked like, thin as a hoe, with a face so wasted away that it could barely contain her features.

It had been more than two months since the maiming of her hand, and she was still wretchedly weak, not from the amputation, but from the extreme effort it took to recall her powers. She still needed attendants, one on each side, to help her walk, but she was getting stronger. In a few weeks she would continue her recovery in Hapsigen, though it would be very difficult to leave the house known as Drogeliv behind. She called it a house, but it was not only a pile of bricks, timber, and stone. It was the soul of the dark woods, the living center of an ancient evil, one so old it had come from the mundat.

The unwelcome thought sometimes came that she herself had infused the house with darkness. But it was not so. The mansion had always been the precinct of foul events. Its very halls—and attic, especially the attic—had been malevolent for many years. From what history she had been able to learn, it had always possessed a particular affinity for unusual practices because the first occupants had strayed rather far from . . . propriety.

When Drogeliv was built, a wealthy older man brought his young wife to live here. He had a penchant for cruelty and, with no one else to sate his needs, he used his wife, who over time went quite mad from loneliness and brutality. Unfortunately, the young wife bore several children, all of whom mysteriously died as babes. When her husband buried them in the woods, she could not bear it, but dug up each one in turn and brought them to the attic to tend to, in what secrecy she could muster. Eventually the wife, who was no longer young, drowned her husband in his bath —so it was said—and lived at Drogeliv to her allotted one hundred and fifty, when she hung herself from the chandelier in the very hall where Nashavety was now sitting.

She glanced up at the spreading iron arms of the chandelier. It would have been quite a feat to rig a rope from the fixture. Perhaps Drogeliv dipped it down for her.

In any case, when Nashavety took possession of the manor, it was primed for sorcery. One of her first actions was to use her elemental power to set up defenses at doors and windows. It was not long before the house began to respond by locking doors on its own and emitting noises if, say, a squirrel found access inside. Over time, Nashavety learned that Drogeliv could be trained. With a reward of food, which in its case meant power.

To fully enliven the house required several powers, ones she did not possess, but that were available to her: The birthright powers of her attendants. These she routinely extracted and, with the aptitude of her revived hand, guided into Drogeliv.

A spike of light burst from the hall windows, even though they were heavily draped. She winced at the intrusion. Her sun-induced headaches were so strong that at times she had to be held down lest, in her thrashing, she damage herself.

An attendant, noticing her discomfort, strode to the windows and adjusted the drapery. Then he took his place again, cross-legged on the floor.

Valenty's attack was never far from her mind, and she found herself reliving that. The stealing of Pyvel. The memory festered in her heart, that Valenty and his accomplice had dared to hunt her, had brazenly pierced her defenses to take what was hers. And that it should be Valenty! Valenty, the craven and weak. Now she saw that it had been an act, how he cultivated an air of debauchery, all the while being Anastyna's lackey and Yevliesza's defender. It would be sweet to extract a penalty for his deception.

And Yevliesza. Yes, the ruined girl who rose and rose in Numinat power, despite all of Nashavety's efforts. And a girl who bore *markings*. Extensive, elaborate—even beautiful—markings. The wings of deepest envy swept over her, touching her face with their light but unbearable touch. What did the transformed scars portend? She sought to know, but that was not the nature of powers, to speak, to answer questions. The only way to know was to pry the information out of the girl herself. But with her ensconced in the castle of Osta Kiya, it was not going to happen soon.

Foremost, however, she wanted to know how Valenty and the man with him had evaded the *house*. Even she was afraid of the great, hulking thing. She feared it had become something she might not entirely control. The animal viciousness of the thing was a warning that she could take things too far.

She started to laugh, but the skin around her mouth was tight as a belt. Take things too far? She had already gone down a long road of trespass, with bodies on every side. She it was who had taught Volkia how to enliven war machines. Once she had seen her finger re-growing, once she had, with a cool, darkened heart, resolved to break every taboo, she saw how powers could be directed into creatures, metal, and skin.

It was inspiring to see how far a little creativity could take you if you were not afraid to improvise.

As she looked out on her assembled servants, she allowed herself a moment of satisfaction. She had come back from Anastyna's terrible penalty, come back stronger than ever. And today she would enjoy the company of a prince of state.

Commandant Prince Albrecht would spend the day with her, conferring on the necessities of war. She looked forward to hearing of his endeavors. He was, she admitted to herself, a most interesting man, unafraid of her quest for mastery, determined to prevail by whatever means—whatever means she provided him.

In teaching him to use elemental power for war implements, she had won his complete allegiance. A productive trade with Albrecht von Treid, prince of this realm: her secret of elemental propulsive power for his shelter and protection. Eventually he would trade much more for her assistance, although for now he still thought himself in control. It would not be long before she was able to travel to Hapsigen. There she would be able to instruct him, and temper some of his untutored impulses.

He must master a more careful deployment of machines. There would be no point in conquering realms only to lose them in some kind of disastrous upheaval. One must tip toe up to the point, but not exceed it.

All in good time. For today they would catch up on things, at least for a few hours. He never spent the night in this place, not that she blamed him.

But now, to work. It was time for the infusion. Drogeliv had enormous feeding needs, since nurturing powers obtained in this way gradually leaked out.

Summoning her intention from the nether regions of her heart, she raised her left hand and reached toward her attendants. She traced her fingers over their heads in great circles and began to pull the Deep from them.

Chapter Thirty-Nine

"Two men on the roof," Kierach whispered.

On a moonless night Tirhan and Kierach took stock of Glenir mansion from a prominent hill overlooking it.

Tirhan responded, "Our archers will dispatch them first. Then we send two of ours up the side." The grappling hook would make a loud noise, but by that time the alarm would already be raised.

They had been watching since sunset, noting which rooms were lit by hearth or by manifesting. His men had scouted the other sides of the manor to identify defenses and anything they could see of shapes or shadows in the windows. Tirhan set a high priority on knowing which rooms his mother and sisters were held in.

Around them, crickets filled the darkness with their unending song. He had sixty-seven warriors as well as two dozen men from the local clan who had agreed to join their ranks. And eight creaturalists who might be the key to it all.

When Tirhan and his second descended the hill, they joined Morwen, her hair braided and bound, her knives in their harness.

She came to Tirhan's side and would not leave him until the fight was done.

Tirhan and Kierach conferred with the scouts who had just returned.

"Three guards patrol the grounds, my lord," young Bridan reported. "Another at the main door."

"Wolves?" Tirhan asked.

"Four, as we expected."

Demyr, their strongest warrior, came forward for final instructions. He would lead the first attack, approaching from the east side to distract the defenders from the primary attack, a direct assault on the main door to the south.

Lodwyn, who had been huddled a few paces away with the group of elders, approached. With his height and bulk, he looked a capable warrior, not the contemplative he had become.

Kierach nodded to Lodwyn. "Our scouts have confirmed that there are four wolves. Once you separate the creatures from their controllers, we will take out the guards. Ignore us, and do what you came for."

Lodwyn turned to Tirhan. "We fend off the creature power," he told him, "but we will not kill."

"That is service enough," Tirhan said. "But there will be deaths this night. Once the wolves are freed, my warriors will fight. The wolves stay close to their guards. Let Bridan show you where their positions are, and you can decide how to assign your people—two on each wolf to break the controller's power."

"I will," Lodwyn said. "But the best we can do is to bring the wolves to our side. Thus we do not so much break creature power as replace it with our own. Once we have a creature, we will lead it away and try to release it."

Tirhan noted the *try*. A wraith wolf might turn on its new captors, but Tirhan's force was not large enough to spare defenders for the elders. They would take the wolves into the wood and hope that they valued freedom more than revenge.

Lodwyn motioned for the seven other elders to follow him toward the manor, including three aged women who had blackened their hair for camouflage.

"All in place?" Kierach asked Demyr.

"Aye, my lord. Waiting behind our warriors, the men of Angewyst, who lend bulk to our attack. They are not fighters, but shepherds. Still, their voices will join our battle cry and create the noise of a larger force." Demyr gave a feral grin. "We will get their attention."

The group dispersed in three directions: To the manor's west side for scaling the wall, to the east for the first wave, and to the south where they must breach the front doors, with Kierach commanding. But first, the wraith wolves.

Tirhan and Morwen crawled forward to crouch behind one pair of elders, who waited for the signal to bring their creature power to bear on the guard's wraith wolf. The wolf seemed no more than a puff of fog at the door, but when it fully entered the world, it would be a fearsome killer.

By Tirhan's side, four men with the improvised ram, the trunk of a small oak. Arrayed behind them, twenty-five warriors covered in cloaks and invisible even to Tirhan. They made not a sound as they all waited for the signal.

Tirhan reached for Morwen's hand, and she gripped it hard, not looking at him, her attention all on the dark zone between them and the wall of the manor and the deeper black of the portico. With the moon just a remnant, most of the light was shed by the stars that filled the sky.

I love you, he wanted to say to her in case he could never say it again. But he knew she would not approve such an unwarlike utterance.

The signal came as the hoot of an owl, faint and eerie. Several archers rose to their feet in the field behind Tirhan. Arrows flew at the sentries on the roof.

The soldier at the door gave a warning cry, and a wraith wolf materialized from the porch, leaping down the steps. It raced toward the archers, as arrows flew from Volkish archers on the roof. From the east came a great roar as Demyr's force charged forward.

Two elders stood and reached out their hands toward the wolf, now plunging through the brambles as though the underbrush did not even exist. At the same time, the men with the ram rushed forward. Behind Tirhan came the screams of men wounded or slain.

More archers appeared on the roof. More than two, enough to overcome Tirhan's men who must even now be climbing the wall. A crash of caving wood sounded from the portico like the tread of giants.

Arrows rained down from the roof, but few found a target in the darkness. The Volkish soldiers on the roof, however, were outlined against the stars, and Tirhan's bow men let fly, finding their targets with more accuracy and driving the archers on the roof behind the parapets.

By now the doors were flattened and Kierach led the men forward, plunging into the gap, followed by Tirhan and Morwen. In the large entry hall only a few soldiers met them, rushing down the open staircase, swords drawn, but outnumbered ten to one. Kierach met the first one and the ring of sword on sword clanged through the hall, along with the grunts and cries of the combatants. With the staircase cleared, Tirhan and Morwen raced up to the next floor. He looked right along an open hallway with a wooden railing. He noted that Bridan, who was to lead several warriors to the left in the search for the queen, was still engaged down in the hall.

A great shout drew his attention.

Looking past the railing he saw, striding from an interior room, a tall, inhuman creature. It burst into the hall, swiping one of Tirhan's men to the side like a cup from a table. In dismay, he saw it was an iron cladder. His heavy stride shook the floor. An Alfan warrior kicked a table over in the cladder's path, but the armored man thrust it aside, heading for Kierach, who had dispatched his opponent and turned to face the cladder, taller than he by an arm's length.

Tirhan twisted around and rushed down the stairs to join the group now converging on the cladder. Morwen pounded after him, shouting "No! Leave them!"

But Tirhan motioned her to follow. As he came to the bottom of the stairs, he grabbed her arm so that he could be heard in the pandemonium. "Warding, Morwen!"

One of his men had the same idea and raised his left hand toward the beast, but the cladder lowered one of his arms and released a fountain of fire, felling the warrior.

Fire. Not only impossible armor, but explosive fire.

Morwen hissed, "Find the queen!"

"No," Tirhan said. "We have this creature to face, be it now or later." He charged into the group that had begun circling the cladder as he ponderously turned his head to see their numbers and positions.

"Warders!" Tirhan called, and Morwen ran to Kierach's side, deflecting a stream of fire that would have cut him in half.

As two other warders joined her effort, they shouted, "Shield, shield!" The cladder stood swaying for a moment, then lumbered away from them, lifting a table and pushing off the wards that had entangled him. The warders separated, coming at the cladder from three directions.

Tirhan could add nothing to the warding and turned to the stairs again, taking them two at a time to the upper story. No sounds of the fight in this direction, but he heard women's screams. He tore down the hallway toward the sounds.

Around a corner came two soldiers, swords drawn and, seeing him, advanced.

In the narrow hallway, Tirhan met the first one, slashing down his weapon on the opposing sword. His sword slid down the blade of his opponent barely deflecting it but striking the man's hand. With a yell of pain, the soldier dropped the weapon and, crouching, jammed his head into Tirhan's chest, sending both of them to the floor. Struggling to raise his sword, Tirhan braced himself against the wall and, as the soldier stepped forward to strike, pierced the man's neck with his sword. Pulling his sword free, he turned to meet the second man's sword thrust. Tirhan heard his sisters crying out in the room just behind him. "Cadris!" he shouted to his oldest sister. He traded blows with the soldier, stepping over the body of the dead one, blood pumping from his neck.

Tirhan's new opponent was strong and fought furiously, driving Tirhan back along the corridor, gaining speed in the hopes of making him lose his balance. He staggered backward under the unrelenting blows. He met them, but he was weakening.

A crash came from behind the soldier, and someone burst out of the door where his sister had been calling him. Tirhan's opponent took no notice of the sound and, advancing for the final blow, raised his sword. Tirhan twisted out of his way and, as the man staggered, pushed him over the railing.

He turned to find Cadris, with a sword in her hand. Her pale gown was streaked with blood and her hands, covered in gore from wresting the sword from the dead soldier's hands.

"This way, Tirhan!" she shouted as she rushed to the next door down the hall. She nodded at him to break it down and, with a vicious crash of his boot, the door gave way. His mother waited inside, armed with a candle holder as long as his arm. She dropped it and came to his arms.

He quickly hugged her, then turned to Cadris. "Where is Hanavar?"

"Back in our room!"

As they turned, Bridan had already found Hanavar and was leading her down the hall. "Quickly now, Mother," Tirhan said, gripping her arm. She nodded to him, knowing that his men were still fighting for their lives.

They hurried down the hall to the railing overlooking the hall. From that vantage point, Tirhan saw the iron cladder lying immobile on the floor. As he and Bridan led the queen and his sisters down the stairs, Cadris moved ahead of them. She carried the bloody sword, giving the impression that she had used it and planned to again.

"Which are the enemy?" she asked Tirhan.

"The ones in uniform, but kindly give your sword to Bridan."

"I shall not," she said, looking around for someone to kill.

The hall and its contents were in ruins. The iron cladder lay on his back as though someone had tipped him over. But he did not stir. Five of Tirhan's men lay strewn and bleeding. Kierach was kneeling by one of them, talking to him. Four bodies, then.

Tirhan went to Kierach's side. "I have Queen Gwenid and my sisters. Is the manor secure?" He knew it was, because Kierach would not be tending to the wounded otherwise.

"Aye, my lord." Kierach looked to one of the warriors still standing. "Bring the horses, quickly." The man nodded and strode to the door.

Morwen was crouched over the cladder. No one else approached the dead cladder, fearful of the diabolics that contaminated it. With a yank she pulled out a knife that had gone deep into one of the helmet eye gaps. It came out bloody. She wiped it off on a tasseled pillow and returned it to a sheath in her knife strap. The blood proved a man was inside the heavy armor. Tirhan had known that men propelled the cladders, yet how could they?

It would be impossible to move a single pace with such weight of iron.

Kierach glanced at the queen, standing at the bottom of the stairs with her daughters. "A glorious day for Alfan Sih, my prince," he said with quiet emotion.

Tirhan nodded. "How many lost?"

"We do not know yet. At least six." He glanced at the machine, lying on its back as though asleep. The machine that had killed four of his men.

"My lord," came a voice from the entry. "The horses are ready."

Tirhan went to his mother and sisters. "You must ride now, fast and hard. Are you able?"

"We are, my son," his mother said, smiling, because she was an expert rider.

"One of you should come with me. It is best that we separate for the long journey back to camp."

Cadris volunteered, and the queen nodded her agreement.

Tirhan quickly embraced Hanavar, wanting to hold her fast, but knowing that the Volkish would soon be arriving and wanting the royals back. He led them outside, where Demyr waited with an escort of warriors for the queen and Hanavar.

As Hanavar mounted her horse, he turned to his mother. "Your freedom will give every Alfan hope. I have thought about you every day since my return, but we were not strong enough. You know the manor had wraith wolves ensorcelled?"

By her expression, she had not known. "Is it even possible?"

"We saw them, and they were under creature control." He paused. "I was told to be patient before I attacked Glenir. To wait until our own people with creature power could free them."

She cocked her head in confusion. "You were told? Who orders a king-to-be?"

He lowered his voice. "One whose influence you called upon."

A smile lit her face, and age fell away from her. Her hair was streaked with white, but her eyes were a pale green, like silverwood leaves, and she looked no older than forty summers. "My son, it will all be on your shoulders now." She put her hand on his forearm, her eyes glittering. "You are ready."

"Still, Mother, the clans do not know me well. But since they know you, they will all take heart. So ride well, but hard."

She mounted her horse with assurance and accepted a skin of water to strap over the heavy jacket she had been given. Hanavar looked stunned and very small on her mount, though she was all of fourteen years. Tirhan approached, giving her encouragement for the ride. "I will see you very soon," he told her.

Demyr was already mounted on a stallion barely under control in all the chaos of the battle aftermath.

Turning to him, Tirhan asked, "Were any of the elders hurt?"

"One of the women is dead, Lodwyn says. But the wolves have gone home."

Home. Wherever that was.

The queen and her entourage headed to the tree line, already outlined against a faint gray dawn.

Now that most of Tirhan's family was gone, Morwen approached Tirhan, nodding an acknowledgment to Cadris.

"The full count of the fallen is ten, my lord," Morwen said, "if Bridan's brother Cynod recovers from his wounds."

Tirhan absorbed the news. Harsh losses. But they might well have been worse, with nothing to show for the sacrifices. He caught his sister's gaze and said, "Princess Cadris, this is Morwen, my shield and foremost warrior, but for Kierach and Demyr."

Morwen bowed her head.

"You are a fighter?" Cadris asked, noting with surprise her sheathed knives and leather trousers.

"I do my part, Princess," Morwen said wiping a splatter of blood from her cheek.

Tirhan's men brought forward mounts for them.

Onto another horse they secured the body of Rhibina, the elder who was killed by the wraith wolf. Lodwyn held the reins.

"Will you take her body back to Talfyn Sid?" Tirhan asked.

"No, my lord. We will bury her among the silverwood trees. There is a stand nearby. It is at least an hour out of your way. We will return the horse."

"No need, Lodwyn. I am coming with you."

The largest contingent of Tirhan's forces were leaving the area surrounding the manor, heading into the woods where they had left their horses.

With Tirhan's smaller group came his chief advisor, his sister, and his lover.

❦

THEY FOUND THE SILVERWOOD GROVE ON THE EAST SIDE OF A rounded hill in the valley of Llanaden. The tree branches were gilded in ice from a recent snowfall that had melted and then quickly frozen. Errant gusts of wind stirred them, creating a bright, tinkling sound. With the silver of the trunks, the copse seemed a slice of another world, devoid of color, but shining white.

Tirhan's escort would have dug the grave, but the elders chose to do it themselves, with Lodwyn digging the hardest with one of the small shovels that the partisans carried for such duties.

When the grave was ready, one of the women began to sing, and her voice was sweet, carried in the breeze. Wrapped in her cloak, Rhibina was brought into her burial place in Lodwyn's arms, the strongest of the elders. Another voice took up the song as they covered Rhibina with soil, and then, one by one, others took up the song, and when Lodwyn nodded at Cadris, she took the next line of the burial dirge, her voice high and strong. Finally Lodwyn took the song, his bass voice discordant, since he could not carry a tune.

When they had sung her to rest, Lodwyn said to Tirhan in a lowered voice, "I doubt any other elder will ever have a king at their burial."

"If I am ever a king, it will be thanks to Rhibina. And all of you."

When they separated into two groups for their departure, Tirhan said to Lodwyn, "I did not think one of the wraith wolves would turn on its rescuer."

Lodwyn smiled. "It did not turn on her. It ended her life in this world and then left with her, taking her to the next."

Chapter Forty

Yevliesza woke far before the bedroom drapes were framed with the dawn. It was no good to sleep, with thoughts like shards of glass stabbing at her nerves. Today they were leaving. Tonight.

Throwing the covers off, she entered the bathroom and washed, trying to calm herself. As she looked at her wan face in the mirror, she thought of Martel, kind and brave, hanging on the wall of the enclosure. Reinhart had done it, and Albrecht had approved it. But she had played a part in his death, a thought that sickened her to her core. And this might not be the end of the bloodshed. But these thoughts could not help Martel whom she had to banish from her mind at least for today, when she would need every ounce of her courage and attention.

She pulled on her robe and, at the window, pulled the heavy curtains back to look out over the city, into the far distance, imagining herself far from this palace of vipers. Her thoughts went to Valenty and the bittersweet longing to hold him and be held. The need to tell him what she was and share with him the burden of it. He would know what to do. She thought he would know. But just to be with him. Dear God, to be with him.

In the parlor, she sat down to sew on the jacket until Breta arrived with the breakfast tray. She worked on the hem of the second sleeve, trying not to have the stitches show on the outside.

Albrecht's clock was ticking with maddening constancy, sounding strangely loud in her ears. It was 7:16. What harm would there be in stopping its mechanism, since she would never see Albrecht again? But Breta would notice.

When Breta came in with the breakfast tray, Yevliesza nearly cried out in startlement.

She pushed the jacket under the chair and rose. The sleeve extended from underneath. She kicked it back in. Once. Twice.

"Porridge and fruit today, miss." Breta said, as she laid the food out. "And a round of bread just out of the oven."

Yevliesza went to the table and cut a piece of bread, as though she was hungry. "Fragrant," she cooed.

"The cook's savory bread. It is the best, miss." She turned to the bedroom. "I will make up the bed."

"Oh, you know, Breta, I think I will do that myself this morning."

At the maid's surprised look, she went on. "I was used to doing so at home, and sometimes I long for the ways I used to do things. If that is all right?"

"Of course, miss." She looked around for something to do.

"You can come back for the tray."

Breta looked at the dress lying on the divan. "Maybe . . ."

"No, let's not sew this morning. I want to enjoy my breakfast and have a few peaceful hours." She took a seat at the table and added, "I would like to see you this evening, after dinner. I have a surprise for you."

"Really, miss?"

"It's a small gift. To say thank you for all the help on the gown."

"Oh. Thank you, then."

"You will be sure to come by after dinner?"

"Yes, miss." She headed for the door, then stopped, turning back to Yevliesza. "I'll help you to dress in a little while."

"Oh, no need. I'll wear my plain dress today. But we can work on the gown after lunch."

When Breta finally left, Yevliesza let out a long sigh. She hoped she hadn't seemed tense in that interaction. Making the bed, that was to assure herself that Breta wouldn't find the things hidden there: the finished uniform trousers, the pair of boots that Tanfred had found, and the sleeping potion.

She ate her breakfast without noticing it, her concentration on the sequence of events—a choreography, really—to reach the boundary gate.

Tick, tick.

First, the uniform jacket. She had nearly finished the sleeves. Next, she'd move the buttons over an inch or two to tighten the fit. That should be done by lunchtime. Then she would place the jacket with the trousers under the bed.

The afternoon would be taken up with sewing on the green dress with Breta. It would be excruciating, but there was no help for it.

After dinner, Breta would return with a pitcher of wine as requested. Yevliesza would pour two glasses and send her into the bedroom for her surprise present on the dresser, the furthest piece of furniture from the door.

She would have only seconds to stir the powder into one of the wine glasses. Then she would act the cheerful part of having a companion to drink with. Breta's present would be opened, thank-yous received, and glasses raised to the gift . . . and to every other cause that Yevliesza could think of. If Breta thought the wine tasted odd, Yevliesza would declare it delicious and say that she hoped Breta was not disappointed with the quality. The girl would probably drink more of it to prove that it was fine. Tanfred had assured her that Breta needn't drink all of it, that the potion was enough to put a grown man down for the night.

Once Breta was asleep, Yevliesza would drag her to the spare bedroom and bind her hands and feet with ribbon, gagging her with some torn lining from the green dress. Then, in the bathroom she would use the scissors to cut off her hair, taking pains to cut the sides and back very close.

Then, the signal at the window. Tanfred had supplied a flint for her to strike a flame. With a lit candle on the windowsill of one of the windows, Tanfred would see it from one of the downstairs windows perpendicular to her wing.

At that point he would inform his coachman that he had received word of an urgent matter, and they would have to leave Hapsigen immediately, bringing a guard with them. It would take some time to bring the horses out, during which time Yevliesza would dress in the uniform and rumple the bed, throwing back the cover, to make it look like she had been wakened in the middle of the night. Not that this would delay pursuit. They would certainly find Breta almost immediately.

While the coachman was seeing the two pairs of horses put in harness, Tanfred would collect Yevliesza at her apartment, helping her to finish with the haircut if necessary. Then the duke and she would descend the nearest staircase to the yard, and she would disappear into the carriage while his man was preoccupied with the horses, their gear, and supplies.

Over and over in the last few days she had been picturing the carriage speeding through the dark streets of Hapsigen, the horses thundering, the jostling carriage, the fog and smoke of the city parting for them as the horses charged on for the city wall checkpoint and the road beyond.

And all this was possible because of Tanfred Wilhoffen, a man she had at first pitied for his delusions and for what she had taken as his thoughtless support of Prince Albrecht. But one thing she had never questioned, and that was his love of his country. Now he was taking on a desperate action that showed a calm courage that amazed her. And that she intended to emulate.

The clock ticked on, sounding now like a rat's claws on the window.

THE LUNCH TRAY WAS CLUTTERED WITH DISHES AND USED utensils, the dome sitting beside it like a great silver beetle. Yevliesza had pushed the food around the plate enough that it might look like she had eaten some of it, but her appetite had fled.

It was 12:49.

With the alterations finished, she had nothing whatsoever to do. It was impossible to sit still. She paced around the room, finally stopping at the window seat to check the weather—windy and clear.

A commotion in the hallway drew her attention, and she turned to the door, her chest tightening in anxiety.

The apartment door opened without a knock. Albrecht stood there, a faint smile on his face, but eyes, so cold. Something had happened.

Her first thought was Tanfred. Had he been arrested? But things could not collapse so suddenly, could they? Behind Albrecht, a soldier, both he and the prince in riding gear.

"How is the gown coming along, Yevliesza?" Albrecht asked.

She swallowed the bile that was building up in her throat. "As you see. It is not finished."

"And will not be."

A small place under her rib cage swelled, full of fear. Holding an aloof pose, she watched Albrecht, her thoughts frenzied, seeking refuge from what was coming.

He strode into the room and headed for her, picking up the

green dress on the divan as he came. He cast it onto the floor behind him. Grabbing her arm, he dragged her to the divan, pushing her onto it.

He stood before her in his riding clothes and cloak, a glacial calm in his eyes. "You are not the creature you have been pretending to be. All this while you have lied to me, a castle of lies. You have used subterfuge and cunning, betraying my every trust."

"Not true, my lord."

He struck her across the face, a blow that sent her to her knees. She lost the capacity to think for a few moments as the pain took over her mind. Her hair, dislodged from its net, curtained off her face, giving her some refuge from the dark lord who stood before her.

"Say that you have betrayed my trust," he demanded. "I want to hear what truth sounds like from you." He bent down and lifted her chin with his hand. "Say the words, but only if they are true."

"I betrayed your trust." She was afraid to lie, even though all her instincts told her to hide, to keep him at bay. What did he know? Had he extracted the truth—every truth—from Duke Tanfred?

She looked up at him. He stood so tall in front of her, he might as well have been the army of Volkia. But he didn't need the army or a single guard to help him. All by himself he could kill her, easily.

"Do you have an accomplice?"

"Yes."

"Who?"

"Lieutenant Martel."

"Martel. I see." He turned away and walked a few paces. He wore a winter cloak; his boots, splattered with mud. He threw the cloak on the window seat. Underneath he wore heavy traveling clothes, including a padded outer jacket with a leather cross strap and sheath for a short sword. As he removed the harness and sword, placing them on top of his cloak, the awful, horrid truth settled in for a long stay. Her escape was ruined. In a few more hours she and Tanfred could have been gone from the nightmare of Hapsigen. A few hours. But now, gone.

She was still kneeling on the floor. Taking her arm, Albrecht brought her to her feet and pushed her onto the divan. He fetched a chair from along the wall and brought it to sit opposite her.

Crossing his legs in what seemed an offhand manner, he gazed at her for a long while. Finally he said, "This is all so unnecessary. You could have had much from me. Instead, I will have much from you. Eventually."

Her mind contracted into a small, hard fist. It was over. It was all over. He would maim or kill her or both. Yevliesza thought that he actually looked regretful.

"I have been on a visit," Albrecht went on. "You will recognize the name of the place. Drogeliv." She remained silent. "No? Perhaps you will recognize the name of its inhabitant. Lady Nashavety."

Despite herself, Yevliesza let out a small moan. Yes, Nashavety had gone over to them. But now they had discussed her. Nashavety had her in her sights again.

"Since your people drove the lady out, she came to us for shelter. We welcomed her, gladly. Today, when she learned that you were in my keeping, she told me some very interesting things."

Through her panic, Yevliesza searched her mind, trying to remember what the malwitch actually knew. But Albrecht was speaking again.

"First, that day you and I met in the crossings, you had not been in the Kingdom of Nubiah. You had been in Alfan Sih. You admitted as much at a trial that your princip held after you fled Numinat. You had come into the protection of Lord Tirhan, and your story was that you and he managed to get past Volkish guards at a gateway. It is not likely that you entered Alfan Sih this way. But we will come to that."

A knock at the door. "The maid, my lord," came the guard's voice.

"She may enter."

Breta came into the room, eyes wide with alarm. She stopped dead when she saw Prince Albrecht. "My lord," she whispered, curtseying and noting Yevliesza's hair fallen around her shoulders.

Albrecht gestured for her to approach.

"Bring a pitcher of water, Breta. And a cup for the guard outside." He eyed the green dress lying on the floor. "Take the gown on your way out and dispose of it."

She curtsied, looking lost. As she left, she took the castoff gown, averting her eyes from the guest who was now obviously a prisoner.

During Albrecht's interaction with the maid, Yevliesza let despair fall over her. Nashavety had certainly told him about the strange markings on her back.

It was not exactly the end of the world. But it felt like it.

Chapter Forty-One

A lbrecht had taken off his outer jacket and sat once again facing Yevliesza, now biting his lower lip as he watched her, obviously readjusting his view of her. She was no longer an inexperienced young woman in over her head, but a capable spy who had fooled him into thinking he was winning her over.

"And now we come to Lord Valenty," Albrecht said.

Her breathing came to a halt. She must have looked dismayed, because he snorted a laugh.

"You must tell me what he was doing in Drogeliv. It was very curious that he found Nashavety and did not attack her."

She was astonished. "He is in Volkia?" His silence demanded an answer. "I . . . don't know." She tried to understand what she had just heard. "Valenty is . . . he is in Volkia?"

Albrecht pursed his lips, watching her with some amusement. "It does not greatly matter. But if you hoped he had escaped Volkia by now, you will be disappointed. I have alerted the boundary gateways to keep close watch for three Numinasi men. He and someone else broke into the house. And took the young-ster away, the one that had been your servant."

Now the situation was completely bewildering. "Pyvel?"

"If that is his name."

How could Pyvel have been captured? And Valenty had rescued him?

"What is Valenty doing in Volkia?" Albrecht asked.

"I don't have any idea. It was carefully concealed. They said —Valenty said—he was going to inspect the boundary gates. And then I was sent to you to apologize, and I never knew anything different." The palace word was that he had a mission to inspect defenses. But he had revealed to her that he was going to Norslad. Was that a lie? Or had he even said that?

Albrecht casually said, "It does not matter now. He will never get out of Volkia. And if he comes here . . ." He shrugged. "That would save us the trouble of apprehending him.

"You and your princip can rest assured that his attack on Drogeliv, on Volkia, will not go unanswered. When we capture him, he will hang as a spy." Sardonically, he said, "I am sorry if you favored him."

"But can you mean to hang him, when so little damage was done?"

"He was in civilian dress, as was his companion."

"But we are not at war!"

"Oh, but we are. Numinat has declared war against us."

All the life seemed to leave her, her breath only a meaningless rise and fall of her chest. *Valenty. Valenty.*

"You love him." Albrecht said. "I am sorry, Yevliesza."

She sank further into the divan, pierced by the thought of losing him, a sadness so keen she no longer cared what would happen to herself.

Breta came in with a tray bearing a jug of water and two glasses. She put it down on the small dining table and left quietly.

Albrecht went to the table and poured two glasses of water. Returning, he handed Yevliesza one of them, and she took a few sips. She wanted to curl up on the couch and close her eyes and slip away. The world was a heavy burden, and she had done her best. It was enough. How sweet it would be to not suffer it any longer.

"Yevliesza," he gently said. "We are not done yet."

She looked up at him hopelessly.

"Show me your back."

It made no difference what he saw. Mechanically, she got to her feet and turned her back to him. She began unbuttoning the front of her dress. When she finished, she tugged on the sleeves and pulled the dress off her left shoulder and arm and then took enough of the material in her hand to pull the sleeve off her right arm. With the garment now hanging down at her waist, she took the straps of her shift and drew them off her shoulders, letting the shift fall.

He approached her to look more closely. "What manner of sorcery . . ." he whispered. His hand pressed against her back, rubbing her skin, making her shiver with revulsion. Lifting her right arm, he examined the path of the patterning up to her neck.

After a time, he pulled the shift back up to her shoulders, and she pushed her hands into the sleeves of the black Numinasi dress, buttoning it, comforted by its snug fit. She sat down and faced him again.

"I am sorry to have required you to do this."

Despite the fact that she didn't care anymore what he did, she was relieved to think he was done with the disrobing.

Once he had resumed his seat, he demanded, "What are these markings?"

"I don't know."

"What do you *think* they are?"

During the past weeks she had decided on something to say if a situation ever came to this point. There was one thing she might plausibly claim it to be.

"I can't be sure, but maybe the markings are a sign of a second power, besides aligns."

He raised an eyebrow.

"I think that maybe my late investment of power came to me in a lightning strike when I first came to Numinat and rode on a dactyl to Osta Kiya. You can ask Nashavety. She probably believes that part. Then I received the gift of the aligns, but I always thought I had a second power. It is either taking more time or is permanently blocked."

"Which power?"

"Verdure. My markings look like tendrils of a vine. I think that I am forever branded with a second power that won't come to me—or has not yet come to me. I am therefore, as Nashavety always said, deformed. She isn't wrong about *everything*."

He crossed his arms, resting his chin on his fist, absorbing this story, watching her, perhaps enjoying finally getting all the answers, or confident that they would come.

"We have plenty of time to explore these things, so we shall see."

By *time*, did he mean under torture? She was afraid of that, but not unduly so. It would happen and eventually it would be over, one way or another.

"So then, Yevliesza. The new passage to Alfan Sih. You know nothing about that, even though you and Tirhan entered the realm through that path?"

"I thought it was a secret path."

"So you *were* in Alfan Sih."

"Of course."

He casually nodded, fully in command, relentless in his inter-rogation. "Here is how it is going to be, Yevliesza," he said. "Soon Nashavety will join me here. When she does, everything will change. Marshal Reinhart will be privy to all she knows and all her opinions as well. We will be, we are, at war with Numinat.

I know that you are loyal to your kingdom. I respect that. You are grateful that they accepted you back, grateful that a high Numinasi lord took you in. You undertook a mission to placate me and then took advantage of knowledge that came your way. I will not say *spying*. That is a word we will not use. Because I choose not to.

"So. Do you see how your position has changed? That everything is different now?"

She nodded.

"You may not know much, but whatever you do know, that you will share with me. Therefore you will stay here. You have value to me. I will treat you well, if I can. If your power, that second power that you think your patterning means, comes to you, you are now under an obligation to tell me. For your life." He paused. "Yes?"

"Yes." But once she cut away her finger, none of it would matter.

"When my military advisors know the extent of your duplicity, as Nashavety will certainly inform them, they will demand punishment. I can protect you from the worst of those outcomes. Torture. Hanging. I can protect you from Lady Nashavety, who has a profound hatred of you, but that can happen only if she and Reinhart and others perceive that we have a . . . close relationship. A personal relationship.

"Do you understand what I am saying?"

She would share his bed. So that he could keep Reinhart from practicing his sadism and Nashavety joining in. And it was not going to end. She would be living in hell.

"Do you see how it has to be?"

She did see. She supposed she was lucky. He was going to protect her. "Yes, my lord," she answered.

"We will begin with that," he snapped. "You will call me by my name. There will be no false formality, no holding yourself aloof. All that is past. You will give respect to Marshal Reinhart. You will cease leading Duke Tanfred to think you are some legendary personage. All those things are over now." He raised an eyebrow.

"I understand."

"I do not relish a forced relationship. You are proud and would find ways to make me regret my protection. So, I have an offer to make you. It concerns Valenty."

When he was sure he had her complete attention, he said, "I am willing to pardon him, let him and his two companions leave Volkia. Provided that you come to me. Come to me with a full heart." He grimaced. "Or as full a heart as you can manage. No resignation, no long-suffering attitudes. You would come to me . . . in gratitude, knowing what your and Valenty's fate might have been."

"And so you would not force me with creature power," she shot back, "to fawn on you and cringe when you frowned."

In his eyes, she saw a flare of anger. He set his mouth. "And no sarcasm, Yevliesza. I know this will be terribly difficult for you. But I do not care."

He stood. "Well?"

"How can I trust that you won't kill him?"

"I give you my word of honor."

She didn't dare question that, of all things. "You could have had me at any time. Why all this elaborate reasoning?"

"Because I would not have had you. Not in any way that was pleasing to me. This will be a simple trade. Valenty's life for your body and your pride."

She stared at the floor, trying to collect her thoughts, to see a way out, to make her way through danger as she had been doing ever since she had come to Volkia, ever since she arrived in the Mythos. But there was nothing to figure out. It was simple. A simple trade.

"Yes, then."

He took a sip of water and placed the glass down on the side table. Then he stood and walked to the divan, taking her by arm and raising her to her feet. "Is there any reason I should wait?"

"No, Albrecht."

He led her to the bedroom, closing the door behind them.

If he touched her, she would pull away. Push him away. But none of that was going to work or be tolerated. She turned to him and put her hand on the back of his neck. She had to do this, had to be the one who came to him, not like a whore, but with as much heartfulness as she could bring to it, or pretend to.

She came into his embrace. The smell of him was of sweat and horseflesh and leather. She clung to him, not even knowing what to do next. Kiss him, she supposed. He ran his hands through her hair, caressing the back of her head, then bringing his mouth to hers, he kissed her so forcefully that he backed her against the door.

After a time, he stepped away and unbuttoned his shirt, flinging it on the bed. Then he began undoing the buttons on her dress, and soon the gown was in a pile around her ankles, and he was helping her step out of the volume of it. Gently, his hands went to her face, down her neck, cupping her breasts.

"I haven't been with a man before," she whispered.

"Valenty was your lover."

"No. He would have been, but no, not yet."

He paused, regarding her now at arms' length. Incredibly, she realized that this mattered to him.

"Perhaps you would rather wait," he said. "To be sure in your own mind."

But she was sure. She would trade her body in an instant for Valenty's life.

Albrecht was keeping his distance, looking at her, thinking

whatever his complex thoughts were about women. About her. "Yevliesza. I can give you time to consider."

"No. Please, Albrecht." She didn't want him to go back on their bargain.

"Well, then. You can give yourself to me in other ways. I will not take your virginity until you are ready, but we can still be lovers."

Lovers. If that was what he wanted to call it. She nodded, and he took her into his arms, in an embrace like a vise.

"Albrecht," she whispered into his chest. "Tell me what you like."

"I will," he said. He pulled her shift off her shoulders. It floated to the floor.

PART IV
A GIFT OF VERDURE

Chapter Forty-Two

Turning before the mirror, Yevliesza tried to recognize herself.

She wore a blue gown, edged in white rabbit fur at the high collar. The garish blue was a color no Numinasi woman would ever wear, halfway between dark and light. It was the only gown in the wardrobe that covered her neck. Not that it mattered anymore.

Her hair fell long in back with side braids fastened behind to hold her hair away from her face. She tried on a smile, but it turned into an awful parody. She belonged to Commandant Prince Albrecht and her clothes had to please him. No black dress, no severe hair style, no longer who she had ever been.

Another thing she saw in her face was anger. Disgust at this reflection of her indentured self. Fury at Albrecht who pretended she had volunteered for this, a pretense she had to maintain, in intimacy with him or at meals, whether alone or, as tonight, with guests. This pretense offended her almost as much as having to touch him. He had decided not to take her completely—what he self-righteously called her virginity. But it was degrading just the same.

Her maid fussed with the gown's skirt, adjusting the drape this way and that.

"Enough, Leni!" she snapped.

"It must be perfect, though."

"If you think the tailor erred, he can fix it tomorrow."

Ignoring this, Leni reached for the fabric again, and Yevliesza stalked away from her, heading for the door. It would be reported if she was rude, so glancing at the mantel clock, she said, "I don't want to be late." Two raps on the door summoned the guard to escort her.

As the two of them made their way to the formal dining room, she discreetly looked down every corridor, in every room with an open door, hoping to see Tanfred. The headquarters palace was engaged in the business of war even into the evening hours now. She tried not to be caught looking for a man with sandy hair and a broad, friendly face, in the garb of a duke.

The uniform for her thwarted plan of escape, formerly stashed under the parlor chair, was now shoved underneath her mattress. If they found it, she thought she wouldn't be able to bear it. But after everything that had happened, it seemed a small matter to lose a disguise. After all, she had lost her self-respect.

Another person she looked for on the brief walk was Breta. Just before they arrived at the dining room, she spied her, carrying a tray of empty glasses.

She stopped and her guard did as well. "May I speak with that maid, corporal? She was my servant."

He gestured to the dining room, about to say no. She thought he hadn't understood her very well. "Can I just thank her?"

He considered this, then nodded, saying something in Volkish, which was likely, *be fast about it.*

Hurrying to Breta, who had turned away upon seeing her, Yevliesza called out her name.

Breta stopped, looking worried.

"Breta," Yevliesza began, "I only have a moment, so please let me thank you for good service. I'm glad you kept your job and that Prince Albrecht is still protecting you. Now I need a very small favor. Can you meet me early tomorrow in the gaming room?"

"They will not let me, miss."

"Take a pail of soap and water to the second floor. Say the game room smells bad from my being sick in there. At least try?"

Breta looked at her, with an expression that might be solidarity with a woman who was being used against her will. "When?"

"Tomorrow morning, at eight thirty. Will you?"

Breta nodded and, curtseying, went on her way.

With her escort again, Yevliesza approached the open double doors of the dining room. Murmured conversation and bright lights filled the air. After the tense moment with Breta, her face felt as stiff as a mask. She softened her expression and took a calming breath. She remembered Albrecht's words of how she was to be around him. *With as full a heart as you can manage.* If she couldn't do that, their bargain was off.

She entered, and all eyes turned to her. Six Volkish officers in black uniforms, Albrecht in civilian dress of trousers, jacket and waistcoat. No other women.

Sweeping into the room, she approached the group of men by the hearth. She nodded a bow to Albrecht.

"Yevliesza," he said, beaming. "Stunning." Turning to Marshal Kenrick, he said, "Blue is her color, yes?"

"Very fine, indeed," Kenrick said, regarding her, his eyes hooded. He didn't approve of her. It was amusing to see the expressions on their faces, that although she had been caught spying, she slept with the commandant. Some of them looked at her approvingly, but it was the look of men who liked to imagine undressing her. She smiled at them all.

"Marshal Reinhart," she said, turning to the one with the rat face and absurd mustache. "It's good to see you again."

"That I doubt," he said.

"Come, Walthar," Albrecht said. "She is our guest." His tone shifted. "She is *my* guest."

The prince came to her side and bent close to her ear. "You are exquisite," he whispered, earning a smile in return.

Albrecht introduced the other officers who nodded to her, faces pleasant but wary. Some of these were under Reinhart's command, and Reinhart was a dangerous man, even for Albrecht. He was not of the nobility, had credible experience in the military, and was popular among the common soldiers. It wouldn't be long before Nashavety arrived in Hapsigen, so Albrecht had told her. But he would protect her from all these threats. A little extra to sweeten the bargain.

While the group had another round of drinks, she pretended that she had foreknowing and knew how each one would die. That one, a *harjat* sword blow. Across from him, an Alfan arrow in the heart. The others: Run over by a diabolical machine; thrown from the great Tower; suicide by poison.

And Albrecht: Valenty would slit his throat.

The mental imagery helped, but only a little. She took a glass of wine from a proffered tray, needing it to take the edge off her mood, lest the Volkish prince think she was not carrying off her part well enough. Yevliesza could see why people drank. To bear their lives.

Marshal Kenrick escorted her to the table, where her place was several seats away from Albrecht. Her station was clear. Protected, not powerful. As she sat in the grand dining hall with its gaggle of officers and their commander, a rift made its way into her anger. A small cleft like a tiny align. It was cold and slow-moving, coloring her thoughts. Sadness.

She was tired of these men and their bizarre ideas. Tired of

Albrecht and his predations. She had a life independent of them, and it was that life she mourned. The one with Valenty. That life, with a man who would love her, honor her. She might still have it. But tonight it was far away, and receding.

She was jolted back to the dinner table when she heard Duke Tanfred's name. It seemed that Tanfred had left for home the day before, returning to his country residence at Wilhoff.

Albrecht was watching her. She made the mistake of meeting his eyes, revealing that she was troubled by the duke's departure. It was excruciatingly difficult to do everything just so, to avoid showing her true feelings. But now that he had seen her disappointment, she didn't try to hide it.

Yes, Albrecht, I wish that you hadn't sent him away. I had a friend, and you mean for me not to.

Her appetite fled. Without even realizing it, she had been counting on Tanfred. Counting on him to work an escape, to have a carriage waiting. She looked at her hands in her lap, trying to steady herself.

Across from her, Reinhart had seen the exchange with Albrecht. As he held her gaze, his mouth quirked into a half-smile.

⚜

IN ALBRECHT'S BED THAT NIGHT, AFTER HE WAS SATISFIED IN HIS usual ways, he turned to her, stroking the hair away from her face, as though he was capable of tenderness. But she didn't know what he was capable of. Despite his wildly inconsistent ideas about honor, she felt that he would spare Valenty's life. Or so she told herself.

But if Valenty was never in peril, then she had accepted Albrecht's awful trade for nothing. Of course, he could still take her by force—it was already force, though he pretended it wasn't

—he could physically force her, but she didn't think he would. He clung to his ideas about honor.

She was not surprised when he cupped her face with his hand and said, "Are you ready to come to me completely?"

He had said it was up to her. For a while, it was up to her.

As he trailed his hand down her body, she said, "It's a decision I have to make."

"Soon," he said, desire in his voice—and something else, something like avarice.

She smiled, trying to be tender yet firm. "But not yet."

Chapter Forty-Three

Valenty and Urik lounged in a sheltered stairway, keeping watch on the brothel across the street. The cobbled streets of Rorrs were dark except for torches set in the doorways of taverns and cheap bedsits. Overhead, a crescent moon wandered through the constellations as though harvesting stars.

Valenty and Urik drank from an empty bottle and now and then swore drunkenly in Volkish. Pyvel sat leaning against Urik as though asleep. From somewhere, a whore laughed raucously.

The quarry they hoped for was an officer, as high in rank as possible and about Valenty's height and build. Even better would be such an officer with a comrade, preferably of Urik's build. If the targets were drunk, all the better.

Valenty stood and took a piss along the wall. It gave him a chance to scan the alley—vacant at the moment—where they hoped to surprise their prey.

A common soldier came out of the brothel, accompanied by a woman with stringy blond hair. Arm in arm, they veered off down the street, nearly falling at every step.

They had been occupying the portico too long and would soon have to find a new observation post. If they had been able to find a higher-class brothel, there would have been plenty of officers, but the search for such a place might have exposed them to scrutiny.

Pyvel, eager to use the fighting moves he had learned, wanted their ambush to include knives as weapons until Urik had him consider whether they wanted blood on the uniforms they were going to steal.

Your body is a weapon. Sometimes feet, but what foremost, lad?

Feet, hands, elbows, Pyvel had recited.

In the doorway, Urik yawned and stood up, none too steadily.

Their signal to set the trap.

An officer had left the whorehouse and turned down the shadowed alley where they planned their ambush. Pyvel shuffled off around the other side of the brothel to enter the alley from the other end.

Valenty noted that the soldier was walking deliberately, not inebriated, but not watchful, either. Urik muttered, "a major," and sauntered away from the steps. Not as high a rank as they had wished, but a major would have to suffice. Valenty followed, while Pyvel, having circled around, was just turning into the alley. He began a credible appearance of being injured or drunk.

When he was sure the officer had noted him, he clutched his stomach and fell to his knees.

"My father . . . my father," Pyvel said in the Volkish words he had memorized, his voice broken by sobbing. He pointed behind him, away from the approaching Valenty and Urik.

The officer drew near. "Here, now, what is this?"

Pyvel collapsed as though losing consciousness. The officer came to a stop, looking down at him.

Someone raised their voice a stone's throw behind Valenty. "Sir? All well?" Another officer strode past Valenty and Urik and came to the major's side. Now they had the two officers they had hoped for.

Judging the street otherwise empty for the moment, Valenty strode forward, closing the gap between him and the major. When the man turned to him, Valenty kneed him in the groin and sliced his hand down against the back of his neck, sending him to his knees. At the same moment Urik grabbed the other officer from behind and, pushing his shoulder in one direction, with one hand pushed the man's chin in the other. The man sank to the ground, his neck broken.

Valenty's blow had not disabled the major, and he rose up, knife in hand. Pyvel was now crouching on all fours. Urik sprang at the man and, with a kick, sent him off balance and over Pyvel's back. As he hit the ground, Urik drew his knife and, using the flat of the blade, struck him on the side of the head, rendering him unconscious.

Valenty was already dragging the other officer toward a sagging door, kicking it open. Pyvel rushed to his side to help, and together they dragged the unconscious soldier inside.

Raising his left hand, Pyvel manifested a pool of light. The room was part of an abandoned building, previously reconnoitered. Concealing their victims in this place would give the three of them a head start in getting out of the neighborhood. Urik dragged the dead officer through the door, and they began stripping the soldiers of their boots and clothes. One of the officers—a lieutenant—was of average size; his uniform would be a tight fit for Urik's greater bulk, but it would have to do.

The unconscious major was now stripped. Valenty drew his knife, telling Pyvel to back away.

"I'm not a child, my lord."

Valenty gave a brusque nod and slit the soldier's throat.

"We could not risk that he would regain consciousness," Valenty told Pyvel. But the boy looked unaffected. Perhaps he had seen worse in Nashavety's foul house.

⚜

THE RORRS BOUNDARY GATE LAY NESTLED IN A GENTLE VALLEY beside a river. It did not have the bleak aspect of Numinat's Lowgate with its stark plains or Numin Pass Gate sheathed in frozen rocks and ice. The rounded hills and narrow river with occasional rapids made a peaceful impression, were it not for the thousands of army tents now surrounding the garrison and the martial drills conducted on the outskirts.

A heavy sleeting rain limited their view of the environs, but Valenty and Urik had known what to expect from intelligence reports. Rorrs was considered impregnable from incursion because, should enemy forces push through the gateway, the narrow valley would funnel them into a wedge, while the slopes of the knolls gave an uphill advantage to defenders.

The three fugitives had taken shelter in an abandoned barn midway between the military fort and the city.

Valenty sat against bales of hay, resting his leg. "They could be watching for us if they think the people who murdered those officers were Numinasi. We should have left hours ago."

Urik spit out a piece of straw he had been chewing on. "And arrive wet with snow."

An officer of Valenty's rank would not show up in that condition. The weakest part of their plan might be that Valenty, their main player, would show up on foot instead of horseback. The scheme had several uncertain aspects; they would have to improvise, depending on what questions they faced from the Volkish guards.

He could imagine some of them, for example, if Marshal Reinhart happened to have passed through the gateway recently. Or was known to be at a war front. Valenty had the haircut, the mustache, and a semblance of a marshal's uniform—which would be supplemented with Urik's strong manifesting powers, the main reason he had been selected to accompany Valenty. But he could only maintain such a complicated illusion for one of them. Pyvel would be Reinhart's nephew, and Urik, a Volkish soldier, who should be high-ranking, but would have to make do as a lieutenant. Pyvel's clothing should be finer, but his small manifesting powers could embellish the figure he cut.

The two of them, of course, did not have the language. Pyvel had been taught to say in Volkish, "But uncle!" seeming to be harping on a request from an earlier conversation, and Urik knew to say "Sir," responding to an order, and "I do not know, sir," in case it seemed called for. For those two, it might be enough. Much of the deception relied on Valenty. He must maintain an attitude of authority and privilege, but have at his disposal impatience, cruelty, and paranoia.

Changing Valenty's face and creating the proper insignia on his uniform would be Urik's main job. He had only seen Reinhart for a few moments, when the two of them, disguised as Volkish soldiers, met him in the crossings. Urik said he would never forget that face, the one that could scare small children. But they also were relying on the likelihood that the guards would not personally know Marshal Reinhart. Valenty just needed to be ugly and brutal.

Simple, the *harjat* had said.

Valenty got to his feet and paced the barn, trying to clear his head and shake his worries about the gate and the snow-turned-to-sleet and having in his care a young man without experience in deception or fighting. Like his companions, Valenty had only caught a few hours of sleep over the past few days. Even so, he was not worried about making a large mistake.

As usual, it was the small things that could bring a good plan down.

Chapter Forty-Four

his was not the time for Tirhan to tell his sister he had fallen in love with one of his warriors.

They were picking their way through thick stands of hemlock and oak, the horses nervous in the dense undergrowth, with roots hidden beneath snow. They rode in silence with a few men riding outlier positions to watch for Volkish pursuit after the successful fight to free the captives.

In two days and two nights of travel, Tirhan and his party had put as much distance as they could between themselves and the slaughter at the manor house. But their pace was slow in the forest riven with defiles down which streams flowed under blankets of ice. Crossing these brooks was dangerous for the horses when, at any moment, their hooves might crash through, causing damage to their feet and fetlocks.

In the quiet of their ride, Tirhan tried out in his mind several approaches to telling Cadris about Morwen. None of them was right. He should inform the queen first. For now, Morwen rode several positions behind Tirhan. She could have ridden forward with him. But then more dissembling in front of Cadris would have been called for. Until now he had not thought past the freeing of his family. He and his sister had not yet acknowledged to each other their father's death and their brother's. That grief that had been deferred. He did not want his sister to think that he had taken this desperate time to enjoy a bedmate. That is not what it was—not that, primarily—but it might appear so.

Beyond how the situation seemed to his sister, was the more important question of how it would seem to his mother. How she would define a suitable match for him and whether he could ignore the clear expectation that clan lord Gryffyd had, of Anwelyth as his queen or consort.

So he said nothing, but kept a watch on the forest and its creatures on the route through bracken and patches of woody, braided vines that unevenly carpeted their path.

"She is welcome to ride with us, brother," Cadris said.

"Who?"

She cast him one of her *this is your sister* looks. "Who? Why, Morwen. I think I should have a chance to size her up."

So she had guessed the relationship already. "That you will not do."

"Of course I shall."

He held her gaze. "No, Cadris. You will not make her uncomfortable. She is not . . . a casual thing."

A raised eyebrow, widened eyes. And silence.

Let her reckon with that. If she wanted to assess Morwen, she had better do so with discretion, or he would have Cadris and Morwen trade places in the file of riders.

A hooting cry from the woods. Kierach peeled off from the group and disappeared over a knoll to learn what the man had seen. They came to a halt and waited, as the horses flicked their ears and pawed the ground.

A short time later, a few of the outlying riders appeared with

Kierach. "Volkish," Kierach reported. "A large party." He pointed over the knoll. "They are on horseback and gaining on us. We are hidden by the ridge, but their scouts will soon come upon us."

Tirhan pointed to the other side of their trail. "We can put that hill between us."

Morwen rode up to them. "No, our only chance is to outride them." She pointed to the descending slope of the path before them. "Once we come into the meadow below, we can separate and fill the flat with competing trails." She looked to Tirhan and then at Kierach.

"Let us move fast, my lord," Kierach urged.

Tirhan nodded, and the party surged forward, careful on the slope, but leaving silence behind. They would be seen at some point. Now they had the advantage of distance and, if they could maintain it, their pursuers would be hard-pressed to follow the separate routes by which the Alfans could braid through this woods.

Cadris had lost her playful—or had it been mocking—look. She followed Tirhan on her mount, watching to avoid tree roots and rocks.

Tirhan's outliers were called in from the other side, and the consolidated group now rushed toward the meadows.

As they came out of the woods, he saw Morwen hand Cadris a knife.

Tirhan told Morwen, "Ward the Princess Cadris."

Kierach brought up his horse next to Tirhan. "My lord, she should not. She must shield you. You will be king." His look was fierce and so was Tirhan's in return.

Cadris broke the stalemate. "This is no time to be gallant, brother. Mother would kill you if you got killed." She smiled at Tirhan and kneed her horse into a gallop.

Tirhan and Morwen followed as the troop splintered to

confuse pursuers. The meadow was a great swath of frozen bog this time of year and stretched so far that the line of trees that marked the perimeter seemed no more than a line of black. Cadris was the best rider of all of them and was soon a distant figure as Tirhan, Morwen, and their group thundered behind. Morwen's cape streamed behind her like the wings of a dactyl, and Kierach, who always rode the most powerful horse, but not the fastest, brought up the rear.

At last plunging into the woods, Tirhan reined in to see if they had found refuge unseen. He was not sure they had. Across the expanse of snow-locked grasses the first Volkish horseman appeared as a tiny figure, but which group of partisans he had caught sight of—if any of them—Tirhan could not tell. Until the horseman set out again, gesturing more soldiers to follow him, directly on a path to Tirhan.

The others were waiting for him ahead.

"Go!" he said. They rushed on, but it was no use; the deadfall and snow made it impossible to make much headway. They were down to six in number and, one of them, Cadris, could not fight.

Tirhan pointed to the saddle of the hill to one side. The slope to it was steep, but not so much that the horses could not climb it. Near the top were jutting rocks behind which they could hold off a greater number, with plenty of time to take bow aim as the enemy scrambled up to dislodge them. With no shelter for the horses, his two men, Lodd and Osric, took the mounts the short distance over the ridge, where they would hobble them until needed.

"If they kill us," Cadris said, hunkered down and watching the stand of woods below, "at least we will have saved the queen and Hanavar."

Kierach gently said, "They will not kill you, Princess. You are too valuable to them as a hostage."

She glanced at Tirhan. He had heard the exchange of

comments and nodded at his sister. No one said, but everyone knew, they *would* kill the future king. He was not afraid if they let him die fighting. Waiting to fight, that was always a time when fear took over, when you had time to think of all the ways to die. But when the enemy was almost upon you, all you could think of was, *I am ready. Come and get me, you sons of hell.*

Chapter Forty-Five

Dreiza and Arlaty were enjoying the roof deck of the domicile on a stark winter afternoon. The sun burnished the snowy landscape with a cold glow. Behind them the peaks of the Numins towered, and below lay the stepped hills of the ascent to Zolvina.

They sipped from their steaming cups and watched as, down the slope, an enormous bird circled. Arlaty leaned forward in interest. "A bearded vulture," she said. "See how its head feathers ripple in the wind?"

"Beautiful!" Dreiza said. "I hope it finds a meal."

"It is looking for blood in the snow."

Dreiza pulled her wool cape more closely around herself. The breeze, frigid from its sweep across the snows, artfully threaded into the slightest gaps in their clothes.

Arlaty was the no-nonsense member of the *satvadeya*. Forbidding until you knew her, then as caring as the High Mother herself, dispensing herbal infusions for every need. With her dark skin she was the only one who looked good in the pale color they all wore.

The *satvadeya* had welcomed Dreiza into their circle with its secrets and its rituals. And she had finally learned why these sisters sometimes left the compound—and where they went. The cave of her initiation ceremony was only the entrance hall to a larger system of tunnels and caverns, some so profound that they remained warm through the winter.

Down-valley something moved on the snow. Dreiza watched, wondering if it had only been a shadow cast by a vulture.

"Something, sister?" Arlaty asked.

"A dark shape against the snow," Dreiza murmured. "Gone now, behind that ridge."

"Dark?" Arlaty asked. "Then not a snow cat. And no bear is out this time of year." She sat back down, but Dreiza continued to watch, squinting her eyes against the glare of the winter sun.

The view was stunning and, though it inspired, underneath the joy of the afternoon lay the curling dread of what she had learned in the initiation cave, of total peril, even the end of all things. Because it was too much to grasp, it lay sleeping just under awareness, but the latest news from Osta Kiya brought it to the fore: Numinat had declared war on Volkia. Staggering news that seemed to herald even worse things to come.

"Sister . . ." Dreiza began. She did not want to sound rash, but it was needful to take steps sometimes, as the Devi Ilsat had admitted. "Is it time to ask Kassalya what the future holds for Yevliesza?"

"If we could only do so without disturbing the girl. High Mother says she must learn to let go of foreknowing. What an awful burden, to detach from one's gift."

Yevliesza in the hands of the Volkish. That too was an awful burden. What must Valenty be suffering?

The black shape again. Dreiza leaned out over the half-wall. "Someone is coming." Arlaty joined her. "I think it is a man," Dreiza said.

"Likely, since the visitor has a long beard," Arlaty quipped. "I will inform High Mother."

"I can go," Dreiza offered, as she was the youngest of the *satvadeya*. It was important news and should be delivered swiftly.

"Yes. Hasten, and I will bring the cups."

Dreiza hurried down the stairwell and composed herself for a purposeful, but not unseemly, rush through the east wing of the domicile to the mother's study. No one was there. Dreiza looked out the courtyard window to see if she might be at the frozen numin pool, but there were only two *satvars* there, combing the snow with delicate rakes and forming river patterns for the delight of their sister renunciates.

At last, she found the Devi Ilsat in the dining hall lingering over her noon meal.

"Mother, there is someone approaching on foot," she announced, trying not to sound breathless, which she was.

The Devi Ilsat tipped her bowl to spoon up the last of her soup. "How many?"

"One. I think. I did not wait to see."

The High Mother swallowed and wiped her lips with her napkin. "Kindly ask the sisters to open the gate."

"Before we know his business? What he intends?"

"If harm, our sapling gate will hardly deter him, my daughter. Let the poor fellow in and bring a nice hot drink to the vestibule."

Dreiza went down to inform a dozing *satvar* to open the gate. Dreiza was surprised by her level of excitement at the arrival of a visitor. It was uncommon for a man to visit under any circumstances and, added to that, during the season of the ice moon, approach on foot was almost impossible. Not that this traveler would be more interesting than a spiritual sister . . . oh, she had forgotten the hot drink. Circling back to the dining hall and entering the cookery, she put a pot on to boil.

Eventually it came to a simmer and into the cup went a liberal sprinkling of dried something-or-other—one of Arlaty's staple herbs.

She left the steaming cup on the stove to keep hot and went to the courtyard to watch. The man's cloak was so heavy that it barely stirred as he walked. He did not look like a *satvar*. The beard, for one thing, and what seemed to be his muscular build, though that was hard to judge beneath the heavy cape.

When he arrived at the open gate, he said, "I beg admittance to your sanctuary to speak with the Devi Ilsat. Please pardon me that I have no permission to come. My name is Father Ludving."

He had a Volkish accent! Dreiza sent the astonished sister next to her to fetch the hot drink and bring it to the vestibule where the High Mother always met with strangers.

"Be welcome, Father," Dreiza said. "Please follow me, and we will see to your comfort." His title was *father*. So he was from a men's *satvary*. But he was Volkish. They had different ways in that realm. It was all very surprising. If he had just come from Volkia, she wanted to ask him about Yevliesza, but that was ridiculous. He could know nothing of her.

The visitor was quite tall. In fact, he towered over her, his bass voice that of a man still young. When they reached the small entrance hall, she offered to take his cape, and he unhooked a chain that kept it close around his shoulders. When he relinquished the cape, heavy in her arms and frosted with ice, she stared at his chest.

He wore a cross on a thong.

By the Nine, he was a churchman.

Chapter Forty-Six

In the light of day, Tirhan and his company counted their pursuers. The Volkish horsemen had taken refuge in a grove of trees out of bow range. Twelve, to Tirhan's five, not including Cadris, who was untrained as a fighter. With the advantage of the hill, he counted that an even match if the enemy did not gain reinforcements.

The slab of uplifted rock gave Tirhan's group cover, but they needed to come around it to use their bows. They had slept sitting up, the only way they all had concealment. As soon as it was light enough, Osric, one of his best archers, had climbed to the top of the rock, judging that a man could do damage from the position if his balance was good.

In their favor, the sun was behind them, forcing their foes to face the sun at least in midmorning. Lodd was their second archer and had taunted the Volkish by ducking outside of cover and drawing a slew of arrows until the attackers gauged the range too far. Aside from Osric and Lodd, two more besides himself could fight: Morwen and Kierach.

"The sun will soon be cresting behind us," Tirhan said. "Let us urge them to strike now."

"I will walk out," Osric said, volunteering to be a target.

Tirhan nodded. "Wear leathers." He glanced at Lodd and Kierach, who shrugged out of their riding vests.

Cadris was listening to all this. She was only seventeen, but carried herself like a seasoned fighter, cold-eyed and steady-handed. "When you pretend to fall, I will scream," she said to Osric.

"No," Kierach said. "They do not know a woman is in our group. They may guess who you are and bring the main force."

Her face tightened at this rebuke, but she did not argue.

Osric donned the extra garments and left the shelter of the rock, lurching onto the hillside scree, trying to make the cover of the next boulder. A flight of arrows hit downslope, and then a second wave was airborne and scattering around him. Just before he made the shelter of the boulder, he cried out as though wounded and fell to his knees.

Kierach and Lodd shouted curses and, the trap, as thin as it was, got the reaction they hoped for. The soldiers streamed out of hiding and came at the hill in two groups, left and right of the refuge. Once they started up the slope, Lodd let fly an arrow from the top of the standing rock. It buried deep in a soldier's chest.

Eleven left, Tirhan counted and, nocking an arrow, stepped wide of the hiding place and shot, quickly stepping back to the shelter of the rock. From his perch, Lodd called, "Yes!" Ten, then.

Morwen bided her time, knife in hand.

One of the soldiers was almost to their position, but he was hidden by the rock. Tirhan waited with his short sword on one side and Kierach on the other. When the attack came, Kierach met the soldier, lunging at him with his sword and causing him to stagger backward and fall. Kierach jumped downslope and quickly killed him. As he turned back to the barrier, an arrow pierced him in the side. It was a solid strike, but he managed to fall toward the protection of the rock where Cadris and Morwen dragged him out of danger.

Tirhan met an assailant on the other side, and the fighting was close, more suited to knives than swords. Tirhan bloodied his attacker, finally sending him crashing downslope, as Morwen's knives flew at the next wave.

With the sun now streaming over the hilltop, Lodd stood, uncaring of exposure at the top of the shaft of rock and drew his bow again and again. Tirhan ranged downslope with his sword and, from the opposite side by the boulder, Osric was still making lethal strikes.

Morwen joined Tirhan then, and he became invincible, or so it felt to him. Arrows deflected from her warding and, as the remaining enemy converged on him, she timed her warding to allow him to strike if he had the advantage. At last there were two enemy remaining, but one was infused with fury and, despite blood flying from his wounds, he closed again and again with Tirhan.

A soldier appeared from the woods. Bow in hand, he aimed for Lodd on the rock and struck him in the head. Tirhan heard rather than saw Lodd fall.

From somewhere the thought came, *there were thirteen,* even as he kicked savagely at his assailant and, toppling him, thrust his sword into his chest.

The bowman came out of the woods, throwing his bow down and drawing his sword. Tirhan went to meet him, and the first blow from the Volkish soldier clanged against his own sword with a force that nearly paralyzed his arm. He twisted away and, coming at the man from his sword-side, slashed at his weapon arm, but the man danced away. Only to take a knife in the mouth from Morwen.

The fight was over. They rushed up the hill, climbing past the bodies. Tirhan sent Morwen and Osric for the horses, as he made his way to Kierach's side, where Cadris was cradling his head in her lap.

An arrow had pierced his side. Having given his vest to Osric, he had lost the protection of it and the arrow had penetrated far. Kierach did not stir, but his eyes fluttered.

"Steady, my friend," Tirhan said, kneeling by his shoulder. He placed his hand on Kierach's side. The arrowhead had gone cleanly in, with blood only seeping past the shaft. By his healing sight, Tirhan knew the arrow had pierced Kierach's spleen. He could not survive and was fading even as Tirhan knelt by his side.

"We have won," Tirhan told him, leaning in so his friend could hear.

He took his hand. "You have made me and Alfan Sih proud. Always."

The older man's gaze went beyond Tirhan's face, perhaps far beyond. He murmured something, and Tirhan leaned close to his lips.

"My Lord King," he whispered. In moments he was gone.

After a moment Tirhan helped Cadris to her feet and held her, since she seemed to need it, or he needed to hold her.

Soon Morwen and Osric were picking their way over the crest with the horses, finding a goat path down, and Cadris went to help. Tirhan laid his cape over Kierach's body.

They could not pause to bury him and Lodd. Now they had to ride, watchful for the Volkish troops eager to recoup their failure at Glenir. Tirhan, along with Morwen, Cadris, and Osric, left the hillside and slipped into the woods.

Chapter Forty-Seven

Yevliesza walked up and down the hallway as before. Now, however, a guard always stood at her door. She was still allowed in the two large rooms, the reception hall and the gaming room, as well as the roof.

This morning, however, she wasn't walking the hall for exercise, she was getting the guard used to seeing her pace the hallway.

At the appointed time to meet Breta, she wandered into the gaming room to gaze out the window, as though in thought, but listening for her former maid.

Martel's body had been removed from the wall. Perhaps Marshal Reinhart had removed it before Albrecht returned because he knew the prince would not like her taunted that way, even if the lieutenant had encouraged her to talk with the Master of Swords.

Below in the yard, a stableman walked a horse. The winter fog that had moved in the day before was now so thick she couldn't see the city beyond the courtyard walls. The horse and its groom looked as though they were in another world, near enough to discern, but far, far away. It might almost be a scene from a ranch near her old home, a land that she had begun to think of as a *realm*, not the whole world, not the real world in the way she used to think of it. A realm, because all the kingdoms were alter-worlds of Earth, overlapping. From Volkia to Earth was, as Lord Tirhan had once said, a journey without a distance. And it was the great mystery of the Mythos that the Mist Walls slowly uncovered the land that was latent, ready to be born.

The clank of a pail. Breta.

Entering without acknowledging Yevliesza's presence, the girl found the place on the rug with the nonexistent stain and knelt to clean it.

Yevliesza looked to the hallway. No one was in view. "Breta," she said in a soft voice, "I need to protect myself."

"I know, miss. I wish I could help, but—"

"You *can* help. Tell me how a woman prevents pregnancy." Breta's eyes widened in surprise. "I should know. But I don't. And I need to know." She looked up at the doorway again. "Keep cleaning, Breta, but talk to me. How do *you* do it?"

Breta murmured, "My power is warding, miss. I bring my power inside me and forbid entrance. I am able to divert a man's seed from places it should not go. For you, miss, with aligns, you do the same."

"But how?" Aligns didn't keep anything away, didn't prevent anything. At least not that Yevliesza had ever heard of.

Breta continued scrubbing the carpet.

"How?" Yevliesza repeated.

Breta said, "No matter a woman's birthright power, she can use it to protect her body from . . . connecting in the usual way. You just bring your power into your body and direct it with clear purpose. So whatever your gift is, it can be used. Like *elements* could be used to wash away a man's issue. Or *creatures* could swarm and create a barrier—that is how my sister uses creature power in bed matters. For aligns, I am not sure, but however you hold your Deep power, however you think of it in your mind, that is how you think of it when your lover . . ." She stopped, shaking her head. She knew Albrecht was no lover to Yevliesza. He was using her. "I am sorry, miss," Breta said weakly.

The guard came to the door. Yevliesza's stomach flipped, but the guard wasn't angry, only annoyed. An unhappy conversation ensued between the maid and the soldier as Breta pointed to Yevliesza and then at the floor.

Adopting an impatient attitude, Yevliesza sharply told the maid to get on with her cleaning and left the room.

The guard shooed Breta out of the game room, and Yevliesza heard the maid leave, closing the stairway door behind her.

Aligns, Yevliesza thought. She could use aligns when it came to *bed matters* as Breta called it. Already, she had an image in her mind of an errant stream disappearing into the depths of an align. She could at least protect herself that far.

Or should she use her primal root power? But she had never known how to visualize her second power. When it came right down to it, she had never even truly accepted her second power. It was a magic that sat uneasily on her, an unwelcome gift that she did not understand and didn't want to.

Without remembering how she got to the reception room, she sat on the divan, staring at the darkened hearth, thinking about that power.

How do you keep part of yourself totally hidden? How do you live if part of yourself, when known to others, would turn your life upside down, would mean that nothing would ever be normal again? When your power would be demanded by monarchs, feared by your enemies, and make any man you love have to decide between his duty and his heart? Whether to side with a queen or a lover?

She had thought that telling Tanfred was a major step. But that was just the beginning.

For the first time since she grew the path to Alfan Sih, she allowed herself to accept who she was. Who she had to be, whether she liked it or not. And how, by hiding her second gift, she solved some problems but created other, perhaps much worse, problems.

She could not go on this way. But the direction forward remained cloaked in fog.

☙✲❧

ALBRECHT LINGERED AT THE DINNER TABLE WITH YEVLIESZA. Before them, the remains of their meal. Albrecht brushed a few crumbs of oatcakes from his hands. "On Thursday evening the priest at the Church of All Graces will do a special mass for our fighting men. I would like you to attend with me."

She hated the idea of appearing in public with him. "Please, Albrecht. Our two realms are at war. I am already a traitor to my land and to be seen in church . . ." She thought he would understand that she had a lingering loyalty to Numinat.

He pushed his chair from the table. "Always so stubborn."

"But isn't it part of what you like about me? That honor means something to me?" A ludicrous thing to say to the avowed enemy she was sleeping with, but she hoped it would hold some logic for him.

"Honor does not weigh so heavily on women."

"It does on me." Thinking she provoked him too far, she added, "Perhaps a church service when the subject is not the war?"

He nodded curtly to her. "Very well, then." He left, joining the officers who were waiting for him in the hallway.

When she was alone, Yevliesza stared at the table with its food remnants. How strange it was that when large things changed, the little things—the meals, getting dressed, drinking a glass of water—did not change at all. Maybe the little things kept one sane.

Someone stood at the door.

Evah. She approached the table and took the seat Albrecht had been sitting in.

Surprised, Yevliesza made an effort to smile at her. "Evah," she said by way of greeting. She had mistakenly assumed Albrecht had sent her away.

"I have message," Evah said. Her gaze slid past Yevliesza as she looked around the room, perhaps worried that she wasn't supposed to be in the dining hall. Her hair and face were so pale, it seemed as though her features were barely there.

"Message from someone you know. From great duke. Not speaking his name."

Yevliesza's heart stilled. Tanfred. "Didn't he leave?"

"Yes, but not like Albrecht think. Not obeying. Say he go to Wilhoff, but he keep in Hapsigen." Evah jerked her head in the general direction of the city.

Tanfred was still here? A thread of hope entered her heart.

Yevliesza looked toward the door that stood open to the hall. People walked to and fro. At any moment it could be Albrecht. She turned her attention to this frail, confused woman. Why was she helping her?

"Why would you do this? You don't even like me."

An impish smile and some life came into Evah's eyes. "I happy if you leave. Help you leave."

Her rival would be gone. So it was for love. She loved Albrecht in a perverse attachment to a man who played with her soul. If Yevliesza was gone, she would have her dark prince again. She was welcome to him.

Evah slid the fist of her hand onto the table. She was holding something.

When she opened her fist, she revealed a ring. Tanfred's ring, with the cross on it.

Here was proof that Tanfred trusted her. Evah held her gaze. "You take ring to him. Yes?"

Yevliesza folded her hand over Evah's, taking possession of the ring. "Yes."

A noise in the hall grabbed Evah's attention, and she whispered, "He wait for you three nights from now. Night of All Graces mass."

Yevliesza's mind was skittering among many questions, trying to put things in order. Tanfred was defying Albrecht's request that he go home. And he had a plan. Had revealed this to Evah and enlisted her help. Because she, of all people, wanted her gone.

"Father Ludving," Evah went on. "Father you knowing. He ask All Graces priest give mass on night of Saint Leo."

"Father Ludving? He is here?"

"No, but he send word to church. Father is big priest. They do what he say."

She had thought Father Ludving a simple man of the cloth, but she might have guessed that Duke Tanfred would have a major priest as his spiritual advisor.

"Listen!" Evah whispered harshly as though she had detected Yevliesza's straying thoughts. "Thursday night Albrecht gone, many important persons gone. For midnight mass. And man of the ring, he come with carriage."

A clench in Yevliesza's stomach, as she realized she had almost been required to go with Albrecht.

"But what is the plan? How do I get out of here?"

Evah smirked. "Verdure."

Chapter Forty-Eight

The next three days passed in slow minutes, marked by the ornate clock on the mantel. It had taken forever to reach this day, the afternoon of the planned escape.

The clock read 4:23. Night was coming, already darkening the windows of Yevliesza's apartment.

Her maid Leni was, for some reason, dusting the furniture, an activity which seemed suspicious. She wished Leni would leave for the day, but first she had to bring Yevliesza's dinner on a tray, and that would not be until six thirty, and then she'd come back at eight to remove the tray. And finally, Yevliesza would be alone to pace and wait.

During the day she had walked the hallway twice, trying to pass the time and burn off tension, but she gave it up, thinking that too much roaming might lead the guard at her door to think something was amiss.

Three times she had checked to see if the uniform was still under the mattress and the boots under the bed within reach and checked many times out the window to see if the weather was worsening. The fog was thick enough to choke a horse. Not a good metaphor, since their escape was to be by horse and carriage. Sometimes she thought that this business of Tanfred's new plan could be an elaborate hoax, with Tanfred lying dead somewhere, killed for his ring. She did not believe this, but the thought arose.

At the window, the one closest to her bedroom door, she tried once again to look down the side of the building, just to assure herself that the woody vine was still there and hadn't disappeared as though by magic since, after all, it had been created by magic, Tanfred's gift of verdure. Which he had been plying for three days, since Albrecht had stood in her apartment in his riding gear and said, *Do you see how your position has changed? That everything is different now?*

Tanfred had caused a woody vine—a thick, woody vine—to grow some forty feet to her window and had done so in just a few days. He must have been nearby and in danger of being seen. If she had watched closely, she might have picked him out. How she would have taken heart if she had! Or perhaps he had worked only at night . . . but clearly his power came from a great depth. A noble power. The same power which had revealed her to him in the first place, over a great distance, when she made her way through the crossings.

Still, she found herself doubtful about climbing down the woody vine. What if it was not securely lodged in the stone and mortar of the wall? What if it would not hold her weight? She pushed these worries away. Tanfred must know what he was doing.

The mantel clock ticked away, savoring each dreadful moment as clocks were wont to do.

It would be difficult to escape the palace, but even more worrisome was the boundary gate. A place called Rorrs, Tanfred had said. They would be walking right into a Volkish army garrison guarding the way and, with the two realms newly at war, the post would be on high alert. If they got through the gate, there would still be the danger that they would be stopped during their passage, especially if Albrecht discovered her absence tonight.

She knew one way to avoid being detained: to create a new pathway to Numinat. She had created a path to Alfan Sih; perhaps it was not beyond her ability to do such a thing again. But then there would *be* a path. A path for invasion and one which would have no protections or controls, at least for many days. No, they would have to leave by one of the existing Numinat gates.

Leave. The word itself was comforting.

Tonight Albrecht would have a working dinner with his command staff. Shortly before midnight he would leave with his senior officers for the mass at the Church of All Graces. So she had likely seen the last of him, the man who had peeled back her disguises little by little. It had only taken him twenty-five days to overcome her lies, persona, and dignity. He probably felt that he had every right to do it. Even the right to summon her to his bed —and demand that she enjoy it if she wanted to save Valenty's life.

She hoped never to set eyes on him again. Not only because of what he had done, but because, despite all he had done, he thought himself *honorable.*

How very much she wanted to set the Volkish prince straight.

Which was far beyond her power. Now, or ever.

⚜

BY THE TIME LENI TOOK AWAY THE DINNER TRAY, YEVLIESZA HAD calmed down. Now was the time for cold determination, and she gathered it around her like a suit of armor. Whatever happened, she would be ready; whatever needed to be done she would do. Anything. She had already stolen a knife. There could be any number of uses for the knife in the next few hours. At her dinner of mutton, it had been simple to take the glistening, sharp knife. It lay on the floor under the small dining table, so if they found it missing from the tray, she could say it must have fallen.

She had some scissors, but she was not going to use it on her hair. If someone came to check on her . . . no, she would bring it with her and use it in the carriage. Unless she and Tanfred were going to flee on the back of a dactyl, an image that her mind seemed to love, but was never going to be real.

If all went well, by morning she would be in Numinat. Valenty would be there, she desperately hoped. Surely he had secured passage through one of the gates by now. But how had he planned to get past the Volkish guards in the first place? He had no idea of the agreement she had made with Albrecht, so he must have prepared a deception. It troubled her that Albrecht had not told her that Valenty had entered the crossings and left Volkia. But Albrecht might want to keep Valenty's fate in play. Or perhaps Valenty's deception had worked, and Albrecht would never know how Valenty escaped.

She thought of a reunion with Rusadka, and the prospect filled her with hope, hope just to hear her friend's voice again, hope that she was well and finding favor in her beloved *harjat* service. And she would see Pyvel and hear his story, doubtless a terrible one if he had been in Nashavety's hands. What a vast relief it would be when she and Tanfred left Volkia. Although she had received kindness and even sacrifice from some: Tanfred, Father Ludving, Lieutenant Martel, and Breta. Even, in the end, poor Evah.

The night deepened. She sat in a chair with nothing left to do. At times she seemed to float in a calm place outside of all care and thought. Time must be allowed to pass. The mantel clock assured her that it was. She let herself hear the ticking without impatience, let herself hear the sound as the falling of seconds, seconds that would never come again, seconds leading to endings and beginnings.

A knock at the apartment door, and the guard opened it.

Albrecht stood there, a small smile on his face. A good smile, she thought, having seen a hundred styles of them on the man. She stood to receive him.

He looked resplendent in a tailored uniform of greenish gray with broad cuffs and a stiff collar trimmed in red and silver. A silver brocade belt cinched his waist, and loops of silver braid hung from one shoulder, secured by an elaborate shoulder tab. His visored hat was tucked under an arm. It was a uniform that conveyed dominance along with high style and it clothed a man who needed it, since he was in fact without substance.

"You look well in that uniform," she said, allowing her face to soften.

He smiled ironically. "Parade dress. And you look beautiful, even in that simple Volkish gown." He approached and put his hand under her chin. "You hide your beauty."

"I think it's vanity. I feel I look better if my clothes don't outshine me."

He was in too good a mood to take offense, to realize she had suggested his clothes outshone him.

"I am off to church. Wait up for me?" He was looking at her with too much force. He wanted her.

"I will be asleep by the time you get back. Can I come to you in the morning? When I'm sleepy, I'm not at my best."

The desire went out of his eyes, and he considered her with a more appraising gaze. Apparently, he decided she was being sincere, perhaps promising him something special by way of a good-morning.

She smiled self-deprecatingly, thinking, *In church, may God strike you dead.*

He kissed her lightly. And then he was gone.

Chapter Forty-Nine

From their hiding place in the barn, and with the cold fogs dissipated, Valenty and his companions saw that not far from the river a ramp edged in stone descended deeply into the ground. On the embankment above, soldiers stood guard, and behind them lay an extensive army camp. At the bottom of the ramp stood a wide and formidable-looking door. Rorrs Gate.

Urik and Valenty watched the road for any horses or metal wagons that could be commandeered. Valenty, in his guise as Marshal Reinhart, must arrive at the gate in proper form, not on foot.

At last, in the distance they sighted a self-propelled mechanical wagon approaching along the main road. Quickly, Valenty and his companions emerged from their hiding place in the barn and crossed the field to intercept it.

As it approached, Urik stepped onto the road and spread his arms wide to call it to a halt. Valenty spoke with the coachman, explaining that they would need the wagon for the last leg of their trip. Urik, he trusted, was working a convincing representation of Reinhart's face and minimizing Valenty's height, since the marshal was small in stature.

The coachman complied with the order, lacking any reaction to being in the presence of Marshal Reinhart, or even any outward curiosity. For a moment Valenty considered whether he was under creature control, but no one was nearby to cast such a power, and they were admitted into the conveyance without difficulty. The metal wagon was about the size of a small farm cart, tall enough for passengers, with an overhead compartment that housed what might be weapons, judging by the tubes they had seen protruding from openings.

"Drive forward to the gate," Valenty snapped at the coachman, and they jolted along the single road leading to the ramp.

The mechanical wagon produced an occasional hiss from behind the metal walls of their compartment as well as fumes of hot grease mixed with the tang of iron. The contraption lumbered along an uneven road, jostling its passengers, including the Volkish coachman seated in front.

In the gloom of the small cab, Urik's face had fallen into a scowling mask. Valenty had seldom seen the *harjat* in such discomfort, disconcerting after the man's unrelenting flat expression through so much of their mission. It had taken some persuasion to convince him to waylay the machine and demand transport. Urik found machinery abhorrent, but Pyvel was fascinated by the metal wagon, looking around as though he might discern its workings, the powers that it harnessed to keep it moving without outward means. He watched the coachman's every move at the controls.

When the conveyance slowed and stopped, Urik and Pyvel slid open the door and jumped out. Valenty told the driver to carry on with his business. His neck burned as he felt Volkish guards staring down at him from the embankment. Close by was the gate. Bolts the size of fists studded the door, and its panels were embellished with patterns beaten into the metal. The door loomed over the guards stationed there, high and wide enough for four men to walk abreast. A small group of soldiers stood in front of it, while one of them, a corporal, was walking forward, checking the identities of people in the short line. Most of them probably would not be admitted to the crossings, as they were all civilians.

Valenty strode past the line with Urik and Pyvel close behind. As the corporal turned to waylay them, Valenty glared at him, and the man took a closer look at the supposed officers, finally deciding to let the soldiers stationed in front of the door deal with the trio.

The duty officer came to attention. Valenty returned his salute, barking the order, "Open the gate, Captain. We will pass through."

"Marshal Reinhart!" the captain said in formal greeting. He paused just long enough to give Valenty a jolt of fear. "Sir, my commanding officer will wish to be informed that you are here."

Valenty scowled. "No. I have urgent business at the Alfan Sih front. Open the door, Captain, and be quick about it. I will tolerate no delay." He narrowed his eyes at the man, letting a sneer form on his lips.

The captain's gaze went to Pyvel.

"My nephew, who accompanies me." Valenty lowered his voice. "I will conduct certain inspections, and I will do so without advance notice, yes? No one is to know I have passed through. Do you understand?"

"Sir!" The captain was trying hard to weigh the consequences of hesitating under a direct order.

It had become a staring match. Valenty was a Numinasi spy and, here and now, everything could come undone.

Pyvel whined, "Uncle Walthar . . ."

"Silence!" Valenty hissed at him, returning a fierce gaze at the officer.

The captain nodded to the guards standing ready to open the doors.

With a clang of iron, the soldiers slid open the reinforcing bar across the doors. Marshal Reinhart's party passed through as a string of salutes followed them.

They were in the crossings. The tunnel ceiling soared high above them, much higher than the valley floor would have allowed. To enter a gate was to enter a passage not made of stone and soil, but of primal workings, built not with artifice, but with powers.

The immediate vicinity was heavily guarded, a spacious, cave-like enclosure with a barricade massed some distance from the gateway. A high-ranking soldier had been standing nearby and, having been alerted by his group, turned to greet the newcomers with a salute. "Marshal, sir!" he snapped out.

Valenty returned the salute. "We come on a sensitive matter, Colonel. You have not seen us, do you understand? Your men are not to discuss this among themselves or with anyone, is that perfectly clear?"

"Sir!"

Valenty nodded and clapped his hand on Pyvel's shoulder, urging him forward. Pyvel started to speak, to use his "But, uncle" phrase, and Valenty dug his fingers into the boy's neck. "Mouth shut," he whispered in Numinasi. The three of them left the barricaded area, as soldiers who had been moving about on business stopped to salute.

Once into a deserted section of the crossing, Valenty whispered to Urik and Pyvel, "Beyond the next turn, we run."

⚬⚬⚬

THE CROSSINGS GREW EERILY QUIET. THE THREE OF THEM hurried along the major path, passing side routes to the realms of the Lion Court and the Jade Pavilion. When a major route bisected their way, they found more foot traffic: messengers and

Volkish military units both coming and going. They passed the junction to Norslad, the second front of the war.

In the warm environs they pressed on, sweating in their wool clothes. Pyvel carried his cloak. The presence of a young boy attracted attention from the few soldiers who passed them.

Urik spoke low to Valenty. "We should head for Numin Pass Gate. It is the least-watched."

"Numin leaves us far from Osta Kiya," Valenty whispered. And in the mountains, difficult to traverse in winter. "Better to go through Lowgate."

"Not worth the risk. We will be questioned again."

Valenty knew he was right. But Lowgate would get them the closest to Osta Kiya, and he was eager to return to Yevliesza, who presumably would be there.

"Numin Gate is not barricaded by the Volkish," Urik persisted.

It was why he and Urik had used that gate when they came through previously. Volkia considered the gate too inaccessible for Numinat to use for military purposes, especially in winter. But there was more to Valenty's reluctance. He was watching for Yevliesza. He expected to see her—a wild hope—but one that kept him watching for a woman with black hair wearing Numinasi clothing. Pyvel had said she had been sent to Volkia on some purpose, a purpose unknown to the boy. That she would be passing through the very paths they were using was not completely unlikely. She would be coming from Volkia and heading toward the Numinasi gates. Volkia would not keep her, even with Anastyna's declaration of war. Why would they hold her hostage? She was not a personage of note, and the first offensive from Numinat had not yet begun.

But he could not risk the lives of the two under his command, not simply for his wish to find Yevliesza and know that she was well.

"Numin Pass Gate, then."

Eventually they came upon the side path leading to it. If they were seen at this point, the story would be that Prince Albrecht had sent his head of intelligence to speak of an accord between Numinat and Volkia. It might work, even if the choice of gates would appear illogical.

But they came to Numin Gate without incident. Urik pounded on the door and shouted the watchword. As the door began to open, Valenty took a last look into the crossings. He could almost convince himself that he saw Yevliesza in the shadow of the last turn.

With frigid mountain air flowing into the crossing, Urik waited for him at the door. He stood aside for Valenty to pass, but Valenty stopped and gestured for Urik to go first. Their eyes met. Valenty would have been dead three times over had it not been for this man. And he had grown to regard him as a friend. Pyvel, of course, worshipped him.

As Urik walked through the gate Valenty said, "You can release my disguise now."

"Already done," the *harjat* muttered. "The boy and I were sick of looking at you."

Pyvel laughed and followed them through the door.

Chapter Fifty

Tirhan led his party on their horses down a steep hillside. The temperature had dropped and dropped. It was too cold to snow and the sun was only a hole in the sky, shedding no warmth. Of the four of them, including Morwen and Osric, Cadris bore the most bloodstains, with the skirt of her gown streaked red from Kierach's last moment.

Their path through the snow would be easy to follow if any of the Volkish units came this far. But Tirhan's worries were all for the queen and his sister, even though they had the larger escort, including Demyr, who was worth any three men. How the Volkish had learned of the Glenir Manor attack so quickly puzzled him. Mirror sendings could not convey more than prearranged symbols. He supposed *enemy attack* would be one of them. But it might also be that a clansman in the holding near Glenir where they had recruited fighters had sent word to the nearest Volkish post. It was always a risk to approach lands where the loyalty of the clan lord might change depending on the fortunes of the hostilities.

The memory of Kierach's death shadowed Tirhan's heart. He hated having left his friend's body behind, but they needed speed, for Cadris's sake if nothing else. She was next in line to accede to the Silverwood Throne, and he had begun to think she would make a fine leader.

At the bottom of the hill a wide valley came into view, one dominated by a broad frozen lake huddled under robes of snow. Osric pointed to the sky. A dactyl flew in the near distance. Tirhan bade his group remain in the trees in case the dactyl was under compulsion and carried a watcher. The creature soon disappeared over a ridge, having remained too far away to allow them to discern if it had a rider.

Morwen said, "They may hunt us still, and we will be easy to pick off in the valley. We can take a trail along the ridge." She looked to one side of the valley. "I know it well."

"The horses will have no fodder there," Tirhan said. "And we are close now. We go on."

Cadris narrowed her eyes at Morwen. "Do you think the dactyl was mounted? Do they attempt such things?" It was exceedingly strange to think of a dactyl so restrained, those great beasts that had never known human rule in Alfan Sih.

"I have not seen it," Tirhan said. "But our enemy did compel the wraith wolves."

Cadris pursed her lips in disdain. "By the Mythos . . ."

Tirhan led them into the open. The wind scoured down from the hills, whipping out strands of new-fallen snow like an old woman's hair in a squall. The Creigath Forest was a dark line on the horizon. He did not know who he would find in the caves that were their destination.

Nor, apparently, was the otherworld guide of a mind to tell him or advise him. Perhaps the old man/warrior/messenger considered his job done. The wraith wolves were free. And the realm of the living and its conflicts might be to that spirit like a fading dream of events long past.

Once they penetrated the forest, they stopped at the base of an enormous fir tree with branches spreading far out from the trunk. Morwen brought forth two locks of hair. One was from Kierach, a man who had been a high lord, adviser to the Alfan king and then his son; the other lock was Lodd's, an expert hunter in his ancestral clan, and a skilled archer for his sovereign lord.

Tirhan dug in the hard soil with a small shovel until he had a good depth.

Tirhan's sister asked Morwen if she might convey the locks to their resting place, and Morwen gave them to her. Cadris placed them carefully in the ground and, with Tirhan kneeling at her side, they both scooped the soil back into place with their hands, sprinkling fir needles over the patch of bare ground.

It was not long before they heard a cooing signal from the distance. Osric gave the return call, and after a few moments two riders appeared through the trees to meet them. They nodded to Tirhan and then to Cadris. As Tirhan's group stopped for a brief rest, the scouts shared out food and ale from their saddlebags, first assuring Tirhan that the queen and young princess had arrived safely and that the other bands from the Glenir battle had evaded Volkish pursuit. It was glorious news, shaded only by Tirhan's losses.

Soon Tirhan and his group were making their way up the cliffside. Calls flitted through the woods, conveying news of the prince's approach, so that by the time they reached their wintering quarters in the Creigath cave system, Tirhan's mother and sister were on the ledge, waiting to greet them.

"My son," Gwenid said, as though there had never been a doubt of his safe arrival. Tirhan went to one knee, and she raised him with a lift of her hand. She was not queen in her own right, but neither was Tirhan the king until the clans met to decide.

"Lord Kierach fell yesterday, my lady. We fought off a small band, and Lodd died also."

"That is heavy news. I am very sorry." She turned to Cadris.

"By the blood on your shredded gown, I conclude that in the fight you acquitted yourself well?"

"I was useless, madam," Cadris said. She turned to Morwen. "But Morwen fought like a denizen of hell."

Gwenid turned to look at the woman fighter, noting her leathers and knife belt. "We shall hear more of this," she said with some reserve.

Morwen nodded like a man, and then the group was enfolded by their fellow warriors, everyone eager to hear tales of the Volkish pursuit. Cadris looked pointedly at her brother, conveying the necessity—which he already understood—of telling their mother what Morwen's status was.

His intentions were quickly told. Gwenid had known Morwen from the time before; she had visited at court with her mother and had been in the group that surrounded her son. He had liked her, and that led to friendship and now with the Volkish occupation she had been at his side as one of the partisans. His shield, in fact. But what might have been a brief love affair had grown into a strong bond. A bond that Tirhan wished to make permanent.

Tirhan knew that Morwen did not bring with her a clear political advantage. On the contrary, a powerful clan lord had all but offered his warriors for the liberation fight in return for a marriage with his daughter Anwelyth. Gryffyd's holdings were vast, and the men he could bring to the cause might turn the tide.

But a nagging doubt hung around the offer. How long would Gryffyd last in the conflict if his motive was a royal marriage and not clearing Alfan Sih of the oppressor? Tirhan did not dislike or blame Anwelyth, but her father's plans stank of ambition and dishonor. Kierach had acknowledged as much but had urged him to understand and accept the hard choices of kingship. Tirhan had always responded that a Queen Morwen who had bravely fought the enemy would ignite people's imaginations and lend a legitimacy to his reign—if a reign was in his future, but even as the words came out of his mouth, he had known that going against the custom of choosing a wife from among the great clans was a risk. And if Gwenid was against it, Morwen would find no welcome at the Silverwood Court.

Nor for that matter had he and Morwen discussed it outright, always dancing around the disparity of their stations, with her straddling the line between paramour and subject, at least in front of Tirhan's small band.

The partisans rested until the evening meal, Cadris falling dead asleep, and Morwen keeping her distance from everyone, her expression dark as she sharpened her knives. Tirhan spoke with Demyr, making him second-in-command, a position he well deserved.

After the meal of stew and hard bread, Tirhan found Morwen in the node of the cave that sheltered the horses.

She was currying her mount with a precision that suggested she needed to do it more than the stallion needed to have it.

"Morwen."

She looked up, making a quick connection with him, then went back to her work.

"Let one of the men to that."

"I choose to do it."

"You do not have to make a show of knowing your place."

Her eyes flashed. "And you do not have to tell me how to act."

He put his hand on her forearm. Morwen turned to him, and words fell away from them. He did not know what to say, nor did she. She came into his arms, and they remained in the embrace, wordlessly sharing the burden of all they had been through and what it had meant, of sacrifice and hope.

He pulled away from her and held her at arms' length. "The queen asks you to join her at the fire."

❦

GWENID HAD HER OWN SMALL FIRE AT THE BACK OF THE MAIN cave, and there the men had made seats out of flat rocks and logs, so the women did not have to sit on the ground. Morwen was Gwenid's only guest, and it was all the warriors in the cave could do to keep from watching them, wondering what the outcome would be, since the two women were sober in their aspect and sometimes frowning.

Tirhan knew he must keep out of this meeting. Cadris and Hanavar sat with him around the main fire and told their stories of the Volkish invasion, their swift capture after fleeing the royal house, and their imprisonment. They were events that Tirhan had wanted to hear, but this night half his mind was at the other fire, and he grew restless and then incensed by his mother's long grilling of Morwen.

"What are they talking about?" Hanavar asked, voicing the very question on Tirhan's mind.

Cadris watched him for his answer.

"The queen is deciding Morwen's future."

"As what?" Hanavar asked in surprise.

Tirhan did not answer. As the moments passed, eventually Hanavar said, "Oh. I thought . . ."

Cadris snapped, "Do not think, Hanavar. Wait."

But it was too much for Tirhan, and he stood up, striding to the queen's fire. He might be a prince who needed to practice patience, but he was also the heir to the throne and by the Nine he was not going have Morwen questioned like an erring servant.

"My Lady," he said to Gwenid. "Have you not had enough time to get acquainted?"

Morwen took a slow breath and kept her attention on the snapping fire.

Gwenid looked up at her son with a small smile. "If she is to be your queen, she deserves to know what she is getting into." His mother's smile grew in depth. She gestured for Tirhan to take a seat next to Morwen.

Every eye in the cave was upon them. Morwen slipped her hand into his, and her grip was strong and easy.

Chapter Fifty-One

Dreiza had not ridden on horseback for a very long time, and every joint in her body grumbled. The other *satvars* did not appear to have fared any better over the three-day, punishing ride. Father Ludving, however, being a young forty-seven, appeared as fit and unaffected as a young *harjat*.

Everyone in the group except Dreiza were healers, and at their camp the previous night they worked their powers on each other to ease the pains of the hard ride, hands resting on sore limbs and aching bones.

In recognition of her past connection to Yevliesza, Dreiza had been put in charge of the group by the High Mother. The current endeavor, approved by the High Mother, acknowledged to Dreiza's satisfaction that there were times when *satvars* took action in the outside world.

They came within view of Causeway Gate. At this hour of the night, the fort and the strip of land bisecting the lake were lit by torches flickering in the wind. On the surface of the lake, a rippling image of the crescent moon.

The garrison crouched in the middle of the causeway

stretching across the lake, a strange place for a boundary gate, it seemed to her. Of course, there was no apparent boundary. Behind the fort was only the rest of the causeway and the far shore and, beyond, the flat scrub steppe. But in the ground far below lay access to the crossings.

Before the procession of eight *satvars* and a priest had even set foot on the causeway, the fort opened its entry door, and Numinasi soldiers held torches to welcome them.

The party was ushered into a warm hall where hearty soup and fresh bread waited for them. Father Ludving drew attention. The soldiers did not hide their mistrust of an enemy priest in their midst, even if the princip's order was to let him through. His presence was needed because once in the crossings, they would encounter enemy checkpoints and, being Volkish, the father would add credibility to their tale. They would style themselves as an order of healers benefitting those injured in war. They called themselves the *Satvars* of Mercy and hoped that the idea would seem plausible, especially with a Volkish priest involved.

They descended the steps into the crossings, bearing sacks of bandages, ointments, and blankets, as well as healing broths in leather skins.

Sister Yarna was tall and solidly built. She could carry a heavy load, but when she came to the foot of the stairs, she put down the saddlebags and looked around, captivated.

Dreiza understood. She herself had only been in the crossings once, but she remembered the feeling of awe that came over one in the presence of the Mythos pathways for the first time. It was an environs unlike any other, with a peculiar, though not unpleasant, smell of a living creature. Its subtle light shone without a source. Also strange, the flexing, pebbly walls and floor, the latter giving with each footstep as though this were the body of the Mythos itself.

It appeared that Yarna was overcome with wonderment, even

veneration. But they had no time to lose. Father Ludving kindly took up her saddlebags and the group proceeded toward the main pathway, expecting at any moment to face off with Volkish guards. The soldiers had no right to forbid passage, but they had been doing so for a month.

Around a bend in the path, a barricade came into view. Three soldiers came forward, their expressions stern. Father Ludving spoke to them, at times gesturing at the women behind him. Soon a superior officer joined them and appeared to scoff at the proposal. As planned, Dreiza, who had a smattering of Volkish, came forward and talked excitedly about providing care to the wounded without regard of homeland. What harm could a few *satvars* do? It would benefit the soldiers. Ludving put a hand on her arm to restrain her, turning an ironic look on the officer and apologizing for the outburst.

The soldier left Ludving's side and demanded that the women open their bags. Soldiers searched through them as Dreiza fretted over unrolled bandages and hastily repacked supplies. Finally the officer insisted that the *satvars* drink from the skins of broth. Dreiza cast a furious look at Ludving, who shrugged, urging her to do it.

That test finished, they were allowed through the barricade. Volkish guards took them to a great widening in the cave where wounded or exhausted soldiers were lying down or leaning against the corridor walls, bloodied bandages binding their wounds. Some patients looked uninjured physically, but stared at nothing, their eyes blank and faces slack.

"We begin," Dreiza told the group, and they spread out to assess the wounded, with the worst of them receiving the first attention. Father Ludving was gratefully received by the men and soon the *satvars* were as well.

It was a ruse. But it was also true healing, as they set bones,

cleaned wounds, refreshed bandages, and lay hands on trauma-
tized bodies, bringing comfort to young Volkish men who had
been sent to two fronts: Alfan Sih and Norslad. And soon, they
feared, to Numinat.

Chapter Fifty-Two

Yevliesza watched from the reception room window. That room gave her a view to the circular road in front of the palace's main entrance. She did not actually see Albrecht enter the carriage, which worried her, but Reinhart had climbed in as well as another officer. And it *was* Albrecht's carriage.

She wandered back to her apartment, pretending to stifle a yawn, and shut the door behind her. It was 11:42.

In the bedroom, she took off her gown and put on her robe and the men's socks she had stashed. Making a thick braid of her hair, she secured it with a black strip she had taken from one of her Numinasi dresses. Back in the bedroom, she rumpled the bed enough that it might look like she had slept at least partway through the night. She took off her shift and tied a wide band of black cloth across her breasts.

At that point she was ready to put on the uniform and boots. Her hands shook as she pulled on the trousers. Then the jacket of heavy wool. Sitting in a chair, she laced up the boots. The soft army cap went into her waistband lest it fall off during her descent. Now was no time to check her appearance in the mirror, but she caught a glimpse of herself as she rushed from the room, seeing a slightly built soldier with a worried expression.

Her heart pounded in her chest, in her ears. What had she forgotten? The knife. She charged back to the mattress and retrieved it. It went into her boot, and she lowered the trouser leg over it.

At the window, she released the mechanism that held the two panes together and opened them. Frigid air embraced her. She raised one leg over the sill, straddling it and looked at the twisting wood branches down which she would have to climb.

Since the braid of stalks was very tight, there weren't as many gaps as she had hoped. She swung her body out, leaning over the windowsill, her back to the night and the fog, her legs dangling below her as she stretched to find a foothold. She found one, testing it for strength. Judging that it would hold her weight, she pulled the windows closed as far as she could.

Removing a long pieced of knotted material from a breast pocket, she slipped the pre-prepared loop around the corner of one of the panes and pulled it shut. Then she spent a few moments sliding the noose out from under the window frame and attached the loop to the other window, pulling it shut. She had been standing on one leg for too long, and it protested with shooting pains. In her hurry, she lost hold of the strip of cloth, and it disappeared into the murk.

The whole time she had been shutting the windows she worried about the next foothold. Her arms weren't strong enough for her to go hand-over-hand down the stalk, but she was able to do so for a minute or two as she gripped the woody branches and her feet flailed for the next purchase. Her hands slipped down the branches, tearing her skin. The ground was still far, far below her, a fall that would break her neck. Her foot hit a V-shaped junction in the vine, and she tested it for stability. Her boot slid down it, coming to a stop in the crevice.

She looked down to judge how far she now had to go. The first-floor windows looked to be about twelve feet below her level. Deciding she was being too cautious, she began a crab walk down the vine, sometimes failing to find a foothold, but often finding a slight indentation that took pressure off her hands and arms which were beginning to give out.

The vine rattled with each of her moves, and her boots sometimes thumped against the stone wall. Light blasted from the windows that she would pass between. People were still working in the first-floor offices and might come to the window if they heard a sound. She slowed down and, step by step, searched for and found purchase for one foot or the other. When her boots hit the frozen snow, she almost fell into the embrace of the ground. Instead, she curled up against the palace wall, putting her frozen hands under her armpits in an attempt to bring them back to working order.

It was a good thing that she hadn't sprawled into the snow. A shadow came to the nearest window. Someone looking out. Whoever it was would see only fog, thick as sheep's wool. But if she left the side of the building, she might be spotted against the snow-laden yard.

The man remained at the window for so long that she could only think of how many minutes had passed since Albrecht left. But if Tanfred's coach was nearby, then her timing might still be good. Her calves ached, and she longed to stretch out and rub her legs, but she stayed hunkered into a ball. The fog traveled up from the river in gray waves, some so dense she could not see the outline of the man at the window, or even if he was still there.

Standing at last, she flattened herself along the wall and moved farther away from the watcher. All the windows were lit. She would have to cross the yard in front of one of them. And did. She set out slowly, her feet crunching into the crust of old snow with a sound of shattering glass. Leaving the deeper drifts of snow against the wall, she soon was moving rapidly through shallow snow, approaching a thicket of brambles. She knew these bushes. They formed a distant border to the palace. For cover, she would walk along the riverside edge of them. She hurried through the first barrier of them, holding her arms around her face to keep the twigs from tearing at her.

After a few minutes she realized that she had gone too far. The hedge should not be this thick. She had been following a map in her mind. Go through the hedge. Turn left and follow along its far side until you reach the road. But the map was wrong. Nearby the river sluiced by, but she could not see it. The thought of tumbling over the embankment visited—*of course* it did—but she shoved it away.

Beyond the hedge, Rothsvund Palace loomed distant and high. She had counted on staying out of sight of the sentries on the roof by hiding behind the hedge, but she must have come to a place where the hedge curved down to the river. She had to retrace her steps. But as she forced her way into the brambles, she became less and less sure of which direction she was now headed in. Furiously, she went on, but at last she found herself so far into the hedge that her sense of direction vanished. She knelt among branches and roots, trying to think of what to do. Somewhere out there, the river moved like a great, slithering monster. Close, very close. She despaired to think of the time she had wasted. Crouching in the midst of the bushes, she listened to her breath and the heavy river flowing.

Something moved in the thicket. Something big. A dog? She stared hard. It was a shadow of a shadow, a low, bulky shape made of snow and fog. Not a dog. It was a wolf.

It stopped some four or five feet away, facing her, its green eyes catching a light from somewhere.

Time came to a stop. She stared at the beast and it at her. *Begone*, she wanted to say, remembering it was what Valenty had said to dispel the likeness of the thrall Nashavety had sent. But she could neither speak nor move, or at least neither seemed like a good idea.

The wolf looked to one side, as though it had heard something. Then it took a few steps in that direction. It stopped and turned its head back toward her, its green eyes the only color in the whole world. It wanted her to follow it. Didn't it? Isn't that why it was still looking at her, even as it took another step?

But it was heading back in the direction she had come. The last thing she needed to do was to follow an animal—*toward* the palace—but she had become desperate, almost losing her ability to think.

She remembered having once seen a wolf in the woodland where she had taken arcana training. That wolf had appeared to be watching her, showing itself, almost, because it had been fairly close to her. When it went behind a tree, it disappeared.

Desperate now, she followed the wolf in the thicket of bushes. It walked easily through the labyrinth of branches and roots, sometimes vanishing as a curtain of fog sailed through, then reappearing again, always looking back for her.

Suddenly she was free of the thicket. The wolf was still there, just ahead. It led her up the incline toward the palace, then turned into bushes again. Following it, Yevliesza entered a narrow opening in the hedge. There she discovered a clear path forward.

The wolf was now moving faster, and she hurried after it. Was this wolf a *sympat*—if wolves could even *be sympats*—and if so, might this one belong to Tanfred's coachman or, ominously, a palace guard?

As the hedge ended, the creature disappeared into the fog again. She stared into a gray miasma lit here and there by haloed lights from the palace windows. This was the side of the palace with the courtyard and stable. She had seen riders arriving here—

including the ugly mechanical wagons. Nearby, she knew, was a road.

The wolf came into view again, leading her into a flat expanse of snow. Now that she was free of the thicket and its panic, she felt deathly cold. It burned at her face and hands. From time to time, she heard a horse whinny from the courtyard . . . unless it was from the nearby road.

Sometimes she walked blind, unable to see where her next step was, always watching for the shadow in the fog, the animal that seemed to know the way. She had started to believe that it was a wraith wolf, and she couldn't fathom why it had come to her. At times it disappeared entirely. Each time it reappeared, it corrected her course. People had told her that these creatures could pass in and out of the spirit world. She shouldn't trust it like this, but truthfully, she had little choice.

Without warning, a great bulk emerged out of the fog. A carriage with two pairs of horses stood waiting. She'd had little sense that she was right next to the road, but she was.

A man's form swirled out of the fog, causing her to gasp. She drew back, but then he spoke.

"Yevliesza, it is me." Tanfred.

She hurried up a gentle incline to the road and threw her arms around him. He hugged her but spoke over her shoulder to his coachman and then quickly ushered her into the coach, closing the door as the carriage lurched forward. She sat back on the bench next to Tanfred. As the carriage jolted from side to side over the uneven, shoveled road, she closed her eyes, trying to calm herself.

They took a sharp turn onto another street, one that ran parallel to the back of the palace, but at a good distance. They were leaving the Danstree River behind and traveling at a sedate pace while still in view of the palace. Yevliesza imagined every lit window had a Volkish soldier looking out and wondering why a carriage would be on the streets this late.

"Can we not hurry?" she asked.

"Not yet, but my man has his orders to make all haste once we are out of view of the palace and the church."

The Church of All Saints. They would go by *there*?

"We will not go close," Tanfred reassured her, "but this is the quickest way to the city gates." He paused. "I thought . . . I thought they had caught you."

"I got lost in the fog," she said, thinking how close the matter had been and how desperate her situation would have been if the wolf hadn't come.

"Thank God," he whispered.

"How long did you wait?"

"Not long," he said, but she wasn't sure he was telling the truth. "Now we must cut your hair. If you do not mind?"

"Oh, God, I forgot the scissors!"

"I brought one. I will cut it off to shoulder-length."

She took off her cap, and he untied her braid. Spreading her hair out around her face, he began to cut, throwing the pieces out the window. He fussed with the length, snipping here and there and struggling in the bouncing coach to make the sides match. Once, he jabbed the scissors into her neck, apologizing profusely.

"Tanfred, no one will notice if it's uneven," she pleaded.

He stopped snipping at last. "It should be parted in the middle," he said as he drew out a comb. When he had parted her hair, he squinted at her, frowning. "No. I'll pull it back and tie it."

Using the strip of cloth she had used for her braid, he pulled her hair back tightly and tied it off.

On the seat beside him was bundle of what looked like clothes. "Put these on; they will be better than the uniform. Civilian dress will work better at the gate."

Her hands were stiff with cold as she undressed, shedding the uniform she had spent so many hours altering. Tanfred tucked the discarded uniform under the bench seat and turned to look out the window as she undressed, ever the courteous duke. The clothes were of fine cloth: A shirt with ample sleeves; a pair of soft wool trousers, and supple, short boots. When he judged she was decently dressed, he helped her into a jacket lined in fur. Last came a leather cap with a brim that she could pull down a little to help obscure her face.

The pace of the carriage was still maddeningly slow. After the haircut and the change of clothes, she had time to think what came next. It was sobering. If Albrecht found her gone, he would come after her in a rage. If captured, Tanfred might be in more danger than she would be. Albrecht might still regard her as useful, although who knew how terrible his anger would be?

Down one of the streets she caught sight of the Church of All Graces. Its great lancet windows glowed with yellow light, in the fog looking like some distant heaven where God sat on a throne and judged his creatures, one by one. She didn't know how such a being would judge her, if it came to that. What had she ever done that raised her actions to a level of self-sacrifice or mercy? It was one of the questions that she would have to grapple with if she ever had the chance. Because living as she had been was not the answer.

Once past the church, the carriage heaved forward, as the coachman urged the horses to speed. She wanted to look behind them, but this was a carriage, not a car, and looking for pursuers wasn't possible. She didn't know if a coach with four horses pulling it would be faster than men on horseback, and she decided that single horsemen would be faster. So everything depended on the priest at All Graces giving a long sermon.

"How far to the boundary gate?"

"Two hours," Tanfred said. "But remember, Albrecht will

always be an hour behind us, even if he does come to your room." He patted her knee, but his hands were shaking.

She hadn't noticed until now how glassy-eyed he looked. He was terrified. "Tanfred. What is the worst that can happen?" When he didn't answer, she said, "They might kill us. We have to accept that it could happen. It's one outcome. The only question is, are we ready?" She thought *she* was, because staying with Albrecht was worse than dying. It would be death masquerading as life. But Tanfred . . . he was giving up a comfortable life, an honorable one. "Are you ready for what might happen?"

"I am. Of course I am."

"Then we won't worry about it. You are the richest duke in the world. The guards are likely to fall all over themselves being gracious to you."

"I am hardly the richest."

"All right, but you love your kingdom and are prepared to die for it. You're a hero, even if they win."

Reaching into her pocket, she took out his ring, the one that he had given Evah to prove that he trusted her. She handed it to him. "It was good that you thought to do that. I don't think I would have trusted Evah otherwise."

He took it from her and put it on, rubbing the cross protruding from the surface. "Would you not have? She wanted nothing more than for you to be gone."

"But it was hard to know what her feelings really were. Sometimes she seemed so childish."

"Perhaps." He paused. "Who knows what she might have been like, had not Albrecht subdued her with creature power?"

They raced through the city streets, passing homes with darkened windows, streets devoid of people or conveyances. In a few alleys she glimpsed a shadowy figure or two Val in the murk. Sentries stood at some of the intersections. The city seemed tense; its people, hiding.

"What happened the day that Albrecht came back?" Tanfred asked. "I worried terribly for you, because he was in such a fury. Did he hurt you?"

That was a story she would never tell. It was a bitter thing, a degradation. She wasn't prepared to talk about it. She could barely think about it.

"He struck me. Nashavety had told him things, things about the new path to Alfan Sih. She revealed that when I was questioned by the Numinat court, I told them I had been to Alfan Sih with Lord Tirhan, something I had never admitted to Albrecht. He was furious."

"He did not beat you. . . ."

"No. But he told me I would never go home. He suspected I knew something about the creation of the new path, or I never would have maintained my stance of *not* having gone to Alfan Sih. And then: how my presence had been detected in the crossings. So he couldn't afford to let me go."

Tanfred shook his head bitterly. "I have brought this upon you. If I had never spoken to Albrecht about the *Eibelung*, none of this would have happened."

"You didn't know. You couldn't have known how it would turn out. Please don't blame yourself. I don't know what I would have done without you."

She went on. "But Nashavety told him about the markings on my back."

Tanfred looked affronted. "And he . . . he saw them?"

He had some very strong ideas about propriety. Thank God someone did. "He did make me show him. That was all there was to it."

"God," he whispered vehemently.

She couldn't bring herself to share how awful that day was. She had nothing to be ashamed of, but neither did she have to describe it, to stir anger and pity from a man who could do nothing to change it or make it a matter of justice.

"I told him that the patterns were the mark of a second power, and I suggested it was verdure. A wild claim, but he didn't call it a lie." Tanfred kept shaking his head, taking blame on himself, and she wanted to ease his sense of responsibility. Anastyna was responsible. And Yevliesza herself, for hiding what she was.

"Tanfred," she said. "Whatever happens in the next few hours, I will always thank God that I met you. There is only one other person I have told what I can do. Rusadka, a *harjat* and close friend. You taught me that sometimes I can trust others. It was a revelation to me that day on the palace roof when you said you would help me. I will always be grateful."

He looked greatly moved, but she thought he would always regret his early actions in warning Albrecht. How much worse he would take it if he knew what Albrecht had really done when he confronted her.

As they sped through the city streets, spraying sleet from under the carriage wheels, Yevliesza told him—so that she wouldn't be the only one who knew—that a Numinasi noble named Valenty had been, so Albrecht claimed, on a secret mission in Volkia. Nashavety had revealed this to him. Albrecht was on the lookout for him now and threatened to hang him if he was apprehended. She related to Tanfred that Valenty had rescued a boy from Nashavety's hideaway, a boy named Pyvel. If she didn't make it back, he should tell the princip this.

Up ahead, torches on a high wall. The city gate. They readied themselves. "You are a duke, Tanfred. No one will contradict you," she whispered. They slowed and the coachman brought the carriage to a halt.

A soldier approached. Leaning out of the window, Tanfred drew his attention and, when the soldier was at the carriage window, Tanfred wished him good evening in Volkish.

The two of them exchanged a few words, the duke adopting a tone that conveyed power and casual privilege. The guard peered in, seeing what Yevliesza hoped was a young man in the duke's company. They had decided she would wear the cap inside the carriage to add to the masculine appearance and, for good measure, she looked out the far window, averting her face.

In another moment the carriage moved through the gated city wall. She shivered, despite having talked about not being afraid to die, and at last they were on the road to Rorrs Gate.

Chapter Fifty-Three

They approached the boundary gate. On the road they had stopped to dispose of the army uniform. Tanfred threw it down a ravine. Then they rushed on. The fog that had surrounded Hapsigen had thinned, then evaporated on the road, but in the dark they could not see much of the valley where Rorrs Gate nestled.

Yevliesza and Tanfred had rolled up the leather blinds of the carriage window to see any sign of his promised diversion, the distraction mounted by several hundred primordialists. He had contacted dozens of them and urged them to share the word that their ninth-power hopes desperately needed help.

Pinpricks of light, hundreds of them, lit the fields near the army outpost. A crowd had gathered. Now and then, a cheer erupted from the throng.

It was a diversion meant to distract the guards, at least to some extent. He had asked his fellow primordialists to come to Rorrs Gate as though to cheer on the troops, but in fact to help him save the *Eibelung*. The garrison commandant had them cordoned far away from the gate and the encampment, but their presence was clear from the flickering candles they held. Tanfred felt sure that the crowd wouldn't be driven off, given that they had come to support the troops. But the diversion could not be a dramatic one; they did not dare protest or pose a real threat.

Tanfred knew she was not the *Eibelung*, not the one who could save their land in the way that they believed. But perhaps she could in a different way—one she had yet to determine. Tanfred believed that and was bringing every resource he could find to making sure she survived to do so.

The coach slowed, now approaching what looked like a ramp descending into the ground. A cheer went up as the guard was changed on the sides of the ramp. A woman broke free of the roped area and ran toward them. She carried something in a cloth. When soldiers forced her back into the group, she submitted, but urged them to take the bundle.

"They brought freshly baked bread," Tanfred said. "Now that they have seen us, they know to make a clamor." It would occupy some of the guards' attention.

Several soldiers were approaching the coach, coming at it from both sides. Had Albrecht alerted the gate? Had he come to her room after all, deciding to wake her? She pushed that thought below the surface and tried to fall into her role of Bertoldt, a young man in company of his important cousin.

Tanfred murmured at her, "Look unhappy, frown." A soldier's face appeared in the window. A short, Volkish acknowledgment of the duke. Tanfred answered. For the soldier approaching her side of the carriage, she had a few sentences ready, but at the moment she could only remember one, *You must ask my cousin, the duke.*

This soldier glanced inside, seeing there were only the two of them. On the other side of the carriage, Tanfred was opening the door and stepping out. He turned to her and gestured for her to follow him, calling her by her assumed name.

Sliding over on the bench, she stepped down to the carriage footrest and onto the road. The night lay vast above them, scattered with stars, an inversion of the spots of light in meadow. The soldiers wore half capes, making them seem all the bigger and more menacing. Tanfred lifted his hand in her direction to bring her to his side and they walked toward the gate. Tanfred turned to the coachman, who by necessity had been brought in on the deception. He nodded to his man. The coachman had decided to remain behind, an innocent driver, now directed to drive the coach back to Wilhoff Manor, the duke's residence. He was considerably more compensated than he ever had been before.

Close behind them came their escort, now descending the ramp with them. Torchlit and lined with sentries, the ramp was made of stone, as were the abutment walls. The door they approached loomed, foreboding and armored. And yet it was the door to freedom. Soon they would be on the other side.

More soldiers stood directly in front of the enormous door. Someone in charge, tall and thin-faced, approached and saluted Duke Tanfred. Tanfred came to attention and returned a nod. He took charge of the conversation by pointing up the ramp in the direction of the field with its people and candles, apparently asking a question about their presence, and the officer replied. Reassured, Tanfred nodded his understanding. He kept Yevliesza behind him and, as planned, he explained his need to travel, having to do with an urgent diplomatic mission to Numinat that Prince Albrecht had asked him to undertake.

The officer in charge kept his face neutral, asking a question, keeping his tone respectful. Tanfred's expression tightened, and he responded stiffly and at length, with some annoyance. Tanfred had warned her that soldiers at the gate might expect that Prince Albrecht would have given the duke a letter requiring the army's full cooperation. But it seemed that they accepted its absence.

The officer snapped something at the guards, and the soldiers began pulling aside the bar keeping the double doors locked in place. The bar screeched on its iron brackets, leaving the doors unsecured. They opened. Before Yevliesza had yet figured out that they were approved, Tanfred was ushering her ahead of him into the crossings.

They were met with a gust of warm air with a scent of baking dough. Yevliesza drew the air deeply into her lungs. It seemed to travel through her body, releasing an unbearable tension she had not even known was there.

Another checkpoint lay in front of them. This one faced outward toward the crossings. She had expected this, for it was the same arrangement as when she had come to Volkia through a different gate. The light was much brighter here than the torchlit ramp, and she squinted as her eyes adjusted.

Another officer came to converse with Tanfred. A friendlier one than before, and this officer turned to her and said something. The next second seemed to last minutes. It was a friendly remark, by his expression. Should she answer? It would appear odd if she didn't. She lowered her voice and said in Volkish, "You must ask the duke," keeping her eyes averted in case the answer would appear rude and not worthy of someone well-born.

Tanfred shrugged and said something apparently witty, because the officer who had spoken to her laughed in response. They left the barricade then, walking past the sentries. Soon they were striding down the corridor.

They had made it into the crossings, had passed each checkpoint. She and Tanfred exchanged a look, and she was happy to see him smile. She felt a calm descend, pressing through her body and easing her mind, but it was not just their success so far, it was the crossings. It was her affinity. She opened to it, and as she walked, she felt that the crossings knew her, knew her at the level of the Deep. She couldn't explain it to herself, but as she recognized it, she heard the familiar soft clicking sounds. It was the sound of the pathways growing, growing imperceptibly, taking long centuries to enlarge.

When she had been in these pathways the last time, she had thought of the clicking sounds as the crossings talking to her, but that wasn't right. She just perceived them at a level other people couldn't. The pathways would never tell her what to do or why. A flicker of disappointment ran through her. In this magical world, she had hoped for magical answers. But of course, answers had to come from *her*. And though she was only a refugee from the mundat, a minor citizen of Numinat, her dilemmas still had to be resolved in her own heart and mind. She pushed that heavy thought aside. They weren't out of danger yet. She needed to stay alert.

They passed through one of the cave-like enlargements, where the ceiling bulged high. Many Volkish soldiers rested here, and one group of soldiers looked as though they had been passing through but had stopped, making room for another unit to pass by in the opposite direction.

Tanfred boldly threaded through the tangle of soldiers, and they gave way for him. By his formal dress with its medals and brocade, he was taken for nobility and given precedence. As the two of them moved through the crowd, she saw a few women in pale tunics and trousers. They were administering to the wounded. She had heard that *satvars* dressed in this way, but surely Numinasi *satvars* would not be welcome in the crossings, since they had been taken over by the Volkish. It was odd, but Tanfred kept her to a determined pace, and soon they were into a narrower pathway.

They encountered crossroads to various destinations. Somehow, she knew where they led to, a realization that surprised her, but that she gratefully embraced. They passed the branch that connected to the mundat, but she barely acknowledged it to herself. It was Lowgate they needed.

The last time she had been in these paths, she had been determined to hide what she was, and in Volkia, she had needed to. But now she wasn't so sure. The path was quiet here, and no soldiers passed. She stopped and moved to the wall, putting her hand on it, finding it coarse and warm.

"Yevliesza?" Tanfred asked, stopping.

Her fingers pressed into the wall, a quarter inch, more than she had expected. Then she set her will for that section of the wall to open slightly, to recede from her hand enough to form a niche. It did so, melting back from her hand, creating a small, round indentation.

Tanfred stared as this happened. She could tell that he didn't want to stop but was mesmerized by what she had done. He waited.

"The crossings bend to me," she whispered.

"I know."

She came back to him, filled with ani understanding she could no longer push away. "Tanfred. I can't hide any longer. It just doesn't work."

He looked at her with great compassion. "I know, Yevliesza, I know." He took her hand. "We are close to Lowgate now. Let us hurry."

In a few minutes they approached the Volkish station that had formed outside Lowgate. There were dozens of soldiers crowded into the area. Again, a high-ranking officer came to deal with them.

As Tanfred and the officer talked, Yevliesza heard the soldier say Prince Albrecht's name. He gestured down the pathway. In dismay, she realized what that must mean: Albrecht had arrived at the crossings.

Yevliesza turned around to look in the direction from which they had just come, listening for a sound of running or raised voices.

Tanfred continued his conversation with the officer, until finally they seemed to be in agreement. He turned back to

Yevliesza and lowered his voice. "Albrecht has come," he said. "We must hurry."

Albrecht had sent a message with a mirror. But they couldn't communicate details that way. The message must have been ambiguous enough that they weren't going to detain the duke.

"They wondered if I might want to confer with Albrecht," Tanfred said. "I have persuaded them that my mission urgently needs to continue."

"I'm not going, Tanfred."

His mouth opened to say something, but he couldn't speak, his look, incredulous.

"Albrecht is here," Yevliesza whispered. "Now he's in my territory. And I'm not going to hide."

"That is madness!" Tanfred's eyes were wild. "He will take you in an instant."

"I'm in the one place I can fight. Here. And I'm going to."

When he saw her determination, he almost moaned, "Yevliesza, no."

She whispered to him. "You will go, Tanfred. Tell Anastyna everything, but not about my second power. Tell her about how the terrible machines are powered. And if I don't get out, say we were separated in the crossings, and you don't know what happened to me. Which will be true."

"I cannot let you do this," he said, his expression desperate. "I forbid it."

"You can't, Tanfred. I have my own duty, and no one can force me to do what I think is wrong." *Not now, not ever,* she promised herself.

He looked anguished. She knew he was terrified for her. And she was afraid, too. But she was also sure. "Now go, Tanfred. Go with my thanks forever."

She watched as he reluctantly left, making his way past the

soldiers to the door. Then through the door, revealing for a moment the stairs to the fort. The door closed behind him.

She walked back the way they had come. She very much wished she could have reassured Tanfred. He wanted to save her, and she would have let him if she could.

But Albrecht was here. And it was her job to stop him.

Chapter Fifty-Four

During a quiet moment in the crossings, when Yevliesza
neither saw anyone nor heard footfalls, she turned to
the wall of the pathway to open up a recess. It needed
to be large enough for her, and her plan was for it to become a
connecting passageway to other tunnels.

Her left hand trembled with the force of her concentration as
she touched the wall and willed it to open. To her relief it began to
melt back, soon forming a small crevasse and then a much larger
one some eight feet high. She held a strong vision in her mind of
a tunnel. She pushed through, entering a narrow cell. The wall
had responded to her visualization and, though she had expected
it to, a numinous awareness of its mystery enveloped her. At the
same time, she was calm, even though her next moves might
bring her into terrible danger. A spike of worry rose through her
and disappeared. She was calm, her thoughts clear.

Just as she picked up the sound of people running, she remembered to close the gap behind her. Leaving open a thin fissure, she
watched as Volkish soldiers ran by, swords in hand. They would
quickly reach Lowgate, but Tanfred was already gone.

The compartment she stood in began to elongate, becoming a

passage, seeking nearby pathways, as she intended. She willed it to continue.

Outside her hiding place was one of the main pathways, the route between Volkia and Numinat, but it was not the only path. The crossings were a network of paths, some more direct than others. Ones used as trade routes grew under constant use, and seldom-used routes remained small, but some were still possible to traverse. In her mind, a map of the pathways was opening to her, like an ancient memory recalled.

She waited for Albrecht. It was likely he would pass this way because he would be directed down the pathway that she and Tanfred had been seen to follow.

Was there a better goal than to kill him? She didn't think so. Albrecht had led his country into two brutal wars of conquest and now threatened Numinat. Thousands were dying because of him. He threatened the stability of the Mythos itself with his use of machines, devices running on the Deep elemental powers of his own countrymen. He had to be stopped before he brought everything down. The idea that she was about to take such an action seemed unlikely but, at the same time, certain. She didn't know when she had decided to fight: when Albrecht took complete control of her; when Reinhart killed Martel; when she passed the Church of All Graces and wondered if her soul would survive close scrutiny. She had wanted, intended, to know her role. And then she did.

This was Numinat's best chance to be free of Prince Albrecht. You either submit, or you fight. You either flee to safety, or you risk everything to stop the evil. If you are able. She was able. How to do this was coming clear to her.

Then he came. Albrecht. He walked by, not hurried, not slow, but looking like there was only one thing on his mind. He wore parade dress. Reinhart and several other officers accompanied him.

Albrecht walked out of view. More soldiers came in his wake. When they didn't find her, they would look for her along other paths, narrower ones. They would split up. She would find Albrecht alone. She turned toward the tunnel that lay before her and began walking, expanding it.

◎◈◈

AS SHE WALKED, WILLING THE TUNNEL TO CONTINUE, SHE NOTED whorls in the fabric of the place, small concentric rings like the pattern of a rock thrown into a pond. She decided to try one node, placing her hand upon it. The whorl enlarged rapidly, leading her into another narrow pathway.

For a time she wandered, finding side paths and pursuing them, each one extending the map that her mind held ever more clearly. She had known that the pathways were more extensive than a few main routes. They had grown over time, like an ancient tree that produced branches and twigs from a buried pattern.

She came to a place where the pathway flared out into a wide, funnel-shaped cave. Muffled voices came to her from beyond the wall. She placed her hand on the wall to create a small fissure. Silently, it formed, and she could see out the narrow gash.

It was a cavern along the main path. A number of soldiers lay on the ground or sat up against the walls, a few civilians administering to them. This was a major chamber at a junction of pathways. She had seen it when she went through just an hour earlier, with women in light-colored tunics and trousers nursing the soldiers. She thought they were *satvars*, by what she had heard of their style of dress. One of them rose from ministering to a soldier and placed her hands on the small of her back, stretching.

It looked like Dreiza. It *was* Dreiza. And tending Volkish soldiers. Yevliesza couldn't put the pieces together, why she would be aiding enemy soldiers, unless it was something expected of those who took the pale. Dreiza seemed to be looking right at her. Her face took on an alert expression, along with a small frown of confusion. But she couldn't see through the wall. Or did she have a foreknowing, sensing through that affinity how close Yevliesza was? The sight of her brought a strong memory of Osta Kiya and the people whom she had loved there. Rusadka, Pyvel, Tirhan. And Valenty. She yearned to see Valenty, while fearing that he was receding from her. She wondered if she was pushing him away because she could never give him what he wanted. *No,* she firmly told herself. *It is still possible for us. Somehow, it is still possible.*

Looking through the narrow slit her vision was restricted, but she saw Reinhart come past with a group of soldiers. The search was spreading out. That was helpful to her purpose. Let them come into the side tunnels. Let Albrecht come.

Yevliesza sat down and leaned against the wall, weary and thirsty. She could not continue much longer without water. Closing her eyes to rest for a few moments, she fell into a profound stillness. Her breathing slowed. A scene came to her mind: the pattern of the tunnels. She was looking down on it, and saw each path and intersection and node. She saw herself sitting there, her head tilted back against the wall. In some areas, soldiers were entering the side paths from the main tunnels. They were far from her, or far enough.

Albrecht was among them. She stood up. It was obvious which one he was, the one in the uniform with braided cords at his shoulder. Opening her eyes, the vision of the network became less clear to her.

To keep the map of the routes clear—the map in real time— she closed her eyes again and saw the way to go. Now she hurried.

She laid her plan. It began with finding a moment when there was a gap between Albrecht and his men. Even a small gap would do. But she needed to find a path that was close enough to his course that she could quickly emerge and get his attention. As he walked on, he sometimes afforded her that possibility, but only intermittently. She would have to be close to him to take advantage of any time he was alone, but the paths did not often provide her close access.

She rushed ahead of him to a likely interception point, all the while aware of how far away he was and whether he paused, but sometimes he and his men took a side path and she had to backtrack.

Then she saw him coming. She saw the junction where their paths could meet. And it happened that his soldiers were a few paces ahead of him. Rushing into a pathway leading to him, she opened the wall. He was just turning a corner.

"Albrecht," she whispered. He turned. And charged at her. Leaving the gap in the wall open, she dashed down the tunnel and turned into a side path, one that connected to the labyrinth in a way that suited her. She heard him behind her, just far enough. He thought he was in control now, but it was the opposite. Maybe she had lost her mind, not to be afraid. But she didn't want to be governed by fear, didn't want to obey, to cower, to say, *Tell me what you want, Albrecht, and I will give it to you.*

"Stop!" he shouted, when he had lost her. "It is no use to run. You know it is over. I have soldiers everywhere."

She had the map. She knew it like the rooms of her house in the mundat. And he did not.

"But, Albrecht, your soldiers are ignorant."

By her voice he knew her direction, and she hurried on, leading him deeper into the maze.

"I killed your Lord Valenty," he said from very close by. "I had him hung."

Her concentration faltered. Collapsed. Not true, not true . . .

he would say anything to intimidate her. The map faded from her internal sight.

And then Albrecht was in sight, emerging from a side path. He lunged for her. Grabbed her forearm, yanking her toward him. His face was drenched in sweat, his eyes flashing in the fey light surrounding them.

"You traitorous witch," he rasped, "you will pay for this, pay dearly."

She struggled against him and, furious, he threw her against the wall, pinning her forearm against the surface of it.

"Let go of me!" she hissed at him.

His lip curled as he held her in place, lifting her arm so high on the wall that she cried out. She closed her eyes against the pain, and as she did so the map came back into her perception. She saw him holding her arm against the wall, saw him bring up his other hand to strike her. He gave her a ferocious blow to the side of her head, but even so, she told the wall to soften and recede. In the next moment the strong fist with which he held her had sunk into the wall. Alarmed, he pulled back, but she willed the wall to form around his hand and not release it. For a moment she could not move her arm either, since it was folded over with the substance of the crossings. She started to panic, but when she began to pull away, she sprang free. Albrecht was pinned to the wall.

But he still had use of his other hand. He grabbed her by the neck, his fingers almost closing her windpipe. "Release your spell, or I will break your neck!"

She struggled, trying to position him even closer to the wall so that wall would enfold more of his arm. With the last of her breath, she sank into a crouch. He had to release her and did so, while furiously trying to pull his fist—and now forearm—free. Her hand went to the knife in her boot, and she slipped it out. As she rose, she jammed it into his groin, using the strength of her thighs to add force to the thrust of the knife.

His scream was terrible to hear in the close confines of the path. Some distance away, shouts responded. She yanked the knife out, and blood followed.

She had hoped to bring him further into the depths before she allowed him to seize her. Now soldiers would find him, and quickly. She backed away from him. "You have lost all your honor, if you ever had any," she said to him. "Volkia will despise you. The Mythos already does." She kept backing up, keeping him in sight, because there were things she wanted to say, things she *needed* to say, but her last words to him before she fled were only, "And *never* call a Numinasi a witch."

She slid her knife into her boot and ran.

SOMETHING WAS WRONG. SHE WAS IN THE MAIN CROSSINGS, heading toward the group of *satvars*, when she realized she had to sit down.

Can't sit down.

She stayed upright and, after what seemed to be an absurdly long time, she found the nursing station, or whatever it was. Dreiza was waiting for her. She quickly guided Yevliesza behind a makeshift screen that gave the women privacy to relieve themselves into a basin. She instructed her to disrobe and, fetching the clothes of a *satvar* from a corner, told her to put them on.

"Do what?"

"Put these on," Dreiza said. She squinted at her. "You have a huge bruise on your face."

Yevliesza had not even remembered being hit. *I stabbed Prince Albrecht,* she wanted to say in reply, but shed her clothes instead and begged for water.

"Water," Dreiza told someone just outside the screen.

"Well, that will serve our purpose," Dreiza said, beginning to wrap her head with a long length of bandage.

"What will?"

"The bruise." Dreiza continued to wrap her head and then rubbed something into the small amount of hair that showed out the back. "We cannot have a young *satvar*. This is barley flour to lighten your hair." She went on: "Your story is that you fainted and when you fell, you hit your head. You are light-headed, barely able to walk."

"I *am* light-headed."

"Exactly. It will be perfect."

A *satvar* appeared with a cup of water. As Yevliesza downed it, Dreiza instructed the other woman, "Tell them we are ready."

"How are you here? At the exact right time."

"Father Ludving."

That did not explain much but helped to check her surprise when she saw the priest waiting for her outside the privy.

"And Tanfred?" he asked her with concern in his eyes.

"In Numinat." She began to tilt toward the floor, which seemed very inviting.

"Lean on me," he said and, with Dreiza supporting her other arm, they walked toward the boundary gate.

"Now you may begin moaning," Dreiza whispered.

Yevliesza gave a whimper. People made way for them as they hobbled forward.

"You have a good bruise," Father Ludving murmured.

"Thank you."

"How did it happen?"

"Maybe you won't like to hear." She had tried to kill a man. The priest would be disappointed in her.

"With respect, Father," Dreiza said, "keep her quiet."

At the barricade to Lowgate, Father Ludving made an explanation and, after an officer inspected Yevliesza's injury, they were allowed to pass.

"The *satvars* . . ." Yevliesza began. "Albrecht isn't dead yet. He might be soon, but not yet. The others should come."

Dreiza banged on the heavy door.

Ludving said, "They are packing up and will follow us directly." He frowned. "Albrecht has been injured?"

"Yes." She thought the crossings would let go of Albrecht's arm, eventually. Or his men could dig him out.

The boundary doors swung open. Taking a last look in the direction of the main tunnel, Yevliesza saw that things were still calm and orderly.

"The *satvars* should hurry."

"They know," Dreiza said. "Now come, my daughter." She smiled and with great warmth stood aside as she ushered Yevliesza through the door.

Chapter Fifty-Five

Yevliesza turned over in her sleep, waking just enough to be confused about where she was. It was dark in the room, with wintry moonlight falling in a pool on the wood-plank floor.

A man sat next to her. Large, bearded. She sat up in fright, gasping.

A bass voice: "Yevliesza, it is Father Ludving. All is well."

Confusion fogged her mind. She remembered someone, a Volkish priest. . . . A wave of nausea gripped her, hard. The man came to her side, holding a basin for her to be sick in. She threw up as spasms clenched her throat and belly.

The priest took away the basin and brought a wet cloth for her to clean her mouth. She frowned from sharp pains in her head.

"Are we in Numinat?" she asked, trying to find a few more pieces of what was going on. They had gone through the boundary gate. Dreiza had been there.

He brought her a cup of water. While she sipped at it, he said, "We are safe at Lowgate garrison."

"Is Valenty here?"

"Who?"

She closed her eyes trying to recall things.

"Yevliesza, you are not well. The blow you took was worse than we first thought, and you blacked out. It is my turn to sit with you."

"I fainted?"

"A few hours ago. I believe you suffer a commotion of the brain."

"A concussion?"

"Yes. I have worked with you and endeavored to reduce the consequences of the blow. Sleep, now. It is the best medicine."

She lay back down, closing her eyes. "Duke Tanfred . . ."

"He is here."

"Why are *you* here?"

"The duke sent word to me that the two of you would try to escape and reach Numinat. He asked me to think of some way to help. I made my way to Zolvina and asked the High Mother to watch for you in the crossings. We formed a group of healers and offered our services to the Volkish outposts there."

"I didn't think the renunciates ever left the . . ." What was the word?

"The *satvary*. They seldom do. And Yevliesza, I also asked her to offer you sanctuary, and she agreed. If you wish to go to Zolvina, they will make you welcome for as long as you need."

She needed sanctuary? "Why?"

"Because I knew that you were lost in spirit. Are you not, Yevliesza?"

She tried to sink into the question, but her mind felt like a still, cold pond. Nothing going on. Plus, it was a far harder question than she could begin to answer, when she was just trying to understand how she lay in a sickbed with a priest of the church taking care of her. She let go of thinking and let sleep enfold her.

Over the next few days, she recuperated. No one asked her about how the Volkish had treated her, or why she had not come home sooner. She was glad, because she might not trust herself to tell the story as it needed to be amended. Most of all, she must avoid revealing her primal root power, which was still dangerous for people to know about. Dreiza learned from her that Valenty had been on some kind of mission to Volkia, and she prevailed on the garrison commander to try to find out if he had returned. But no one had any word of him.

One day Yevliesza felt well enough to walk outside the fort, and Tanfred accompanied her. He was leaving for Osta Kiya to report to Anastyna most of what had transpired. Father Ludving would go with him. It would be strange for two Volkish to be in residence at Osta Kiya, but both had been instrumental in helping Yevliesza return from captivity. People would like their stories. Well. Not Sofiyana. But they would have the princip's thanks.

"Will not the princip expect you to report?" Tanfred asked her. A light fall of snow furred Tanfred's cloak and muted the view out to distant rocky promontories.

"I don't know what to say to her. But please tell her that I did apologize to Prince Albrecht. And that it didn't seem to be what he wanted from me." She stopped and turned to him. "Tanfred. I don't know what to say to people. I may have killed Albrecht. He almost killed me. I don't know whether I did well or will be punished."

"Punished!" he spat. "They would not dare."

"Anastyna will want to know what happened in the crossings, so now I'll tell you, so that you can honestly repeat my words. As we fled through the tunnels, trying to evade Volkish soldiers, we were separated. Albrecht found me and we fought. I used a knife against him and might have killed him, but I can't be sure."

Tanfred knew what she had done in the crossings and knew how she had done it. He also knew that, as part of his agreement not to reveal her second power, he must not disclose the specifics.

As the snow fell harder, they retraced their way to the fort entrance. She looked at the rounded hill in front of her. It was there that she had seen her first dactyl. At this moment the sense came to her with more clarity than she had known that first day, that she was in a land of myth. Now she knew it at a level that she doubted even her fellow Numinasi did.

"What will you do?" she asked Tanfred. "Will you stay at Osta Kiya?"

"I think I must. For now. If the princip allows it." He paused. "The more important question is, what will *you* do?"

"I'll join the fight, in some way that doesn't jeopardize everything. But I'm going to fight, whatever it costs me." It was a strong conviction, but it didn't mean she knew how to maneuver within royal politics or how to set limits on her dangerous power.

"If you see Valenty. If he gets back to Osta Kiya, tell him what you are free to tell Anastyna. But ask him to come to me in Zolvina. Will you?"

"Of course." He paused. "He is in your special regard?"

"Yes."

"I hope, for your sake, that he is safe. I will pray for you both."

She thought it couldn't hurt, and she liked that he had said it.

"One other thing, Tanfred. Please tell the real story to Rusadka. To her, you can tell everything."

Chapter Fifty-Six

L ate at night by a crackling fire, Dreiza sat with Yevliesza. It was their second night out from Lowgate and, with Yevliesza's head injury, they had been traveling at a gentle pace. The tents of the *satvars* made a circle around the fire and most had already retired to them.

Yevliesza was improving, her headaches subsiding, and her train of thought more coherent. Dreiza knew that Yevliesza was worried about Valenty. *She* was worried about him, now that she knew he had been on a clandestine mission to Volkia. Prince Albrecht had told Yevliesza this, having learned of it through Nashavety. Nashavety! The banished *fajatim* who had disappeared but had actually gone over to the Volkish.

Above them flowed the River of Night, its stars so thick they faintly illuminated the prairie with its frozen grasses and scattered trees. In this vastness, with the fire alerting anyone to their presence, Dreiza felt vulnerable, keenly aware that she was responsible for Yevliesza and wishing she had not declined the garrison commander's offer of an escort.

She had used her mirror to communicate with the High Mother that Yevliesza was on her way. The High Mother, in answer, sent a vision of the numin pool, frozen but swept of snow. Dreiza supposed that meant something and on the ride had given her attention to the possibilities, finally settling on *We will be waiting for you.*

In the distance, a wolf called out, a long, plaintive howl.

Yevliesza looked in the direction of the sound, turning her face so that Dreiza saw the bruised side. "Do you think wolves can be *sympats*?"

The question surprised Dreiza. "Wolves? Yes, it happens."

"A wolf appeared to me. On the palace grounds the night of my escape."

"Appeared to you?"

"That's how it seemed. When I got lost in the fog, suddenly it was there. So close I could see the pupils of its eyes. I followed it, and that's how I found the carriage waiting."

"A wolf," Dreiza mused. "Had you seen this wolf before?"

"I saw a wolf once, when I was practicing aligns in the woods near Osta Kiya."

Dreiza frowned. It could not be the same wolf, not if Yevliesza's sightings had been in different kingdoms.

"This one—the one in Hapsigen—acted almost tame. But it also disappeared a lot."

"Into the fog," Dreiza said tentatively.

"It was a heavy fog," Yevliesza admitted. "But I think it was a wraith wolf."

They considered the strange possibility for a few moments. At last Dreiza said, "Wraith wolves can visit the next world at will. But they are more wild than normal wolves. Some people say they are dark spirits."

"If it comes again, should I avoid it?" Yevliesza asked.

"We of the *satvar* way do not believe dark spirits exist."

Yevliesza placed a heavy branch on the fire. A few of the logs collapsed beneath it, flaring. "But what happens to bad people when they die? Couldn't they become evil spirits?"

"My order teaches that such people's essences dissolve at death."

"Then if any *sympat* comes to me, none will be evil or sorcerous?"

Dreiza paused. Nashavety might control an animal with creature power. But to make it behave in explicit ways like providing assistance . . . it did not seem possible. True, Nashavety had harassed Yevliesza with her thrall. But in one instance—near the tower stairs of Osta Kiya—it was a manifester's creation. And in the other instances, when Yevliesza was housed in Raven Fell, the thrall had just stalked Yevliesza in what might be a normal way.

"I would trust it," Dreiza concluded. "See what it does. But you should ask the High Mother." She gazed at Yevliesza, at the good side of her face, and thought how little one knew other people or guessed their depths. Especially this young woman.

"How long can I stay at the *satvary?*" Yevliesza asked.

"How long would you like to?"

Yevliesza did not immediately answer. Then: "Maybe I should become a *satvar*."

"Of course you should not! For one thing, you are too young, and youthful *satvars* are not accepted." She did not say, *And you must remain in the world and do good.*

"A month or two?"

"However long you need to, you may stay."

"Does the High Mother feel that Anastyna did badly by sending me to Volkia?"

She had answered this before. "The High Mother knows what happened to you. Father Ludving told her of your captivity. She is concerned for you." Dreiza wanted to say more, but the High Mother had instructed her to wait.

She sat up, alert. In the distance, a shadow moved. It might be an animal. Dreiza rose.

Yevliesza came to her feet. "What?"

"Someone is coming. A rider."

Yevliesza pulled something from her boot. A knife.

It shocked Dreiza to think that Yevliesza had taken the weapon out so quickly, prepared to use it.

As the rider drew close, he dismounted some distance away and approached, leading his horse by the reins.

"Oh," Yevliesza breathed.

"I cannot see so far," Dreiza said. "Is it a *harjat*?"

"It's . . . it's Valenty."

Dreiza's tension slipped away. Why would Valenty be out here? Whatever the answer, it filled her with relief.

At the edge of the camp, he stopped. "May I join your circle?"

His face was still in shadow, but Yevliesza knew it wasn't just her imagination. It *was* Valenty.

Dreiza put her hand on Yevliesza's shoulder. "Go and bid him welcome."

Yevliesza slowly walked toward him, still thinking she might be wrong, that it could be someone else, yet she knew it wasn't.

And there he was. She remembered his face, she remembered the miracle of him, and where he had been, and that he might never have come to stand before her again.

"By the Nine," he whispered, dropping the horse's reins.

She took another step toward him, and he strode forward, closing the distance, pulling her fiercely into his arms. They held each other without speaking, without moving. The stars traveled a little, and a breeze carried the scent of snow.

At last, he held her at arm's length and looked at her swollen face. "Who do I have to kill?" he gently said.

"It's all right," she whispered. "*I* killed him."

"I must hear of this," he said, bemused.

"Valenty. How did you find me?"

"I came through the gateway at Numin Pass five days ago."

"You knew I was here?"

"I've been searching for you," he said, bringing her into his arms again. It felt like heaven. It felt like home.

"Come," he said, putting his arm around her and walking with her to the fire.

Dreiza stepped forward to greet him. They embraced. "Back from Volkia, then," she said.

"Ah, no." Yevliesza heard his tone, that voice conveying, *and do not ask.*

Dreiza let his non-answer pass. "And now you are somehow here?"

"The Numin Pass commandant had a message from Lowgate that Yevliesza and some *satvars* arrived from the crossings." He cocked his head. "*Satvars* in the *crossings*?"

Dreiza shrugged. "I will tell you tomorrow." She told Valenty and Yevliesza that they must have her tent and that Yevliesza had suffered a serious blow to her skull and must rest. Her inflection left no doubt as to the thorough rest she was prescribing, even if the two of them shared a tent.

Dreiza bid them good-night and was soon asking to share the tent of one of the other *satvars*.

Yevliesza and Valenty sat side by side, absorbing the fire's warmth, and Valenty quickly told his story, more interested in hers. In addition to much else, she learned that Pyvel had been kidnapped and what the boy had endured in Nashavety's lair. And that a *harjat* who had been at Valenty's side through his mission was accompanying Pyvel back to Osta Kiya.

In turn, Yevliesza told Valenty what she had planned to tell him: some of what had happened, but not all. Some details she wasn't going to share, and one thing overshadowed everything, but it was too much at that moment, about what the lightning had actually brought to her all those months ago.

"I have been wild with worry," he told her. He cinched her tighter to his body, until they could scarcely be any closer. "I almost killed Nashavety. I *should* have killed her. But her guards outnumbered us, and we might not have come out alive. Still, I would have killed her, but for Pyvel. Tell me she did not hurt you, that the demon did not touch you."

Yevliesza wanted to comfort him. If he had killed Nashavety . . . she would not have suffered half so much at Albrecht's hands. If, if. What good to think of what either of them might have done differently?

"She didn't touch me. But she's still in the world, brewing ugly things, helping Volkia. It's terrifying."

They stared at the fire, holding things in, not willing to let the world entirely intrude on their reunion.

Valenty turned to Yevliesza. "Come. You must sleep." He rose and held out his hand for her. "I have slept in the open since Numin Pass Gate; you may have the tent."

"I don't want you to leave my side." She tried not to think about how soon they would have to part.

Inside the tent there was only one blanket. He lay their cloaks on the ground and had her sit while he removed her boots. He put their boots in a corner of the tent and secured the door flap, then laid the blanket over her. Kneeling by her side, he brought her hand up to bury his face in it. "I failed you," he said. "If I had known where you were, I would have come for you."

"I'm glad you didn't." She had so long held on to the hope that he was safely in Numinat.

She looked at him, his form barely a shadow in the tent. "Valenty," she said. "Lie with me."

"You need to rest," he gently whispered.

"No, I don't need to rest. I need *you*." She reached for him and drew him down beside her, and he didn't hold back.

"Valenty," she said. "I love you. I will love you all my life and I will love you tomorrow and every day after."

He pulled her toward him, his arm in the small of her back, bringing her close, kissing her with a lingering, savoring kiss. The taste of him was electrifying. A fire burned in her as she kissed him back. The flame had been burning in the minutes since he arrived and now flared as he whispered her name. She threw the blanket off. "Valenty, come to me." She sat up and shrugged out of her tunic and then began removing everything else. She noted his hesitation as he sat back on his heels, watching her fling her clothes away. "Come to me before I change my mind."

He began unlacing his vest. "Please do not. Do not change your mind."

His clothes were quickly discarded, and he moved onto the pile of cloaks with her, bringing her into his arms.

She pulled back for a moment. "And I know how to prevent pregnancy."

In the dark tent she could not see him clearly, but thought that he was smiling. "That was not foremost in my mind," he said.

"What is?" she teased.

"You. Always you."

Later, lying in his arms, she felt a strange sadness that she had rushed him, almost demanded that he take her. She wanted him to be the first and hadn't been entirely sure that she could decide, that the world would let her decide, who it would be. These thoughts weren't clear to her, but she had needed to claim him, or for him to claim her, out of devotion and not obligation or force.

She wept in his arms and didn't really know why, except the relief of finally giving herself to a man who loved her.

Eventually that night she told him of her second power and why she had kept it secret—all the reasons, including her doubts about his obligations to Anastyna. But first she swore him to secrecy. Would he promise not to divulge anything to Anastyna if she told him something of military importance? Would he trust that she had the right to keep it private, and would he swear to it? He paused, considering this. *Would Anastyna see it as a betrayal?* he asked. Yes, probably. *And yet you would ask this of me?* Yes. *Then I promise*, he told her.

Hearing her story sent him into a profound quiet. He felt the old burns on her back. He could not see what they had become in the darkness of the tent, but she would show him in the morning. She told him how she had helped Tirhan enter Alfan Sih. And that the crossings had helped her trap Albrecht and how it had done so. He slowly trailed a hand across her brow and down her face as though he needed to ground this new knowledge in the reality of her body next to him.

"What will become of us?" he asked simply, more in wonder than in fear.

"I don't know, I truly don't." She told him she was going to stay in Zolvina until she figured it out.

"It is where women go to get rid of me," he said, only half-playfully.

"It's where I'm going to find myself."

They lay thinking about that, her head on his chest, her arm around him and his around her, until they finally slept.

Chapter Fifty-Seven

A round them were mountains. Mountains drenched in white, stark against an arctic-blue sky. Yevliesza and the *satvars* had wrapped furs around their leggings, and their heavy wool cloaks trailed behind them in the snow, making soft scraping sounds as they walked.

On one mountainside, a field of snow separated from the slope and rumbled down in a fog of white. But that was a good distance away. Their path lay through a shallow valley, where animals had walked and trampled down the snow, but it was still hard going. The sun struck the snow with a fierceness that drove into Yevliesza's head like spikes. Yet, with her exertions, she wasn't cold.

They stopped often, sometimes brewing something hot to drink, building a fire with a few bundles of deadfall they carried.

Valenty had left the day before, traveling in the opposite direction. It was very hard to watch him leave, but he promised to come to see her at Zolvina, if the High Mother would allow it. Tomorrow or the next day he would see Anastyna, and their conversation would be a hard one. They might set aside anger and accusation, however, keeping their attentions on Volkia, the coming war and how they could hope to defend against infernal weapons.

She missed him. He had not been with her long enough to fill the hole that their separation had brought. Wiped clean in her mind were any doubts about him. How strange that she had ever put a barrier between them, that she could have lacked trust, or forgiveness for things that now seemed too petty to hold onto.

"There," the one called Yarna said. A tall woman at the head of their line who was the strongest of the group pointed to a ledge in the peaks above them.

Yevliesza stopped to identify the stone building, no larger than a baby's fist at this distance. Zolvina. It looked like a habitation at the very top of the world, impossibly tiny and vulnerable. But it was her place of safety. Perhaps in the ice and iron embrace of these peaks, she would at last find clarity.

"We will be there before dusk," Dreiza said, "if Yarna can continue to lead the way." The two women exchanged smiles, and the group resumed their trek.

Dreiza had been optimistic. Night had fallen as they made their final approach to the *satvary*. Lit torches on the roof were their beacons.

The gate to the sanctuary was open, and a group of five or six women in heavy cloaks waited for them.

One of them left the gate and approached. The woman's cheeks were bright pink in the cold, and she strode forward to welcome them, smiling in such pleasure that Yevliesza immediately wished to put herself in the woman's care.

When she turned to Yevliesza, she said, "I am the High Mother of Zolvina *satvary*. Be welcome and at home here, Yevliesza."

Her companions on the journey passed through the gate, embracing their sisters who met them in the courtyard. "It is very good of you to let me stay," Yevliesza said.

"No, Yevliesza, you have earned a place here. We owe you all our care."

"Owe? I don't think you owe me anything."

"Oh, my daughter, I rather think we do." The old *satvar* put her hand on Yevliesza's shoulder and urged her into the courtyard. "Come and warm yourself by our fires, and we will explain everything."

The gates closed behind them, no more than screens made of saplings, delicate though toughened with ice. She let the *satvars* lead her into the sanctuary.

~*~

Follow Yevliesza, Valenty, and Rusadka as the story deepens in *Servant of the Lost Power,* Book Three of The Arisen Worlds quartet. Coming winter, 2024.

Acknowledgments

Some authors work on their novels in cafes and libraries, but I have never been able to concentrate in such places. Therefore, I can say that I wrote this book by myself. But I was not really alone in that endeavor. I benefited from the help of so many.

My deep thanks to an extraordinary author and friend, Anthea Sharp, for crucial publishing advice and encouragement. And to fellow author Melody Kreimes, who kept me company along the writing path, in good times and tricky ones. My appreciation to Jim Thomsen for his expert copyediting. Heartfelt thanks are due my husband, Tom Overcast, who steadfastly cheers me on, believing in my writing, no matter what, even on page 211 when doubts perennially come to visit.

I am indebted to my advance readers, Michele L. Casteel, Charles Hirst, Marilyn Holt, Morgan Mead, Marisa Miller, Lisa Montoya, Eric Morris, Veronica Rood, Janet Smith, and Leeann Smith. They have contributed to this tale, this book, in many ways large and small, and I am so very grateful.

About the Author

Kay Kenyon is the author of seventeen fantasy and science fiction novels. Her work has been shortlisted for the Philip K. Dick Award, the John W. Campbell Memorial Award, and the American Library Association Reading List award. She lives in beautiful eastern Washington State in the foothills of the Cascade Mountains with her husband Thomas Overcast.

Visit *www.kaykenyon.com* and join the author's newsletter for a free story, plus find out about upcoming releases and reader perks.

CPSIA information can be obtained
at www.ICGtesting.com
Printed in the USA
BVHW042001160723
667189BV00001B/2